GW01326130

MARK
OF THE
WATER NYMPH

Tattoo Trilogy Volume 2

A E KIRK

Published by Three Acre Books

Copyright © A E Kirk, 2020

Layout by Guido Henkel

The right of A. E. Kirk to be identified as author of this work has been asserted by her in accordance with the Copyright, Designs and Patents Act 1988.

All Rights Reserved. No reproduction, copy or transmission of this publication may be made without written permission. No paragraph of this publication may be reproduced, copied or transmitted save with the written permission of the publisher, or in accordance with the provisions of the Copyright Act 1956 (as amended).

Any person who commits any unauthorised act in relation to this publication may be liable to criminal prosecution and civil claims for damages.

All characters in this publication are fictitious and any resemblance to real persons, living or deceased is purely coincidental.

Printed in the U.S.A.

ACKNOWLEDGEMENTS

This book has been in the pipeline for so long and there are so many people I wish to thank. Mainly for their help, dedication and love for Tara and the gang, I want to say a huge thank you to Jen for her amazing longstanding support. Kim and her lovely mum Cathy, though you are far across the Pond, I cannot thank you enough for the near ten year love of the books and my writing. And last but certainly not least, Anna. Words cannot express how much you have helped me, not just this year but every single year this book has been in one stage or another. Thank you for your nit picking.

And also, a big thank you to my husband, Geraint and my parents for their loving support. I couldn't have done this without them.

CHAPTER ONE

"If there is magic on this planet, it is contained in water."

— *Loren Eiseley*

MY HEART PUMPED LIKE THE RAPIDLY ESCAPING BUBBLES FROM AN underwater volcano. Salty liquid coated my palms. I was becoming the hunted, and I was running for my life. I was fleeing those who were trying to take me away from my ethereal existence. I had a mission to complete. I would not let them catch me.

My damp bare feet slapped against the wet concrete as I headed towards the old abandoned pier. It had seen better days, but the world did not need such outdated entertainments.

Barging through the "Restricted Access" barrier with my shoulder, I took the chance to glance behind me. I saw them: four men in black suits. One of them holding what appeared to be a long, metal rod. What they were going to do with that, I was unsure. I had seen something similar on the hidden plane, but I doubted that the humans had hold of that. Zeus would not allow it.

Heading straight to the entrance of the pier, I saw a metal door ahead. The top of which was glass. It was my only option. Springing into the air, I twisted and shot straight through the window, landing on the other side and rolling to gain back some momentum. My forget-me-knot silk dress ripped on the shards of glass. I ignored it. My goal was the sea.

As I sprinted towards the iron sea, I called home; it suddenly dawned on me that I was returning alone. He had left me, abandoned me, but why? It was because of him that I was running for my life, now alone on the surface world. Was there anyone who could help me?

Suddenly, the air around me began to fizzle and crackle; charged with high amounts of electricity. I turned and saw it. A human was holding the metal rod, and a blinding white bolt of lightning flashed. I had no time to move, no conductor to stop the shock penetrating my body and rendering me useless. How did the humans have hold of Zeus' staff? How did they know about it? Their ridiculous Greek mythology did not even mention it. It was a secret kept from humans for a reason.

Screaming in pain as the white-hot electricity zapped through my body, I felt myself go floppy. I hit the wet wooden pier with an almighty thud!

The running men came closer but then slowed as they approached. They feared me still, and so they should.

'Ah, my dear Thera,' one of the men said slyly, panting a little from running. 'What a find you are and my master would be all to pleased to add you to his Cabinet of Idols.'

Unable to move or speak, I tried to make a connection to my brother, to reach out through our unique link and use his powers to help me. However, I could not find it. The link had broken.

'Turn her over,' the man snapped to his subordinates. Rolled over by a shoe, I faced a stern human with salt and pepper hair. He stared back with an evil glint in his eye. 'Nice to see you, oh Mother of Water Nymphs. Oh, yes, I know who you are. I know what you were created for.' He smiled knowingly at me. 'Your ilk disgusts me. Every legend is like vermin to me.' Bending closer, he asked, 'Do you know who I am? Well, I shall tell you. I am a man with a very bold idea,' he laughed mockingly and reached out to stroke my hair.

Disgusted by his touch, I knew who he was; I was no fool. He was part of a mercenary group who bartered and traded legends like me. I was a favourite. If they seized me, they had half of the world, and I was not exaggerating. If any human possessed my powers and my brothers collectively, they could use us to destroy the planet. It is probably why my brother, Santorini, left me. Together, he and I were unstoppable, a destructive force not to be reckoned.

I remember our creation thousands of years ago. A massive volcano erupted. The explosion caused devastation around the Mediterranean during the time the humans call the Late Bronze Age. My brother and I formed out of the volcanic rock that cascaded out into the unsuspecting sea. When we cooled the Ocean Herself gave us a new life. Given powers and new names of Thera and Santorini, we existed to obey the mistress of the sea.

Not so long ago, there was a rumour on the tides. A war was coming. Santorini and I stayed out of it and decided to return to the hidden plane. However, something went wrong. We had become separated when the portal to the other world closed. I tried to retain the link with my brother, but it did not last for long. Distraught at his loss, I was cast away on the ocean foam but, unexpectedly, the group of mercenaries discovered me. Since then, I've been running for my life.

One of the men grabbed me roughly by the arms and dragged me to a standing position to face the man who had been hunting me. He smiled in satisfaction then motioned for the other men to take me back down to the front of the pier.

My head lolled to the right. Through my thick black hair, I saw the sea sweeping up against the stilts of the pier, almost beckoning me to return to it. I wished and prayed with all my heart, but the waves could not reach me.

'Sir, the sea,' one of the men said worriedly, just as we were about to enter the arcade.

'We are nearly there,' he replied, sounding tense.

Carried through the dusty old arcade, where the paint peeled off the walls, graffiti decorated the "No Entry" signs and human games had been smashed and broken, I wondered who his master was. It was someone with a substantial amount of power and influence, but the only people I could think who could do this was the Ancients, and they would not dare get involved in capturing legends. They despised all legends; they were not in control of them. Also, what was the Cabinet of Idols? Did it consist of other immortals such as me? Was it full of others legends and if so who?

The men brought me to a shiny black van. Tyre marks on the road showed it had screeched to a halt just before the bollards near the front of the pier. Getting some feeling back in my body as the effects of the staff were thankfully, only temporary, I tried to struggle free. Shoving me against the van, one of the men drew close to me. So close, I saw the whites of his eyes.

Within the first five minutes of knowing this man, I found out he was aware of my existence and that he knew about my powers. That was never a good sign. Only a handful of legends knew. The most damning thing about this man, however, he possessed the Staff of Zeus. Whoever had given it to him had betrayed the entire magical community.

Unceremoniously they shoved me into the back of the van like a sack of potatoes. Hitting the cold, metal floor the door was shut quickly, throwing me into darkness. Unexpectedly the men began to shout. The sound of the staff cracked above. What on Atlas was going on?

'Jane! Get us out of here!' someone yelled. Then the air was still and the shouts ceased.

'Hello!' I said as loud as I could, which was pathetic. The staff had sapped so much of my power; my voice came as a whisper. 'Hello, is anyone there?'

The van door suddenly opened and bright sunlight and warm fresh air pooled in, blinding and confusing me. Wasn't it night-time? And why could I taste sand in the air?

'Oh look, she's in here,' said the barely audible voice of a very tall black-haired girl. I straightened myself up and looked at her. Her beautiful green and grey clothes were not human-made. They were hand-made by Silkies and had the aura of Forest Elf protection. She wasn't from this plane that was for definite.

'Who are you?' I asked, shielding my eyes from the glaring sun to get a better look at her.

Her eyes immediately went wide. 'Renita,' she smiled. 'Your voice is barely audible.'

Rolling my eyes, I nodded slowly. The wind suddenly whooshed up at me, and brazen red sand met me quite suddenly; I felt momentarily sick.

'Leave me in here for at least twelve hours, don't ask why. Understand?'

'Um, yes I understand,' she nodded, still smiling.

She withdrew and closed the van door slowly. I caught a glimpse of three other figures staring in my direction, but I couldn't see their faces in the strange dusty haze. Taking a deep breath, I closed my eyes and waited for hours to pass and my powers to return to me.

KNOCK, KNOCK, KNOCK!

The van door slid open loudly, and three people loomed over me.

'Hello, um, bonjour?' said a soft male voice with a Norwegian accent.

'You idiot, she speaks English!' snapped another male voice, but this one sounded like he had more backbone.

Opening my bleary eyes, I sat up, checking my arms and legs before laughing; I stood up and breathed a sigh of relief. I was myself again and felt my familiar power restored. 'Well that's much better,' I smiled at the small group of people who had gathered around me. 'Shoo, shoo.' I waved them back as I got out of the van. 'And as a matter of fact, I speak every language since...well since a very long time. So, let's start from the beginning-.'

'Who are you?' It was the girl from earlier, Renita. Clearly, from her attire and accent, she was of Greek origin.

Thinking about her question, I thought it odd. Surely, they should know who I was. I mean, no one miraculously stumbles upon mercenaries who just happen to have me stuffed into the back of a van.

'Are you, Thera?' a girl with braided blond hair asked. Looking at her once again, I could tell she was not human. Though her clothes were not as ethereal as Renita's, they certainly had a flare of Ancient Rome about them. It wasn't a toga per se, more like a strange cross between a brown linen-coloured wrap and a cloak. She must have been hot. Then something else occurred to me; where on Atlas were we? It was scorching.

Gazing around all I saw were miles and miles of open desert. We were high up on some sizeable red rock... 'Oh no,' I cringed, looking around in fright. 'Please tell me we are not on Uluru!'

'What?' Renita asked, confused.

'Right, let's get these questions over and done with now before something bad happens,' I said nervously. 'Yes, my name is Thera. Right, now my question: Who are all of you? What are your names and your, um powers?'

'Ooh me first!' Renita laughed, jumping up and down on the spot. 'I'm the daughter of Pygmalion. I can make inanimate objects come to life.'

'Jane,' the blond-haired girl said, holding up her hand. 'Daughter of Janus. I can see into the past, and the future, although only occasionally. But I can open doorways.'

I smiled. I had gathered someone had the power to get us here from Britain. 'So you're the one who can phade?' I asked.

'Um, yes,' she replied.

'Ah. Well, you cannot open doorways, not like a portal. What you do is call phading.' smiling at her. 'Did you mean to travel literally to the opposite side of the globe to get away from those men?' She nodded once but didn't make eye contact with me. 'And you are?' I asked, turning my attention to the puny looking hazel-haired boy. Extremely pale and gangly, I was surprised he was still able to stand. He wore a small, simple leather jacket over a beige long-sleeved shirt and brown trousers. What intrigued me was that he didn't have an air of power about him.

'Tyr,' he replied softly. 'My, my name is Tyr,' waving a stump where his hand used to be.

'Tell her who you are,' Renita said encouragingly, smiling at him.

'I'm the s-son of Modi, the Grandson of Thor,' he muttered.

My Norse myth was a little rusty, but once I heard the name, it clicked. 'Oh Mother Nature,' I said feeling sick. 'You're the offspring of the most-', but I instantly stopped myself as poor Tyr withdrew and went off; dragging his feet along the floor, utterly dejected. Something was up with that boy.

'Well, that was tactless,' said the other boy. With one glance, I could tell he was trouble. With straw-coloured hair and wearing a long grey robe, it was like being back in the Middle Ages again. 'Did you not know he is moody and has no faith in himself? You've just made it worse for us.'

'And your name is?' my voice monotone.

'Dagen,' he said proudly.

'And you're the offspring of which mythological Abbot?' I asked, hiding a smile.

'I'm not an Abbot,' he snapped. 'I am an apprentice of Merlin himself,' he smiled, trying to look down at me as though I was worthless.

Rolling my eyes, I shook my head in despair. 'Alright, whose joke was it to send you after me?'

'How did you know we were sent?' Jane asked a frown etched on her forehead. 'We didn't mention it.'

'No, but it's obvious and believe it or not, I'm quite clever,' I smiled at her. 'You came to help me right, to stop them from collecting me?'

'Collecting you?' Renita asked, folding her arms in thought. 'The Cabinet of Idols. Is that what you mean?'

'You know about it?' I asked her cautiously.

Dagen sniped at me, 'I thought you were clever.'

Ignoring him, I looked into Renita's eyes, her face faltered. 'Your brother sent us. He had moments to make a decision. The main portal became distorted, and he knew it was a one-way trip. He sent us here with an important message for you. "Keep away from the Cabinet of Idols and ensure the Staff of Zeus remains in the right hands." Does that mean anything to you?'

Sighing, I turned away from them to think. This Cabinet of Idols sounded terrible. Those mercenaries wanted to give me to whoever was in charge of the collection. What more could they gain if they had the power of the staff? Did they have any idea what that thing was capable of doing and how dangerous it was? What struck me as odd was what the Salt and Pepper haired man said. He didn't want my brother to know, not just yet. But know what? My brother already knew he had the staff.

'The Staff of Zeus, where is it?' I demanded, making them all jump.

'We took it back from them,' Renita said, half smiling, 'but then we lost it.'

I was dumbfounded at their carelessness. 'You...you lost it? How could you lose it? Do you know what would happen if it fell into the wrong hands?'

Jane looked sad. 'I'd never heard of it before. We knew it was powerful when we saw it. It had Zeus' emblem on the tip. It was throwing out lightning, but that's not all that it does, is it?' She asked me. Glancing at her, I shook my head. 'I thought so, I can tell by your eyes.'

'For the love of Atlas,' I snapped. 'How is it that a bunch of semi-myths come to rescue me? Where are all the others?'

'For your information,' Dagen drawled, 'every myth has left for the magical plane. They fear what is happening here in the human world. We are all you have. Also, I'll have you know I am quite old. That lot,' he said, indicating with his thumb, 'are teenagers compared to me. I'm nearly seven hundred and twenty-eight years old.'

'I'm three thousand six hundred and thirty-six,' I snapped. 'Grow a pair.'

With his jaw-dropping in horror, Dagen, thankfully, shut up.

Moving to the edge of the rock, I looked over and saw what I had been dreading. We didn't have much time. 'Right so,' I said quickly, turning back to the group. 'The Staff of Zeus, what happened to it?'

Everyone looked at Tyr. 'I...I dropped it when Jane phaded us,' he said, looking like he was about to cry.

'So basically it could be anywhere between here and the South-West of England. Brilliant. Now we've got that sorted, Jane how about you phade us someplace else?' I asked her, smiling.

She looked shocked as I addressed her and began shuffling her feet. 'Well I could, but sometimes it doesn't work like that,' she mumbled. 'I mean, I'm not as good as my Dad,' she laughed dryly.

I felt my eye twitch. 'Uh-huh, well I'm just going to put our situation into perspective so that you can all understand. I am in the desert, there's no water, and since there is no water, I can do absolutely nothing about the problem that we will face in about...oh...less than three minutes. Also, none of you has the power to help us. So one more question: Do you believe in Ancestor Worship of the Australian Aborigines?'

'Huh?'

Hearing their ragged breath behind me, I yelled, 'RUN,' and headed to the opposite side of the sacred rock.

The girls screamed behind me, and Dagen yelled, 'Jane, phade us now!' Nothing happened. All I knew was that, after we were off Ayres Rock, we would be safe from the evil spirit energy coming to engulf us.

Careening down the giant red rock, sending flecks of earth raining down on those at the bottom, we slipped and tripped as we tried to flee. As we slowly descended, the unmistakably angry energy began to dissipate, but I still felt the hairs on the back of my neck standing on end. They weren't giving up easily. After all, we were the ones who had dumped a black mini-van on top of one of their highly active spiritual sites.

After making it to the bottom, I continued to run; I didn't want to linger.

The others followed. No one asked questions, and no one turned around until I knew we were a safe distance from Ayres Rock. Collapsing into a heap amongst some dry thorny shrubbery, I finally looked back to see the looming ancient rock almost laugh at me in spite.

'Yes I know we shouldn't have landed on your rock,' I panted as I sat on the floor. 'It was an honest mistake. Just let us be, and we'll go,' I said then laid back on the sandy ground. I was exhausted and needed water desperately.

'Who were you talking to?' Renita asked me, as with wobbly legs, she stood up and dusted herself down.

'The spirits that still reside in, on, and around the rock.' I sat up and pointed at it. 'Uluru, or Ayres Rock, is very sacred to the Aborigines,' I told her, still trying to catch my breath. 'They use it for their Dreamtime, stories of their ancestors,' I explained as she gave me a puzzled look. 'We have just trampled all over their history, and their Dreamtime is a lot older than me. So, respect your elders.'

I heard Dagen snort from behind me, but I ignored him. I felt like for most of this trip, no matter how long it was going to last, I would be ignoring Dagen and his snide remarks.

After catching our breath and feeling relieved that we had stopped being chased, I faced an easterly direction and began to walk.

'So, how come you were sapped of all your power when we found you?' Jane asked me as Renita and Dagen led the way. Tyr trudged beside me, glancing at me now and again, he still couldn't make up his mind whether to talk to me or not.

'The Staff of Zeus. It zaps your powers for a while,' I told her, evading her statement. 'The Salt-and-Pepper-Haired man knew he didn't want me anywhere near the ocean. I was rendered helpless. I couldn't use my powers,' I said more to myself.

'How come?' she asked, sounding genuinely quizzical.

'My brother and I have a special connection. We can see pieces of each other's futures, but never our own. When we bolted for the portal to the magical plane, he went first and got a vision of me and realised I needed help. The portal closed, and I was left behind.'

'So, he had a vision of you and the Staff of Zeus and then went into the other plane to send us to help you.'

'Correct, Jane,' I sighed.

'No offence, but why did your brother leave you?' Tyr asked, moving in front and turning around to face me as he began to walk backwards.

Cringing inwardly, I didn't want to tell them this early on the trip, but I guess if I had to say to them, now was a good a time as any. 'The Cabinet of Idols,' I began. 'It's like a prison for legends. He left me here probably because the cabinet is in the magical plane. You see, if they had me at full power, they would have half a chance of destroying the planet. With my brother as well, they would have the means to destroy the entire planet. So, from his logical point of view, leaving me here stranded by myself, gives the world a fifty-per cent chance of surviving.'

After a while, I noticed that I was the only one walking. Each stood with their mouths wide open.

'Can we keep moving please, I am a tiny bit thirsty,' I suggested. 'Mother of all Water Nymphs here,' I chuckled, 'emphasis on water.'

'You can destroy the planet?' Renita asked, looking afraid of me. 'But how? The only ones who can do that are the Ancients themselves.'

'Thera's a legend,' Dagen interrupted her as he stormed right up to me, standing inches from me in a threatening manner. 'It's true, isn't it? You aren't a human creation. You're a myth's creation ergo, a legend.'

'Very good, what else do you know?' I asked him carefully.

Shrugging nonchalantly, he replied, 'the Ancients can't erase you from human history. They could erase us, but not legends.'

'Um, define legends to me, because funnily enough, I thought they were the same as myths,' Jane piped up looking confused.

Groaning, I turned around and began walking, urging the others to follow. 'We can talk and walk at the same time, isn't that marvellous,' I shouted.

With the scraping of feet, the four of them caught up with me, all eager to hear the definition. I found it annoying that I was discussing this with them, surely they shouldn't care. It didn't concern them, not directly at least.

'So,' I said in a teacher-like tone, 'when humans lived during the Neolithic era, um about nine thousand five-hundred years ago, they started creating their Gods. Which then led to religion, mostly Ancestor worship, but it wasn't widely known. However, during the Early Bronze Age, technological advancements swept across the globe and with it, religion. It was during this time that the Ancients decided to create myths, the ideas of human Gods and Goddesses.'

'But why, why create us? Why not just have it as a belief and leave it be?' Tyr asked me.

I shrugged. 'Why not?' He looked puzzled but remained mute. 'Why not make magic real? Why not give them hope for something better in life? The amount of faith that one human had during those times was paramount in their life. If they didn't believe, they had nothing to live for.'

Dagen looked at me from the corner of his eyes. 'What do you mean?'

'Seeing is believing.' I smiled. 'What the Ancients did was help the humans keep their faith by creating real myths. Each God and Goddess has a unique role to play. To make the sunrise, to ferry the dead to the Underworld, to keep the crops nourished. The ideals behind each divinity have a great purpose. For that purpose of sustaining humanity, the Ancients created myths.'

'Sorry,' Tyr mumbled getting my attention, 'but if you're not one of us, what exactly are you?'

'I am a legend — a creation from a myth. My brother and I were born from a volcanic eruption in the Mediterranean. We were born from the magic of Ocean Herself. The Ocean Herself is Mother Natures' sister in a way.' I added. 'However, together, our powers can do insurmountable damage to the planet. It's our fault Atlantis sunk,' I confessed still feeling guilty.

'Whoa,' Jane gasped. 'That was you! How did you do that?' she asked in a scandalised voice.

Cringing at the thought, I explained. 'A slight mishap when we shifted the tectonic plates to release some pressure to divert a magma stream. We didn't account for Atlantis being within range of a tidal wave.'

'Moving the earth's plates,' Dagen said, smiling in thought as though he had solved the puzzle. 'So you can essentially shift the world, ergo destroying it if you wanted by drowning it in water.'

I shot him a look of contempt and took a step towards him. 'I can do worse things to this planet than merely sprinkling it with water, my boy. You mark my words: death will swoop down upon this world as though Hell itself made its home here.' Looking at their frightened, startled faces, I changed tack and quickly smiled at them, 'but that's only if my brother and I are together. The most I can probably do by myself is a tsunami, or a whirlpool, or an underwater earthquake and possibly spout off a massive geyser, that's about it. Although, in answer to your question, the Ancients did not create me. My mother, a myth, created me and a creation of myth is a legend. My will is my own, and I cannot be killed by the Ancients, only by my creator and my mother would not destroy me. I'm far too valuable.' Falling back into step with me, we continued in silence.

CHAPTER TWO

'JANE,' DAGEN SNAPPED AFTER FOUR HOURS OF WALKING, 'ANY TIME NOW would be good.' Jane folded her arms and looked away from him.

'I told you it doesn't work like that,' she barked at him. 'I have to have enough energy to phade us thousands of miles anywhere. Why don't you magic us away?'

Glancing at Dagen, he looked almost ashamed but then quickly recovered when he noticed I was looking at him. 'I don't want to resort to using my magic. Besides, I'm too hot to do anything.'

'Well it is Australian summer,' I told them, glancing up at the blazing sun.

With no warning, Dagen angrily snapped, 'Why can you not take us away from here? Are you the daughter of Janus or not?'

Scared, Jane backed off a little and shook her head, her two ringlets flapping around her face. 'I-I'm sorry but I can't,' she mumbled. 'I can't just switch it on and off like that. It's mostly if I'm in danger and we need to escape.'

He made a threatening advance towards her. 'Do you wish me to put you in danger?'

'Please,' Renita squealed, getting in between them. 'Please, don't fight, we'll find water soon, I know we will. We just have to keep going.'

I interjected. 'Renita is right, we need to find water.'

'Why do we need to find water anyway?' Dagen drawled.

I rolled my eyes. 'Because then I can transport us anywhere we want. Plus, it'll make me feel better. Let's keep going.' Together we continued to trudge on.

After a while of nothing but desert, I decided to give the others a break. Perched on a rock by myself, I surveyed the endless sand and scraps of dried weeds. My heartfelt heavy. I missed my brother and I missed the ocean. I could not understand how I had got into this situation. It was beginning to irritate me the more I thought about it. There must be something I had overlooked, someone who could shed some light on all of this. Turning to look at the others it quickly became apparent it wasn't any of them. Though they had certain useful powers, they could not help me.

Pondering on this I asked out loud, 'Will you give me a sign or do I have to find you?' Turning around in a full circle, I looked at everything, giving every rock, bush or piece of dirt my utmost attention. After a few minutes of nothing, I gave up and sauntered down to the others. Then I felt it underneath me.

'It's an earthquake,' Jane yelped as everyone began to stagger and lose their balance. Hitting the floor, I pressed my hands against the earth and smiled. It wasn't an earthquake. Sand began to sink into the ground in a strange shape. Snaking and dancing around the earth it moved from left to right, then abruptly stopped.

'That was strange,' Renita said as she looked on the floor. 'What are those markings?'

'It's a...well I'm not sure,' Dagen said, tilting his head, but he wasn't going to understand, not at this level.

I glanced up and found a small clump of rocks nearby. They were high enough to see what had happened to the ground. Standing, I ran towards the rocks, calling to the others to get out of the way. As I reached the pinnacle, I glanced down. 'So that's your game,' I smiled. 'Well fine, be that way. No doubt it will be difficult, annoying and potentially dangerous but that's what you like, isn't it? It's all a game to you when you know the ending.'

'What is it?' Dagen called from below.

Motioning the others towards me, they ran up to see what I was looking at.

'It's a message in the ground!' Jane gasped.

'*Find Us.*' Tyr said looking puzzled. 'Who are we finding? And how do we find them in the desert?'

'No, the question is: Who did you contact?' Dagen snapped his head in my direction.

'Stupid boy, you don't contact them, there's no need,' I laughed, as I walked back down to the bottom. I put my hands on the ground and scrubbed the message off the earth. 'Right, there's a second plan.' They shuffled down to meet me. 'We need to find the Moirae. They have a permanent residence in this plane. They'd never leave for the magical world. It's not their style, there's no fun for them in the magical plane because no one dies.'

'Oh no,' Renita groaned. 'Please, let's not. I mean no disrespect, but they are a bit horrid.'

Looking at the others, they seemed puzzled. 'The three Fates.'

'Oh the Fates,' Jane smiled, 'yes we don't call them the Moirae, that's only in Greek mythology,' she said, folding her arms and looking at Renita.

'Um,' Tyr said putting his stumped arm up to speak, 'what are they?'

Giving him and Dagen a mystified look, I asked, 'Don't you know any other myth apart from your own?'

Scoffing, Dagen said, 'of course *I* do. I have immense powers that outshine you all so, clearly, I do. The Fates yes um they-'

'Decide whether you live or die,' Jane interjected. 'Plus they see the past, present and future.'

'Yes, I knew that, if you would let me finish,' Dagen hissed.

'Enough,' I bellowed. 'We don't have time for this. There is something I need to do first, but Jane, we need to phade, now. It'll take a long time until we find a massive body of water. We can't wait that long.'

'I told you, I can't,' she hollered, stamping her feet like a human child.

'You've done it before. Look, maybe we can help you.' Holding my hand out for her, 'and you,' I snapped at Dagen. 'If you do have powers, then you can help as well.'

'How dare you!' he said waspishly, looking affronted. 'I do have powers.'

'Then, prove it! Tyr and Renita stand anywhere inside this circle,' I ordered them as I pointed my finger to the ground and magically created a small circle around us.

Giving Tyr a small smile, Renita asked, 'Do we need to hold hands?'

I shook my head. 'No. You two are in the circle, there's no need. Jane and Dagen, hold hands with me.'

Disgruntled, Dagen quipped, 'This isn't going to work.' I shot him a dirty look and he shrugged. 'I'm just saying. Besides, why haven't you done this before? I thought you said you were clever.'

Sighing, I didn't want to voice my opinion but decided it was for the best. If Jane knew how much she was valued, maybe she would step up a gear. 'I was giving Jane a chance to collect her energy, but we don't have time for this. The Moirae know something and they want us to find them. Though, I berate myself for not asking them sooner.'

'But where do we look?' Jane asked as she and Dagen grasped my hands. 'I sort of need a direction or place to make this work.'

'Just let us use our powers to help you. You can get us to the coast of anywhere for all I care,' I told her. 'Once I'm in the water I can sort things out and I can give you an exact position.'

Taking a deep breath, she nodded. 'Alright, I'll try.'

'Good. Now Dagen, I just want you to focus, so-'

'Yes, yes I know already, concentrate and pool my energy into her. I know how this works,' he said irritably.

Calming my nerves, I looked at Tyr and Renita. 'Just stand still,' I told them. They nodded and gave each other a small nervous look. 'Alright, Jane, when you're ready.'

Giving me a stiff nod, she closed her eyes. I felt Dagen's hand tense up. Out of the corner of my eye, I could see his face was red from concentration. Hiding a giggle, I closed my eyes to concentrate. As I did, I saw Renita reach out for Tyr's good hand.

'Phade,' Jane whispered.

'NO!' I yelled, but it was too late.

Pitching forwards into a brilliant bright white light, the circle swirled around my head making me feel extremely dizzy. Then with a tremendous and painful whack, we landed on something wet, freezing and slippery.

Opening my eyes I smiled at the familiar scenery but I was also annoyed. I stood and looked at the damage Renita and Tyr had done to themselves.

'Oh my, where are we?' Dagen asked, his teeth beginning to chatter as the frozen winds swept around us.

Helping Jane up I said, 'We are in Antarctica! Welcome to the land of the perpetual sun. Well, for several months out of the year.'

Glancing down at what used to be Renita and Tyr, I sighed. I couldn't undo what they had done, but I could at least make everyone comfortable.

I walked to the water's edge and smiled. It was good to be home. Raising my arms, I brought forth a large ball of water. Spinning around I threw it in the direction of the others. In the air, the water moulded itself into frozen blocks and fell neatly on top of one another, forming a complete igloo around them. 'Stay there and keep warm,' I called.

'Who in Pluto is this?' I heard Jane shriek.

'I'll be back in a minute, just stay there and don't say anything to... them,' I cringed.

Yearning for the water, I smiled and ran; diving into the refreshing icy blackness of the sea. Instantly I had every magical sea creature imaginable in my mind. They were worried and restless. I had merfolk, who had no time to escape, yelling in my head about how to get into the other plane. I had Silkies, Ahti, Dakuwaqa, Hapi, Ceto, Charybdis, Susanoo and Enki all asking me stupid questions about what to do next.

'ENOUGH,' I shouted, quietening every one. Though a lot of them were thousands of miles away, I was connected to them all.

Sinking to the very black abyss of the freezing coldness of the Antarctic waters, I tried to soothe the worries of the inhabitants of the seas. 'Remain still,' I ordered them. 'There is a threat on this planet and it concerns all myths from every culture. The main portal to the other plane has gone, but do not worry,' I said as I suddenly felt their pain begin to surface in my mind. 'If you remain hidden you will be safe.'

'You need help, Mistress,' Hapi whispered to me. 'I was on the other plane when I met them. Neptune and Poseidon invited them into their Kingdom, they were human before but now they belong to us.'

'Who are they?' I asked a little calmer. But Hapi's mind left my own and slunk below the depths of the abyss by the deepest part of our world. 'Who knows of their existence? Someone, tell me,' I demanded. 'Charybdis,' I commanded. 'Were you not summoned from my presence not long ago? To a small islet in the bay of Ha Long?'

'Yes, mistress. It was by a Water Nymph, much like yourself but not entirely complete,' she spoke softly, with a hint of secrecy in her voice.

'Not complete? Explain.'

'She did not understand her powers Mistress. She commanded me in the old way. At first, I thought she was a new legend, but no one can compare to Mistress and Master,' she cooed.

Closing my mind to her, I inhaled a deep lungful of cold salt water and thought. How could someone summon Charybdis or any sea creature? It was so old-fashioned, and I should know, I invented it. Summoning was a sure-fire way of getting the attention of any sea affiliated myth. Santorini and I made it abundantly clear that we found no need to summon any more. But, this Water Nymph didn't seem to understand the rules. All of my Water Nymphs were old enough to know better. Someone had slipped under my radar.

Opening my eyes to complete darkness, I scowled. There was something I didn't understand, something that I was missing.

Casting my mind open to every remaining water myth, I spoke carefully, 'I will be out of contact for a while. But I ask a favour first, tell me where The Fates are.'

Images and whispers floated through my mind as the myths banded together to help find the Moirae. An image of the thundering sea crashing against a cold snow-capped cliff, with the screaming wind as its only company, hit my mind in a torrent. Flying over the snowy hills, I suddenly dived through the thick ice-covered lake. Bubbles blurred my vision as I began to sink lower into the water. Then as the world above me dimmed, a faint glowing green light appeared below.

'THERE,' they all bellowed in my mind. Filtering across my field of vision, I saw a dark grey cave that seemed to have formed under the lake with a natural air pocket. Large stalagmites and stalactites, rocky plinths and brilliantly coloured stone formations decorated the otherwise boring cave system. Deep in the centre was a green floating orb, with a merciless looking black pupil in the middle. 'We see you,' came a strange low ragged breathless voice.

Shaking the vision from me, I rose quickly to the surface. I knew the place where the Moirae lived and it was going to be dangerous. I just hoped Tyr would be up for it. Well, I was sure he would if he was himself.

Bursting out of the water, I thanked the myths for helping me. Hitting the frozen desert of Antarctica and minding some annoying wayward penguins, I made my way to the igloo which, was being battered against the icy blasts of snow. Crawling on my hands and knees, I entered inside and saw Dagen and Jane at the far end of the igloo scared to death at the mangled mess of Renita and Tyr. 'Evening,' I said pleasantly, making my way towards them and sitting down.

'You're sopping wet,' Jane chattered, her lips turning a shade of blue. 'Are you not cold?'

Shaking my head I placed my hands onto the icy ground, a warm pool emanated from beneath. 'There, that should warm up this place a bit. Now then,' I said turning to the strange form in front of me, 'I need to think.'

Jane and Dagen scrambled out of the way and shoved against each other to get to my little hot spring as I tried to think about how to undo the damage.

'Who-who is it?' Jane asked from behind me.

'Well you can either call it a 'her' or a 'him' or a 'they'—depending on your preference,' I said tilting my head as I looked at the mess.

Prodding my back, Dagen said viciously, 'Make sense, will you! What happened?'

'They merged, to put a finer point on it.' I looked up at Jane. 'When you phaded they held hands and now are a mute mangled mesh of two beings in one.'

'You mean to say that mass of flesh is,' Jane began, sounding ill, 'Renita *and* Tyr?'

I nodded. 'They will be alright for now, but I wonder...'

'Wonder what?' Dagen asked me, a slight panic in his voice.

Turning around to look at him I said, 'It's not good to keep them like this. I can't undo the merge, but I can at least make them comfortable, give them a face at least and maybe some hair on their head and-'

'Yes alright I get the point,' he snapped. 'So what are you going to do about it?'

'I need this.' I moved Jane and Dagen's hands out of the way and dipped my finger into the warm, slightly steaming pool. The waters glittered and an image of a golden shimmering tree appeared before them. 'This is The Amber Tree. I created it. Well, that's a slight exaggeration, Santorini and I created it.'

'It's a tree?' Dagen asked looking puzzled.

'The Amber Tree was made within the first couple of decades after Santorini and I were created. It was like a pet to us. As far as we are aware, it is the very first underwater tree that the Ancients have no hold over. It has incalculable powers, but it's tricky as we never sought to find out what powers it has.'

Scoffing, Dagen sat back on his heels and looked disgusted. 'Surely if you created something you should be aware of its powers.'

'Not if it took on a mind of its own.' I said shrewdly. 'It grew and adapted to what we were learning. Being in the ocean it learnt so much in such a short time. Jane, be a dear and hold my ankles. I'm getting my tree.'

'What?' she asked, looking confused and scared, but there was no time to explain.

Pitching forward, my arms, head, neck and upper torso headed straight into the warm pool. I felt hands grab my ankles.

The tree was at the bottom of the mountain in the Mid-Atlantic Ridge. I took hold of it around the trunk and moments later I was being pulled out of the water by my ankles and back into the frozen plains of Antarctica.

Placing it beside me, I gazed at its splendour. The tree was like my child surprisingly. It had been with Santorini and me for so long, I couldn't imagine being without it.

'It's so beautiful,' Jane sighed, looking at the glistening leaves.

'You see,' I said, touching a branch gently, 'they think you're beautiful too.'

'Are you insane?' Dagen asked, looking at my tree as though it was strange. 'A tree can't hear you.'

'It's a magical tree,' I snapped at him, feeling hurt. 'Don't say such things. It's got feelings and can sense who is being nasty or nice. So,' I said, turning to my beautiful tree, which was now emanating a light apricot glow. 'I need to reverse a mishap. Two bodies became one and they are a mess. If you can help in any way, please do so. Even if it's just to make them comfortable and give them an actual face,' I said, cringing as I turned around and stared at the mess. After looking a little too closely, I saw one nostril, but it wasn't a pleasant place for it to be in.

To my relief, the tree began to glow brighter.

'Yuk, what is that it smells like oil?' Jane pointed to some green sap that began to ooze out through the bronze coloured bark.

'Medicine, I hope,' I said, as I wiped it off the bark and smeared it onto the face of the smelted couple. 'Stand back,' I warned them.

Doing as I asked, they moved to the very end of the igloo; recoiling from the now quaking mass of Renita and Tyr.

The green gloop suddenly began to fizzle and boil; spreading around the mashed heads. The tree's substance got to work and within a matter of moments, two mashed bodies became one whole person.

This new person had brilliant shining amber eyes, an almost symmetrical face with a sleek smile, high cheekbones and sumptuous shimmering blond hair that faded into black at the bottom. Just by looking, I could see a bit of Renita and Tyr but melded together to perfection.

I was stunned.

Out of the corner of my eye, Jane moved forward slowly. Raising her hand to speak she said softly, 'um, is it me but, is that more Renita than Tyr?'

Shuffling forwards, but remaining behind Jane, Dagen replied 'no I see more Tyr than Renita.'

Silencing them with my hand, I took a confident step towards the fused pair and asked, 'What is your name?'

It turned its head slowly to look directly at me; I instantly got shivers down my spine. With an intrigued look it said, 'We are one,' both of their voices spoke eerily together.

'FREAKY!' Jane squealed.

Sympathising with her, I tried not to show my perturbed feelings and smiled at them. 'What is your name?'

'We are one,' they said again, their eyes boring into my soul. 'You may call us by our name.'

'What does *it* mean?' Dagen whispered, sounding a little edgy.

Frowning in concentration, I looked more closely at them and said, 'Renita?'

Blinking quickly, the amber in their eyes vanished and was replaced by her azure colour. 'Yes, what is it?'

'Oh my gosh!' Jane squeaked. 'She's Renita but she still looks like-' but I cut across her.

'Renita, what do you remember, from before we phaded?' I asked her, but giving me a perplexing look as though I asked her the distance from here to Mars, I elaborated. 'Do you know where we are and how we got here?'

'How we got here,' she repeated my words. 'We are,' she started as she touched the wall of the icy igloo and stared at her wet fingers. 'How did I get here?' She blinked the stared at everyone. 'Thera, where is Tyr?'

Dagen sighed but added, 'That's a good question.' Folding his arms he nodded at her. 'I guess he's in you!'

'Hey, zip it,' I snapped at him. Turning back to Renita, I told her about the circle and the little mix-up. 'It is fixable, don't worry,' I told her ashen face as the words began to sink in. 'Just breathe.'

Dagen coughed and motioned at Renita. 'I'm not sure if this will work, but it's worth a try. Tyr.'

Seeming as though Renita was given an electrical shock, her mouth opened into what could only be described as a silent scream. Within moments, her eyes turned a deep brown and the black hair crept up into the skull and became short.

'That's not normal,' Jane gagged. 'Even by magical standards.'

In disgust, Dagen tutted at her. 'Some myth you are. Can't stomach a little magical change? Ever seen changelings?'

Tyr, even though he looked terrible, was elated that he had his hand back and marvelled at it while I carefully explained what had happened between him and Renita. He didn't seem like he understood but promised not to annoy anyone and to remain quiet.

'You can't remain quiet,' I told him, as I looked at the others. 'I need your help. I know where The Fates are, where the Moirae are. They are in Ruoššasuolu, Norway.'

Jane and Dagen looked worried; Tyr, on the other hand, looked elated. Lifting both hands he positively beamed, 'I'm going home!'

Chapter Three

'So explain this to us again,' Dagen moaned in a suspicious voice, as Tyr was admiring his new hand while we prepared to set off for Norway. 'Jane can't just phade us to where the Moirae are?' he asked me, as I began to snip leaves off my tree. There was no way on Atlas I was going to Norway without some help.

Sighing, I shook my head, 'Nope—well not unless you can breathe underwater,' I tried to hide a smile. 'Now then,' I said, clapping my hands then rubbing them together, 'who wants to go to Norway?'

'What, now?' Jane asked, looking at Tyr's excitement as he quickly stood up and jumped up and down, saying 'me, me I do!'

'Yes Jane now, the sooner the better. Though I do love the refreshing taste of Antarctica, I must say that it is time to press on and find out what is going on with the Staff of Zeus, how to un-meld him,' I looked at Tyr, 'and who is controlling the Cabinet of Idols.'

Everyone stood up and gathered around me as I said goodbye to my tree. 'I'll see you soon,' I cooed. 'You can stay at the bottom for a while. No one knows where you are, so you shall be fine there.'

Out of the corner of my eye, I saw Dagen grit his teeth; trying to refrain from saying anything. Hiding my smirk, I placed my hands on the ice and opened up the thick frozen ground for my tree to slink into the ocean. 'Be good and don't do what I would do—be like a tree and leaf,' I laughed.

'Oh for the love of Atlas,' Dagen snapped, 'can we go now?'

'Um, quick question,' Jane asked in a small voice, raising her hand. 'Can we not go into another cold climate without the proper attire? I'm freezing as it is.'

'Ah, good point,' I said, as I picked out three leaves from my tree. 'Not sure if this will work but it's worth a try.' Flicking my eyes to Dagen, I saw him relax a little, but why? Before I did my little magic trick, I looked at Dagen and asked, 'why don't you conjure up some clothes for everyone? I don't particularly want to waste my magic leaves.'

Outraged, he waved my words away. 'Pathetic and trivial. My magic is not to be used for such childishness.'

Tyr gave a low whistle and looked away in embarrassment. I frowned at Dagen's words I had a sneaking suspicion that he wasn't all that he said he was. He would have to use his magic sooner or later. If I knew the Moirae, they wouldn't just let us walk right up to them; there would be a lot of trials and tribulations to get through and I was worried.

Groaning from impatience, I brought the leaves to my mouth and exhaled hot breath on them. Removing my face from my hands, the leaves shimmered. 'Take one each and eat it quickly,' I told them, showing them the magic leaves.

'What have you done to them?' Jane asked, as she picked one and popped it into her mouth. 'Oh it tastes like…a sweet, soft but…do you know I can't put my finger on it. What about you?' she asked Tyr.

Taking one gently, he smelt it first before nibbling the edge. Scrunching up his face, he glanced up as though searching for the right word. 'I'm not sure, I get the sweet softness to it, but you're right. There is an actual taste to it,' he told her before shoving the rest of it in his mouth.

Grabbing the last leaf Dagen shoved it in his mouth, chewed quick then swallowed it. 'It tastes like magic. Can we go now!' he sniped, giving me a satisfying glare. I had to give the boy some credit, he did know a little bit about magic but why-

'Magic? Oh, Thera it was divine.' Jane clapped happily, throwing all thoughts out of my head, bar one.

'Uh-huh, just don't throw up,' I added, as I grabbed Tyr and placed him in the middle. 'Alright everyone, just like before, please. Dagen, please concentrate. Jane, we need to go to Ruoššasuolu. Just keep repeating the word in your mind and hopefully, it should work.'

Glaring at me she said waspishly, 'I know how my power works.'

Rolling his eyes, Dagen grabbed mine and Jane's hands. 'Get it over with.' I felt his cold hand wrap around my own. At least the leaves were working.

Jane phaded us to a small peninsula near Ruoššasuolu. Granted it wasn't exactly where we wanted to go, but it was close enough.

'Gods above it's...not that cold,' Dagen clarified, as the icy winds began to blast him as we arrived. Bending down, he touched the snow gently then retracted his hand. 'I feel the cold, but it doesn't bother me. It's a very strange experience.'

'Your bodies are adapting to the climate,' I told them peering up at the dark, looming mountains before us. 'Though you can distinguish the cold from the nippy, you won't be complaining that you can't feel your toes,' I told them. 'I'm not sure how long the spell will last, so if any of you feel the cold, please tell me.'

'I would never feel the cold. I'm home!' Tyr exclaimed, as he ran and sprang into the air, landing in the thick snow. 'Ah, it is good to be back.'

'How close or far away are we to the Moirae?' Jane asked as she trudged her way through the crunchy snow.

I shook my head and shrugged. If anything, it would be down to Tyr or at least Dagen to find them. Because of the simple fact that this was Tyr's homeland, and Dagen, because he, at least, could sense magic.

Though I, too, could sense magic, I can't pinpoint it on land. That was my only flaw. For example, as soon as we phaded here, I felt at least four different types of magic. Threatening, protective, ancient and evil and each worried me. Glancing at Dagen I wondered if he could sense the same thing, though he did not say anything. I was starting to wonder about his magical capabilities.

'We better get a move on,' I told the group as Tyr stood up covered in snow with a beaming smile on his face. 'Let's head for the mountains in front of us. The higher we are the better the advantage.'

The icy winds lessened as we began to walk towards the foreboding mountains ahead, however, the four types of magic that I had sensed previously unexpectedly began to merge, signalling that something was going to happen. I glanced in every direction, frustrated that I couldn't see it.

'Dagen,' I started to ask. But turning to look at him, his face was pure horror.

With his wide scared eyes looking dead ahead, he began to back away. 'You'll see it in a minute.'

Moving in front of the group, I placed my hands over the snow ready to draw power from the frozen water. I wasn't going down without a fight. I heard it before I saw anything; a rattling sound of thick heavy chains, metal clinking against metal. They kept in beat to someone or something that was very slowly dragging itself towards us.

'No,' Tyr breathed in horror. 'It, it can't be.'

'Explain,' I demanded from him, but he shook his head in fright. 'Tyr-' I began, but I abruptly stopped as I heard a loud dog-like howl. Whatever it was, it sounded big.

The others scrambled behind me as the sounds of the chains grew ever closer. My heart rate picked up as I faced the unknown danger. Scanning ahead, I saw a shimmer of purple light in front of me as though there was a tear in the air, ripping from unknown seams. Several heavy, rusty links from a large chain fell out of the rip and clinked to the white powered ground below. Slowly, and dripping in what I could only imagine as thick black tar, a thin right leg extended out of the rip. As soon as its pad touched the pure white snow, the concentration of evil and vengeance suddenly blasted into my face, making me shiver in fright. Its mangled chest followed its right leg, and within moments, the head and neck of the most disgusting, frightening wolf I had ever seen in my life emerged.

'Fenrir,' I heard Tyr gasp in terror as the animal fully materialized. With bared yellow teeth, wherein tar mixed with bloody drool dripped from its jowls, the wolf stared solely at Tyr. 'I thought I was your friend,' Tyr began, but the wolf suddenly snapped loudly to shut him up.

The thick chains wrapped around its body, cutting deep into him; it almost seemed like the flesh and metal had fused in places, making the wounds appear festered.

Flicking my eyes at Tyr I saw so much pain on his face. What had happened between these two?

'You, wolf,' I said to it, mustering up all of my courage, 'be gone from this place. Go back to the hell that spat you out.'

Growling in anger, the wolf bent low to the ground, about to pounce.

'No,' Tyr moved in front of me. 'Do not attack my friends. You are angry and so you should be, but I am angry and sad too. You killed my grandfather who was avenged by my uncle, and yet in spite of that, your hateful spirit wishes to attack and harm me and my friends? What ails you to warrant such an attack against me? The only one who cared for you? Can you not remember, Fenrir?'

Snapping with quivering jowls, the wolf nodded its head slightly but did not calm his angry white eyes. Instead, the wolf took a strong step towards Tyr, growling all the while.

'I am not your master and I am not your enemy,' Tyr told him gently, putting his hands up in a gesture that said he was not going to fight. But, that was a bad mistake.

Without any warning, the wolf launched its mangled, chain-covered body towards Tyr. 'NO,' I yelled loudly, pushing Tyr out of the way and pulling up a shield of ice from the ground, Fenrir hit square on. 'GO! MOVE!' I shouted to the others, as I ran right.

Following me, we sprinted through the deep snow, but I wasn't going fast enough. Annoyed, I lifted my hands and called out, 'Clear a path.' A long strip of snow began to melt into the solid dirt below. The path was just wide enough for us to run along. 'Get in front of me,' I yelled at the others, as I tried to push them past me.

Screaming, Jane grabbed hold of Tyr and ran in front of me. Dagen however, was still trailing behind.

Unexpectedly, I heard the wolf's loud angry howl again making me jump from fright. It echoed around us and sounded scarily close. Grabbing Dagen by his shirt, I dragged him forwards. 'Stay ahead of me you idiot, you can't stop him!'

Not arguing, Dagen went in front and ran after the others, kicking up grit as he went.

Hearing the growl and the snapping maw of the vicious wolf, I upended the drifts of snow along the path; creating a semi blizzard to reduce the animal's visibility. I wondered how long that trick would last.

Picking up speed, I caught up with the others, 'Tyr, how do we stop him?' I called out

'It's me! He's after me,' Tyr called back.

'Right you lot, protect Tyr, unless…' I said but then stopped myself and blurted out, 'Renita!'

Suddenly the person upfront fell from view; Jane and Dagen tripped up and were sprawled across the path.

Spinning around, my heart pounding from fear rather than lack of energy, I saw the shaggy mangy wolf lunge for us. About to make another shield of ice to protect everyone, the wolf suddenly vanished in a gust of snowy air, followed by its evil magical presence.

Panting, I looked around for an ambush, and after a few moments, I breathed a sigh of relief. 'It's gone.' I turned around to see the others picking themselves off the ground.

'Where am I?' Renita quivered, looking scared. 'I was in an igloo and now I'm here...'

'You are in Norway,' Jane said hugging her. 'Glad to have you back.'

'This switching people thing is getting tedious,' Dagen snapped at me. 'Why can't you fix this?'

Feeling slightly insulted I rounded on him. 'Why don't YOU fix them? You are meant to be the apprentice of Merlin. As far as I was aware, Merlin was the best wizard in history. Yet I have not seen one ounce of your capabilities, nor have I *ever* heard your name in mythology!'

'Please don't argue,' Renita said softly as she came between us. 'It's not going to help matters. Besides, can someone fill me in on why we are here?'

'I will,' Jane said happily, 'but let's do it while we walk. Thera, can you create another path towards the mountain please?'

Obliging, the group began to trudge along the small path. Jane and Renita happily chattered away while Dagen and I remained silent. There was something up with him, I just didn't know what it was but I was determined to find out.

CHAPTER FOUR

WITHIN A FEW HOURS, THE THICK CURTAIN OF WINDS BEGAN TO DIE DOWN leaving a new powdery cover of soft, brilliant white snow that reflected the half-moon, hidden behind the shadowy clouds above.

'Wow, it's a nice place here when we're not chased by a tar-covered wolf,' Jane sighed happily as she linked arms with Renita, leading the way. 'So are we heading upwards then?' she called.

Dagen and I trailed behind. I had been staring into space thinking about Santorini and wondering what he was doing. I felt so lonely and lost without him. Why did he do this to me? Did he not know I needed him to complete me? Idiot brother.

'Thera, did you hear me?' Jane called again.

'Yes, up,' I snapped, then immediately felt bad for being so blunt. 'Sorry, I just miss my brother.'

'What was he like?' Renita asked as she turned around to face me.

Dagen stopped and let me pass him. 'I don't want to be involved in this conversation,' he said grumpily.

'You weren't going to be anyway,' I hissed nastily catching up to the others. 'What do you want to know?'

'You said that the Ocean made you both into Water Nymphs, what is the Ocean like?' Renita asked, smiling at him, a little twinkle in her eyes.

Sighing happily, I smiled back. 'She is my mother and I love everything about her. She knows everything that has ever sailed across her many seas or dived into the deepest trenches. The only sad thing is when she gets sick,' I said feeling the pain of the many times my mother had to endure the pain and suffering of the mishaps that have happened in her life.

'What do you mean, get sick?' Dagen asked from behind me, sounding intrigued.

'Battles, explosions and spillage from humans,' I told them, 'it doesn't help her. That is why she entrusted Santorini and me to help look after the seas for her as well as water-related myths and legends.'

'Wow, you do a lot of work, don't you? Is there anything else you do?' Jane asked me, her eyes lightening up.

I nodded. 'We monitor the earthquakes in the oceans as well as underwater volcanoes. Many times you'll get tidal waves which can cause a lot of damage. Naturally, we try to stop them, or at least slow them down but um Atlantis was our biggest mistake. We will never do that again.'

'What about Pompeii? Were you responsible for that?' Jane asked me, but I vigorously shook my head.

'Nope, it was land-based. We had nothing to do with that. Not sure who was responsible for it actually.'

'By responsible you mean purposely causing it?' Dagen asked me, a slight tone of disgust in his voice.

'Mother Nature causes it,' I said in a scalding way, 'but she has helpers who deal with-' but I suddenly stopped talking and quickly said, 'shh.'

Immediately everyone stopped, my heart was pounding in my chest again. Something was with us and I could not see it. 'Dagen,' I said quietly, 'do you sense it?'

'Yes,' he said breathlessly, 'but I don't know where it is coming from.'

'Above,' Jane said, clasping her hands over her head as though in agony. 'There's two of them, they mean harm. They want to sow the seeds of the dead. I can see them. We have to get out of here.' Was this her other power?

Suddenly, she grabbed Renita and began to run. 'Hey wait, what's happening?' I asked feeling utterly confused. 'What do you mean to sow the seeds of the dead?'

'It's Odin's ravens,' she squealed. Then no sooner had she mentioned them, two large ravens that were the colour of night itself, suddenly dropped from the dark velvety sky above and attacked.

'Run!' Dagen yelled, trying to beat the birds away, but it seemed impossible; they were relentless, continuing to peck and scratch at our heads as we ran.

'Where to? There's no cover!' Jane yelled back.

'Protect us,' I gestured at the snow. Within seconds, the snow in front of Jane and Renita curled up and over like a wave and crashed over us, forming a protective dome.

'Thank you,' Jane panted, smiling slightly.

'This isn't going to protect us for long,' I said worriedly as I heard the top of the dome take on some heavy damage. 'Jane, what did you mean about sowing the seeds of the dead?' I asked as the others looked at her, shock etched on their faces.

'Dragons teeth,' she said, 'they are going to drop dragon's teeth.'

I groaned at my stupidity and kicked a snowdrift in front of me.

'What…what does that mean?' Dagen asked confused.

Taking a breath I said, 'Drop dragon's teeth into the soil where battles have been fought and it will raise the dead, and not just the random dead, the warrior dead. We are standing in a country that has been through a lot of bloody battles with a lot of bloodthirsty warriors.'

'Can't you use your magic to help us?' he asked in a pompous manner.

Whipping round to face him, I glared at him angrily. 'Can you please understand something? We are trying to be cautious to get to the Moirae. They have many myths defending them, the first was the wolf, and the second is the ravens with warrior backup. We are outnumbered. They are having a grand old time watching us suffer like this!'

'What can we use to defend ourselves?' Jane panicked.

Dagen snorted. 'There's nothing here to defend ourselves. It's a wasteland of snow and rock.'

'Rock-' I gasped as I turned to look at Renita. 'The rock Renita! Form it into something that can protect us.'

'Are you mad?' she asked looking offended. 'I can't do that. It takes time and precision.'

'We don't have time for precision,' Dagen snarled at her, 'just make a big rock-giant or something.'

'Thicket,' she snapped, 'I need an object to work from! I can't just bring up a rock from the ground.'

I smiled. 'You can't, but I can.' Making the dome wider, I made everyone back against the walls. The ravens continued to hammer down, but I was lucky they hadn't broken through just yet. Melting the rest of the snow that was under our feet, I pressed my hands to the ground and concentrated; after all, it was much easier doing this in water than on land. My hands suddenly glowed red and began to sizzle. 'Huh, interesting.'

'Phew it's hot in here,' Jane said fanning her face.

'I used to be lava remember?' I told her. 'I'm used to bubbles when I mould the earth,' I explained to Renita as she seemed puzzled at my words.

After a while, I managed to grab a decently proportioned piece of the rock, roughly about twenty feet tall and slowly began to lift it out of the cold ground.

'Your dome is melting,' Dagen said covering his head as the roof began to drip on him.

Sighing impatiently, I waved my hand at the dome and it re-froze. There was silence from outside. 'Hmm, it seems the ravens have stopped attacking, that can't be good.' Quickly, placing my hands onto the extremely hot rock, it began to cool so that Renita would be able to mould it.

Standing back and smiling at my genius, I motioned to her. 'Right you get on with it. We'll get the attention of the birds to give you some time, alright?'

'What? You're going to leave me?' she squeaked, her eyes looking fearful as she glanced between Jane and me. I didn't want to leave her if truth be told, but I guessed she would need some time to create this giant and if Jane said that the birds were going to drop dragon's teeth, it was only a matter of time.

'Artist's are best left alone,' Jane smiled and clapped her on the back. 'Good luck!'

Before we gathered, there was a sudden rumble of the earth.

'Oh no,' Jane whimpered.

Quickly placing my hands on the frozen ground, I tried to understand what the rumble was but as far as I could tell, it wasn't warriors rising from the dead and it certainly wasn't an earthquake. 'I don't know what it was,' I told them feeling annoyed that my powers weren't helping me. 'Look, forget it, it didn't feel life-threatening, let's move.'

Opening a small hole in the ice dome, the three of us ducked out and ran.

'Where are we going to run to?' Jane hollered through the frosty winds that had picked up again.

'Just head up,' Dagen said. 'The higher we are the better it is for us.'

Cringing at his logic, I briefly turned around to see the look on his face. 'How do you think it's better for us?'

'Because you can avalanche the warriors when they turn up,' he yelled to me.

Seething in rage at his stupidity, I was about to yell at him when the mountain began to shake again.

Jane and Dagen lost their balance and fell over. I spun around and saw a shadowy figure looming ahead.

Standing in front of the others, I braced myself for an onslaught of warriors but as the figure got closer and became clearer, I blinked in confusion. 'Etrician?'

'What up girl!' he said smiling. With his ever muscular bronze toned body hidden behind a rust-coloured shirt and beige shorts, his intense eyes locked onto mine. How I missed him. ''Ow is it I find you 'er on me, rock mon. What are you doing 'er?'

'Your rock?' Dagen snapped, standing up and brushing snow from him.

'Yeah little man, my rock.'

Stifling a laugh I folded my arms and stared at him. 'You like it in Jamaica then? You've got the accent down pat.'

'Only one that flows right wid me,' he said, making a wave motion with his hand, but dropped his accent after I gave him a stern look. 'Besides, I blended right in with the crowds. It's how I got these!' He pointed to his dreadlocks. 'Now, why are you here?'

Stepping between us, Dagen shouted to get attention. 'Wait, who is he?'

'This is Etrician,' I introduced him. 'He is a son of Mother Nature. In other words, a legend. Mother Nature needed someone to help tidy up and to keep an eye on things on land, so she made him,' I told Dagen and Jane.

'Incoming!' Jane suddenly screamed, as she pointed to the sky.

Spinning around, I glanced up and saw the movement of two silhouettes flying fast in our direction. 'Etrician, we need to hide in this mountain, they won't be able to get us in a cave. Help us and I'll tell you all you need to know!' I added as he looked like he was about to abandon us.

'Follow me,' he said, taking up my path and running up it.

'But what about Renita?' Jane called back looking scared.

'She's a big girl, she can take care of herself,' Dagen bellowed, following immediately behind Etrician. Though Dagen was right, I didn't want to leave Renita on her own.

The four of us headed upwards, quickly followed by the loud flapping of wings and then suddenly: *plop, plop, plop* of something hitting the snow.

'Etrician, get us in the mountain NOW,' I yelled at him my nerves wracked with fear at the prospect of warriors of the dead coming to fight us. It didn't matter how many times I had to bury the dead when they sunk their ships at sea; the visual appearance of skeletons still upset me.

Sprinting past a large drift of snow, Etrician curled his hands into fists and punched the rock in front of him. A perfect archway opened up in the snowy ground admitting us. Etrician stood back to let the three of us pass but when Jane stopped as it was too dark, I heard Etrician muttered cursed words behind me. Moving me to the side, he slapped the inside of the newly built rocky passage; within seconds bright green crystals flowered from the ceiling, guiding us deeper into the mountain.

'You guys stay down there,' he called from the entrance. 'I'll wait for your friend.'

A little frightened and out of breath, the three of us came out of the small tunnel and into a semi decently sized chamber where the fluorescent green rock glittered brightly from large clumps around us, creating various spooky dark green shadows.

'Your friend is good with rock,' Jane laughed shakily.

Groaning I shook my head, 'Don't tell him that, he'll think he's the king of the rock.'

'I am the king of the rock!' Etrician laughed down the passage. 'Yea 'av dat!'

Chuckling, I closed my eyes and stared at the floor. 'Now we have a short time to breathe,' I said worrying about Renita.

'I think we drew them away from Renita,' Jane said as she hugged her knees to her chin. 'But we need to think of a plan to go back and help her.'

I nodded then turned to Dagen. 'I have something to say. Dagen, are you some sort of idiot?'

'I beg your pardon?' he asked indignantly. 'An idiot? I think it's a fair assumption to call *you* the idiot. Your brother asked us to help you, not the other way around.'

'Well I don't see you doing your job!' I snapped at him. 'Asking me to make an avalanche, are you crazy? Those skeletons are relentless. You can't kill the dead. You can maybe slow them down by lobbing off their heads but they'll still walk! For the love of Atlas, don't you think?'

'Oy lava,' Etrician called to me, 'cool it down. I 'av to concentrate. I cannot think with your eruptions.'

'It's interruptions,' I mumbled. Folding my arms, I turned away from Dagen; I didn't even want to look at him. Jane was right though, Renita was the one we needed to help. After all, she was two members of our group.

Out of the corner of my eye, through the tinged green room, I saw Jane clutch her head. Moving swiftly to her, I stared into her pained looking face. 'Breathe,' I told her softly. 'Is it your visions?'

Without saying a word, she nodded.

Placing my hand on her forehead, I closed my eyes. I could not help her control her vision, but I could at least try to take some pain away. Letting out a sigh of relief, though still clutching her head she told me, 'She's made the giant but...' she frowned and tilted her head, 'it's abnormal.'

'Forget what it looks like,' Dagen hissed from beside her.

'Ignore him,' I scowled at Dagen. 'Just concentrate.'

'She's surrounded,' Jane said loudly, 'she's surrounded, help her...HELP HER!' she screamed.

Jumping up, I quickly left her side and headed through the passage. As I got to the entrance, I saw Etrician race down the snowy mountain like a rocket heading towards what appeared like the fray of the battle.

I smiled and dug my hand into the snow nearby and drew out an ice-sword. 'CHARGE!' I yelled, running pell-mell down the path, the ice-sword waving madly over my head as I ran towards the silent deathly warriors of old.

As I arrived, Etrician had the same idea as me. In his hand was the more favourable material to behead magical walking skeletons, a perfect diamond sword. He thrashed away at the oncoming onslaught, grinning madly and shouting, 'Av that you skull 'ed.' Glancing to my right was a large bizarre rock creature charging up the path with Renita perched on its shoulder like some strangely elongated parrot.

With one leg and one arm shorter than the other, the strange living formation limped its way to the skeletons and bashed them on the head, laughing childishly as the skulls cracked underneath it.

'Oh charming,' I winced as I could feel each crack the monster made.

'Are you going to just stand there or are you going to help?' Etrician said, snapping me out of my bewilderment.

Raising my sharp-edged sword, I swung it towards three oncoming skeletons and chopped their skulls off, each one of them falling to the floor with a sickening crunch.

One skull rolled towards me. I kicked it, making it fly in an arc towards the gimpy rock monster. Seeing the flying skull coming towards it, it used its hand as a bat and whacked it towards the icy cliffs behind me, smashing the skull into smithereens.

'Nice shot!' I laughed as I barrelled towards another set of fleshless humans.

'Take 'dat an 'dat, ya sick twisted freaks,' Etrician guffawed, lopping the heads and legs off the skeletons that advanced towards him.

After twenty minutes into the fight, Etrician wasn't laughing any more, and neither was I.

'How do you stop them?' Renita called out, as her rock monster now took it upon its being to smash the skulls and any bones it found to smithereens; just to ensure they wouldn't rise again, but it didn't work. Within minutes the smashed skulls and bones reformed themselves, making up the skeletons again.

As I had told Dagen, they were relentless.

'There's only one way,' I told her, slicing a skeleton in two and jumping out of the way as one ran towards me, but then it promptly smacked into one of its fleshless comrades.

'I'm listening,' Etrician said.

'To kill Odin's ravens. They are the Planters.'

The skeletons now decided that the rock monster and myself were threats and turned around, heading west. Following their direction, I saw Etrician on the ground in the snow, his sword beside him, motionless.

Panicking, I ran towards him, slicing off the skulls of some advancing skeletons who had got too close for comfort. Skidding to a stop, I grabbed onto Etrician's face, forcing him to look at me. 'Etrician, what's wrong? Are you injured?' Looking up the skeletons had pieced themselves back together. With their old swords and shields in hand, they ran at us again.

'I was so close,' he said softly, as though in pain. 'I was so close...'

'So close to what? You're not dying, are you? You idiot you can't die from a sword wound!' I said. My heart began to beat loudly in my chest as panic filled every part of my soul. I didn't know what was wrong with him, he seemed perfectly fine not five seconds ago.

'I was so close…to becoming de-manned,' he said, almost crying. 'That last skeleton nearly snapped off my man parts.'

Suddenly realising what he was talking about, I exploded.

'WHAT!' My hands suddenly turning a bright red from the heat I was emitting.

'Hey, you have no idea what it's like losing your family jewels.' He frowned, cupping them protectively. 'And let me tell you, I got me some big jewels.'

'ARGH!' Pouncing on him, I throttled him with my scorching hot hands. 'YOU BLITHERING IDIOT YOU ALMOST…MADE ME… CARE ABOUT YOU,' I said, beating his head against the floor.

'Hey guys, a little help,' Renita asked from behind me.

Turning around, but still seething from Etrician's idiocy, I saw the skeletons amassed and gather around Renita and the rock monster. Renita's energy was draining from her quickly and the rock monster was slowing down.

Glancing back to Etrician, I said slowly and dangerously, 'You are going to protect the boy. And when we are safe inside the mountain, you will seal up the cave. Do I make myself clear?'

'Yes ma'am,' he gulped in fear.

Standing up, I picked Etrician up with me, holding him still. Spinning around, with my right hand I shot out five blasts of blazing red-hot fire at the skeletons; scattering them instantly. Usually, I wasn't able to do this. Being a Water Nymph you're meant to have a cool head, but it wasn't my fault I was originally lava. Mother always did say I had a temper, but it usually appeared when someone I cared for was in danger or…if someone I used to care for annoyed me…yet again!

'I'm sorry Renita,' I said through gritted teeth. 'Come forth Tyr.'

Cringing, Renita fell forwards to the snow in agony.

'Etrician, stop that wolf,' Letting him go I ran to the quivering form of Tyr by the rock monster who had stopped moving completely as though life had been snatched from it.

'What wolf?' Etrician asked but no sooner had he asked that, a howling wolf's call sounded nearby, followed by a low menacing growl.

The atmosphere suddenly changed into revenge again, making me cower from it, but I had to be strong for Tyr.

Struggling to get up, I was by his side and began to help him to his feet. 'Fenrir, he is back,' Tyr said, sounding upset.

'We have another problem; Odin's ravens have brought the dragon's teeth. You need to stop them,' I said, giving him a meaningful eye.

He shook his head. 'I cannot destroy the last remnants of my grandfather. They guard Valhalla with their very souls. I can ask for them to stop, but whether they will listen to me is another matter.'

I nodded, understanding. Tyr leaned on me as I took him towards the passage ahead.

Taking a deep breath, Tyr tossed his head back to look to the darkening yet flurrying sky. 'Huginn and Muninn I call you to me.'

My eyes darted to the skies, but there was nothing. 'Try again,' I begged him. 'Please.'

Puffing out his chest, he stood up boldly and said a little more loudly, 'Hugninn, Muninn, I call you to me, Tyr, grandson of Odin. Come to me and listen to my words.'

My heart lifted as I heard two screeching squawks of two very large birds above me. Still holding onto Tyr, I felt him sigh in relief as the two ravens swooped down and landed close to us; their heads bowed in respect, which was a good sign.

'Call off the seeds of the dragon's teeth. Odin would not allow another myth on his land that goes against his kith and kin! Be gone and take them with you!' Tyr said strongly and confidently.

The Ravens gave a harrowing squawk in reply and one by one the skeletons slowly began to collapse; leaving nothing but the pasty white lifeless bones in their place.

'Right, we can run now,' I said, picking him up and carrying him towards the passage. 'Etrician, get a move on!'

'Yeah I'm coming woman,' he yelled.

Diving into the passage, I pushed Tyr in front of me. Tripping up, he rolled down the rocky hole in the ground, but I was worried about someone else now.

'GARH!' I heard him scream from somewhere close by. The howling of the wolf was scarily closer then I had previously thought and I hoped and prayed that Tyr would be safe underground, at least for the time being.

Hearing the crunching of snow, I saw Etrician's looming figure. Moving out of the way, he dove into the passage and quickly closed it behind him. 'You owe me big time! What on Atlas is going on?'

Chapter Five

All snug and safe from ghostly Fenrir above, everyone gathered around a large glowing green gem and looked at Etrician like a strange intruder. He, on the other hand, glared at me in a threatening manner. 'You,' he pointed at me, making everyone jump. 'Are you going to tell me?'

Sighing, I rubbed my temples and stood up. 'So, Santorini is stuck in the other plane, as far as we are aware. This lot,' I pointed to them, 'are myths; apparently, Santorini sent them to help me. Although, a team of men in black suits are after me because of the Cabinet of Idols.'

'You've been marked for da Cabinet of Idols?' he asked, looking shocked. 'Dang girl, what 'av you done to deserve dat?'

'That's not the half of it,' I began, traipsing around the room in thought, 'they had the Staff of Zeus.'

'No way. Dat's impossible, who would give it to humans man? Dat's crazy…Wait-' he frowned cottoning on, 'you said had…'

I gestured to the others. 'They dropped it.'

'Oh you are not funny,' Etrician said standing up and moving away from them like they were diseased. 'Don't day know it's dangerous?'

I shrugged my shoulders. 'Apparently not,' I told him, 'but we are on our way to the Moirae to get some answers.'

Still frowning, he folded his arms and stared at me with a perplexed attitude. 'They're here? In this place? Well, good luck.'

After a few seconds of silence, Dagen asked, 'Have you two finished insulting us?'

'Ignore him,' I told Etrician, who was about to say something.

'No,' Dagen shouted, 'I will not be ignored! Who is this man anyway? First, he springs up from nowhere, then you both run away, and now she's turned back into a boy,' Dagen said pointing to Tyr, 'and the wolf is back. What is going on? Who is he to you?'

Feeling slightly embarrassed I sat down a little ways from them and looked away. I did not want to get into this conversation. It was embarrassing for both of us and judging by the look on Etrician's face, which was very similar to mine, he didn't want to talk about it either.

'Leave them alone,' Jane said at him, 'can't you see they don't want to talk about it. Shouldn't we be thinking of a way to get out of here and get past Fenrir?'

Etrician nodded and clapped. 'Well said. See a lady who knows sense.'

'Yes, because you don't know or have any,' Dagen snapped.

Etrician suddenly saw red. He had had enough. With his eyes turning a fiery crimson, he waved his hand and a large piece of rock clamped onto Dagen's mouth and, by the looks of it, was unable to come off.

Stifling a giggle, I turned away as Dagen got up and began mumbling incoherent words at Etrician.

'W-what have you done to him?' Tyr asked with wide eyes.

'It's obvious isn't it?' Jane asked him. 'He's shut him up so they don't have to talk about their private lives. I think it suits him.'

Glancing around, I saw Dagen shoot a filthy look towards her but was unable to say anything. Folding his arms in disgust, he glared at me as though it was my fault.

Etrician importantly straightened his jacket then grabbed my shoulders gently. 'Look at me girl.' Sighing, my eyes flew up to his and I felt better. Though we'd had our differences in the past, Etrician was there for me when I needed him, even if Santorini wasn't. 'No one knows who or what you are to me apart from us. So, you want help out of this cavern?'

I nodded. He turned to address the group, but I stopped him and grabbed his hand. 'Thank you for coming when you did. I know it was accidental,' I laughed softly, 'but it's appreciated.'

'Hey, girl. What have I told you there are no accidents. Everything happens for a reason. But I will tell you 'dis;' Drawing close to me he whispered, 'watch out for Dagen. That boy has a mouth on him and when he realises what he can do, you'll be in a world of trouble.'

'Hmm,' I agreed, but he quickly withdrew from me and headed towards the group before I had a chance to ask more.

'Right den,' he said slapping his hands together and rubbing them in enthusiasm. 'Let's get you to your destiny.' He smiled and moved to the back of the cavern; glancing over his shoulder he winked and snapped his fingers. With a small rumble, a clean-cut tunnel appeared. Bright green luminescent rock shone brightly on the ceiling. 'After you,' he motioned.

Dagen waltzed right up to him, prodding him in the shoulder then pointing at his mouth. Looking stern Etrician moved closer to him and whispered in his ear. As Dagen's eyes grew wide with fear, he quickly nodded. Putting a supportive hand on his shoulder, Etrician removed the rock from his mouth and, without a word, Dagen headed off into the tunnel.

Curious, I was about to ask Etrician what he had said, but he turned and shook his head. 'In good time.'

As we all entered the tunnel, Etrician guided us deeper into the mountain but after ten minutes of walking, stopped. 'Dis is as far as I can go, I cannot go any deeper. It's not my place to take you.'

Moving past the others, I caught up to him and roughly spun him around. 'You know something. You got a vision from the earth didn't you?' I demanded. 'Tell me what is in store for us?'

He appeared sad and gave me a concerned look. 'There are things which I do not know and cannot say, but know this: believe in them or else the world will fall to its knees.' Cupping my cheek with his warm hand, he bent forward to kiss me on the head. I closed my eyes and pretended we were alone together, away from all of this; back on the island, we had designed for ourselves before arrogant Aphrodite took it over. But when I opened my eyes he was gone. The only thing I could still feel was his warm hand on my face.

Turning my back on the others, I hid my emotion. For centuries, I had been trying to keep it under control; I couldn't let them see me cry. It would show them I'm weak. The sea was never weak. It was strong, heartless and cruel. With a deep breath, I strode on, hearing the others follow me without uttering a word of complaint.

My feet slapped the wet floor of the Etrician-made tunnel and I began to wonder about everything to this point. How we got here, why we were attacked and what were the chances that the Fates would answer our questions. Something was niggling at me, yet I was unsure what it was. What was I missing?

Stopping I turned to face the group. 'Why are we here?'

Glancing at each other in confusion Jane and Dagen shrugged their shoulders. My eyes stared into Tyr's. He frowned in thought, saying, 'we were attacked.'

'Elaborate.'

'Your friend made this tunnel to escape from the skeletons,' his voice sounded cautious, on the edge of understanding something. 'But not just the skeletons, from Fenrir as well.'

'Why is he after you?' I demanded my voice strong and penetrating. 'What does he want? No ghost can want revenge in the way he was attacking you.'

I saw it, out of the corner of my eye Tyr's right hand twitched nervously. With one move my hand reached out and grabbed it, 'tell me, what is the purpose of your right hand? Why did you not have one before? Who are you Tyr?'

Yanking it away he cradled it tenderly as though nursing an old lost friend. 'I sacrificed my hand a long time ago.' Sighing heavily, he held it up for us all to see. 'My grandfather Odin sacrificed his eye for wisdom and me, my hand, for the greater good and safety of the Gods. I fell from my Godly plinth in Asgard and now I watch as my grandfather takes my place and rules over the skies. I am not a full god anymore but a fallen one; a half-god, cursed to have Fenrir follow me whenever I am in my homelands. However, a long time ago, I fled to the other plane to be at peace. I knew Fenrir could not follow.'

'So, you have one now because you are fused with...her,' I said, mindful of my words. With another heavy sigh, he nodded. Turning my back on him, I began to walk again; everyone was quiet as Tyr's truthful words sank in, giving them plenty to think about. However, I was wondering about the only option in separating the two.

As I had seen, it was an increasing strain on both of them to swap personalities, almost damaging their souls. It was also taking a toll on their bodies physically and mentally. I was beginning to think that if Tyr's hand was once again severed by Fenrir the wolf, there may be a chance to split them out of one body.

My mind though constantly went back onto Dagen and who he was. Etrician knew and he warned Dagen, but I was unsure. I had a suspicion that Dagen was a liar, but it was his choice to tell us. However, if he did not tell us soon, he may put us in danger and that was something I was unwilling to tolerate. 'Idiot brother,' I mumbled. It was his fault.

Without looking where I was walking, my foot clipped a rock and suddenly I tripped up and fell over. 'Thera' Jane yelled, as she and Tyr came to my side. But I just laid there on the floor and, without knowing why, I suddenly burst out laughing. 'Um, are you alright?' Jane asked confused, as I creased up, tears pouring from my eyes.

I nodded and rolled over, looking up at them. 'Well, my foot hurts, but apart from that I'm alright.' Tyr offered a hand and helped me up. 'Well that's better,' I sighed in relief. 'Too much serious thinking and it drives me mad. Anyway, I've thought of a way to un-fuse you and her,' I said to Tyr. 'The thing is, it involves your hand.'

Clenching it into a fist he nodded solemnly. 'I thought you'd say that.'

'And it also involves Fenrir.'

'What?' he barked, 'I won't let him come near me.' Tyr's eyes had dark circles underneath; he was nervous, yet there was a sense of weariness.

Jane put a reassuring hand on his arm, 'I think we should listen to Thera, we need to trust her. Right Dagen?'

With three sets of eyes staring at him, Dagen the know-it-all just nodded. My eyes slanted at his strange behaviour.

'I'll do what you say,' Tyr said sadly, looking forlornly at his appendage. I smiled at him warmly and placed a comforting hand on his shoulder and nodded.

The tunnel soon stopped and the four of us came out into a very dark, still world. On the other side of the small mountains, it was as though we had travelled into another land. It was deathly quiet over the tundra. The moon above now hidden behind thick dark clouds; only the faintest of light shone through, but not enough to show what was hidden around us. It got my back up instantly. A large bowl-shaped valley that gave the impression it was completely devoid of life lay before us. Situated in the centre and drawing my attention was a great, black frozen lake. My eyes suddenly shot to it. The vision the myths of the oceans had shown me was this lake, or rather, what was below it. 'We're here,' I told the others as they crowded around me, all of them staring.

'It's down there, isn't it? Under the ice?' Jane asked breathlessly, taking a nervous step towards it. Staring at the lake, I saw her eyes glance rapidly back and forth, as though she was mentally preparing herself. 'What else do you think will be waiting for us?'

Shaking my head, I remained silent. I didn't have a clue. The witches of destiny were ruthless. They would have more tricks up their sleeves to prove our worth to meet them. If anything, just meeting them would be a trial unto itself.

Carefully, we began to climb down the steep mountain; using craggy rocks as purchase to ensure a safe descent. Mindful, I found safe paths to tread. My eyes never wavering from Tyr and Dagen, they were my top priority.

Reaching the bottom, I called everyone to a stop and searched around. I strained my eyes and ears to pick up the slightest movement or sound, yet I saw and heard nothing. It was as quiet as the grave and a deathly silence was never good…

Jane bent down and touched the edge of the frozen lake, applying pressure. 'It looks thick enough to walk on, let's get going.' Before she took a single step, my arm flew out and stopped her.

'Ice can be deceiving and not in the way you'd think,' I said as I bent down to examine the hoarfrost. Placing my right-hand flat on its surface, I smiled. 'What message is it this time?' I asked. With a small push, the entire lake vibrated, quickly followed by the sound of cracking ice and splashing water.

Tyr, Jane and Dagen stumbled back looking shocked and frightened as parts of the ice-capped lake suddenly fell under the dark ominous water. When the ice stopped breaking, I could tell that there was a message that the Moriae had left for us, but it would take too long to walk back up the mountain to get a good look; after all, this was a very big lake.

Pondering how to do this, I turned to the snow behind me. 'Right, let's see if this will work.' Flicking my hands out, I stretched them wide. I wanted as much snow as possible. 'Up and over,' I called, lifting a layer of snow. Turning around carefully, with the deposit of snow hovering about twenty feet in the air, I placed it over the ice. 'Mirror,' I commanded strongly.

The snow glittered in the waning moonlight and crunched together, forming a slick sheet of reflective ice. Smiling at my genius, I lifted it higher and stared at the mirrored writing in the black ice.

My brows furrowed instantly as I stared at the peculiar reversed letters.

'That's, that's runes,' Tyr whispered, stepping to my side. 'That is the language of my people.' He moved closer craning his neck to get a better look. After a moment or two, he frowned and said, 'It's our names and…'

'And what?' Dagen asked apprehensively.

Tyr turned to face us, looking confused and scared. '*It's impossible to escape from what is destined.*'

CHAPTER SIX

THE MESSAGE THAT TYR TRANSLATED WAS PUZZLING AND FRIGHTENING. For the longest time, I stood there by the side of the black frozen lake in silence, trying to understand what it meant. It's impossible to escape from what is destined. Why was it impossible? Surely, you carve your destiny by walking upon a path that you create. If the Moirae already knew our destiny, then what was the point in life?

In deep thought, I was shaken awake by a small hand from Jane. Snapping out of my stupor, I looked to her as she pointed. 'The lake is glowing green. I think it's time to go.'

Gazing ahead, I sighed. We had come this far, we may as well continue to find out at least some answers to our questions.

Facing the others, I could see their scared faces. They were worried about what was down there and though I could only hazard a guess, I was not about to tell them my thoughts and motioned for them to fall in line behind me. 'Hold onto one another,' I told them, facing the frozen lake. Raising my hands abruptly to the dark overcast skies, the lake suddenly parted and the ice instantly broke, screeching and crashing together in a way that would make your teeth itch. As a path was made, heading to the centre of the lake, I began to slowly walk down it, hearing the others shuffle behind me.

'I don't like this,' I heard Jane mutter, her words full of fear. 'I'm getting a bad feeling about this but I can't see anything,' she said, referring to her visions.

'You won't,' I said softly, 'the Moirae will be blocking your powers. It would annoy them if there was some myth who bettered them at their own game.'

'And what game are you referring to might I ask?' Dagen quipped quickly.

I turned my head slightly. 'The Gambling Game of Fate. They hold the strings of everyone's life. It would spoil the fun if they could not control everyone's lives.'

Nearing the entrance, I could feel the power emanating from within. Though my nerves calmed as I felt neutral energy coming from inside the cave, I was still apprehensive. Ushering the others inside, I froze the entrance to the cave so no water could seep through.

Entering the wet cave I began to see the stalactites and stalagmites erupt from the ceiling and floor of the vestibule, shining various colours from white to pink with a tinged blue-grey colour. They fascinated me; they took so long to form and each was shaped differently. As I admired them, the others gaped at the large green light that was shining very brightly in front. Taking one glance at its source, I heard Tyr gasp in shock. From out of the corner of my eyes, I saw the look on his face and began to understand.

Moving towards it, the group stopped when we heard the slithering sound of feet dragging across the wet gravelly floor, waiting patiently for the person to approach us. The horrifying appearance of a frail, old woman came into view. She had white fraying hair, sunken hollow pupil-less eyes, baggy wrinkly skin and a drooping posture.

With a fragile bony elongated hand, she extended it towards us then, with a chilling crack of her knuckles, her index finger curved, beckoning us.

'Come on,' I said confidently to the others. I felt Jane clutch my arm like a small child and the boys followed in my wake as we carefully moved towards the haggard-looking old woman by the name of Atropos.

As we neared, she turned around and slowly moved to the left of the cave. The bright green orb, which emitted the light, floated right past us. It was clear on Tyr's face how much that orb meant to him, but now was not the time to discuss it. We had other things to do.

Putting her hands up to stop us, Atropos clapped once and in a large puff of deathly red and black smoke, her sisters Clotho and Lachesis appeared both looking as worn and haggard. Leaving Jane, I took a cautious step towards them and bowed. 'Your trials were entertaining,' I smiled weakly.

The sisters tittered and gazed curiously at me. 'We thought you'd enjoy them,' Atropos spoke with a raspy breath. 'We wanted to give you a challenge, but you haven't passed yet. Not until that boy is whole again.'

'And not until he speaks the truth,' Clotho snapped waspishly, her finger pointing to Dagen.

Dagen moved back, casting himself in my shadow. I moved in front of him, getting the full attention of the Moirae. 'I've come for some answers as you know. Tell me and we shall leave quickly.'

Like a gaggle of dying geese, they chortled until their laughs soon turned into hacking great coughs. I waited patiently until they got their breath back.

'The Cabinet of Idols,' Atropos said. 'I could tell you, but what would be the purpose? Wouldn't you feel better by discovering anything yourself?' Gritting my teeth, I knew where she was heading but remained silent. 'You have battled with this before have you not, Thera Mother of Water Nymphs? You came to us wanting answers, but matters must be addressed first,' she said. Taking a step towards us, she withdrew her finger. 'You, boy. You who speaks his mind and has much to say for himself. You will tell the group, tell the world who you are and what you've done or we shall speak no more.'

All eyes fell upon Dagen. He refused to come out of my shadow. Turning to face him, I sighed at the pained look on his face. He didn't need to say anything. He had already admitted to us what he wasn't and what he couldn't do by his actions or lack, thereof. Nevertheless, there must be a reason why. 'Tell us the truth Dagen,' I asked softly. 'What are you to Merlin?'

Looking away, he stared at the floor, his haughty spirit was gone and I guessed it was due to Etrician's words. 'I was an apprentice of Merlin but I...' he began, talking to the floor, 'I was cast out. He said I didn't have what it took to make a magician. He said I was better off as a stable boy.'

'But you were created, so there must be something you can do,' Jane said, trying to lift his spirits.

He stared up and met the sunken hollow eyes of the Moirae. 'Go on boy.'

'I'm a thief' he said sadly. 'I stole Merlin's powers, not all of them,' he added quickly, as though trying to redeem himself, 'but I did steal from him.'

'But he did not teach you how to use his magic,' I said, closing my eyes and searching back through my memory of all the times Dagen was unwilling to help. 'You did not help because you did not know how to use them.'

With a short nod he turned his back on us. He was genuinely ashamed of what he had done, but it didn't help us.

'He did help though,' Jane piped up. 'He gave me the power to phade us to Antarctica and to here as well. That counts doesn't it?'

Everyone was silent, unsure of what to say to Dagen or each other. Taking a deep breath to clear my mind, I opened my eyes and stared at the Moirae. Brittle yellow teeth smiled back at me. What were they smiling about now? 'Is that all?' I asked them, but it was pointless, nothing with them was ever easy.

In unity, they raised their hands and pointed to Dagen. '*Incarcerate!*' they spat.

Appearing out of nowhere, thick brown ropes flew out of their hands and wrapped around Dagen's body. Unable to hold himself up, he crashed to the floor, the platted magical cord twisting and entwining around his neck almost choking him.

Jane and Tyr quickly rushed to his side but I backed away. It was not within my power to help Dagen, nor was it Tyr or Jane's. This was Dagen's battle with himself. We should not interfere. 'Tyr, Jane,' I said loudly, getting their attention as their hands scrambled around the thick ropes, trying to free him. 'Come away. We cannot help him,' I said sadly.

Staring at me in puzzlement Jane ignored me and continued to help but Tyr saw the truth in my eyes and stood up, backing away.

'You boy,' the fates hissed again. Tyr and I looked over at them and they inched towards us. Grotesquely, their salivating mouths, quivering lips and sunken eyes seemed to fixate on Tyr and it worried me. 'You who are two whole people will die if you do not separate. You must save the girl who is as strong as a brick and save yourself who is quick on his feet. Be gone!' they screeched.

'Thera,' Tyr yelped, as an invisible something grabbed the back of his jacket and dragged him out of the cave back to the surface, with Tyr screaming all the way.

'TYR,' I yelled as I began to run, but something tripped me up and I fell with a loud thud to the floor. Rolling over, I saw the Moirae looking down on me, smiling in such a ghastly way I felt repulsed.

'Tyr no!' Jane yelled. She was still trying to help Dagen, but nothing she tried was working.

'Come with us Mother of Water Nymphs,' the Moirae said together.

Getting up I followed, but not before moving swiftly to Jane. 'You cannot help him,' I told her hurriedly, 'leave him be, he needs to find his power.'

'But what about Tyr?' she snivelled. 'I need to help.'

'It's not your knot, it's Dagen's. He has to undo it.' I stood up and glanced to see where the Moirae were going. I didn't have time to explain. 'I have to go, but leave him be,' I warned, running after the witches of destiny.

Following them round to the left, I came across a sunken pool that shimmered in white and blue light. 'The Pool of Truth,' they said, gesturing to it.

Grabbing a long white stick, Lachesis touched the pool lightly then withdrew staring at me. Curiosity got the better of me. Inching forward, I gazed into the pool and saw snippets from my past. 'I am the Fate of Past. I have seen your birth. I have seen your mistakes and your triumphs and all that ever was. I give you this message. Take your lessons from the past and use them for the future. Your past creates who and what you are. Do not forget that.'

Lachesis gave her stick to Clotho. And with a sneering look, Clotho tapped the pool. Within seconds of seeing the images in the lapping waters, I realised this was the Fate of Present.

She asked, 'Need I say anything? Betrayal, pain, torture. You are doing this to yourself by thinking too much. By all means think, plan, escape. However, be aware of your enemies. When once you had none, you now have the world against you. For now, do not let what may happen, be the reason for influencing your choices now.'

I smiled at her wisdom and she passed the stick onto, Atropos the Fate of the Future. It was she that I needed to talk to, yet I knew what she was going to say.

'It's impossible to escape from what is destined,' she said, not touching the Pool of Truth with the stick.

I laughed dryly. 'How did I know you were going to say that?'

Smiling with her wizened face she said, 'because like me, you do not want to know the future, you want to find out yourself and I respect that.' She sighed and shook her head. 'I know you want to know about the Staff of Zeus, but I cannot help you.'

'Do you at least know where it is?' I asked her, but she shook her head again.

'No, the Staff of Zeus is unwilling to be located. Nevertheless, those who matter have put things in motion. You need to search for two myths that are off our radars. Those who have been given the power of myths by humans.'

'I beg your pardon?'

'Hear what I say,' sounding impatient, she shooed the other two fates out of the way. 'The world has been given a date to end. However, there is a way to stop it and begin anew. This is not the end of the world; it is, on the other hand, the end of magic. It is the end of meaning and belief in something beyond humans' understanding. A war has begun and the humans started it. Your brother went to the other plane for fear of being captured by the Cabinet of Idols. But you knew this.'

I remained silent as she continued, though I felt fresh pain stab at my heart at his mentioning. I missed him dearly. I loved my brother with all my heart and soul, and being this long away from him was torturing me day by day.

'This war was started by a group of humans who became myths. It unbalanced the world and the Ancients had to get involved and turned them back into humans.' She held up a bony finger, 'my only message to you is to track two of them down.'

'And where are these two humans I need to find?' I asked, hopefully.

The Fate of Future smiled and shrugged, 'How in Hades underworld am I meant to know? For some reason, like the Staff of Zeus, I cannot get a reading on any of them. So far as we know, they are called Hannah and Darren and they live in England.'

I felt outraged by the fact that I needed human help to find the Staff of Zeus. It was insulting. Placing my hands on my hips and staring at them incredulously I asked, 'How can they help us, how can they do anything? Look at Dagen, he's a myth yet he cannot help himself. These two will never be able to help us, they're human!'

She shrugged, not seeming to care. 'You wanted our help and that's what you are getting. These two humans are your ripple effect.'

For the longest time, I had found humans superfluous. The majority of them had stopped believing in magic, they destroyed their planet, waste resources that keep them alive and yet somewhere, the universe was telling me I needed their help. It was a personal insult. After asking the Moirae how they could reclaim their powers, they told me I didn't have to know. For all-knowing myths, I found them extremely unhelpful.

I went back to Jane and Dagen, both of whom were still struggling against the ropes. Sighing, I sat on the floor, putting my knees to my chin and stared at them as though watching an interesting magic show. 'Look, it's not going to work,' I said to Jane, as she pulled at the ropes, making them tauter. 'You're making it worse for him. He's got to figure it out for himself.'

'What is going on?' Dagen panted, twisting and turning against his bonds. 'What is this rope?'

In despair, at his lack of knowledge, I replied, 'You have been entangled by the Gordion Knot and it can only be solved by a bold stroke. The person trapped within its coils is the only one who can figure it out and that's you so hurry it up, will you? We don't have all day.'

'Did the Fates tell you what you wanted to know about the Staff of Zeus?' Jane asked as she gave up and sat next to me. 'Oh, and the Cabinet of Idols?'

Shaking my head, I leaned against the wet rock. 'Nope, but two humans can help us.'

'I beg your pardon?' Dagen asked in an offended tone, as he craned his neck to look at me, looking like a flailing sea slug on a hook. 'Humans? But they can't help, what are the Fates playing at?'

Shrugging, I tilted my head and stared at him. 'They are some type of magical humans called Hannah and Darren. They became myths, unbalanced the world and the Ancients made them human again. Anyway, the only clue we have to find them is that they live in England. Atlas knows how they are going to help us, but we'll have to wait and see. Although, we can't do anything with you being tied up in the way that you are and Tyr fighting for his right hand. How on earth did we get into this situation?' I asked glancing up at the rocky ceiling to anyone who would reply.

Shrugging Jane replied, 'Dagen's an arrogant liar who doesn't think about anything but himself and Tyr is a sweet boy who doesn't want to cause trouble, yet trouble follows him around. Your brother has a sense of humour by picking us out.'

Barking out a laugh I tilted my head back and stared at the colourful rocky formations around. 'You have no idea. My brother has a rather interesting sense of humour.'

Dagen was now kicking out his feet, trying to slip out under the coils, it was a vain and fruitless attempt, but funny to watch.

'Oh yes, he's hilarious! Remind me to ask you about pointless anecdotes of your brother once I'm free of these wretched bonds,' Dagen spat.

'Your knot, your problem,' I said simply. 'Or, it's *knot* my problem,' I laughed.

Enraged, he shouted curses at me, but I closed my eyes and ignored him. Hearing Jane giggle beside me, I smiled and waited for Dagen to figure it out. 'I wonder how Tyr is doing.'

'It's worrying me that he's not back yet, maybe we should go looking for him?' she suggested.

Opening one eye, I glanced at her. 'By *we* you want *me* to go, right?'

With a childish smile, she replied, 'Well, I can look out for Dagen and encourage him to *knot* give up,' she laughed.

'Am I going to be punned at now until this is over with?' he yelled in annoyance.

Standing up I brushed the dirt off me. 'Yes and sheesh, don't get so up-taut.'

Jane burst out laughing, adding, 'Yes you're getting yourself all frayed.'

Chortling together like idiots as Dagen screamed and yelled in frustration, I walked away but turned suddenly to face them. 'Hey Jane, Jane, I have a good one. Knock, knock?'

'Who's there?'

'Knot me!'

Hardly able to keep myself from laughing so much, I stumbled out towards the mouth of the cave. Hearing Dagen's profanity mixed in with Jane's raucous laughter, kept me giggling all the way there. I stopped laughing as I saw my thick ice-wall in front of me, thankfully still intact. 'Move aside,' I ordered.

Obeying, the ice fell like thick droplets of dark rain, and water immediately began to pour in. Holding my hand up quickly, the water stopped, reflecting the shimmering green orb behind me that was yet to be addressed. Maybe when Dagen had released himself and Renita and Tyr were separated, the Moirae might discuss it with us. If not, then it was up to Tyr.

Walking into the refreshing dark water of the hidden lake, I sealed the entrance behind me and shot towards the surface. Landing gracefully onto the frozen bank, I was suddenly blown away by a great gust of wind. 'Catch me,' I ordered the water below. Spouting out a plume, it caught me before I fell and gently placed me on the ground. I peered out into the darkness to see who had cast such a strong wind. 'Tyr, have you got your powers back?' I called out into the night.

There was a small pause and then, 'Um yes kind of. Though would you mind shutting up, please? Fenrir is still after me.'

Within seconds of him speaking, there was the sound of a loud, spine chilling, wolf's howl, 'Oops.'

Snarling and snapping with viscous, yellow drool that swung from his jowls, Fenrir bounded into view and headed towards a drift of snow, which was large enough to hide a frightened myth.

'Tyr he's coming for you!' I called to him, unable to do anything. Fenrir had ignored me. He was after Tyr and Tyr alone. It wasn't my fight, but I could suggest things to him...perhaps. 'He's coming up fast.' Without warning, a blast of icy cold wind and snow shot in my direction nearly unbalancing me. 'Hey, watch it!' I snapped.

The drift of snow was gone in a flurry of icy silver flecks and so, by the looks of it, was Tyr. With no Tyr to chase, the wolf growled and snapped its jowls in annoyance, tossing his head back and forth trying to find his prey. The wolf caught a glimpse of me but skulked off uninterested.

'Tyr, let him take your hand,' I called to him. 'It's what he's after. We both know it, besides; I think it'll separate the both of you.'

'How can you be sure?' he called from somewhere in the darkness ahead of me.

'Erm.' Suddenly I felt unsure about it. I was never questioned by Santorini when I came up with random thoughts, he just agreed with me and things got done. Suddenly, the wolf spun around and charged to where it thought Tyr was hiding. 'You're just going to have to trust me. He's coming, Tyr,' I warned him. 'Just let it go.'

Quickly bursting out of the snow in a flurry of flakes, Tyr threw himself towards the ghostly form of Fenrir, with his right arm stretched out. 'Take it and be gone!' he yelled mournfully, glancing at his right hand with such sadness in his eyes.

Snarling in revenge, the wolf pounced and grabbed onto Tyr's right hand, biting through the sinew and bone, breaking it clean off.

BANG! Tyr's entire body suddenly erupted into pure white light and energy. I looked up to see Tyr floating in the air with frozen water flowing around him, the faint sound of high-pitched screaming echoing in the background.

The screaming became louder, in such a tremendous crescendo I had to cover my ears and squint my eyes. Tyr's body suddenly moved sideways with such a sound of a great tear of energy that made my teeth itch.

Renita's body abruptly flew out from the left, cast aside into the snow. Scrambling up, I ran after her.

'RENITA!' I yelled, hurrying towards her. Skidding to her side, I brushed the excess snow off her face and gently lifted her head. 'Renita, can you hear me?'

Bending down, I pressed my ear to her mouth and sighed with relief. I heard breath but it was very faint. Looking up at Tyr, my jaw dropped. The whirlwind of snow was gently letting him down, though he too appeared a little worse for wear...a bloody stump on the end of his right arm.

'Thera?' Renita stirred. Her eyes found mine and she smiled.

'Well, you two have certainly made tonight interesting,' I laughed. 'And hey, look? No wolf. And I can say both your names and there'll be no funny business.'

I saw Tyr's right eye open and he smiled. 'There never was any funny business.'

Tittering I stood up, brushing the snow off me. 'Renita, are you capable of moving? Dagen has got himself in a bit of a knot,' I laughed at my pun. 'I don't like the fellow; I think I perhaps tolerate him. But we should be there for him.'

Laughing, Tyr sat up. 'Well said. Tolerate, I can go for that.'

'Same here,' Renita smiled. 'So let's get going.'

As the three of us approached Dagen who was still struggling and still bound. Renita laughed. 'The Gordion Knot? Well, good luck with that.'

'Glad to see you are yourselves again,' Dagen said venomously.

Jane stood up and hugged Renita and Tyr. 'It's good to see both of you again, you know, whole and separate.'

'It's good to be well,' he showed his stump, 'nearly whole,' Tyr smiled sadly. 'Just as long as it doesn't happen again,' he eyed Renita. 'But this whole experience has given me my powers back so...'

'You have powers?' Dagen gasped, arching his back to look at him. 'What can you do then?'

'He has the power of the sky,' Renita smiled, 'so wind, snow, rain, anything to do with the weather I guess.'

Tyr nodded.

Dagen suddenly stopped struggling and laid still. 'I can't do this,' he said defeated. 'I don't know how to undo the knot and you're all just standing there mocking me.'

'What did he do?' Renita asked, looking confused.

The corners of my mouth lifted into a small smile. 'We're not mocking you anymore Dagen, we just want you to try.' Gently shaking his head, Dagen's shoulders slumped and he moved no more.

'Tyr,' I whispered to him. 'I think you have to deal with that,' pointing to the floating green orb. 'I saw the look on your face when you saw it. It means something to you so I think you need to sort it out.'

'Ooh, do you know what it is?' Renita squealed as all eyes, apart from Dagen, snapped to the orb. 'I saw it on the way in, but I didn't say anything in case I was seeing things I shouldn't.'

'What do you mean, seeing things you shouldn't?' Jane asked her, a puzzled look on her face.

'Um,' Renita said, twiddling her thumbs, 'nothing you need to know.' She smiled widely.

'Uh-huh, anyway,' I intervened. 'Tyr, go and sort the orb out and we can stay here with Dagen and help him through this.'

'Can you come with me?' he asked shyly.

'What am I, your mother?'

Shuffling his feet he stared at the floor and shrugged. 'No, but, I just need to tell someone who won't mock me.'

Jane burst out laughing. 'You should have seen her mock Dag-'

'Jane,' I snapped, 'be quiet. Stay here and help Dagen.'

'How?'

'Snap him out of his great depression,' I shrugged, following Tyr to the orb.

Hearing Jane mumble obscenities, I walked in Tyr's shadow, heading towards the ominous green orb magically suspended in the air. Nearing it, I felt a sense of tragedy mixed with profound enlightenment. 'So, you know what it is?' I asked, glancing at his head.

He nodded briefly. 'My grandfather Odin's eye,' he said simply.

'Oh right because that is, um normal,' I scoffed, looking at the orb in a new light. 'Why an eye? My Norse mythology is a little vague.'

'It was for wisdom. He sacrificed his eye for wisdom and it seems that the Moirae have it, though I am unsure why.'

'Hmm.' It was odd that Greek myths mingled with the Norse. Maybe it was for protection? After all, if this group in black suits wanted powerful legends, they may want high-status myths too. The Moirae wouldn't see them coming if they had the Staff of Zeus. 'Well, the Moirae are vulnerable because of the Staff of Zeus. They left Greece to hide out here. If the staff ever fell into the wrong hands, it could potentially cause a lot of damage.'

'But, how was that even created?' Tyr gasped.

Thinking back thousands of years ago I replied, 'The staff was made by Zeus and all of the Greek gods and goddesses combined. However, the Ancients took the staff off them saying it was too dangerous. It was placed in the Ancients care thereafter.'

'So, does that mean that–'

'One of the Ancients is a betrayer, or foolish,' I finished. 'But personally, that under-credits them. They are anything but foolish. No,' I sighed, not wanting to voice the truth, but I felt compelled to say it, 'one of them has got an agenda, though I don't know why.'

Tyr hugged himself and glanced around nervously. 'They are meant to be neutral, creating both good and bad myths, to keep the balance.'

'Yes Tyr, you're right, but the humans messed up that balance. We've got two humans to track down and ask for their help,' I snorted. It was a wonder I was asked to do something so ridiculous.

Tyr laughed. 'Not a human fan are you?'

Shrugging my shoulders, I stared at Odin's eye. 'They have their good moments. However, in the last few hundred years, I've just seen too many bad moments. They don't have the privilege of knowing why they were created. It's one of their life's ambitions to know, "Why are we here?" yet it eludes them, constantly. Though it is ironic that when humans find out why they were created they become Ancients.'

CHAPTER SEVEN

'COULD YOU COME WITH ME TO THE MOIRAE? I WANT TO KNOW WHY they have my grandfather's eye,' Tyr asked, staring at me with pleading eyes.

Sighing I shook my head, 'It's not my place, I'm sorry Tyr. You have to face them yourself. It's your family, not mine.'

Looking hurt, he nodded. Giving another fleeting glance at the eye, he walked off, heading towards the lair of the Moirae. I felt sorry for him. He was probably more confused about all of this than I was, but it wasn't my fate to know, it was his.

I headed back to the others, who had promptly given up trying to free Dagen. 'Right,' I said in an exasperated tone, 'let's start from the beginning, I don't want to spell it out for you but-'

'I know a 'bold stroke', I got it,' he snapped. 'Renita just told me.'

'For someone intelligent, you're not helping yourself,' I snapped back. 'Think outside the box!'

'Oh, I get it!' Jane said happily, clapping her hands. 'It's so easy!'

Rolling my eyes, I leant against the wet wall and closed my eyes. 'Any time Dagen.'

Finally, his hands gently began to stroke the magical ropes. Within seconds, they relaxed around him. Squirming out of them, he kicked them aside in a blind rage. 'Curse you to the depths of hell!' he spat, pointing his finger at them. Suddenly a loud green crackling projectile shot from his finger, and with another crack, the ropes were gone.

Jane and Renita backed against the wall in fright as Dagen's eyes blazed an angry yellow. 'Don't mess with me!' he yelled out happily.

'Well, it's nice to know you've got your stolen powers back.'

Dagen laughed in a jubilant manner. 'I'm going to practice,' he added, then scarpered off.

'That was scary,' Renita quivered as she and Jane came close to me for protection. 'Who knew he could do that?'

'I bet he can do more than that,' Jane said wisely. 'I wish I had better control of my powers.'

I smiled, 'Jane you have very interesting powers. The reason they fail sometimes is that you didn't need them on the other plane. The same goes for you Renita. The pair of you have been in the other plane not needing your powers at all. Being here, you have to all the time.'

The green eye of Odin that was hovering just out of the corner of my eye suddenly pulsated; a ring of pure energy blasted towards us.

'What the-?' Jane gasped, picking herself off the floor.

'You two get back!' Scrambling up, I headed for Tyr. Something has gone wrong.

'LIES!' Tyr screamed. As I approached, I saw a great vortex of wind sucking dust and nearby rocks inside. 'Tell me the truth!'

The Moirae looked complacent by their strange pool. The Fate of Past was holding the strange stick.

'Tyr what's going on?' I asked but he ignored me.

'You horrible old witches!' he spat, 'how dare you besmirch the name of my people, the name of my religion, and cause so much devastation! Go back from whence you came!'

'Tyr!' I shouted at him, this time grabbing his attention. 'What is going on?' So much for not interfering, the boy needed help. Whether I could give it to him, however, was another matter entirely.

'They took my grandfather's eye. They said they need it to help them but they won't tell me why,' he cried angrily. 'I say that they are lying. That eye belongs with the gods, not in their disgusting grubby hands. I want it back!' he yelled, the wind intensifying; whipping up my hair like a dangerous storm.

Edging closer, I took hold of his stumped arm. 'Tyr, don't do this.' I pleaded. 'We have other things to do that are more important. I promise once this is over, we'll come back and you can take your grandfather's eye. But right now, we need to leave.' He stared at me, tears pooling in his eyes. 'Please.' I nodded and admitting defeat, the wind died down.

Tyr slumped to the floor and Renita ran to him, throwing her arms around his neck. Dagen came bounding into the chamber with a confused look on his face.

'We need to leave,' I said to everyone. 'Jane,' I said turning to her; 'as far as I am aware we need to go to England. That's where these humans are.'

'No go to Wales first,' Dagen cut in. 'You'll want help. I can get you undercover help,' he smiled devilishly.

'Oh yes, from who?' Renita asked scathingly.

'From a wood nymph who owes me,' he replied smiling at her. 'I know for a fact that she didn't return to the other plane because she's been given orders to stay behind and help out this wood called Hafod. So, to Hafod we shall go.'

Looking at me for a sign, Jane gave me a hopeless expression.

'Let's just go,' I sighed as I held her hands.

Gathering in a circle, Tyr and Renita stayed inside though they folded their arms so they wouldn't touch. They didn't want to get stuck together again and I didn't blame them.

'Right, Jane, when you're ready,' I said, squeezing her hand in support.

She closed her eyes and whispered one word, 'Hafod.' Immediately a bright blue light erupted all around us, pitching us forward into the merciless blinding void. My hair danced around me as we travelled hundreds of miles South-West, over mountains and seas, across snowy tundras and frozen fields. Then the light vanished, our feet on solid ground but in a different country. It was still dark but considerably warmer than Norway. The snow, however, was present, freezing the grassy ground like the sky's own white fluffy comforting blanket.

Jane had phaded us to the outside of a large wood. Huge dead-looking trees splattered with snow menacingly loomed over us. A few owls perched atop their branches watched hungrily for little rodents waking up from hibernation too early.

Turning a full circle, I saw that behind us was a large meadow, completely carpeted with crunchy snow, which illuminated the area around. The air was still and silent as though goading you to speak and break the peacefulness of this place.

'Well done Jane,' I whispered, 'you're getting better at phading.'

'Look, there's a human house down there,' Renita said happily pointing to my far right.

Several hundred yards away, a little thatched farmhouse with flickering lighted windows from a warm fire within was tucked away in this beautiful countryside. Sometimes humans didn't know how lucky they were.

'So this wood nymph of yours,' I addressed Dagen. 'Finding her any time now would be a good idea.'

'She's usually chatting up some troll by a bridge,' he frowned looking towards the forest. 'Come on we'd better go.' Following Dagen, we all entered the eerie looking forest.

The owls flew off at the sound of our thunderous feet through the thicket. Every animal seemed to be on high alert as we barged into their quiet domain. I felt a strange presence of foreboding as soon as we passed the threshold of the forest…We were being watched.

'A troll?' Tyr groaned, 'they have the worst sense of humour ever.'

'I've never met a troll,' Jane piped up. 'What are they like?'

'It depends on which type you meet,' Tyr answered. 'Mountain troll vary in sizes and colours depending on the mountains they inhabit. They need to blend into their surroundings. Nasty creatures sometimes,' he shivered. 'The trolls in Norway are idiots, though.'

'I have a question,' Renita piped up. 'Who issued the order for Trolls to give out a test? They do right, at bridges? It's usually a riddle isn't it?'

As everyone remained silent, I piped up, 'Yes, you're right. And it was Etrician, he has a wicked sense of humour. He handpicked the trolls and told them to ask whoever wanted to cross the bridge a riddle or a stupid question.'

Pushing on through the silent, dark forest Dagen began to slow down as we walked around a large clump of thick pine trees. The rest of us slowed to a stop as Dagen edged around the clump to see the path ahead.

Jane and Tyr looked at me for answers but I merely shrugged, I had no idea what he was up to. 'Stay here,' he said then disappeared around the corner. Hearing his slight footsteps across the frostbitten ground, several twigs snapped beneath him. The echoing breaks bounced from tree to tree, ricocheting like a bullet. I felt the air shiver around me. From the corner of my eye, I saw the clump of trees move of their own accord. With quick reflexes I dove out of the way, rolling across the cold floor before springing up. Tyr, Jane and Renita were unexpectedly enclosed by the pine trees.

Abruptly there was a loud crack from behind. Spinning around a tall, tanned lady with long berry-red hair and a dress made entirely out of leaves emerged from a large tree. Brushing off little bits of wood she made her way towards us, her eyes blazing with fury. She dragged a misshapen sack and threw before me. 'Ow!' it yelped.

'Who are you and what do you want?' she barked.

'Ivy!' Dagen mumbled from within the sack. 'We need your help.'

She kicked the sack. 'What part of *'Never step foot in this forest'* did you not understand?'

I took a step forward. 'Regardless of what Dagen has done, we do need your help.'

'On what?' She eyed Dagen as he tried to free himself.

Stepping over him, I closed the gap between us. 'We need to locate two humans. They are special humans; they were given myth abilities. That's all I know.'

Her eyes went wide. 'How can you not know about them? All of the fairy clans around Britain, as well as a few centaurs, have cloaked the entire house in magic after an Ancient's decree. No one goes in and out without their say so.' We were all stunned into silence. 'Atlas above, don't you know anything?'

'We've been in the other plane,' Tyr told her. 'And Thera here is The Mother of Water Nymphs. She doesn't go onto land much.'

'Look,' she began, 'whatever you have with these humans, I would leave them well alone. You cannot talk to them whatsoever. Two of them are former Sirens and two of them have been marked for the Cabinet of Idols.'

'Whoa!' Tyr, Jane and Renita said in unison. I suddenly felt their eyes on me.

'I have been marked as well,' I told her, 'yet here I stand.'

'You have the power to protect yourself,' she snapped, 'they don't. The Ancients took it from them.' Groaning she paced backed and forth. 'Look, I'll tell you what I know. The T.A.T known as *Tattoo of Arcane Technology* was a secret organisation led by humans. They take myth's blood and inject it into special humans to create new myths.'

The girls gasped in horror. It was a frightening notion that humans could become magical in such a ghoulish manner.

Ivy nodded. 'Yeah, but that's not all.' She unfolded her arms and, freeing everyone, including Dagen, gestured for us to sit down. 'After they all became full myths, it unbalanced the world and it nearly began a war. We believe it was planned by the T.A.T. from the start. Two of these hybrids, Sirens, ended up having a battle in the middle of London. So the Ancients got involved. They then forced them all to become humans,' she held her chin and frowned, 'though it's odd that they still have magical protection. Makes me think that there's something else the Minister has in store for them.'

'Minister?' I asked, confused.

'We've called him the Minister because he looks like a politician with his salt and pepper hair. He is determined to capture powerful myths for his boss.' The night I was almost captured at the pier came to the forefront of my mind. So that is who he was. The Wood Nymph stared at me. 'If you've been marked you need to hide. You cannot get caught.'

'What is the Cabinet of Idols?' Jane asked her. 'What does it do?'

'We are unsure of what it does,' she said vaguely. 'All we know it's a prison for those with power.'

'They had the Staff of Zeus,' I told Ivy, the thought suddenly occurring to me. 'The Minister, he had it. But it was dropped when we phaded away from them. These two humans from this T.A.T group can help us find it.'

'The Minister had the Staff of Zeus?' she asked, her face going pale. 'That's not good, that means-'

'We've been betrayed by one or if not all of the Ancients. But why would they want to destroy their creations?'

'Hmm,' she said in thought but didn't voice her opinion. 'Did you come in contact with it?'

Agreeing I explained, 'I got zapped by it. It rendered me powerless but I recuperated quickly,' I smiled. 'Even if they continued to zap me they wouldn't be able to destroy me.'

'How is that possible?' she asked in awe. 'The Staff of Zeus can be used against legends such as yourself and if used by-'

'Only my mother can destroy me,' I told her. 'Though forgive me, but I am not going to divulge my secret of staying immortal.'

Putting her hands up, she shrugged her shoulders, 'Far be it for me to annoy a legend like you.' Standing up she gave us all a pitying look. 'Well, good luck to you. It's time I headed back into the wood.'

'Wait a minute, Ivy,' I called, catching up to her. 'The house, please tell me where it is. I know you know.'

Sighing she said, 'I didn't tell you this,' she whispered, 'but it's in Bristol near Durdham Down on Queen Victoria Road number forty-five. There's a large hedge in front of it, but I wouldn't go near it if I were you. Fairy guards are posted there.' She scoffed. 'So, now that I've warned you not to attempt to interact with these humans you obviously will.' I didn't give her a response. 'Just don't go to Greece. Anyone who is left is fleeing the main island for a reason. I tell you this now, once you've been marked there is no fleeing from it. They will get you... eventually.' Looking at the expression on my face she gave me sympathetic eyes, 'whatever you do, good luck.' She turned away and headed to the trunk of a nearby tree. Seconds later, she vanished into it.

'This is ridiculous,' Dagen moaned as he and I held hands walking down the cold icy street of Queen Victoria Road. After waiting for the morning, Jane had phaded us to a nearby park close to the road were these hybrid humans were staying. Telling the others to remain in the park, I decided to check out the road with Dagen and forced him to act as if he was a boyfriend, just to blend in.

'Just shut up and put up,' I snapped at him, holding onto his hand tighter. 'I don't like it any more than you do.'

'Why did you drag *me* along?' He sneered. 'I was perfectly fine staying in the park with the others.'

We came onto the road Ivy had said and I began to count the house numbers. 'Tyr has had a tough time as it is-'

'Oh and I haven't?' He snapped. 'Being tied up by that Gordian Knot for hours and then thrown in a sack by a Wood Nymph hasn't given me the privileges of having a time-out?'

Stifling a sigh, I ignored him and slowed down my pace. Checking the odd numbers on the right-hand side of the road, I came towards house number forty-three and abruptly stopped. 'I-I can't move,' I said suddenly feeling a little worried.

'Neither can I,' he said giving me a fearful look.

An old ginger tomcat came towards us, but as it approached number forty-five, it immediately turned left and walked around it. It was as though something was forcing it away from the house.

'Centaurs and fairies,' I sighed heavily. 'Ivy told us about them but I honestly didn't think that they would...arh,' I added in annoyance.

'So what do we do?' Dagen asked as we turned around and backtracked.

Thinking deeply, I didn't notice that I was heading for a collision with a human and suddenly smacked into him.

'Oh I'm sorry,' I said, as rectangular pieces of paper fell out of his gloved hands. Helping to pick them up I noticed his strange attire. He wore a strange blue uniform with a matching cap. A shoulder pad informed me he belonged to the Royal Mail, whatever that was.

'Thanks for that,' he smiled, as he flicked through the pieces of rectangular paper.

Grabbing my hand Dagen was about to drag me off, but I held my ground. 'Excuse me, sir,' I asked as he was about to head towards house number forty-five. 'I'm new to this country and your er uniform is intriguing. What profession are you in?'

'I'm a postman,' he smiled cheerfully. 'I deliver the post,' he said lifting the pieces of paper to show me. 'Aren't you cold?' he added, looking between Dagen and I. 'It looks like you've come from a Medieval Fair or something. New Years was two weeks ago you know.'

'Yes,' I smiled politely. 'Well good day,' I bowed and walked off with Dagen. Waiting a few seconds, I turned back around and saw the postman walk right up to the house and push a few rectangular pieces of paper, through a small bronze slit in the door. As he walked back towards the pavement, I turned around and dragged Dagen back to the others to tell them what we'd seen.

'I think that they are trying to make it seem like a normal house and only certain human members of society are allowed to the door, past the barrier,' I told the group as they sat on a strange circular platform that swivelled around on the spot. Turning around too many times they fell off the platform and wandered around to the next strange object in the park, not paying attention to anything I was telling them.

'This is a strange road isn't it?' Jane asked Renita as they placed their hands on the red and yellow ground. 'It's spongy but it has lovely colours.'

'This swing is odd,' Tyr called as he sat on a small black frame that was connected to two chains on either side.

'I think you're meant to sit in that seat thing,' Jane told him, 'but you're too big for it.'

'Excuse me!' I said, grabbing everyone's attention. 'Will you stop playing around and listen to me. We need to go back and check out the house again, try and view it from a place where we won't be seen.'

'Oh, I can help with that,' Renita said as she jumped off a strange coloured horse that was attached at the bottom by a large spring. Being mindful of some humans who were walking their dogs, we followed her into a copse to hide. Placing her hands onto the ground, Renita dug out a small rock and placed it in her hands. Closing her eyes she mumbled something and then, opening her palms, slowly blew gently over the rock.

Before my eyes, the rock broke into small pieces and out jumped a tiny insect. 'And who says rocks don't have eyes...or ears,' she smiled. 'This is Jim.'

'Jim?' Tyr laughed. 'Funny name for a rock.'

'Hey,' she said covering Jim with a hand, 'he has feelings too you know. Anyway, Jim here is going to be our eyes and ears. I doubt that fairies will notice a small little bug, like Jim.'

'Aw I think he's cute,' Jane giggled.

'Girls,' Dagen and Tyr moaned.

Ignoring them, I asked Renita, 'How is he going to be our eyes and ears?'

'Like this,' she said placing Jim on the ground. 'Βλέπε και ακούω,' she said in Greek, which translated to, "I see and hear". The little rock insect suddenly began to make a strange circle on the ground, pacing faster and faster, then with a quick bright light, the ground was a small shiny and portable circular mirror.

'No way!' I gasped, 'It created an Extensive Mirror,' I gasped, smiling at her brilliance.

'No not an Extensive Mirror,' she said sadly, 'I'm not that good. It just shows us what he can see and hear, sort of like a two-way mirror. Get him as close as you can to the house and I'll take it from there.'

Passing Jim to me, the others crowded around the mirror in the park as I took Jim back to the house. Dropping him before the barrier, I headed to the opposite side of the road and leant up against some black-painted railings.

Watching I saw little Jim make his way to the pavement and through the magical barrier. 'Well done Renita,' I breathed.

Beside me, trundling along in a strange white van with its sides removed, the vehicle stopped just before the house and a human in a white uniform got out. 'Morning,' he said to me smiling as he went to the side of the van and grabbed a small orange crate with a handle that carried glass bottles filled with white liquid. 'These guys sure go through a lot of milk,' he laughed as he saw the expression of confusion on my face.

Noticing Jim, the little bug hid underneath the first step to the house. The human walked up to the door and knocked gently on the solid oak wood. With the sound of chains and other metal clanging, the door opened and a girl with long raven black hair and brilliant blue eyes stood in the doorway. She wasn't looking at the man, she was looking at me. 'A Siren,' I said as I looked at her pretty, pale face. Her features were unmistakably that of a Siren, regardless that she had no powers left. My eyes flicked down and I saw Jim scarper inside.

'Your milk,' the human said, offering her the orange crate.

Breaking the staring match, I closed my eyes and walked back towards the park. My job was done, all we had to do was sit back, enjoy the show and see if there were any loop-holes to get these two humans out of the house.

As I got back to the others, they glanced up and shook their heads. 'You have already made a nuisance of yourself and you were only gone fifteen minutes.' Dagen snorted as I sat down next to them.

'What did I do?' I frowned.

Sighing, Renita said, 'Rewind.'

Looking over their shoulders, I saw a frayed pale green carpet and a tall white pipe.

'Thanks for the milk,' a girl said then there was a loud bang. 'Okay guys, I think we have a stalker.'

Two feet covered with a pair of white socks moved into Jim's vision then turned around and went out of view. The little bug moved forwards a few inches then stopped; its head turned right to see an open room with a settee occupied by three people.

'What do you mean a stalker?' asked another voice, female though Jim couldn't see.

'Just went to get the milk and I saw a girl standing opposite me, staring at me. It was kinda weird; I got this odd impression from her.'

'What kind of impression?' a boy asked who was sitting on the settee staring ahead holding a black object; his thumbs moving around it like he was trying to wrestle with it.

'Sam, I'm not going to talk to you while you have your head in Nathaniel's idiot-box,' she barked.

'It's not an idiot box,' a dark haired boy replied, who had similar features to the Siren. I wondered if they were siblings. 'It's an X-Box okay. And don't diss it just because I kick your arse at Halo.'

'Don't care. Oy Henry, Darren, the milk's here,' the girl called. 'But seriously, I think I felt something from her.'

'Er, Tara, please take your bi-tendencies away from my breakfast please,' a blond girl quipped as she watched the moving pictures in the box.

'Shut up, Saskia,' the girl called Tara sighed and left the room.

There was a sharp snap of a door and thundering feet came down what sounded like a flight of stairs.

'Good morning,' a husky male voice said. Jim turned his eyes to look up and I saw a tall boy with dark brown hair and deep bottomless blue eyes that were filled with so much love and affection for the long black haired girl.

'Here's your milk, Henry,' she sighed, giving it to him, then sauntered off down the hallway towards another room.

'Hello crunchy nut breakfast!' another boy said, slapping his hands together and rubbing them. But as he rounded the corner of the stairs he stopped and went into the room, turning his head to the right. 'Morning Saskia, I see you already have breakfast.'

'Yup,' came the reply.

'Do you want any tea?'

'Nope.'

'Do you want me?'

'Nope.'

'Do you love me?'

'Darren, get stuffed will ya,' she yelled, a square cushion sailed towards his face. 'I'm trying t'watch the T.V.' So, he's our first target, I thought.

Picking up the cushion, he stared at it then placed it down by the settee. Looking hurt, he turned around and headed down the hallway with Jim hot on his heels.

Entering a plastic floored room, Jim turned right, hid behind a cupboard and began crawling up it carefully, being mindful of several spiders waiting for their hapless prey.

'What's wrong with you?' Henry asked.

'I saw a girl outside of the house staring at me. She was dressed oddly too; her clothes were blue and floaty. She must have been freezing.'

Hearing things being opened and metal clanging again, Jim managed to creep up towards the surface, his eyes locked onto four occupants within.

A girl with long reddish-brown hair was reading something by a table. Whatever it was it looked extremely interesting, as she didn't seem to pay attention to what the girl was saying.

'So let her freeze, it's her fault,' Darren said.

'No but that's not what's making me feel a little anxious,' she hurried on in a frightened tone. 'I got a sense of... authority from her. I'm not sure if she was watching me, or that she was there to capture me or-'

Coming into the room with a wad of papers in his hand he rolled his eyes, it was the boy who may be her sibling. 'Tara you make yourself sound so important. Just shut up.'

She stared at him as though her eyes were daggers. 'God if I had my strength back I'd smack you so hard Nathaniel-'

'Well you don't,' he said matter-of-factly. Ruffling the pages, he calmly looked at her. 'Tara, we are protected, no one is going to get us, your strange kooky dream was just that, a dream.'

'But everything is just odd,' she continued. 'I mean, Hannah and Darren got those weird blue stone bracelets from a Mr C whoever that was.'

'Chris Cringle,' Darren told her, 'how many more times must I say that to you?'

'Tara, you are stressing yourself out way too much,' Henry said. He inched towards her and kissed her on the forehead and enveloped his arms around her waist. 'Just chill out, it's a new year. Forget everything that happened last year. We can all look forward to a better future.'

Pulling away from him she stared lovingly into his eyes and shook her head, 'No, something is coming. I can feel it.'

'Turn it off.' Standing up from the group, I paced back and forth, thinking. Renita obeyed and looked up at me with a puzzled face. 'They are already suspicious. I thought about the kidnapping but now I'm not so sure.'

'At least tell the fairies that you mean no harm,' Jane told me. 'Then they can tell this Tara girl and the others that Hannah and Darren will be looked after but they are needed, it's their destiny to help us.'

'Those bracelets though,' Tyr queried. 'From a Mr C, do you think it was Chris Cringle?'

I agreed. 'Almost definitely. The Fates said that it was being taken care of. Chris has many powers for both myths and humans. He gives gifts and I would bet every grain of sand that he gave Hannah and Darren the bracelets. I have a feeling I know what they will do once they put them on, especially if each bracelet has a slither of Aqua stone in it, which is a blue stone.'

'What's that?' Dagen piped up looking intrigued.

'It's a special gem that enhances water abilities.' I replied. 'Basically, any water orientated myth becomes stronger if they are near the gem. But having it on you constantly, well it would be a sight to behold.'

'So what's the plan now?' Tyr asked, laying back on the ground, staring up at me.

'I'm going to send Hannah and Darren a letter. It's the only loophole I can think of. They need to know what's going on. I just hope and pray that Tara and the others don't find out. It doesn't involve them.'

CHAPTER EIGHT

WITH THE LETTER WRITTEN AND THE POSTAGE STAMP MAGICKED ON, Jim was nestled in the corner of their living room as the rest of us sat around the park watching the daily activity in Renita's two-way mirror.

For a few days, we watched their daily routines and found it interesting. Their language was different from ours, their attire and how they interacted with each other in some aspects bizarre. It reminded me of a very dysfunctional family. But, suffice it to say, we learnt a lot about them.

'I feel very nervous. Are any of you?' Jane asked as she and Renita leant against each other watching the action slowly unfold.

The sound of the letterbox squeaked and the post fell to the floor.

'Post!' Lottie jumped up in delight and headed out of the room into the hallway. On returning she flicked through the post and came to the discoloured letter that was addressed to Hannah and Darren. She stared at it for a few seconds. 'Um Hannah, you and Darren have a letter.'

'What?' Tara, Hannah and Darren said together.

Suddenly standing up, Tara ran forwards and tripped up over Nathaniel's stretched-out legs. 'Where do you think you're going?'

'Ow,' she moaned, rubbing her right elbow. 'You could have seriously hurt me,' she snapped, slapping his legs.

'Get off!' he said, pushing her out of the way. 'It's not your letter. Hannah, Darren, take the letter and open it in the kitchen. I'll keep miss nosey in here.'

With a strange expression on her face, Hannah took the letter off Lottie and walked out of the living room. Jim quickly followed behind.

Turning right again, Jim crawled up the cupboard, just missing the door that one of them had closed behind them.

Hearing some tearing of paper, Jim ascended the board. The little spy bug approached the top and saw Hannah and Darren at the table; with their backs turned we couldn't see their reaction.

As we watched them, the tension grew to such intensity I could have sworn I saw electricity in the air. We were on the edge, hoping and praying that they understood the letter.

'Do you think it's a fake?' Hannah asked, turning to look at Darren, though I was unsure of the emotion on her face.

Shrugging, he picked up the letter and stared at it. 'Dunno, but what if it's not?'

'Well if it's not, then there is a Water Nymph waiting for us to help her. We were told we had a destiny, maybe this is it.'

'But without the others,' Darren added. 'It just doesn't make sense. It's too vague and we have to decide now?'

'She said that time was "of the essence". I don't blame her if she needs a quick decision.'

'Alright, but what about this line, "If you agree, just say yes and we'll come and get you." She didn't leave a return address so what does that mean…'

Gasping she turned around and stared at the kitchen. 'She could be watching us.'

'Can't be,' Darren said simply. 'The fairies won't allow anything magical approaching the house.'

'She must be, she knows about the bracelets.' She showed him her right wrist. 'She may have found out something that the fairies don't know… Oh my gosh, what if she's been watching everyone? What if she isn't who she says she is?'

'Okay, now you're been paranoid.'

'I'm not paranoid,' she huffed. 'I'm just trying to look at everything from all angles. Hannah sat down at the table and sighed. 'If it is true…we can't tell the others.'

'Why the hell not?' Darren demanded. 'They will want to know where we're going. If not, you know Tara will end up coming after us.'

Shaking her head Hannah glanced up at him in a sad way. 'No, she won't. She didn't come after us when the sea called to us. It's doing it again. I know she'll let us go.'

Taking a deep breath, Hannah stood up and placed a reassuring hand on his shoulder. 'I'm in… I'm going to pack.'

'What, now?' Darren asked, looking confused. 'It's too soon, I need time to think. What about Saskia and Nathaniel?'

'They'll understand.' She gave him a watery smile and headed out of the kitchen, leaving Darren staring at the letter.

'Garh!' he yelped after a minute or two. 'Fine, I'm in. I'll tell the fairies you're coming.' Glancing up from the table, he did a full turn, his eyes slanted and cautious. 'Damn, I hope I'm not talking to myself or I may check myself into the nearest insane asylum.' Pocketing the letter, he headed out of the kitchen.

'Right,' I began, startling the others from their stupor. 'I'm going to greet them. Renita, you and Tyr stay in the park, we'll come to you later.'

'Oh this is going to be fun,' Dagen grumbled as he and an overly excited Jane got up. 'Save me a seat next to the cold rock by that root,' he pointed to the floor.

'Oh come on Dagen, it's going to be fine,' Jane laughed as she dragged him away.

'Be careful you two,' I warned. 'If these humans have got protection, others may be after them. When the barrier goes down the magical community will sense it.' Glancing around the field, my senses heightened, I didn't see any danger, but it didn't necessarily mean there wasn't any.

'What makes you think they need to let a barrier down and what do you mean by "sense it"?' Renita asked.

'We've been watching those humans for a few days now. Don't you think it's odd that every time they want to go outside they suddenly forget? Or they have something else to occupy themselves? They are housebound. No one goes in and no one comes out. It's the fairies rules. Although, if they have a real purpose to leave the house, it will be beyond fairy magic. The mythological world is doing a lot to protect them and in so doing, they've stirred up the wrong attention. I wouldn't doubt it for a second that the Minister already knows where these humans are. We need to be extra careful.'

'Come on Thera,' Jane beckoned from the edge of the park.

Waving at her, I gave a meaningful look to Tyr and Renita and headed off to catch up with the others.

'Jane,' I said quietly, as we turned the corner onto Queen Victoria Road. 'Be prepared to phade us back to the park as soon as we get the humans,' I told her.

As we neared number forty-five, we slowed to a stop just before the invisible barrier. Glancing up and down the street, I saw and heard no one, not even birds chirping or cars from the main road behind. 'Something's wrong,' I whispered to the others. Instantly they were tense. 'Jane, do you see anything in the upcoming future?' I asked hurriedly, my eyes continuing to sweep across the frosted silent road.

Closing her eyes she took a deep breath then, 'No nothing. I'm sorry, it's like something's blocking me.'

Wracking my mind, I tried to think of something that would stop Jane's powers and encapsulate the entire road in chilling silence. It was as if—how could I have been so blind! Some random memory flittered across my mind, hitting me and snapping me to attention. Flicking my head up, my eyes searched the skies above. Though I saw dingy mournful looking clouds and a partial scattering of blue sky, part of my brain was telling me I was being paranoid, but the other part remembered what Ivy had said. It was a memory of a conversation about the centaurs.

'Dagen, shoot a bolt of magic into the sky,' I commanded, grabbing Jane and testing the invisible barrier in front. Damn, I thought, as I felt it repel me.

'Why?' he asked as though the request was illogical and stupid. 'Someone might see.'

'There is no one to see! Just do it!' I hissed.

Just as Dagen put his hand in the air, I heard several metal clicks from the door of number forty-five.

Our heads whipped in that direction, our eyes peering through the thick bush, which obscured the view of the living room window.

'Can you see anything?' Hannah's voice came in a whisper.

'We're here,' I said, moving forward. But the barrier stopped me.

'Are you...Thera?' Darren asked.

Seeing his mouth through the foliage, I smiled, 'Yes it's me.'

'Have you got your bracelets from Chris Cringle?' Jane asked them in a childish tone.

'Who's that?' Darren demanded defensively.

'That's Jane. I've brought two myths with me for your protection,' I said, the tension in my voice. 'Ask the fairies to take the barrier down. Only for a second so you can come out.'

Slowly the humans descended the steps towards the edge of the path when all of a sudden I heard running footsteps and strange whooshing noises from behind me. Spinning in the opposite direction, I saw Tyr and Renita at the top of the road, their faces pale and scared.

Three men dressed in black suits rushed around the corner after them. Gasping in fright, I immediately felt the barrier behind me go down. Before Tyr said it, I already knew what was happening. I already knew this was going to end badly if we didn't leave now…

'THERA IT'S A TRAP!' he bellowed out my worst fear.

'Dagen, shoot the sky!' I yelled, as within seconds everything around me began to darken like something or someone, had thrown a blanket over the sky.

'Why?'

'JUST DO IT!' I screeched.

The idiot was just standing there gaping at the men chasing the others down the street. He hadn't listened to a word I had said.

'DAGEN!' I screamed.

He threw his hands up in the air and shot a large bolt of green coloured energy. Zooming up into the air sounding like a strange fizzing firework, it made contact with the sky, shattering the illusion into a million pieces. The broken spell, the Mirror of Reality, cascaded down around us. It was a spell that only centaurs could cast, to create a perfect world where they can hide or place other myths in. The sounds of birds, dogs and traffic instantly blasted all around us.

Glancing around, I saw that Tyr and Renita had outrun their pursuers and bolted straight for us. Feeling the fairy barrier go down for a fleeting moment, Jane and I reached out and grabbed Hannah and Darren. Jane held onto my hands, waiting for the others to join us.

'Going somewhere?' a deep familiar voice asked, almost dripping with evil.

Spinning on the spot, I saw a familiar figure emerging from behind a small white rusty van on the other side of the street. My insides turned cold as I remembered the last time I had clapped eyes on the salt and peppered haired man. It was the Minister.

He smiled sadistically and calmly walked towards us. Letting go of Jane's hand I stepped in front of them. 'Not another move,' I growled.

Sweeping his salt and pepper hair from his eyes, he glanced to his right. Renita and Tyr had stopped running. Not sure what to do, their pursuers crept closer to them. 'Don't you even think about it!' I ordered, holding a threatening finger at them.

The Minister put his hand up to stop them and they edged backwards, holding their palms towards Tyr and Renita, magic ready to fire. With a flick of his hand, several more men in black suits appeared from behind cars or round the hedges in the residents' front gardens. My eyes whizzed to the men, counting them. There were eight in all. One thing I noticed was that only the two men who had chased Tyr and Renita had a small chain pulled taught against their necks. What was that all about?

Walking cautiously towards me, Tyr and Renita closed the gap between us. Feeling a warm hand grab my own, I braced myself to help Jane phade us, but not without some small talk first.

Staring at the Minister he stared right back at me, his eyes showing a composed intrigue. 'How long have you been here?' I asked him, a strange sense of calm washing over me.

'Oh, I've had my eye on this place for a while now.' He smiled charmingly as though I was an old friend.

'Just who are you?' I demanded. 'You seem to know about magic very well. I have not yet felt any magic from you.'

He chuckled. 'Well, I am human after all… with magical benefits.' Out of the corner of his eye, he glanced at the two men with the strange, chained collars. 'Do you like them? They are legends, like you. Only, they answer to me.'

'You're a monster,' I seethed.

His laughter became a faint titter and he shrugged his shoulders. 'I prefer to think of myself as an idealist in the mythological world. You, however, find yourself an optimist, no? Trying to solve the clues to your fate… Oh, I know about the Moirae and your little trip there. It's just a shame I couldn't follow you. You have a neat myth behind you, she transports you to where you want to go, does she not?'

I remained silent.

Shrugging his shoulders again, he looked past me to Hannah and Darren. 'Doesn't matter to me, my attention has turned to those two behind you, but I can't touch them. Not just yet. I have to be patient, so I give you a friendly warning. Don't be a hero. You'll come to see our way of thinking soon.'

'Ha,' I spat. 'You want to collect me and shove me in the Cabinet of Idols. How could you possibly think I'll come to your thinking?'

Smiling evilly he said, 'Because you can't escape your destiny, Thera. You may know it, you may not, but rest assured I will have a hand in it.' His attention turned to Hannah and Darren who were behind me, his cat-like eyes found their pray instantly. 'You two are now in the open. Thera will slip up eventually and when she does, I'll be waiting for you.'

'Sir orders to shoot?' one man asked, who crept up towards us but stopped, unsure of what to do. The Minister hadn't given any orders thus far to shoot at us.

'Where do I go?' Jane asked me, high-pitched sounds erupted around me as palms were raised and aimed.

'Shoot the insipid one,' the Minister sneered, pointing at Jane.

Three pairs of hands turned towards her. Magic concentrated in their palms. 'Oh no,' I gasped.

'Madagascar,' I heard a soft voice from behind me.

With a blinding flash of blue light, the echoes of magic firing, the frightened shouts of the group, the Minister and dismal January Bristol were quickly left behind.

There were a dull thud and splash that came from the group and warm clear saltwater flowed around my body as Jane phaded us to the white beaches of Madagascar. The others spluttered and coughed as they dragged themselves out and walked further inland.

'Thera, you coming?' Renita called.

It was night, and the moon hung high in the sky, shining its brilliance down on us, illuminating the palm trees that bowed towards the water's edge.

After a few minutes relishing the water, I stood up, shook excess water and sand from me, and followed the others into the jungle.

'Can anyone tell me where we are and where we're going?' Hannah called from upfront.

'We're in Madagascar,' I answered. 'And presumably, we're trying to find shelter? It's January after all. It may be stifling hot, but there's high pressure around us. Thunder is on its way.'

'Why did you bring us here?' Darren asked. 'What the heck is out here anyway?'

'I didn't bring us here,' I called back.

'I did,' Jane admitted.

'And who are you, exactly?' Darren asked. 'I take it you're some sort of teleporting myth?'

Shooting daggers with her eyes she flicked her blond locks from her face. 'It's called phading,' she said waspishly. 'My name is Jane. I'm the daughter of Janus. I hope you two know about your myths and legends?'

There was silence from them both.

Moments later, we emerged into a clearing. Ahead I saw the looming stretch of jagged rocks, a small mountain range that ran almost through the entire stretch of the island. I heard Tyr ask Jane, 'Why exactly did you bring us here?'

'I... I had a vision.' She muttered. Then as I reached them around the clearing edge, Jane turned to me looking apologetic. 'I'm sorry I came here. I should have mentioned it first, but I-'

With a smile, I put a hand on her shoulder. 'Don't worry about it. You got a vision to come here, so obviously we're meant to be here.'

Darren frowned at me. 'Are you meant to be their leader then? From the letter you sent us it sounded as though you were under orders from someone else.'

Renita and I shared a look. 'It's complicated.'

Sitting down on a fallen tree Hannah replied indignantly, 'well, you're not *my* leader.' Her blazing hazel eyes stared at me, unafraid. I had to admit I admired her. 'The others can follow you around like little lap dogs, but you don't look very important.'

Tyr whistled low and looked away.

'Do not speak to me like that,' I chided, feeling heat rise from my fists. 'Your human leader, Tara, is not here; therefore I am responsible for both of you. Until you get your powers back, oh and believe me you will,' I added, seeing a slight sparkle in her eyes as they flicked at the bracelet, 'you will listen to what I have to say for your safety. Do you understand?'

There was a slight pause between us when she stood, her eyebrows knitted tightly together. 'Look, I don't understand things and I don't like not knowing what's going on. You've explained nothing to us. I should never have left the house.' She walked away from the group and Darren ran to catch up with her. They didn't go far and sat down on a clump of moss-covered rocks nearby.

'Keep an eye on them,' I told Tyr. 'I'm going to find some shelter.' Nodding to Jane and Dagen to follow me, we headed past the clearing and back into the jungle.

The jungle was fresh from a thunderstorm that had washed away the grime of dust and pollen that had built up over the day. Large leaves glistened in the rays of the moon that peeped through the canopy above. The howls of the Indri and other nocturnal animals like the Fossa, Fanaloka and the many varieties of lemur, chattered in the trees above or scurried away from our presence as we descended into a thick part of the jungle.

'Hey, what's that?' Jane pointed ahead.

It was a large vine-covered rock formation that appeared smooth from age and weathering. But what was interesting was a man-made hole that had been carved below.

'Let's check it out,' Jane beckoned. Nearing we saw that it was the entrance to a deep cave. 'Oh, look at that tunnel!'

Dagen clicked his fingers and a green flame appeared in his palm. Raising his hand high into the air, we all gasped in awe. There were carvings all over the walls from a rather old civilization, which I recognised instantly.

'We need to get the others here. They may need to see this.'

'What are these for?' Hannah asked, as she came right up to me, shoving her left wrist in my face. Dagen had fetched the others, and just in time, as the clouds quickly flew in from the east, covering the moon completely and throwing down large globules of warm rain.

The silver bracelet reflected Dagen's eerie green flames that he'd created in the corner of the entrance to the cave. Hannah's bracelet, just as I expected, had part of an Aqua stone, polished to shine just as powerfully as if Triton himself carved it from his trident. My eyes glanced to Darren's wrist. He wore his too. It was identical to Hannah's.

Jane and Renita sat together and whispered amongst themselves. Tyr gazed at the carvings, muttering to himself. Dagen was watching Hannah and Darren carefully. 'You got them from Mr Cringle didn't you?' I asked sitting down next to Jane and Renita who had abruptly stopped whispering.

'By Mr Cringle, you mean Father Christmas don't you?' Darren asked me. I had piqued his interest.

'He has many names, but yes the very same,' I told him. 'He knows something went wrong with your group to warrant him giving you something so precious.'

'Precious?' Darren and Hannah asked together.

Gently touching the silver bracelet that Hannah showed me, the stone lit up in a wondrous array of blue light that flowed and danced around the chamber in such a way it seemed as though we were underwater. 'They can restore your powers, but I cannot help you,' I said. As I let go of her hand, the stone dimmed. The cave lit up briefly as lightning flashed above followed with a loud clap of thunder and the familiar sound of rain pelted the ground just outside moments later.

Gasping for breath, Hannah clutched her wrist and gave me a strange look. 'I felt power coming from the bracelet, coming from you. But I had no idea you were that powerful. I just thought you were an ordinary Water Nymph like I used to be.'

'She could destroy the planet if she wanted,' Dagen said sarcastically, 'but of course, she can't because her dear brother isn't here.'

SLAP!

Shocked at what I saw, Jane's hand was perched over Dagen's reddening hand-printed cheek. All of us were motionless as his face lit up like a Belisha beacon. Expressly embarrassed at what Jane did to him in front of everyone, he rose to his feet and wordlessly stormed out of the cave. 'I'm sorry but… but don't be mean to her,' Jane called.

Moments later, we heard Dagen yelling in panic. Tyr and I locked eyes and quickly darted out of the cave, the others on our heels. Coming to a stop just outside, Jane and Renita jumped backwards in fright as a small tribe of men and women, who came to the height of my knees, surrounded us. Dagen was on his knees, his hands behind his head. He was already saturated from the storm that blew in from the north, though that didn't seem to bother him. From the flashes of light that cascaded across the night sky, I noticed stone-tipped spears pointing at his Adam's Apple.

'They've um… found us,' he muttered.

I counted fifteen tribesmen and women. Every member had brightly coloured paint in the form of familiar symbols on their bodies. They were all wearing various colours of loincloth that wrapped around their midriffs. Intrigued by the symbols on their bodies, I was about to question them when the tallest of the tribesmen walked forwards and stared up at us.

Gesturing for us to move back into the cave, we silently filed in behind the chief.

All dripping wet, the group pushed us on, deeper into the cave. 'Do we do anything?' Hannah whispered as we traipsed onwards, ignorant of where we were going or who these people were.

Shaking my head, I remained silent. Provoking these small, unknown natives wasn't a good idea.

The chief skittered forwards into the darkness; a few sparks ignited before me and a torch came to life. Turning to me, he beckoned us on. I got the impression that they didn't want to hurt us. On the contrary, it was as if they were guiding us.

I caught glimpses of the symbols on the chief and they swiftly reminded me of an ancient tribe called the Wengye's. This particular tribe spread across the Pacific around two thousand years ago and ended up settling on the African continent. Though a few hundred years later, I'd heard they promptly vanished, their entire culture and religion gone, eradicated by humans and by the Ancients.

It's what awaits all myths when their culture is lost and forgotten; they are destroyed. The Greeks, Egyptian, Norse, and Celtic myths are hanging on by a very fine thread, which the Ancients have threatened to cut.

Quite abruptly, the chief stopped and pointed his torch at the right side of a slimy-looking cave. Apart from it coated with moisture, it also bore beautiful decorative scenes in vibrant colours. Unable to decipher what they were, the chief said, 'Birth of Creation.'

I heard gasps coming from Dagen, Tyr, Renita and Jane, but not the humans.

'What did he say?' Darren whispered to Hannah, though there was no point in asking her, they wouldn't be able to understand the language.

Quickly turning to Darren and Hannah I said in a rush, 'you won't be able to understand what they say, so just keep quiet and I can translate when I have the time alright?'

'Where do you hail from?' the chief asked Dagen, as he grabbed the front of his jacket and shook it slightly.

'Many places,' he said in a shirty manner, grabbing his jacket from the chief and flattening it down. 'I am from Britain, he,' he said pointing to Tyr, 'is from Norway. And they come from Italy and Greece,' he indicted Jane and Renita in turn.

The chief looked at me with inquisitive eyes, as though silently asking me to tell him who I was. 'I come from the ocean,' I told him truthfully.

Nodding respectfully, he glanced to Hannah and Darren. 'They are like us, though they are not like you.'

'Yes, they are human,' I confirmed. 'May I ask why have you brought us here?'

'Our God Telaluk told us of his demise in the Birth of Creation. Though our language is still prominent in our decaying culture, the power to read and write was lost to our scholars who left our paradise many centuries ago. In venturing into the world to discover new lands, they never came back.'

Slightly shocked at what I was hearing I asked, 'Are you...are you the Wengye people?'

The chief's face lit up. 'You must be very wise to know our real name. The local people on this island ignore us, believing we are evil spirits. They call us Ratsy Fanahy. My name, however, is Chief Galtway.'

'Thera,' I smiled.

Hannah waved her hands at me. 'Can you translate now?'

'These are the Wengye people,' I explained. 'This,' I gestured around us, 'is the Birth of Creation.'

Darren put his hand up. 'Er, which creation? There's quite a few.'

I asked the chief but he replied, 'A window to the other world can be seen behind me.' Flicking the torch around, I saw nothing but the gigantic face of a boulder. He passed me the torch with a smile.

'Wow,' Tyr whistled low. 'I didn't know there was one here. But,' he looked at me, 'I thought all of the portals were closed a few days ago. Was this one missed out?'

Standing beside him, Renita shrugged. 'It must have been.'

Apart from Hannah and Darren who couldn't understand, the rest of us stared at each other in worry. The Minister could use it to get to the other side.

Though it was a golden rule that no human could enter the other plane, if any human tried, they would turn into an Ancient.

As the Staff of Zeus was no longer in the hands of the Ancients, it was another cause to believe that we had been betrayed by an Ancient, and recently too.

CHAPTER NINE

'SO, QUESTION,' HANNAH ASKED, AS TYR AND RENITA SPOKE WITH THE chief on how to get to the portal. 'This portal behind us, no one has used it for a long time?'

The chief caught my eye, I translated and he shook his head.

'Not that we know of,' I admitted. 'But that doesn't mean to say that the Ancient's don't know of it. All of the portals should be closed. If this one is still active, it'll only work one way. You can go through, but you can't come back.' Hannah was silent and I turned my attention to the craggy rocks around where the light touched. 'Galtway, your entire history,' I breathed, 'it's all over the cave, even the ceilings.'

'It is forgotten history though,' Galtway said sadly. 'As I said, the scholars left centuries ago, taking the knowledge of how to read our culture's writings. Though with you here, maybe you can help us.'

'How can we help you?' Jane asked looking excited as we all gathered closer to the forgotten pygmy people.

Galtway grabbed a sharp rock off the floor and knelt towards the ground, drawing strange misshapen circles in the mud. 'This is what the cave system looks like,' he pointed. 'Here is where we are.' Indicating half a semi-circle where the boulder was. 'There is a large cavern deep within this cave system, under the mountain,' he marked with his stone. 'Within this cavern is the Holy Walls of Time. Though we cannot understand it, we know it tells of the spirits that have come to help us. We know that it describes a band of saviours who help restore the order from which something terrible has befallen the world.' With a deep frown on his forehead, he looked into our eyes. 'The walls speak a horrible truth about the Anceti.'

'The Ancients?' I gasped.

He pointed to his map. 'The Holy Walls of Time explain about the coming of the eighteenth Anceti –the unbalanced.'

'Well that sounds promising,' Dagen snipped sarcastically.

'May we have a look?' I asked him, ignoring Dagen's comment, as usual, my heart pounding from fear and excitement all in one.

'You may,' he said permitting us, 'but be careful. Our ancestors would not let you go willingly into our cave that is why they placed the black pool there. We dare not cross it.'

'Black pool?' Renita asked, glancing up from the map. 'Thera, have you heard anything like it?'

I nodded but did not reply. It could be anything if truth be told, but I'd have to see this pool for myself to know why these people fear it so.

'The pool is only one of the objects that block your path,' Galtway explained, 'to get to the Holy Walls traps are stopping you from reaching there. But, the portal to the other world is within a chamber all by itself but we cannot reach it and dare not to.'

'Let me guess,' Renita piped up, 'there are a lot of traps and other such things in the way?'

Looking scared, Galtway shook his head, 'not a trap no, the Blue Fire of Death. Cross it and you will be no more.'

'Good luck,' Dagen and Darren said together as they looked up at me.

'Why aren't you coming with us?' Jane asked them.

Darren lent smugly against the cave wall, putting his hands behind his head. 'I don't see the need to do something that Hannah is capable of doing on her own,' Darren gestured to her. 'I'm perfectly fine, waiting for her.'

'Likewise,' Dagen smiled.

I scoffed. 'Dagen, you don't want to come along because you can only do one thing with your powers, ignite your hand. Big whoop!'

He scowled, his smile wiped clean off his face.

'I'll stay with the boys,' Renita volunteered with a sly smile. 'Plus, I want to speak with Galtway about his tribe. I find it fascinating.'

I beckoned them all. 'No, I think we all need to go together and no backchat, please,' I added throwing the boys a scathing glance.

Thanking the pygmy tribe, we all built up the courage to venture into the darkness of the cave. After Renita had used her power to move the boulder carefully, without causing structural damage, I led the group down into the bowels of the cave system with the flickering torch held aloft in my hand.

Staring around the human-made tunnel, it gave me the time to think about the others and how far they had come. Tyr had gained his powers and much of his confidence, Renita had come out of her shell and Jane was becoming rather adept at phading. The only problem was Dagen. His power came from Merlin. And though he had no idea what he could do. The more I thought about Dagen and the mythology surrounding him, he'd be better off getting his hands on the Book of the Mage. It would at least help him control his gift. But in this current situation, I didn't particularly want to take a trip to Avalon if I could help it.

'He means he doesn't want you to get hurt,' Jane said soothingly, stopping my train of thought. I had completely zoned out of the conversation the others were having.

'We would be better with a T.A.T. approved torch.' Hannah complained. 'It's better than the old one Thera is holding.' Hannah came to my side and said smugly. 'It shines like the sun.'

'No torch shines like the sun,' Tyr piped up in my defence. 'Not a human-made one anyway,' he scoffed. 'Your T.A.T. couldn't possibly create such a thing. You were a pathetic group of false myths who have started a ripple effect which caused a war and has got us into this mess.'

'Whoa,' Jane gasped. Tyr had never spoken to anyone like that before and it even shocked me.

'Oy, we didn't know, it's not our fault.' Hannah complained.

'Enough!' I bellowed. 'File behind me and keep quiet. I need to think.'

With everyone doing as I ordered, we moved slowly through the wet earth-smelling passages. Continuing through the gloom, even with the torch, parts of the ceiling became rather low and the walls narrowed, making it a tight fit; neither of these would be a problem for the tribe, however. Soon enough, as the ceiling lifted and the walls widened, I stretched my hunched back and took in the scene of remarkable formations. We stopped and stared in awe. The vista before us, quite literally, astounded us. Columns of stalactites and stalagmites, which joined over time, were sporadically dotted around, looking as though they were bearing the weight of this staggering mountain range above. The wind from the mouth of the cave behind us blew in pathetically but somehow managed to sound like a small Banshee yelling out her pitiful cries. Drips from the ceiling above splashed down heavily into the clear pools below and with it, the small sounds crescendoed in the cavern. Each drop echoed off the rocky plinths, knobbly columns, and smooth calcium covered walls. It was the beautiful, natural sound of a cacophony of a living cave.

Tyr moved around and was about to enter a second tunnel when he stopped. 'Um, I can't go any further.' I noticed a small inscription of Wengye on the lintel above him and made a mental note of it. He moved his left hand around, pressing an invisible wall. 'There's magic here stopping me from going any further.'

Reaching out to where he was pressing, my hand went through. 'Huh. I seem to be able to pass through–'

Without warning, I felt the earth shake beneath me. Immediately I glanced up at the calcite straws and stalactites that clung from the ceiling and hoped they wouldn't come crashing down on top of us.

'Is it an earthquake?' Tyr asked as he flattened himself against the walls of the cave, his eyes flicked up to the ceiling too.

'No, it's–' Jane began, but her words were cut off as there was an explosion of rock from behind us.

Renita and Hannah screamed in terror, as the cave suddenly filled with dust. Jumping out from the darkness, I saw him and his worried face. Relief quickly spread as he rushed towards me pushing me away from the tunnel.

'Are you alright?' he asked, his voice became normal, his accent dropped. Holding onto my shoulders tightly, I nodded silently. Searching my face for any hidden emotion, he sighed. 'This place, I cannot believe you would come here.' He pulled me away from the others so we'd be out of earshot. 'It's dangerous.'

'You know that this cave was a portal?' I asked. 'A working portal?'

He bobbed his head. 'It's more than that. This place was created by the Ancients. I spoke to one; I hadn't met him before so I'm assuming he is new.'

'New?'

'Yes. He seems a nice guy, very easy to talk to,' Etrician smiled. 'If I could hazard a guess, I'd say he was from Texas. Got to love those guys from the West, yee-haw,' he laughed slapping his thighs.

'Don't do that again,' I chuckled. Out of the corner of my eye, Hannah and Darren shared a look but remained silent. 'Sorry,' I pulled Etrician back to the group. 'This is Etrician, a legend for Mother Nature.'

'Okay hang on a minute,' Darren said putting his hand up. 'None of you have explained to Hannah or me what a legend is. Now in my book, a legend is someone awesome and no offence, but can you really say that you're-'

'Shut up, Darren!' Hannah shouted. 'Don't joke, not now, okay?'

Briefly explaining the difference between a legend and a myth, I was surprised to see how well they understood and they asked no further questions on the matter, which was a great relief.

Renita tilted her head, staring at the formations in thought. 'If this is a working portal, then maybe this is where the Staff of Zeus was passed into this world.'

Etrician and I nodded; I had already come to that conclusion a while back.

Unexpected Dagen said, 'You know, I've been thinking.'

'Ha, don't hurt yourself,' Darren spat.

He ignored him. 'I bet you anything that the reason why every myth is fleeing Greece is probably because the staff is there. It explains why the Fates fled for their lives. They know they can be destroyed by it and also why most of the myths have gone to the other plane or are in hiding.'

Shocked by Dagen's theory it sounded like it could be a possibility, however, we could not go leaping into action and get the staff back. If myths were fleeing from Greece, then it was clear that someone had it and knew what it could do, giving me yet another reason to worry.

'Thera, in your letter,' Hannah said slowly, 'you said that the Minister possessed the Staff of Zeus. I take it he's human?' I nodded. 'Okay. But you didn't say what the staff does.'

'If you are a myth and are shot with the staff, it can destroy you.' Jane shuddered, replying for me. 'The staff has the power similar to the Ancients. It can erase myths from the face of the planet.'

'And does the Minister have the staff?' Darren asked us.

'I don't think so,' Tyr said. 'I think he's still looking for it. He may come to the same conclusion that Dagen has. That it is in Greece. He won't be chasing us anymore.'

I scoffed. 'Yes, he will. He still needs me. I've been booked free of charge into the Cabinet of Idol hotel. And you two,' I pointed at Hannah and Darren, 'you have been offered a room too and so has the rest of your group.'

'But why?' Hannah asked. 'What is the Cabinet of Idols and why does he want us?'

I shrugged. 'It's my quest to find out. But, that's by the by. Your mission is to get your powers back while mine is to stop the Minister in getting the Staff of Zeus and finding out which Ancient is betraying us all.' Everyone remained silent. Tyr fidgeted, uncomfortable with what I was saying. 'Look, I know it is dangerous and all we can do is prepare. For one, there are things I have been thinking about with regards to Hannah and Darren.'

'What like?' Darren asked suspiciously.

'Your bracelets. They have the Aqua gem set within them it can hold immense power to a myth. There was a reason why Mr Cringle gave them to you and I need to talk to the only person I know who may have something to do with them.'

'Who?' Hannah asked, sounding intrigued, but I shook my head.

'It is not for you to worry about right now,' I sighed heavily, realising that it was another thing I had to worry about. 'At this moment in time we need to understand why you four' I pointed at Dagen, Tyr, Renita and Jane, 'cannot pass through the barrier. Answering my question, I think I know why and how.'

'Enlighten us,' Dagen asked, folding his arms.

Pointing above him I transcribed the writings, 'You who are bound by rules of the Ancients may not enter the holy chamber unless invited. Humans and legends are not bound by Ancients, so we may pass. But you four cannot.'

Spinning around, the four of them stared at the wall above them and groaned. 'Atlas be damned!' Dagen cursed. 'All these rules and yet the Ancients are breaking them!'

'Calm yourself, Dagen,' Jane said in a frightened tone. 'We must think of how to cross the barrier… if we can only be invited by an Ancient, and to be honest I do not like the prospect of summoning one here, maybe we can try and find another way around it.'

'What like phading?' Tyr asked a small glint in his eye.

Grabbing onto Tyr's stump, the others grouped around; grasping hands with each another, all focussing their energy on Jane. 'Um, I don't think that's a good idea,' I began but it was too late. Within seconds a blinding blue flash of light erupted in front of me and within moments the group of four were standing next to me, all looking very pleased with themselves.

Hastily I backed up, pushing Hannah and Darren out of the way. I could almost count down what was going to happen next. Without warning, a loud booming voice resonated around us. 'RULE BREAKER!' it shouted.

With an almighty BANG, the four of them were pulled back towards the barrier, smashing into the rocks with such force they created long cracks in the walls, which spread up towards the ceiling like creeping ivy.

'Whoa,' Etrician said, quickly placing his hands on the walls to seal up the cracks and to stop the columns from breaking around us. 'You shouldn't have done that. Someone is bound to hear that.'

'Go,' Jane urged in a panicked stricken voice. 'We'll be alright, I'll take us somewhere.'

'Where?' Dagen asked, looking around him as he and Tyr picked themselves off the muddy floor. 'We need someplace safe where no one can find us.'

Rattling my brains the only thing I could think of which was protected was Ireland. 'Country Antrim,' I said, as Etrician, Darren and Hannah entered the tunnel. 'Giant's Causeway, meet us there you'll be safe,' I promised them, there was another reason why I wanted to go there for Hannah, Darren and Dagen's benefit.

'Good luck,' Jane said, as she and Renita clasped hands and grabbed onto Dagen and Tyr. Without a second glance, they vanished in bright blue light.

I sighed with relief but only for a second, as Etrician grabbed my hand and dragged me forwards into the tunnel with nothing but jagged rocks. 'Open your maw,' he said in a powerful voice. Hannah and Darren gasped as what appeared to be a toothy mouth opened. The top half revealed a smooth ramp behind. Etrician placed his hand on the wall and luminous green crystals blossomed, guiding the way into what appeared to be a secret hidden chasm.

'Holy cow!' Darren exclaimed as he came to an abrupt halt on the other side. With little room to move, I edged around behind them and gasped a little at the sheer drop to unknown darkness below.

'Close,' Etrician ordered the rocks and with grinding and a rumble they obeyed and returned to their normal state.

'That is one big drop,' Hannah said breathlessly as she peered with one eye open into the drop below. 'I don't like heights. God knows how Tara does this, just jumps off buildings and cliffs and rooftops and the like. It would give me a heart attack just thinking about it.'

'Well she was afraid of heights wasn't she?' Darren chortled. 'But she got over it. You can too.'

'Don't need to do I? Water Nymph remember? I'll stay in the water thanks.'

'You're not a Princess of the Seas yet,' Etrician reminded her. 'Though I do wonder how you will be…' he left the sentence to hang in the air for me to answer it, but I remained mute on that point. If I told Etrician who I had in mind to help me, he would forbid me to go. It wasn't like Poseidon had any leeway over me; it was more in the protective factor that would be contributed to meeting up with him.

'So now what?' Darren asked, thankfully changing the subject. 'I'm going to say, we don't jump into the depths of Hell.'

'Don't say that,' Hannah quivered as she looked away. 'Although, it does sort of remind me of that archaeologist movie.'

'Huh?' We all asked her.

'Well in the film, the main guy came to something similar to this. He had to walk over an invisible bridge; he had to take a leap of faith. He jumped and he found himself on a rock bridge that was camouflaged. He found the path by sprinkling dirt over it.'

Testing her theory, I bent down and picked up a handful of small pebbles and threw them into the black void and they promptly fell into the large black pit below.

'Hannah your theory sucks,' Darren hissed.

'Well, you try and come up with something then?' Hannah snapped and tried to turn round. But it was the wrong thing to do. Suddenly her foot slipped and she lost her balance. Flailing her arms like a windmill, she caught Darren's shirt and pulled to regain her balance, but it only unbalanced Darren as well, and he began to fall backwards.

'NO!' I screamed as I reached out for them. Pitching forwards, Etrician reached out for Darren, who managed to twist round to grab onto the ledge as a screaming Hannah fell backwards into the darkness.

Hitting the floor on the small narrow ledge, I grabbed Darren's scrabbling hands but there was little purchase for him to pull himself up. His pallid scared eyes stared at me as if to say, 'This can't be it, can it?' and without another word, he slipped off the edge.

I heard them falling into the darkness, screaming in horror all the way. Etrician placed a steady hand on the ground. His voice broke the sudden haunting silence and whispered, 'There's water at the bottom of the chasm.' As soon as he said that I heard two distant splashes of water.

Without a second thought, I flung myself off the ledge. The wind whistled past my ears, covering Etrician's terrified shouts. If there were a chance I could save them, to get to them, I would try.

The darkness engulfed me quickly, but I had no time to feel afraid of it, I was afraid of losing the humans, afraid of losing my new friends.

Smelling the purified water below, I called it to me to search for Hannah and Darren. Plunging into it head-on, I immediately sensed two bodies floating in a southerly direction, heading towards the ocean. My heart lifted as I sensed they were still alive, but barely.

Hurtling through the water at such a fast pace, I caught both of them with a small wave. 'Etrician!' I yelled behind me, my voice bouncing off the walls. 'Etrician I'm down here! Curse whoever forbade me to have night vision!' I spat, clinging onto Hannah and Darren's cold wet bodies.

Feeling another body enter the water, I waited patiently for Etrician to turn up. Coming within meters of me, I pulsated the water and pulled him up. 'Hello,' I smiled.

'I cannot see a thing,' he coughed. 'Let me give us some light, where's the cave wall?' he asked.

Sensing the water's edge as it sloshed against the slippery wall, I moved him slowly towards it. Hearing him place a wet hand on the rock, bright blue crystals sprouted all over, lighting up the whole cavern, giving off an eerie glow. My eyes rested on the half-drowned bodies of Hannah and Darren. I felt the water within their bodies that was clogging their airways and quickly revived them. Spitting up the excess water, they inhaled deeply and coughed.

'Welcome back to the living,' I smiled down at them. With bleary eyes, they glanced up at me appreciatively. 'You took a bit of a tumble and found this natural river that comes from the top of the mountains. Luckily, it caught you, you should be thankful.'

'With water,' Darren laughed, 'I always am.'

'Ditto,' Hannah coughed as she tried to stand up, but couldn't.

'Do not move just yet,' I told them. 'Etrician,' he admired the rock with great enthusiasm, 'any signs of getting up and out or finding the portal?'

Turning to face me, he grinned. 'It's above us. There's a tunnel leading towards it and,' he paused and laughed, 'there is a rock bridge directly above us. It seemed the Wengye tribe moved along a ledge to get to a natural bridge. From what I can tell, an old column collapsed, maybe due to a large earthquake of some sort and made a path over the chasm.'

Moving towards Etrician, I grabbed his arm and commanded the water to push us upwards, towards where this natural rock bridge was. Lo, and behold within seconds we came across a misshapen, bumpy column that broke off many years ago. Gingerly placing us on the bridge, Hannah and Darren staggered to an upright position and slowly all of us crossed safely.

Hannah and Darren led us to another enormous chamber ahead where the old Wengye scripture covered the walls. There were histories, poems, love songs, and even what looked like pieces of plays. It was amazing and it was brimming with energy.

'Is this the Holy Wall of Time?' Hannah asked as she approached a wall close to her.

My first contemplation was a resounding no but as I read it, I began to laugh.

'What's so funny?' Darren asked, staring at me as though I had gone mad.

Going to Hannah's side I pointed out the instructions and turned to Etrician, 'Look,' I pointed.

He pulled a face as he came over. 'It's instructions on how to make rice. In fact,' he said looking around him, 'there seems to be a lot of rice making on nearly every inch of this chamber.'

He wasn't cottoning onto what he was reading. So, I asked, 'How do you measure time?'

'By the sun,' he said in an off-handed tone but then laughed as he realised what I was getting at. 'No, you think?'

I nodded and laughed. 'I do, I really do!'

'What? What are you two talking about?' Hannah asked, sounding upset that she was left out of the conversation.

'Humans measure time by the sun, yes? I mean you have watches now, but years ago people measured it by the sun, or the lunar cycle, or by water by using a clepsydra, or a Candle Clock if you were Chinese or Arabian. But if you did not have any knowledge of how to measure time in a sense of say, how long would it take to boil a bag of rice, what would you use?'

'I have no idea,' Darren said bemused.

Laughing I said, 'I just answered it for you. The native people of Madagascar cannot tell you how long in minutes it would take you to walk to the beach. Their answer would be "boil one bag of rice," or in your terms about ten to fifteen minutes.'

'That is weird and cool at the same time,' Hannah laughed. 'But why are you telling us?'

'This,' I gestured to the entire cavern, 'this is the Holy Wall of Time. Originally, I thought it was well... I didn't know what I thought, to be honest. It didn't occur to me until now their meanings and implications of their knowledge of "time". But it's pure and utter genius as you humans say.'

'That is very true,' Hannah laughed. 'But, now what?'

'Now, we read,' I sighed.

Sitting down on a rock, Darren and Hannah appeared extremely bored as Etrician and I got set to work on the cave writings. Within minutes, we deciphered which parts would be interesting to know and which wouldn't and soon, we found ourselves staring up in the middle of the cavern, where Etrician found it interesting. 'It's devoid of straws,' he puckered his brow. 'I'm sure there used to be some, but maybe they chipped it away, which if they had makes me angry.'

'Okay shove a rock in it!' Darren yelled. 'I've had enough of your slatey-talk, it's boring.'

'Could you at least please tell us what you are reading?' Hannah groaned.

'I'll go first,' I said to Etrician, as I heard him sigh in annoyance. 'So, we have the mention of the arrival of the Acenti, the Ancients, but so far it's just helping out the natives, which I'm guessing was the Wengye tribe at the time. They taught them how to read and write, to farm, keep livestock but there wasn't much livestock on the island per se, it was mostly various lemurs. So the Ancients helped the tribe by giving them a present?' I questioned as I read and re-read the word.

Moving to me, Etrician looked at it and corrected me, 'That isn't a present, that's a reward,' he frowned. Then together we read on whilst translating for the others. 'The reward was the Door of the World, to come and go freely as they wished.'

'The portal!' Hannah and Darren said together as they rushed to our sides.

'However,' we said together, 'the Door of the World could only be used by those the Ancients deemed worthy.' Abruptly the writing stopped and so did we.

'Is that it?' Darren scoffed. 'Well, that sounded pointless.'

'No, it makes sense,' Etrician said in thought. 'Usually, it would be intelligent people or people with wealth that would make them worthy, but not all wealth is in the form of gold mind you,' he added when seeing the look on Darren's face, as though he was thinking there was long lost treasure on the island. 'Wealth came in many shapes, sometimes the bearing of children, sometimes a great poet or a historian. These people were deemed truly wealthy many years ago.'

'So what else does it say?' Hannah asked as she pointed to an indentation in the ceiling where shadow partly hid the writing.

Moving directly underneath it, Etrician and I began to read the first sentence and paused, 'This... this is unbelievable,' I gasped in horror. 'Did you know?'

With wide troubled eyes, he shook his head, 'No, and no one I know is meant to either. I doubt Mother knows.'

'What? What's wrong now?' Darren yelled.

'It is telling the history of the Ancients but why? There is no known location on the planet that talks about the Ancients and yet this speaks about the coming of a new Ancient,' I began. 'They will bring forth terror, destruction and the end of the world. Beware the cunning face who spreads a thousand lies. Beware the beginning of a war between wings. Unless a clan can reach for the stone, he will win with a thunderous voice and an evil grin. Beware of the false myth. Beware of Drayman.'

'Drayman?' Hannah whispered and walked off muttering to herself. 'D-R-A-Y-M-A-N.' She stopped and stared at Darren. 'But, it can't be... it's just a coincidence, isn't it?' Hannah asked Darren as he shook his head.

I snapped my fingers and pointed to Etrician. 'Wasn't Drayman an immortal?' I asked. 'One of the Macrobians who discovered how to stay forever youthful?'

Etrician nodded. 'That's the one. An immortal would be classed as a false myth. They ingest magic, they were never granted it.' He nodded to Hannah, 'You look like you've seen a ghost?'

She clapped her hands. 'Drayman is an anagram of Maynard,' she said finally. Darren's face turned pale. With Darren unable to say anything, Hannah clasped her hands to her head and repeated, 'No it's not him,' over and over again.

'Have you heard of the name?' I asked Etrician. 'You said you met a new Ancient?' I demanded.

'Yes,' he said strongly, 'He didn't give me his name. He just sounded like he was from America.'

'Like he was from Texas?' Hannah asked. It dawned on all of us. 'You met him, Maynard,' she said to Etrician. 'He created the T.A.T group and turned us all into myths.'

Darren scoffed. 'I doubt Henry would call it a myth, he'd say he was turned into a monster.'

Slapping a hand to her forehead Hannah was bemused. 'Wow, he's an Ancient. That makes sense of everything. We knew he had vanished.'

'He probably saved Rhea's life,' Darren muttered anguish etched on his face.

Hannah gasped. 'I bet Maynard is the boss of the Cabinet of Idols! If he knew about this place, he went to the magical plane through the portal, grabbed the Staff of Zeus and got a group together to track down powerful magical entities.' Hannah and Darren were horror-struck and that did not bode well for us.

CHAPTER TEN

SILENCE TOOK HOLD OF US QUICKLY. WE HAD DISCOVERED SOMETHING that was a heavy blow. Etrician and I were frightened. If one single Ancient could bring forth the end, then I didn't want to be here when that happened.

However, everything was beginning to make sense, this new Ancient that Etrician met, the one with the Texas accent was Maynard, the anagram of Drayman. It made me question who knew the Ancient's history and the fate of the world such a long time ago. It was also highly doubtful that an Ancient would write about their subtle flaws on a cave wall in the middle of Madagascar. There must be some connection in all of this something that I was missing.

Glancing around the ceiling, I picked out words that gave me an extra clue in understanding all of this. The Wengye God, Telaluk had similar powers to the fates and was known to have written about the Ancients. From the Ancients point of view, however, Telaluk was dangerous, as he knew universal truths that the Ancients may not even know. It now made sense why the Ancients were "helping" the Wengye by giving them a gift of a portal. The Ancients were destroying their culture and reducing them to barely living, just like Galtway had said.

'Concluded the God Telaluk?' Etrician asked gently, finally breaking the deathly silence. I nodded. 'It was their undoing.' Etrician said wisely. 'The Ancients had to create him. It was their law if enough humans believed in him as an iconic figure. Unwillingly, they gave their "reward," the portal, to the Wengye people. The Ancients knew they would inevitably destroy their culture and beliefs because so many of them left and sought out a new world.'

'Ergo, giving the Ancients a reason to destroy their myths who would know of them,' I finished sadly.

'Why are you talking about this?' Darren asked. 'We told you who Maynard was and now you're banging on about the Wengye tribe?'

'Shush,' I said, trying to think. Burying my head in my hands, I walked around pondering on everything. There was something I was missing in all of this, but what, I couldn't grasp it.

'This Maynard fellow,' Etrician began, my head snapped up to meet his puzzled eyes. 'He knew about the portals?'

'He must have done,' Hannah shrugged. Etrician took his gaze off me to look at her. 'I mean he collected myths to create us.'

'Well our parents were first,' Darren interjected.

'But something must have sparked it off,' Etrician said. 'Some myth must have been caught first for all of this to happen. Do you not see? No myth can be caught unless you know how to and the knowledge is only privy to a myth.'

'So, are you saying,' Darren began as he faced Etrician, folding his arms, 'that some myth betrayed the entire world of magic by telling Maynard about the portals?'

Etrician heaved a sigh and looked at me again. 'We need to find this portal. It must be around here somewhere.'

'Is there a way to close it?' Hannah asked as Etrician went to the cave wall, pressing his hands against it.

'Wouldn't the Phaistos Disc close it?' Darren piped up.

'You know of the disc?' Etrician asked, frowning.

'Tara and the others went to see King Minos a few weeks ago,' Darren paused and glanced at Hannah, 'wow a few weeks and look what's happened?'

'I hear that,' she sighed.

'Anyway, as far as everyone was aware, King Minos was the only one to read the disc, but Tara ended up ordering everyone into the other plane where the disc was and the Ancients took it back.'

'That was when the myths fled this world for the next when the Staff of Zeus was taken from the magical plane.' Etrician spoke softly, 'when your brother-'

'When Santorini left me and I was hounded by mercenaries,' I added bitterly. 'Besides all that, the disc can close a portal. And it's in the other plane. Typical.'

'But without the King of Minos we can't do diddly squat anyway,' Darren sighed.

'Why?' I asked, hiding a smile.

'He was the King, he knew the Minoan language,' he said testily. 'And you don't.'

'Am I not Minoan? Am I not a legend in my own right, to warrant myself knowledge beyond the comprehension of you humans?' I fumed, standing to my full height, towering over him. 'Do not think of me so lightly for you will be testing my patience. Etrician,' I barked at him. 'Find me that portal and once we cross over, we may close it behind us... for good.'

Looking sheepish, Darren and Hannah remained quiet as Etrician got to work on finding the portal. After a few minutes, he stopped and shook his head, 'I cannot sense anything Thera. If there was a portal here, maybe it's gone already.'

'No,' I said in defiance. 'The portal is here. Maybe we have to trigger it. Oh, for the love of ATLAS!' I yelled at myself. 'Why am I not thinking about things that are right in front of me?'

Walking over, I grabbed Etrician and yanked him away from the cavern. 'What, what is wrong?' he asked looking confused.

'Hannah, Darren, stand there,' I pointed in the middle of the room. 'That indentation in the ceiling above us is a little peculiar don't you think, where everything else is flat? I think it's the impression from the portal. The whole cavern is energised, I felt that when we entered. We can't trigger the portal, only they can. They are humans who know the magical world.' No sooner had Etrician and I stood away from the centre of the cavern, it suddenly burst into a gleaming yellow light, flooding every nook and cranny of the natural room. The rays that shone from its epicentre danced across our faces. It was beautiful. Though I knew of portals, I had never seen one. Though, in truth, I've never needed to.'

'But because they know of what it does, won't they become Ancients?' Etrician asked me in a tense voice.

Shaking my head, I slowly approached Darren and Hannah who were awe-inspired by the strange oval portal that emerged before them. 'Not if we hold onto them and guide them through to Ireland.'

'Are you going to tell me why Ireland?' he whispered with a hidden smirk. I met his eyes and shook my head a little. 'We are going into the Sel. It can help us get to where we want to go.' Etrician explained, 'The Sel is like a null void of white space. When myths or legends travel at a great distance they phade through the Sel. Think of it as a stepping stone from one place to the other.'

'Darren,' Hannah whispered to him. 'Lionel, he must have passed through here, you think?'

Glancing at her, he nodded once.

'Right, let's go,' I smiled at Etrician and we stepped into the portal, guiding Hannah and Darren with us. A warm feeling engulfed me, but it washed away into nothing as the yellow light vanished replaced with a brilliant white but plain, boring space. Filled with nothing you could easily lose your mind if you weren't careful. Looking behind me, I saw the cave glimmering in the bright yellow light that the portal emitted but soon that light would stop shining in the cave for good. 'Pre ya'ta den seildo torit,' I whispered. The portal began to close slowly, the light on the other side began to wane and within moments the portal was closed.

'So, you just need to say the words to open and close a portal?' Hannah asked intrigued, as Etrician and I began to focus our energy on Country Antrim.

'Shush,' I sniped concentrating on Country Antrim. Etrician and I held onto Hannah and Darren with all our might. Finally, after a great force of magic between the both of us, a portal opened ahead, gushing freezing yet refreshing air around our bodies.

Walking out of the Sel, the portal behind suddenly closed, leaving nothing but faint traces of magic in the air.

'Welcome to County Antrim, the home of the Giants!' I laughed, my voice echoing all around me. The portal had taken us to the top of a hill that overlooked Giant's Causeway and the ocean. It was so close I could practically feel the salt on my skin.

'L-lovely,' Hannah said through chattering teeth, 'but could we f-find s-somewhere w-warm, please. I'm bleeding f-freezing and still wet!'

Taking the water out of their clothes to dry them, I gave them an Amber Tree leaf each. 'You'll feel a difference for sure.'

Darren sniffed the leaf. 'What do we do with them?'

Scoffing I replied. 'Eat them. Right, we need to find two blonds, one black-haired and one brunette,' I muttered glancing around, but it was pretty pointless, as darkness had followed us once again. 'Why can't we go to places where we can see?' I seethed.

Laughing, Etrician put his arm around me and brought me in for a kiss on the forehead, 'Because nothing is ever simple with you.' He smiled cheekily. 'Oh, and by the way, they are in a Renita-made cave by the Amphitheatre.'

'What did you say?' Hannah asked as colour returned to her cheeks after swallowing the Amber leaf. 'Did you say, Amphitheatre?'

'Yes,' he replied and led me towards the others.

She opened her mouth then shook her head, 'Wait, no. The causeway is a collection of super cooled rocks that look like stepping stones, hence the myth of that Irish bloke and Scottish giant, making a causeway to Scotland to beat him up.' Quickly grabbing her bag she chased after us.

'That was a brilliant play,' I laughed to Etrician, as I linked fingers with him; Hannah approached us looking confused.

He chuckled, flashing me his pearly whites. 'It was wasn't it? Talked about that for decades didn't we?'

Her frown deepened with every second. 'Play, what do you mean play?'

Darren rolled his eyes as though a child said something simple. 'Hannah, you've got it wrong,' He caught up to us, hopping on one foot to get his shoe on. 'I'm part Irish,' he said a little out of breath, 'and I know that it was about two lovers and it wasn't some Irish bloke, it was Finn McCool who loved a lady giant in Scotland and made the stones to go and get her.'

Etrician cringed. 'Didn't like that version so much.'

I laughed at him. 'That's the face you showed me after the play ended. You still don't like it? I thought it was sweet.'

'As modern humans say, it was a chick-flick,' he smiled.

'So they aren't real? They're plays?' Hannah and Darren had stopped walking. Annoyed, we turned around to see their puzzled, irritated faces. Darren looked positively outraged that he had been misled but so was the rest of the human world. It wasn't meant for them to know the truth, where's the fun in that? 'We've been taught in schools about Giant's Causeway, about the myths it pertains to, the history of Ulster and Scotland and the giants and they are plays?' he spat. 'For your entertainment I guess?'

An almighty cold wind blasted in our direction, throwing a strange cry of what sounded like the word, 'Help' towards us.

'Are you going to answer me?' Darren demanded.

'Shush, I hear something,' I chipped.

'I don't,' Hannah whispered, looking around for an invisible source. All four of us stood stock still, our ears open, listening for the slightest murmur...

'Help,' the voice said again. My head jerked towards the sound and without a second thought, I let go of Etrician and ran off. Etrician, Hannah and Darren were on my heels as I sped across the dark windy hills over the causeway. 'Help,' the voice called, sounding louder, but I was heading too far east I needed to go north. Speeding up, I banked right quickly and soon approached a dip which led down to a road. Briefly stopping to see the outline of the road where the pale moonshine filtered through the clouds, I leapt down the dip towards two bodies by the side of the road. One, in a white floating dress, leaned over the second, who was on the floor, not moving and appeared injured.

Approaching them, the one in white suddenly stood up and placed her hands in front of her. Within moments a round golden shield sprouted from her hand. Large enough and grand enough for the wealthiest King in the world, it was embossed by a large hissing snake sandwiched between a lion and a dragon. The eyes for each mammal were inlaid with emeralds.

'I mean you no harm.' I spoke softly, putting my hands up.

'W–who are you?' she asked in Gaelic.

'You called for help,' I replied in the same language. My ears picked up the sounds of galloping feet behind me. Etrician, Hannah and Darren were speeding their way towards me. 'Stop, stay where you are,' I told them, then quickly drew my attention back to the girl. 'My name is Thera, I am the Mother of Water Nymphs.'

'The Mother of Water Nymphs?' she asked, peering around the shield. 'What brings you on land?'

'I'm being hunted,' I told her truthfully.

'We are being hunted too,' she spat. 'Me father... we were attacked. Tried to join the uprising but we weren't quick enough.'

'Uprising?' I asked in shock. 'Where?'

'Greece.' Lowering her shield, she stared at me with large dazzling grass green eyes surrounded by a tear-stained face. However, in all honesty, she was perfect. Symmetrical face with high cheekbones, purest of snow-coloured skin and luscious brown locks that draped gently to her waist. 'Some stupid myth decided it was a good idea to ally with other myths around the world who hadn't fled to the other side. Cowards,' she spat. 'But me father and I went and we fought but it wasn't enough…' she sobbed, 'it wasn't enough.'

'Tell me what happened?' I begged her, as she fell to the ground in a very dramatic way and then flung herself over the wounded body beside her.

'Me father, please help me father and I'll tell you what you want to know,' she said sobbing into her porcelain-looking arms.

Bending beside her, she moved back so I could see the bloodied body of her father. 'What's your name?' I asked her, bringing out one of my Amber Leaves and placed it on her father's gaping wound to the right of his stomach.

'Who is Thera talking to?' Hannah whispered to Darren, who just shrugged.

'Airmed,' she snivelled, ignoring them. 'This is my father, Dian Cecht, the healer of our lands. No herb can heal him, we both know it.'

Startled that I had found them so easily, I was also surprised to see that my little Amber coloured leaf was working. 'No herb can, but a leaf from a tree does the trick.'

'Aye, it must be magic,' she snapped her fingers and glared at the leaf, inspecting it. 'You use magic often?'

'Not all the time.' Standing up I backed away from her. 'Only when needed.'

'Tch,' she tutted in a disapproving manner. 'Magic just gets you into trouble. It got us into trouble, did it not, Da?' Coughing, he put his right hand up and waved. She stood up to face me. 'He'll be alright by the roadside,' she smiled. 'Anyway, nice to meet ya's,' she grabbed my hand and shook it roughly. Glancing past me she saw Etrician, her eyebrows went up. 'Oh, who's the handsome fella?'

'Etrician-' I began, but she pushed past me and headed up towards him.

'Ah, a fair fella you'd be,' I heard her, unsure of who to keep my eyes on, the injured man or the hussy after my own man. I watched her drape her arms over him, her hands gently smoothing his dreadlocks. My blood instantly boiled. 'Don't think you're human friends can see us, but forget them and I can show you me place,' she hissed in his ear.

'Um Thera,' Hannah called to me, as she saw Etrician's strange behaviour. 'What's going on?'

Sighing, I put my hand up for them to wait while I turned towards Dian Cecht. 'Top of the er evening Dian,' I smiled. 'Mind taking off your human wards for a while?' I nodded towards Hannah and Darren. 'Promise you'll be alright. It's just that, my two human friends over there have myth blood in them. It's a long story about the T.A.T. but-'

'They're formerly known as the O.M.C or the Origins of Mythological Creatures Guild,' he smiled in a distasteful manner. 'Oh aye, I know of them. Hannah and Darren. And I know of you, Thera.'

Feeling a strange buzz around me, I heard Hannah and Darren squeal as Airmed suddenly appeared before them.

'Da!' Airmed yelled in a hoarse voice, 'why did you do that? They can see you now!'

'Because Thera and I need to have a little chat,' he said, as he slowly began to sit up. He took the used leaf off his stomach and smiled warmly. 'And I think it's best for you, dear daughter, to find their myth friends too who are clustered together down by the causeway. I can only explain so much about what happened in Greece all thanks to an acquaintance,' he said tapping his nose. 'The wicked shall never rest,' he chortled. 'Because the immortal's never sleep.'

Chapter Eleven

Dian Cecht hobbled along the small coastal road in the dark cold hours of the night, remaining quiet all the way. Still not fully healed, he leant against me for support. Etrician went off to find the others by the causeway, while Dian Cecht and Airmed led us to their home.

With the slow pace that Dian Cecht was walking at, very soon the others joined us and we were bombarded by questions about the cave and the portal. However, out of the corner of my eye, I noticed Airmed flirting with Etrician, giggling like an idiot and prancing around him like a drunken pony. However, she didn't look where she was going and fell over with no grace as her dress flew up in the wind revealing her undergarments to all the boys. 'Brazen hussy,' I muttered as the group burst into laughter.

Jane gambled up next to me, her eyes wide with excitement. 'You found the Holy Wall of Time then?' Though she seemed rather wary of Dian Cecht, who paid her no mind, she focused her attention solely on me. 'We were wondering where you had gone to, but Dagen said to just wait where you told us to...' she added looking sad. I got the impression that when I wasn't there, Dagen was the boss.

With an affirmative smile, I replied, 'Yes we found the wall.' Dian Cecht then pointed left to a bridge that crossed a small gully. 'Interesting information about the Ancients, though it puts us in a precarious situation.'

'With regards to what?' I heard Dagen demand from behind me.

'The former head of the T.A.T. is a man called Maynard,' I responded. 'He also happens to be the new Ancient who will bring the end of the world,' I laughed dryly. 'So not to worry Dagen, I'm sure that every plan we concoct, Maynard will be spying on us to find out what we're doing. We've figured that Maynard is the actual collector and employed the

Minister to track me from the beginning. We need to get Hannah and Darren's powers back soon. They are sitting selkies without them.'

Breaking his silence, Dian Cecht placed a comforting hand on my shoulder, 'Calm yourself mother nymph. It will do you no good to act as brashly as you intend. These things take time and planning if not, you will make a mistake.' Making me feel like an idiot I remained quiet on the subject and brought it up no further.

Passing over the bridge, where I could have sworn I heard a low grumble from underneath. Dian Cecht stopped and waved his hand. On cue, the air shimmered before us. Darren and Hannah let out gasps of awe as a dull sensory fog had lifted and in front, was a quaint little medieval cottage surrounded by small shrubs where their yellow flowers resembled sea anemone. Blue and yellow flowers crept up and around the house and bright shamrocks carpeted the path towards the heavy thick wooden door. The cottage was two floors tall with diamond-hatched windows. As we neared, the zesty smell of wood smoke coming from the chimney swept around us.

'Hidden in plain sight,' Dian laughed craftily.

Slowly making our way to the front door, Airmed took the lead and opened it for us admitting us in. 'Whoever is last, close the door!' She barked. 'The house like's its warmth.'

'The house like's its warmth?' I heard Darren ask, but no one filled him in.

Taking us through a grey slated entrance hall, we took a right and came to a very cosy old living room, which was strangely decorated with old and new objects such as beanbags and an old stained apothecary table, as well as photographs of lakes and forests and tapestries of battles past.

Dian sat carefully on a snug settee; the rest of us knelt on the floor or found a place to perch on the arm of an occupied chair. Etrician found a wooden stool and sat on it, slapping his thighs for me to sit on them, but Airmed got there first. 'Oh you do look after a lady so,' she giggled.

Seething, I ignored them both and sat on the floor next to Hannah. 'So, you said we need a little chat?' I goaded Dian Cecht into speaking. 'Is it a private matter or can everyone hear?'

'Oh you do get straight to the point,' he smiled, as he twisted his body gingerly. Fumbling around in his back pocket, he brought out an old leather pouch and a very long pipe made of wood and clay.

'He reminds me of Father Jack,' Darren whispered to Hannah, stifling a laugh.

'Shush,' I sniped from behind him. Immediately falling quiet, my eyes flicked over to the wound on Dian's stomach and I cringed.

Dian Cecht caught me staring at it and he nodded in such a grave manner it cut through me like an icy knife. 'Yes Thera, it was from the staff.'

So someone had the staff and what was worse, they knew how to use it. Sighing, I buried my head in my hands. For Dian Cecht to speak of it so casually he knew his fate.

'You knew about the staff falling to earth,' he blinked in response. 'And you tried to get the staff back.' He didn't say anything, so I asked, 'How many fell?' I found myself unable to hold onto his gaze and my eyes fell to the threadbare moth-eaten carpet, though I felt all eyes on me.

'A fair few,' he replied sadly. 'But you shouldn't dwell on that.'

Frowning at him I glanced into his emerald coloured eyes. 'Why did you go to Greece? A Wood Nymph from Wales called Ivy warned us not to go. You see, we are being chased by a human called the Minister.'

Shaking his head he shrugged, 'I have not come across those names. But in answer to your first question, we heard rumours that myths fled their homes. The centaurs, Pegasus, the nymphs even the Moirae had gone. We then discovered that the Staff of Zeus was active. Banding together with some remaining myths, we were going to travel to Greece and fight for our right to exist. But we arrived to horrific scenes of carnage,' he added. 'Airmed, tell these good people what you saw as I was zapped and my powers were taken from me,' he asked with a croaky voice.

Forcing myself to look at her, she was sitting on Etrician's lap looking weepy again. 'Terrible,' she wailed like a Banshee. 'Terrible!' Wiping her face as dramatic tears fell down her cheek; she stood up and placed her hands in front of her, the golden shield thrust out of her palms. Turning the shield around so we could see underneath, she waved her hand gently over it and leant it against the wall.

'We arrived,' she began in a thunderous voice then pointed to the inside of the shield as we looked at her. Strange images moved like coloured shadows across the shiny shield, swaying back and forth. She was showing us what she had seen.

Unable to see what was going on, Etrician moved out of her way, giving her the stage, and sat next to me, grabbing me around the waist and pulling me towards him.

'People were running and screaming,' Airmed dry sobbed, her right hand flew up to her forehead in a very Shakespearean "oh woe is me" flare. 'But those people could not see the reason for their screams,' she said, placing her hand over her eyes though she was searching for something. 'They felt the sting of the staff, smelt the air of singed flesh, so they ran in panic. Then,' she shouted, making everyone jump as she lulled us into a deathly quiet, 'a band of brothers and sisters, six in each, marched down with a damned reckoning. They used their magic to stop the Puppeteer, but they drastically failed,' she said in a staged whisper as she gestured to the shield, her arms draped over it and obscured the images.

'Airmed stop doing that you eejit!' Dian growled at his daughter. 'It's annoying and we can't see!'

Pouting childishly, she moved her arms away from the images and then we saw six Grecian forest nymphs who were dressed for battle with Hephaestus body armour and what looked like six male satyrs, with thick Ivory trimmed helmet's which matched their long dangerous looking spears. All linking arms, they took an equal stride, hunting down a small child, which I would say roughly the age of ten, in the middle of the dark field covered in strange blue and yellow flowers. The child, who we could only see the back of, held the staff up above its head and waved it around like some strange toy. Its shoulders moved as if laughing and pointed the staff at the oncoming myths. The staff's quick flashing lightning bolts zapped the myths and they were down in seconds, they didn't even stand a chance.

'Others joined the fray,' Airmed said in a moody manner, as she folded her arms and kicked the shield in a temper, the images changed. Etrician, myself, Jane, Renita and Tyr gasped as we saw a stampede of various breeds of centaurs hurtling towards the child, their shields and swords gleamed in the moonlight above, but when the child waved the staff they fell into the long reeds of the field. The child turned around, what I thought was a boy was a girl with black unholy looking eyes, an evil smile on her face... I didn't know who she was, or which mythology she belonged to, but the scenes were too much for me.

'Enough!' I barked making everyone jump. Standing up, I moved in front of the shield to block it. 'Yes our fears have come true but there is nothing we can do yet. I know what all of you are thinking, but we are not ready.'

'We need to help them,' Hannah spoke, her throat catching as she was trying not to cry.

'You and Darren would not even be able to see the Staff of Zeus let alone the rest of the mythical world. Airmed and Dian are letting down their magic just so you can see them. It is dark mysterious times we have entered into now. Those centaurs protected that forest, along with the other myths in Greece. They tried to do what was right and failed and we would fail too if we barged in and tried to defeat that girl. It is not the way!' I shouted, emphasising the last sentence.

'Then what can we do?' Tyr asked as he stood a serious look on his face. 'We have magic, we can help.'

'You do have magic, but none of you is trained enough,' I said sadly. 'The reason why I suggested Giant's Causeway was to help train you, to develop your powers. The amphitheatre is shrouded in protective magic so humans won't be able to see us, it's safe. Dian's right, we can't go barging in, you need to train up, even myself.'

'What about us?' Hannah asked looking up at me.

'You and Darren will have to wait. If you have any skills as a human, it's best to retrain yourself. The time will come to help you claim back your mythical powers soon, but not yet. For now, be patient.'

Still, in a huff that her father shouted at her, Airmed made some tea for us while we talked amongst ourselves about what I had said. Etrician pulled me to the side to have a private talk with me. 'Train them? Are you sure?'

I nodded once. 'We are heading into a battle of wits and magic. If you noticed, none of those myths knew what was in store for them; they barely had time to use their magic. But that girl she looks possessed almost. If we do this, then they can be the bait while we go and take her down.'

'Take her down? Use them as bait? Thera, what do you sound like?' he asked looking shocked. 'You protect and preserve, you do not wage war.'

'Do you understand the severity of this? We have to get the staff off that girl. The world is unbalancing. This has to stop.'

'Tea!' Airmed called from the kitchen.

Moving forward with Etrician in hand, I heard Renita whisper, 'I'm not sure how we can do this,' but I didn't have time to indulge in her fears. There wasn't any room for fears right now. We had to be strong, all of us.

Grouping around the old stained rickety table that was in the middle of the room, everyone grabbed a cup of piping hot tea and passed the milk and sugar around. 'Here,' Etrician said passing me a cup. 'Just the way you like it.'

Taking it, I inhaled the slightly sweet smell of sugar and hint of milk and blew icy cold air on it, freezing it in seconds.

Etrician laughed, 'Yes, just the way you take it. Frozen solid.'

Up tipping the cup, the frozen tea fell into my hand and I began to nibble on it around the edges.

'That is so freaky,' Hannah said in amazement. 'You can do so much stuff with your powers and I hardly knew what to do with mine,' she added sadly.

'We didn't have long to get used to them,' Darren told her softly.

I made a quick decision. Excusing myself, I motioned them into the entranceway, I had to talk with them. 'Tell me about your transformations. The process, what you knew and what you adapted to.'

Hannah went first. She told me about how the guild started and that her great-great-aunt was part of the original guild called the O.M.C and initially they wanted to destroy all evidence of mythological creatures around the world. However, there was another side to the guild, one that wanted to use the mythological evidence and gain knowledge. 'Only when the T.A.T. was born they used myth DNA to create myths from humans.'

'Our parents were the first in the generation of the T.A.T.' Darren piped up. 'But as we've found out, only certain people can become myths.'

'Nathaniel, Tara's brother,' she said blushing slightly at the mention of his name, 'is an exception to all. He can nullify the myth DNA in our bodies and he turned us human again on request from the Ancients so we could come back to this plane.'

I put my hand up, 'Question. Only actual myths can be in the magical plane. How did you get there?'

'Well because,' she paused then added, 'because Tara commanded me to change into a Water Nymph. What we talk about when she isn't around is that, Tara did this when she wasn't a full myth. Tara is pretty powerful.'

It echoed Ivy's warning to leave Tara well alone. It seems as though the magical world needed her, but when I wasn't sure. 'T.A.T., the first word stands for Tattoo. How did that work out?'

'Ah,' she nodded. 'We were given tattoos to represent what our powers would be. For example, I had been given a trident tattoo.'

That made sense. 'It is relating to you being a child of Poseidon.' I corrected her. 'Meaning that you were a nymph of the sea.'

Bobbing her head, she replied, 'I know that now. But the T.A.T. already knew about Siren's and how powerful they were because they can command.' She continued. 'That's why Tara became our leader and Saskia second in command. Anyway,' she said getting back onto the topic, 'when I became a Water Nymph and she made me summon Charybdis to swallow some furies she was fighting and sent them back to hell.'

My mouth dropped open in shock. 'So you did summon my poor Charybdis?' My temper suddenly rising. 'My mother gave me the power to summon sea creatures but over time I found it wasn't a nice way to go about it and my brother agreed. You have no idea of the consequences of your actions. You were given a power, which you had no idea how to control. Both you and Darren.'

'Hey I can't do diddly squat,' he said in defence putting a free hand up as the other was still holding his tea. 'I'm a merman, that's it. Just a tail, breathe underwater. End of.'

Incredulous child. 'No, it's not.' I rebuked. 'You can control waves and create a maelstrom just to name of few. Honestly, I am appalled that you know very little about the myths you were to become.'

'But we didn't know,' Hannah said, her voice breaking. 'Most of the time we were running for our lives, being chased by a dragon, then by the leviathan-' that instantly sparked off my memory.

Santorini and I were in the Bahama's at the time tending to some wayward mermaids who were swimming in clear waters when we felt the leviathan's presence in our oceans. We knew for certain that the leviathan had gone back to the other plane. However, we were confused it had come back of its own accord. The beast was hard to handle. It has such a bad temper, so we saw no reason to intercept and ask what it was doing.

'-then we were chased by the ugliest harpies you have ever seen. And then in Spain, we meet up with our operator Dave the Minotaur! Then after all of that, I screwed up when I let go of Macie and she ended up in his void thingy. I didn't mean for her to end up there, I let her go because...' Darren was staring at her intently. He hadn't heard this excuse either, 'Because Macie didn't want to be a myth anymore. She wanted to leave. So rather than Tara forcing her to come with us, I gave her the opportunity to leave the group.'

'You horrible cow!' Darren spat. 'You never really explained yourself. Macie still hasn't forgiven you.'

'Yeah? Well, look at what happened after that! Karma's a bitch! It pretty much pushed me over the edge when I saw my best friend turn into a Phoenix where we knew she'd be stuck in that form forever! So yeah,' she turned to me, 'we'd had it rough the past few months and I'm so sorry that we didn't know what our powers were!'

'I did know what I was but I had no idea what powers I had.' Darren informed me as we let Hannah calm down. 'That stupid book that Tara sleeps with more than Henry, and believe me, that's saying something,' he sniggered then abruptly stopped as he saw my unimpressed face. 'Well, it just gives us a list of the myths the O.M.C knew about, but it also shows whether the myths have been found or used.'

I instantly felt sick.

'So,' I said slowly, trying to understand, 'after the both of you transformed you went to the other plane?'

'We were summoned there, yes,' Hannah said gently.

I left it at that, as Renita caught my attention. She sneaked out of the kitchen and headed towards the living room where Dian was still sitting. Maybe she was going to ask if he wanted some tea. Not particularly fazed about her, I headed back into the kitchen where Jane was entertaining everyone by doing impersonations of the group. Dagen, it seemed, was becoming a favourite.

'Why don't you do magic,' Jane imitated with a lower voice, folding her arms like Dagen and stomped her foot on the ground. 'I think you're pathetic,' she snapped like him.

Tyr, Etrician and Airmed were in fits of laughter. Dagen, however, was not. You could say he was a very distinct red colour. Highly embarrassed, he turned his back on them and made himself another cup of tea. Behind his back, Jane copied him perfectly doubling the raucous laughter of the group.

Minutes later Dian called everyone back into the living room. 'If you will stay the night and rest up it would be more company for the house,' he asked, as Airmed helped him to stand. Moving swiftly to him, I checked his stomach and smiled. 'You'll be fine. For a healer, you heal well.'

Inclining his head, he smiled. 'For your act of kindness may I repay you?'

'We are all fit and healthy,' I smiled as I turned to the group who were sat on the floor with Hannah in the middle making strange hand gestures and then it hit me in my chest. I saw Tyr's eyes snap onto Hannah's hands as they danced in front of him, almost cruelly taunting him. Turning back to Dian I said, 'I would like you to give Tyr his hand back.'

The room suddenly stopped talking at the mention of 'Tyr' and 'hand' being in one sentence and all eyes stared at Dian for an answer, but it was Tyr who spoke.

'Thera, I thank you for wanting to give me my hand back, but Fenrir will return, I know it. He will claim back my right hand no matter where I am,' he said sadly.

'Ah but my boy,' Dian said roughly, placing a strong hand on his shoulder, 'the hand I can give you will not be of your flesh, but will be of the finest Goblin made silver the world has only dreamed about in fairy tales. The only thing you must learn is that silver is a difficult metal to pass magic through, therefore you need to practise. But of course, this depends on whether you want a hand?'

Glancing at me Tyr smiled. 'I will,' he laughed. 'I would like a hand.'

Thanking me and giving me a brief hug, Tyr joined the others who all congratulated him and patted him on the back. All of them except one.

Renita was sitting by the window looking forlorn and though something was bothering her. I wasn't going to pester her for answers. If she wanted to tell me, she need only say so herself.

Airmed brought blankets and pillows and turned the living room turned into what Hannah described as a magical student hall, although Darren said it was more like a magical youth hostel. Whatever any of them was was anyone's guess.

Etrician and I huddled together on the moth-eaten carpet, while Jane and Renita slept either side of us. Darren called 'dibs' on the old thread-worn settee, though he got a punch in the arm and moved over so Hannah could share. Dagen and Tyr shared one blanket on the armchair though both looked thoroughly annoyed with the other.

'Don't touch me!' Dagen shouted, sounding scandalised.

'I'm not touching you, I have one hand that I'm using for a pillow,' Tyr shouted back. 'I can touch you tomorrow though,' Tyr laughed, which sparked everyone else off.

'Enough... now... please,' I yawned, Etrician tightening his hold around my waist. 'Mummy needs to sleep.'

The conversations died down, apart from Dagen and Tyr who tittered away about Tyr's shiny new hand he was getting the following morning. Though thinking that I was asleep as Etrician and I had been silent for a good while, Tyr said, 'Thera sacrifices so much to help us. She could have asked anything from that old myth yet she asked to have my hand back. She does look out for us, doesn't she?'

Dagen was silent for a while and then said, 'She does. She reminds me of my mother. I loved my mother very much and every time I see Thera do something nice or helpful, my heart breaks. I like Thera, I look up to her. Don't tell her I said that,' he added in a harsh tone.

'I won't I promise. But we need to look out for her, it's our duty to help her, not the other way round. We promised Santorini.'

Dagen yawned then whispered, 'We will look out for her, don't worry Tyr.'

I closed my eyes to sleep, a happy tear rolled down my cheek as I slipped into unconsciousness.

Chapter Twelve

The early morning light of pale orange woke me up. With bleary eyes, I saw Jane opposite me, snuggled into an old blanket. Gently moving to not disturb Etrician, who was still snoring softly beside me, I got up and headed quietly out of the room.

Crossing the paved entranceway, I tiptoed into the kitchen to find Renita sitting on the table looking melancholy. 'Morning,' I whispered. Jumping in fright, she turned tears fell down her face. 'Renita,' I gasped. I had never seen her cry before. She was always so happy-go-lucky. Moving swiftly to her I put a comforting hand on her shoulder but she shrugged me off.

'Please don't,' she begged. 'I'll be fine,' with a watery smile she looked at me, but it quickly fell from her face as she stared at the ground.

Sighing, I sat beside her at the table and felt the house stir as if it had woken up. The timbers creaked as though stretching and the windows cleaned themselves from a layer of dust to let more light into the room. Then with a quick spark of fire, the agar, situated in the middle of the back wall, surrounded by piles of black soot covered copper pans, came to life.

'This is a fine old house,' I told her softly. 'They're quite rare you know magical houses. Normally they belong to the Elves. But this one it seems was built especially for Dian Cecht and Airmed.' Looking at her from the corner of my eye I saw her nod, but she remained quiet. 'Did you notice the blue and yellow flowers around the house?' She nodded again. 'It just occurred to me what they are. They are called Swiftful Death in Dark Desire. Fili Domtayum yn Nichte Domatra. They were the most sought after flowers in the human world. The blue part of the flowers can kill anyone who eats it, while the yellow part can bring anyone back from the dead. But the knowledge of them has been lost to humans for centuries and they've forgotten.'

'But soon the flowers will go and no one shall see them again, they'll be wiped out from this earth,' Renita said darkly.

'With plants, not so much. Hardly anyone remembers The Amber Tree and yet it is in existence because I know of it,' I told her, but she didn't seem happy about it. I got the feeling that there was something that was troubling Renita more than I could understand. Withholding a sigh, I jumped from the table and grabbed a kettle. 'Tea?' I asked her.

'Thera,' she said my name in such a way it frightened me. Placing the kettle back on the counter I turned to face her. 'I'm going to die.'

An icy feeling gripped at my heart instantly, choking all warmth from me and with a short intake of breath she heard, Renita shook her head as tears spilt from her eyes. For a myth to question their immortality was unheard of…unless they knew what was coming for them. Trying to lighten the mood I asked, 'What's brought all this on? Don't think that the staff will-'

'It's not the staff,' she said in a hard tone, her hands gripped the table threatening to break. 'It's who I am.' She glanced out through the entranceway but I heard no one stir. 'I'm not long for this immortal world,' she said softly. Lifting a shaking hand she placed it over her chest, 'I feel it in my heart, it wanes a little every day.'

'Renita,' I whispered, feeling two clear tears roll down my face. 'The Ancients they… they may be able to help you if…' but what else could I say? This was a first for me. I had never known a myth who knew they were going to be "erased" from human existence. Though Renita had powers and had classical mythological parents, sometimes the children would be forgotten. 'Maybe your father could-'

'He doesn't want me,' she gasped, trying to hold in her agony, 'he wanted his son, he never wanted me. I was the second child and as such, there was no written record that I was even born. It was my mother who pleaded with the Ancients to let me exist. But in the end, both of them knew it was a mistake, that I was a mistake.'

'Don't talk like that.' Moving to her, I knelt in front of her and grabbed her hands. 'Listen to me. You are not a mistake you are needed. I need you; this small slightly dysfunctional family of myths need you. We have to help each other out, Renita.'

'It's not nice to be forgotten.' Her voice cracked. Withdrawing her hands she placed them on her lap. 'Before your brother came to me, the Ancients told me I didn't have long left and explained the processes of what will happen. First, my heart will weaken, then my powers will fade and with it, my memories shall leave me and whoever knows me. They told me it was a gentle way to go,' she said with a watery smile. 'No one can do or say anything to stop it. Ironically, my name means resistant and yet I have to give up so easily.'

I placed a strand of her smooth black hair behind her ear. 'If you want, I can try and help-'

But she shook her head. 'There is nothing you can do and soon, like everyone else you'll forget everything about me. Just promise me you won't tell the others. They'll start to feel the emptiness and will question it, but I am entrusting you with my last wish.'

'If you wish it, I will not say a word,' I nodded in respect.

Silence had fallen between us once more, but before either of us could speak, Tyr bounded into the kitchen. 'I get my hand today!' he cheered.

Smiling in earnest, Renita jumped off the table and hugged Tyr for his happiness, pushing away all the sad recollections that had made her cry. I was proud of Renita for doing that. Though she was tiring and deeply upset about what was happening to her, she didn't want the others to worry. She put their happiness before her own. She was strong and I admired her.

Filling up the kettle, I placed it over the piping hot agar as the others began to wake. Renita helped me wash up the cups from the previous night and poured out the tea for everyone, including Airmed and Dian who cheerfully walked into the kitchen.

'This is a first,' Airmed yawned as she grabbed a cup. 'Usually, I'm the one making the tea. Thank you,' she nodded to Renita and me.

Heading to Dian, I enquired about his stomach. 'You have healed fully?' I smiled. He nodded, sharing my happiness and beamed back. 'I'm glad.'

He chuckled and rubbed it tenderly. 'Still a bit sore, but thanks to you I have recovered from most of my injuries. The tale of how I got the mark is epic but-'

'Mark?' Etrician asked about to take a sip. 'You have a mark, but the Amber Tree's leaf should have cleared it all up,' he frowned.

Looking slightly embarrassed as everyone in the room was staring at him, Dian unbuttoned his shirt to reveal his potbellied hairy torso. But there the mark was, in the middle of his stomach. If truth be told, I hadn't noticed that last night. There was some dried blood around the edges, but visible to everyone was a red jagged scar.

'Did you know of such a mark last night?' I asked him.

He shrugged and looked down at his chest in a puzzled manner, creating a triple chin. 'I knew I would have obtained some form of marking from the staff but it is indeed intriguing.'

'Could someone pass me a wet cloth please,' I asked, holding my hand out to my side as I continued to stare at it. I dabbed at the dried blood and poor Dian gasped at the pain I inflicted. After a few moments, the symbol became clearer and I stared at it in puzzlement. 'Jane, could you come here for a second please?'

Feeling a brush of wind, she came to my side. 'What is it?'

'That,' I pointed at the mark, 'tell me what it is please.' I had an idea of what it was, but if she confirmed it then I was confused even more so.

Leaning towards it, she shook her head in perplexity. 'Well it looks like the symbol for Zeus,' she said squinting. 'A single thunderbolt. But the Staff of Zeus doesn't leave a mark, does it?'

Shocked at her words, I grabbed Etrician and told everyone to stay in the kitchen. Heading into the living room, I slammed the door closed I needed privacy. 'What is it, what's wrong?' he asked in a panicked tone.

'I got zapped,' I said facing him, staring him right into his earthy brown eyes. 'I got zapped by the staff. The staff can destroy myths but it only temporarily stunned me. I think, I think that maybe I got marked as well.'

He gasped. 'What?'

Turning around, I slipped off the top half of my tattered dress and brought my hair to the front, revealing my bareback. 'Do you see anything?'

Hearing him move forwards, Etrician's warm hand touched me gently on my left shoulder blade where the staff zapped me. 'It's a thunderbolt,' he whispered in fright. 'You have it marked on you.'

'Oh, Atlas no.' I whispered, my body shaking from shock and fright.

I felt his thumb smooth over it gently; a cold chill suddenly crept down my body making me shiver. Holding in my tears, I covered myself up and turned to face him. 'The others will know sooner or later, it's best to keep it quiet for now…'

He held me close to him. 'You knew about Zeus' mark before you asked Jane didn't you?' I nodded slightly. 'Then why did you ask her to confirm it?'

'A second opinion?' I shrugged. 'The symbol is important. That's probably what it means to be marked for the Cabinet of Idols.'

Etrician remained silent.

'You know what this means?' I whispered, as a tear rolled down my cheek.

Before Etrician could ask anything, there came a knock on the door. I wiped the tear away and stood apart from him.

'Um,' Dagen began, 'are you going to tell us what's going on?' he asked from the opposite side of the door.

Groaning, I headed to the door and yanked it open. 'No, but let's focus on Tyr, shall we? It's a special day for him after all.'

After everyone had had some breakfast, Airmed decided that Jane, Renita and I were unfit to walk around in public.

'I'm just saying you three look terrible,' she said bluntly as all the girls sat on her bed in her room upstairs. 'Your dress sense is appalling and you have no taste.'

'I have taste!' Jane and Renita said together looking hurt.

Scoffing, Airmed went through her drawers and pulled out some clothes. She picked out a long black crushed velvet dress with lace sleeves and a small dropped 'v' shaped back, it reached to the floor with three light black cotton skirts underneath to fill it out. 'This should be fine for you, it would bring out your eyes,' she said kindly, 'and hide your birthing hips,' she added with a smile.

'Thank you,' I seethed, as I took the dress off her and stormed out of the room. 'Birthing hips?' I hissed to myself as I headed into a spare room to change. 'It would bring out your eyes,' I impersonated her whiny voice. 'Stupid wench.' Taking off my torn dress, I threw it aside and slunk into the one she gave me. 'Brazen hussy.'

Grabbing my old clothes, I headed downstairs and back into the living room where all the boys and Hannah gathered around Dian and Tyr. All eyes were suddenly on me as I entered, making me feel instantly self-conscious. 'Wow,' Darren and Etrician said together, staring at me with wide eyes.

'You only like the dress, that's it,' I quipped, shoving the dirty dress into Etrician's chest.

Hearing the girls come down the stairs, I moved out of the way. Stepping towards me, Etrician whispered, 'I would like you even more without the dress.' Stifling a smile, I blushed childishly and stood beside him. 'We were waiting for everyone to see Tyr's hand being made,' he informed me as the guys wolf-whistled Renita and Jane when they entered the room.

'You girls look beautiful,' Tyr said glancing at Jane and Renita. It was true though and I had to admit, though silently, that Airmed did have a good taste in clothes. Renita was wearing a long royal blue dress with frilly white lace around the diamond neckline and cuffs. Around her waist was a golden woven plat that hung loosely around it, with little sparkling tassels on the ends.

Jane was wearing a dress that looked like it was made from sunshine. A dazzling pale yellow in appearance, it too was long and sweeping with cut off sleeves and tiny raindrop patterned blue crystals inlaid into the corset bodice.

Both girls were beaming with pride with their new dresses, though I was wondering how long the dresses would keep clean before we ran into some difficulty or fighting. Thinking in a pessimistic way, it, unfortunately, was inevitable. Hannah, however, was the only one in the room who looked putout and it was understandable. She wore a mud-splattered plain blue t-shirt, muddy jeans and what used to be white shoes.

'You all look wonderful,' Dian smiled, 'my daughter I see has taken good care of you.'

Snorting, Etrician nudged me in the ribs. I managed to pull off my sarcastic snort as a coughing fit and pardoned myself from embarrassment. Looking at Etrician, he frowned at me as though I was being rude. If only he knew.

Everyone gathered around to see Tyr's new hand. 'Found a spare one as I routed around my trunk last night,' Dian said holding it up for everyone to see. Intricately crafted; it even showed the contours on the knuckles and the lines on the palm. 'It will hurt for a while Tyr,' Dian said carefully as Tyr held out his stump, unravelling the cloth around it. 'But when the hand becomes yours you will be able to use your magic. Understand?'

Tyr nodded but didn't seem to mind. He looked so eager to have a hand I don't think he minded it would hurt him. Knowing that Fenrir wouldn't come and claim it from him, Tyr was positively giddy.

'Very good,' Dian said, as he stood up. 'Now, if the rest of you could back up please that might-'

'Da, perhaps it would be better to do it outside?' Airmed suggested, 'with Tyr's powers, we won't know what will happen.'

'Aye, that's a good idea, my child,' he nodded. Taking the hand, he led everyone out into the front of the house. The sun blazed through the clear blue sky above. It almost looked like it was spring all around; wildflowers grew higgledy-piggledy around the garden next to bunches of native and exotic herbs that wafted strange and almost intoxicating smells that set my mind swirling.

'Make sure you don't stand too close to my Aphrodisia,' Dian warned, as we gathered around. All heads turned to him as he pointed right where I was standing. Jumping aside, I looked behind me and saw the most beautiful flower that glistered in the sun. Each teardrop-shaped petal were the colours of the rainbow, the centre was a deep crimson red. The stalk, which I found rather interesting, was in a twisted shape, yet it grew straight. 'One good sniff of that and you'll try and bed anyone... and I mean anyone,' he said frowning.

Dagen seemed suspicious. 'What do you mean anyone?'

Dian replied with a chuckle, 'I mean your best friend, if they were standing too close.' Everyone edged away from it, apart from Etrician and I. Exchanging looks, we concealed a private thought.

The respectful Irish legend raised the hand towards Tyr. 'If you please?' he asked, looking at his stump.

Taking a deep breath, Darren gave him the thumbs up for support. Holding out his stump, Tyr smiled and gave Dian a quick nod. 'I'm ready.'

Gently taking hold of Tyr's stump, Dian took the magical silver Goblin-crafted hand and placed it on the end. In Gaelic, he said: 'By the powers of my essence, by the work of my friend, I give this hand of silver to a body I will now mend.' Dian repeated this sentence over and over and as he did so, the hand began to glow.

As the magic words sunk in, the light intensified. Then without warning, the hand began to melt and floating in the air in strange globs, made its way to Tyr, making instant contact with his stump.

Tyr suddenly yelled in pain and grasped his forearm with his good hand, squeezing it hard, digging his nails into himself, to relieve some of the pain.

'Hold on Tyr,' Airmed said soothingly as she stood by her father to watch.

The melted silver suddenly began to form into a hand from the wrist up but it was taking some time and with each passing moment, Tyr's pain increased. Beads of sweat sprang from his forehead; his eyes bulged through agony as the process surged through his arm. I suddenly had a thought, 'Does he have to be conscious for this?'

Dian's eyes suddenly locked onto me as he kept repeating the spell, but shook his head.

'He just needs to not move,' Airmed told me. 'Why? What is your plan?'

Grabbing my dirty dress from Etrician, I fumbled for the little bag that I had still within its rags and brought out a leaf from my Amber Tree. 'Deep coma,' I breathed onto it, and slapped the leaf onto Tyr's head and held it there.

Within seconds he stopped yelling, his eyes rolled back into his head, his left hand unclenched itself from his arm, withdrawing bloody fingers nails and he remained perfectly still, rigid as a board. I kept my leaf in place as I was unsure of whether or not if I took the leaf off, he may wake up and start screaming again.

Hannah's eyes grew wide. 'Wow, that is so cool, in a scary way!'

'I had no idea you could do that!' Jane gasped, looking at Tyr's peaceful face.

Laughing, I shrugged my shoulders. 'Neither did I, but I thought I'd give it a try at least.'

After a few minutes, the hand on Tyr's stump had formed completely and soon became solid. Dian stopped speaking his spell and gently touched the new silver hand. 'Ah yes, perfect. You may break your spell now.'

Complying, I removed the leaf, hoping and praying that Tyr came out of it. Within a few seconds, he opened his eyes and yelled out in pain again but it wasn't as loud or agonising as before.

'It aches,' he said lifting it. 'Hang on…what just happened?'

'Thera put you into a coma,' Darren said nonchalantly, as though I did it daily.

'I didn't want to see you in pain,' I told him truthfully as he looked at me in horror. 'But you have a new hand!' I said in excitement.

Beaming, though trying to hide his pain, Tyr twisted his hand to see it from different angles; catching the sun's rays, it shone brightly.

'Try and make your fingers move,' Dian encouraged.

With pained effort and through gritted teeth, Tyr's stout-hearted determination made his index finger move slightly. Then exhaling rapidly as though he ran a hundred miles, he shook his head. 'For the love of Atlas that was difficult to even move that much,' he gasped, inhaling deeply. 'I have a long way to go it seems.'

'Indeed, but you will succeed easy enough,' Dian laughed. 'I have faith in you and it seems, so do your friends.'

'High five!' Darren asked holding his right hand out to Tyr.

We each looked at one another in confusion, 'High five?' I asked Etrician. Shrugging, he grabbed my hand and lifting it kissed it softly.

'We have a lot of work ahead of us if we are going to get this band of myths into shape. How about we start now?' he asked, smiling at me.

'No time like the present. Alright you lot,' I shouted as everyone was admiring Tyr's hand. 'Thank the nice people for letting us intrude on them and let's pack up. We are off to the causeway to start your intensive training and be warned, I don't take no for an answer.'

I was waiting for Hannah and Darren in the entranceway. Everyone was taking their turn thanking Dian Cecht and Airmed for their kindness. Annoyance prickled over me as I saw Airmed swoon over Etrician and pull on his arm saying, 'Don't go, stay here with me,' then giggled like an idiot, flicking her locks out of her face.

With scowling eyes, I stared hard at her. 'Stupid myth,' I grumbled. 'Brazen hussy!'

'Who's a brazen hussy?' Hannah asked, laughing a little as she came towards me, Darren in-toe.

'No one,' I snapped, then made a beeline for the edge of our host's magical protection. 'Well it's been fun,' I smiled falsely, looking at Airmed. 'But I'm glad we could help you and for what you've done for Tyr, we are all very grateful,' I nodded to Dian.

'Ah, you are most welcome,' he smiled, puffing on his pipe. 'And know you're not strangers here and are welcome any time. Providing you bring a sprig of your Amber Tree next time, eh? Would be nice to understand its magical properties,' he chuckled heartily, making his potbelly jiggle.

Inwardly cringing that he wanted to tear off part of my tree to examine it I smiled and instead replied, 'Thank you for everything.'

'Ah you're welcome and good luck with the training!' he called.

I made a point to watch Airmed carefully as Etrician was saying goodbye to her. My blood instantly boiled as I heard her purr, 'Come back to me any time.' Then without warning, closed her eyes and leaned in for a kiss.

Irate and without intending to, I stomped my right foot on the ground in temper, causing a slight earth shake. Immediately everyone yelled in fright. Etrician was the only one who knew where the shake came from and put his hand out to stop Airmed. 'I'm with Thera,' he said smiling.

'Right, we're off now!' I bellowed angrily. As I passed over the magical threshold, the temperature suddenly dropped as the sky became overcast with dark grey snow-threatening clouds. A chilly fresh wind nipped at my face instantly and I relished it. I felt trapped within the suffocating bubble of magic and was quite happy to be free.

'Thera!' a meek voice came from behind. Catching up to me, Jane tapped me lightly on the arm and withdrew it quickly as I span around.

'What?' I barked.

With sympathetic eyes, Jane reached out her hand again to comfort me. 'It's alright. I understand.' She gave me a hug taking the bitterness out of me and the bleak clouds above retreated, leaving patchy sunshine. 'We all know how you feel about Etrician. And you don't have to worry about him turning from you, he never will.'

Before I could thank her, the others passed through the barrier. 'Let's go,' I said walking towards the causeway. I heard one or two people mumble, 'What's up with Thera?' but I ignored them. Jane knew my hot-headed, possessive bad temper, and I think one person knowing such a fact about me should be enough.

Heading down to the causeway, I got the strange feeling that no one was up for training. The look on everyone's faces showed anxiety and fear. Poor Dagen appeared positively petrified.

As we got down to the causeway I felt the pressures of the old magic the centaurs and giants had left behind. The amphitheatre hadn't been used in a very long time. Though it was fun during the old days when all sorts of myths and legends gathered here to entertain one another frequently, I found it difficult to believe that no one would be doing that again. It sort of became unpopular.

Reaching the bottom of the basalt columns that made the stage, I turned to face the others. Etrician came to stand by me.

'Right, Renita and Jane you will go with Etrician. Learn and listen from him.' They each nodded. 'Tyr, Dagen you will come with me,' I said, dividing them.

'What about us?' Hannah asked.

Thinking about it, it was best to split them up rather than both of them come with me, that way it would be equal. 'Hannah, come with me, Darren with Etrician.'

'My group over there by the wall,' Etrician pointed to the seating area that overlooked the rough turbulent sea behind me. To the humans the seating area looked like the columns had been smashed by giants—they were partly true. Each large black column was stepped in such a way as to see the stage below. This was to accommodate all forms of myths and legends. Not all of us were the same size.

'The rest of you can stay with me.' I led them a little further towards the water's edge. 'Right, let's start shall we?'

Hannah put her hand up and asked, 'shouldn't we warm up first? You know, run on the spot, do some stretches?'

Dagen laughed derisively. 'No, that's pointless. Our bodies don't need warming up, but you do so why don't you go and practice over there,' he pointed.

Tyr tutted and turned to her. 'Don't listen to him, I'll do some stretches with you, Dagen can practice with Thera first,' he smiled evilly.

'You, here, now,' I barked to Dagen. Muttering curse words under his breath, he ambled towards me while Tyr and Hannah walked a little further away. 'I think you need to start from the beginning.'

Upset he said, 'I should be able to do magic fluently and I try but I just don't know how to form it coherently.'

Shaking my head, I knew it would have to come to this and I really, really didn't want to do it. 'Dagen,' I began, 'I am going to offer a suggestion. You don't have to take it, it's your choice, but if you do, it will help you. The only problem is, you will have to show respect, keep your mouth shut, and let me do the talking. Do you understand?'

Frowning, he asked. 'What is the suggestion?'

'There is a book to help you, the Book of the Mage. Within its pages holds the key to learning all forms of magic. The only problem is that to get to the place where it is located, you have to have an invite. Requesting an invitation will take too long.'

'Where is it?'

'The Book of Mage belongs in Avalon. You know this?' I asked him.

Familiarity etched on his face and he nodded briefly. 'Merlin spoke of Avalon often. But he dare not reveal the whereabouts of it, nor how to enter onto the island. I am guessing you do?'

I nodded. 'As island within an island. Britain holds so many secrets it's a shame the humans relinquished most of their mythological knowledge.'

'For their own good, I think,' he said darkly.

Dagen stood up and promised he would think about it. It wasn't just a short trip to the isle, it would be dangerous and he had many things to think about before he made a decision. As he went away to ponder, I called Tyr over. But before he even stood up, the whole amphitheatre shook quite violently. Several black, shiny basalt columns broke, scattering shards around us. Renita and Jane screamed as they ducked for cover.

'Hannah, watch out!' Renita suddenly shouted, pointing to her.

Out of the corner of my eye, I saw Hannah wobbling close to the edge. But before I could even take a few steps to reach her, she fell into the rough Irish sea.

CHAPTER THIRTEEN

THE SPRAY VIOLENTLY KICKED UP AND HANNAH QUICKLY VANISHED, swallowed up by the ocean.

'HANNAH!' Renita and Jane ran to the edge.

Without thinking, my legs moved on their own accord, my breathing came in panic-stricken, short gasps, my heart pounded in my chest and I found myself heading towards the place where I heard the splash. My mind quickly caught up to the situation at hand, and I ran faster. I was solely focussed on getting Hannah, but suddenly I felt a weight crash against me, forcing me to the floor. 'No you can't put yourself in jeopardy,' Tyr yelled at me.

'But Hannah,' I gasped, the wind knocked out of me.

'Myths are being murdered left, right and centre,' Tyr held me back. 'We're protecting you, Thera,' he panted, pinning me to the ground to stop me from going after her. 'You can't go in the ocean; you would give your position away to the myths of the oceans that aren't on your side. We can't let anything happen to you, we promised your brother.'

Then in a flash of black and blue, Darren tore past us and dived, headfirst into the ocean. 'NO!' I screamed, struggling against Tyr. Managing to push him off me, I rolled out of the way and scrambling up, I raced to the water's edge. It thrashed menacingly against the sides of the rocks. With each pummelling blow, it felt as though the basalt columns underneath me threatened to break. The seas were angry and unsympathetic.

I was about to leap into the black portentous waters when a warm hand grabbed hold of me. Spinning me around, I stared into Etrician's earthy brown eyes. 'Save them,' I whispered, my voice caught in my throat.

He nodded then pushed me out of the way and dove into the waters without an utterance of a word. Jane and Renita and I stared at the thrashing waves, hoping to see something and then…

'THERE!' Tyr shouted pointing in front of us. About forty yards ahead, Hannah's head along with Etrician's torso burst out of the seas and headed towards us. As they got closer, I called the waves to me and brought them safely ashore.

Rushing to Hannah's side as she coughed and spluttered up the water I suddenly stopped as I saw her. I glanced at her wrist and gasped. 'Where is Darren?' I barked at Etrician, though continued to look at Hannah in shock.

'You need to deal with him,' he said. My eyes flicked to his face, he was frowning in puzzlement and concern. 'I don't understand what had happened in the waters, and now out of them… I am even more confused.' He took a quick look at Hannah's wrist and shook his head. 'Go, get him quickly or else he'll-'

'She can't,' Tyr bellowed, grabbing my hand. 'She's not meant to be in the ocean. We promised your brother we'd protect you, Thera. Risking it all by going into the ocean is idiotic!' he yelled. Through the sheer force of his voice and annoyance he felt, his silver hand made a fist.

I replied softly, 'It's all right. There are other ways to communicate without fully submerging myself and letting every other myth know where I am.'

Still unsure but having no choice in the matter, Tyr let me go. Taking three fateful steps, I knelt and put my hands into the water, balancing myself on the balls of my feet. Instantly I sensed Darren and the situation he was in. He too felt my presence. '*Darren, come here,*' I asked him in my thoughts.

'*No,*' he shouted at me, as though a child who had found out I was about to stop him from playing with his favourite toy. '*I want to stay here. I like it here.*'

Scowling at his disobedience towards me, I inhaled deeply retaining my authority over him and anyone else who claims the sea as their home. '*Darren, you will come here now!*' I ordered him. He had no choice as I created a water bubble around him and dragged him towards me.

Hurtling curse words as though trying to prove a point on how intolerable and hateful I was to spoil his fun, he slowly made his way to me. As he neared I tried to think about how he got into this situation, how he and Hannah both. It made no sense. They'd both been in the water before and yet, this?

When Darren was within reach, I pulled him out of the sea within a sphere of water that hovered just above the surface. Swimming around like some fish in a bowl was Darren, the merman.

As everyone gasped in shock, I backed up and brought the ball of water over land. Darren was swearing at me in my mind, but I ignored him. 'When I break the water,' I said, hearing the sound of running feet getting closer to us as. Moments later the others approached. With open mouths, they stared at Darren in amazement, 'someone put some clothes on him.'

Coming to my side, Renita held out a fresh pair of jeans and nodded. 'I will do. I'm so sorry, Thera, it's my fault I thought that I had control of it, I didn't mean to cause the earthquake.'

'No, no, I'm glad you did,' I said to her as Darren gave me the middle finger, still swearing at me to put him back in the sea. 'I would have never had known otherwise,' I began, looking at Hannah's bracelet that was now gently humming and shining a soft pale blue. The Aqua stone had been activated. 'The bracelets turn you into a myth whilst you are in the ocean. Clearly there was a difference between salt water and fresh,' I said more to myself.

Jane, for some unknown reason, started laughing. 'He looks so funny when he's angry and his tail shows it. Sorry Darren!' she called waving to him.

'Hannah,' I said gently to her, getting her immediate attention. 'How long did it take you to transform into a Water Nymph just now?'

Staring at me with cautious eyes as though she was unsure of whether I would scald her or not, she mumbled, 'Seconds. Then as soon as my head broke the surface, I turned back into a human again.'

Her voice was steady, calm, and emotionless. Though her face showed her lack of emotion in her heart, I knew she was stricken with fear.

I turned back to Darren and cracked the bubble of water. As the air reached him his tail suddenly vanished, his naked body smacked painfully to the floor with a crunch. Renita's cheeks suddenly burned with embarrassment as she threw his jeans to him, hitting him in the face.

I turned away to give him some privacy. He spluttered up water and with deep panting gasps a few minutes later he uttered, 'Okay, dressed.'

Facing him, his shaking body was partly damp yet he remained human. 'I guess you have to be fully submerged,' voicing my thoughts aloud.

'Confused as well?' Etrician asked as he helped Hannah up. Glancing at Hannah, I saw some change in her. She had become taller and looked more ethereal looking. Those bracelets were a force to be reckoned with.

'Partly,' I replied, looking between Hannah and Darren, 'but also partly intrigued. I have never come across this before and I believe it's the power of the bracelets and freshwater versus salt.'

'Well, this is all bleedin' brilliant!' Darren lashed out. 'You two are talking about us like we're freaking experiments!'

'Well you are in a way,' Dagen piped in. 'It's all rather fascinating for us to see you look like an idiot.'

Within two strides, Darren reached Dagen and pulled back his fist.

SMACK!

'Darren!' Hannah gasped clamping her hands to her mouth. As he withdrew his fisted hand from Dagen's nose, blood speckled it.

Yelling in agony, Dagen dropped to the floor; pinching his nose to stem the blood that gushed out like a geyser. While the others laughed at Dagen's misfortune, I didn't. If truth be told, it was unfair to laugh after hearing him and Tyr's conversation the other night. Dagen just needs to learn that being spiteful makes him a horrible person.

Dagen continuously tried my patience and though I ignored him regularly, his words were still as vicious as a viper.

Walking to him, I bent down to see the damage done to his nose. 'It seems that Darren still retains some strength,' I said, inspecting the bleed. He was going to have a bruise for some time, unless... 'leaf?' I suggested, bringing out my little bag containing my Amber Tree leaves. 'It may help with the bruise?'

Scoffing, he shoved my hand away from him and stood up. 'We're going to Avalon,' he said thickly. 'Now.' Dagen went to the water's edge and splashed water in his face to get the blood off.

'What?' Everyone asked looking confused.

'The sooner I get there the sooner I can unlock my magic and repay my debt,' he snapped viciously at Darren.

Darren took a threatening step to him. 'Bring it!' He goaded.

Exasperated by two children, I stood up and got in between them. 'There will be no repaying of debt's that include, fighting, slapping, biting, using magic or nasty remarks,' he added for Dagen's benefit.

'In that order?' Etrician frowned. 'But why Avalon? When did you get an invitation?'

'I didn't,' I said with a wry smile. 'But Dagen needs to go. This group has to work and help each other out.'

'No,' Etrician raised his voice, his finger pointed at me. 'You are not going there. Do you realise what you're getting yourself into?'

'Yes I do,' I said, grabbing his finger and pretending to bite it.

'It's not funny, Thera!' he scolded, grabbing my shoulders and shaking me gently. 'You could get lost in there. Without an invitation, you won't be able to-'

'I know but I'll be fine,' I said, trying to shake him off me. 'I'm not a hapless sprite, I know what to expect when we get there and I promise I'll be careful and I'll get back after the first full moon,' I assured him with a smile.

His eyes were intense but he finally let go. 'You'd better or I'm coming in after you,' he said concerned.

'Wait a minute,' Hannah said putting her hand up as though in school, 'Avalon, as in the final resting place of King Arthur Avalon?'

I nodded once. 'The very same. Jane, I need you to take us to Glastonbury, if that's alright with you?' I asked.

She smiled. 'Of course, specifically where?'

'Chalice Well.' I replied. Tilting her head like a confused puppy, I elaborated. 'To open the gateway to Avalon, we have to walk on the path from the bottom of the Tor of Glastonbury to the top. We need to pass through St. Michaels Tower in a straight line. The site is Celtic and still has some power from Arthur's time but we need to go now while it's still early.'

'Renita, come with me please?' Jane asked her. 'I don't think I can get back on my own.'

'Sure, I'd love to!' she giggled.

Tyr glanced at us nervously all then pointed at me. 'How are you going to get back here?'

I pointed to Dagen. 'I'll have him,' I smiled. 'He should know how to use his magic by then and can bring us back.'

Scoffing Dagen walked to me. 'Of course, I will,' he said in a smarmy tone.

Giving me a swift kiss goodbye, Etrician held my hands and kissed them gently. 'Please be careful. I cannot help you once you've crossed over.'

Stroking his cheek, I smiled. 'I promise you, I'll be fine. I have Dagen, so I'm not alone.'

Jane, Renita and Dagen gathered together and held hands, waiting for me. Quickly grabbing onto Jane's right hand and Dagen's left; we disappeared in a blinding light of blue.

We arrived by a large red-bricked building behind a hedge in the quiet little place opposite the Chalice Well entrance. A natural spring that the ancient Celts worshipped and drank from before they completed their pilgrimage to the top of the Tor it was now an attraction.

I had visited this spring only three times in my existence; entrusting it to a group of water fairies who reported to Santorini and me every few decades or so. Though they were a bit wary of the humans making the well an attraction only half a century ago, they realised that the humans were keeping it safe and so silently worked with them to maintain it.

The sky above was partially cloudy, with a few wisps of light blue sky above peeking through. Thankfully, the winds had dropped drastically and it was sheltered a little. The gravel beneath our feet crackled as we moved past a parked blue car and peered around the entrance of the driveway where Jane had phaded us.

'Do you need anything else from us?' Renita asked, and pointed to where we needed to walk.

I stared up towards the Tor. A strange ominous feeling dowsed me briefly. 'No, we'll be fine thank you. Just keep practising and do what Etrician asks of you. You cannot contact us when we reach Avalon, so try and play nice for mummy,' I laughed.

'Will do,' Jane smiled as she offered her hand for Renita to take. Obliging Renita strangely stared at me; a shadow of grievance passed over her eyes. But blinking a few times, it had passed.

'You'll be fine,' I said to her softly.

Smiling sadly, she nodded and without another word, Jane phaded herself and Renita back to Giant's Causeway with a blinding flash of blue light.

'At least she's getting better at phading,' I sighed, as Dagen and I hurriedly crossed the road.

'Do you take care of the spring?' he asked, pointing as we passed the entrance. The tresses where honeysuckle and roses would creep around it during the summer looked unkempt and aged. Though there were a few cars in the car park, the place seemed a little lifeless.

'Not directly no,' I confessed, as we began to walk up the road towards the start of the hill. 'Santorini and I left it in charge to five water fairies. They are looking after it, so there is no reason to visit them now.'

'What if you need their help?' A car zoomed past, honking loudly and making me jump.

'If and when the occasion calls for it,' I replied, eager to get this finished quickly.

As we reached the corner of the road, Dagen and I hurried across to the start of the path. 'Right, keep behind me and repeat the words, "I come to thee who rest in peace, may I be one with Avalon."

'We're not going to die are we?' Dagen immediately shouted in panic

Stopping before we got any further I shook my head, 'No we're not, it's polite to make oneself known to those who still reside on the Tor and may I remind you right now, no, we won't get eaten.'

'Eaten!' he yelled.

'Dagen,' I sighed, putting my hand up, 'just do as I ask, alright? We'll be fine, I promise.'

'You're making a lot of promises lately, I'm surprised you think you can keep up with them,' he laid into me.

Ignoring him, I pushed on, thinking nothing other than the words of entrance onto the Isle. Technically, when Arthur was around, Glastonbury Tor was Avalon, or more specifically the Isle of Avalon, when water surrounded it. Presently, Avalon and its whereabouts were wiped from human memory, hidden by Merlin's magic. Of course, humans still had an inkling that Glastonbury Tor was a special place and had some connection to Avalon.

As Dagen and I began to head up the path, I suddenly felt a ley line beneath my feet. It was very strong and powerful.

Ley lines were magical, invisible lines in the earth that draw myths and ghosts to them. Humans use dowsing rods to locate ley lines as well as water, yet with myths and legends, we feel it in the earth.

The magnetic ethereal draw was almost enchanting as I walked across it, guiding me up the hill at a nice easy pace. With each step I took, repeating the words in my head, I began to feel several presences that were like my own. They were ancient, respected, gifted and revered for who they were and what they stood for. Sensing that Dagen was still behind me, I began to slow as I approached the top. St Michael's Tower now standing in its reverence before me and there creeping out from the shadows of the morning sun, was a very large dragon. Pewter grey in colour with shiny blue flecks on its chest, it stood up on its powerful muscular legs and growled deeply; the vibrations coursed through my chest. Not fearing it but instead feeling such adoration for the beast, my thoughts stopped and I bowed.

Dagen, who wasn't paying attention, smacked into me, making me unbalance a little, but taking no notice of him I stood up and waited for the dragon to speak. Politeness between us was paramount into getting a free trip into Avalon.

The dragon acted as caretaker to the gateway into Avalon. You were only permitted to pass if the dragon saw your invitation, which I didn't have. Asking Dagen to repeat the words of "Respect for the Dead" was the only way to appear humble and contrite, especially since I was going to ask a very big favour.

'Water Nymph,' the dragon spoke, its forked tongue lashing the air to smell me. 'You have come a long way and yet you are neither dying nor in need of peaceful death. You come here on false pretences.' It growled menacingly, short sharp breaths of smoke blasted out of its nostrils in anger, yet I stood my ground. 'And what is this feculent maggot cowering behind you? It appears human though I detect a dormant and misused magic about it.' The dragon took a large step towards us; its tongue licked the air around Dagen. I could hear him whimper behind me and I wanted so desperately to tell him to shut up, but I dare not speak, not just yet.

'I sense that you have no invitation into Avalon and yes do not think me naive as to know you carry no word to enter the realm of the tortured dead. It is not often myths or legends come so freely to Avalon and when they do, they wished they never requested an invitation.' It laughed deeply; its tile-like scales rattled together sounding like waves washing along shale. 'So I shall ask you only once Water Nymph, why are you here?'

Taking a deep breath, I stared up into its shallow black eyes. 'I am here to guide this myth into Avalon for him to seek help from the Mage.'

'No!' the dragon roared, thrashing its tail, causing whiffs of sulphur to purge my sense of smell. With tearing eyes, I bowed in respect. But I wasn't giving up that easily.

'You say you are not naive though may I ask whether you feel the shift in the balance?'

The dragon looked affronted and snorted smoke into my face. When the smoke had cleared carried by a light breeze, the dragon's enormous head was metres from me, its left eye staring right at me. 'What do you, a Water Nymph, know of the balance?'

'More than you think.' I said testily. 'Something evil is rising in this world. The myths of Ancient Greece have fled their homeland in fear. They hide out in caves and are protected by centaur and fairy magic. The Staff of Zeus has fallen to earth and with it, the devastation it brings to myths, including yourself, is incontrovertible evidence that no one is safe. I and several myths have allied to try and stop these things from happening. This myth behind me, which you have callously called a feculent maggot, is a courageous boy who wishes to help the world by understanding magic in the right way. Avalon is the only place where he can learn his true potential and use his magic to help. Are you denying him his right to learn the sacred arts and side yourself with the evil that will corrupt this world?'

'How dare you!' The dragon roared, stamping its mighty feet causing the ground beneath us to shake violently.

'I dare! I need to know that you are on the right side! To help us in our quest and to get this boy taught in the arts.'

As the ground stopped shaking, the dragon leaned back to look at us both. A trembling Dagen came to stand behind me. Though he tried to stand up tall, I felt him wanting to run away back down the hill. But this was not an option. There was no turning back.

'I understand your plight, Water Nymph, though heed my words and heed them wisely. If I allow you to pass through the hallowed gates and into Avalon, there will be no guide to lead you safely to the Mage. She knows all who enter into her domain and she may dismiss you and your troublesome quest.'

'I understand.' I bowed in respect.

Snorting more smoke into my eyes, I hid a little cough as to not to offend it. The dragon skulked back towards the tower and peered into the archway. Inhaling deeply, yellow smoke suddenly billowed from its mouth. Flowing straight towards the archway, the smoke did not go through it; instead, it looked as though it hit an invisible wall. Within moments, a tall black wrought iron gate was now in front of St Michaels Tower. Written on the top of the gates were old Celtic symbols that spelt out "Avalon."

'Know this,' the dragon spoke before I took one single step. The gates began to open, metal screeching on metal, which made me shiver. 'Since it is a visit, you are only permitted to remain in Avalon until the next full moon. In Avalon time speeds up twice fold. So a full moon would occur after fifteen nights. Also, there is one more thing to tell you…' it said with a sneer, 'there is no such thing as daytime in Avalon. It is in perpetual night and the moon is always full.'

The dragon laughed, a mixture of white and yellow smoke spluttered out of its mouth as it bent low into a bow, admitting us in.

'Let's go, Dagen,' I said to him softly. 'Keep your wits about you and mind where you step.'

'Good luck, Water Nymph,' the dragon grumbled, as we headed slowly to the gates. 'And to you also, feculent myth.'

Approaching the entrance to Avalon, coldness abruptly pressed against my skin, as though dowsing me in Atlantic water. It was almost suffocating in a way, which I found extremely uncomfortable and distressing. The heavy decorative gates peeled back and slammed against the sides of the arch, bits of brick and mortar sprinkled on the ground, though no human would notice.

Originally, where the archway would look out towards green fields in the distance, instead there was only a wall of a dark grey mist. It swirled around strangely, as though the wind carried it, yet no wind came from within.

'Want to hold my hand?' I offered to Dagen as together, we stopped short of the entrance.

'It's not because I'm scared,' he whimpered, 'it's because I don't want to get lost.'

With a weak smile, I nodded. 'Brace yourself.' Stepping forward into the mist, it hit me so hard it made it difficult to breathe. Despair was so thick and oppressive in the atmosphere, it would strip you of your sense of self within seconds.

Pushing on, one foot after the other, the ley line still guiding me all but vanished and so too did the grey mist. Avalon stood before us in all its wonder and veneration.

'Have I gone blind of colour?' Dagen stammered, blinking rapidly trying to lift the spell.

'No,' I gasped, 'you haven't.' My knees buckled underneath me and I fell hard to the cold wet ground below. The oppressive atmosphere had quickly caught up with me, and I soon realised what it meant.

'Thera!' he cried, kneeling beside me. 'What's wrong?'

'Torment, pain, woe, the fear of oblivion; I feel them,' I cried, tears threatening to spill. 'I feel them all. The soldiers who fought for Arthur and the wizards and witches who died at the hands of the Mage; their suffering is all around me.'

'I see you,' a seductive voice suddenly whispered into my ear. 'I see you and your companion. How interesting your search for the Book of the Mage will bring you to nought.'

'He needs to learn,' I spat, angry tears now spilt from me. 'I won't leave empty-handed.'

'Thera, who are you talking to?' Dagen asked, but his voice was thrown out of earshot, as though a slight whisper amongst a torrential downpour of hailstones.

An evil cackle reached inside of my brain, a searing pain licked at the sides of my skull, making them fit to burst. 'You will leave when I TELL YOU TO LEAVE!' she screamed.

Clutching my head as the pain pounded in my skull, I keeled over onto the floor and screamed. 'Stop!' I begged her. 'Please, stop it now!'

'Thera, what's wrong with you?' Dagen sounded horrified and placing a hand on my head, abruptly the pain vanished. I heard her painful screams in my mind and she withdrew.

Panting on the dirt floor, trying to catch my breath even though I hadn't run an inch, Dagen's concerned face peered over me. Though I still felt the oppression of this place, nothing could beat the pain she inflicted on me.

'Well,' I said with a weak smile, 'she knows we're here, she knows she can't kill me and she knows that you have Merlin's magic.' Offering his hand, Dagen helped me up and frowned at me, waiting for me to explain. 'Merlin was the only wizard she envied. His abilities outweighed her own and surpassed her on such a level her magic became the opposite of Merlin's. When he ever used magic against her, she was nullified. Since you have Merlin's power, his magic stopped her hold on me.'

'You mean the Mage is Morgan le Fay?' he gasped in terror.

'None other. I'm surprised you didn't know.' Brushing down my dress, though I didn't see a point as I couldn't distinguish the varying shades of grey, I took the chance to look around. The sky, as the dragon was right, was a dull black with a full moon hanging amongst it but it looked insipid. We were situated on what was an outcrop from what used to be a mountain, but its peaks had crumbled and were lifeless and colourless. But then again, everything was lifeless and completely devoid of colour except grey, white and black. Its the price of wandering into a world without an invitation.

Cringing, I looked down and saw my grey skin. 'Well I guess this is how far I can come to showing my age,' I laughed.

'It's like those black and white movies that Hannah and Darren fight over,' Dagen said, placing his hands on his hips and looking around. 'It's so boring here. Even in the Antarctic had some ice that had a violet tinge to it but this, it's nothing.'

'Well, let's not dawdle in such a place. The more time we spend here the less time we have at finding the book.'

Silently, Dagen followed behind me every step of the way. In truth, I had no idea where I was going. Though I could only hazard a guess that the book was with le Fay herself as she was so protective over it. Of course, she could well have hidden the book where we would be continuously lost in this barren wasteland, spending eternity here and not know it. It was that thought that frightened me the most. The other's didn't have an eternity to wait for us, they had a few days if that.

Slipping and sliding down the path, the wasteland suddenly crept upon us and so did the spirits of the soldiers that resided in Avalon.

'Ignore them,' I whispered to Dagen, as I reached to grab him and make him walk faster. 'If you get involved in their stories they will not leave you alone.'

'How do you know all of this?' Dagen said quietly, walking quickly beside me. 'You are just a Water Nymph.'

Staring daggers, I corrected him. 'I've been around plenty of lost spirits. Who do you think knows the legend of Arthur if not another legend? The Lady of the Lake in under my charge. I know about Avalon. It's not an old legend as some, but those of us who have been around a bit longer tend to know these things. Concentrate on walking and don't listen to what they say. Don't be pulled in by their tales. It won't do you any good.'

No sooner had I said that three soldiers, dressed in Roman attire, from the 2nd century A.D., came towards us. 'Tell my wife I tried,' one of them said. 'Tell my son I love him,' another asked.

'I can't,' Dagen stammered.

I prodded him in the back. 'Don't say a word!' I reprimanded at him. 'You'll make it worse.'

'You know my son right?' one of the men asked Dagen. 'I know you have seen him in the village, talking to that pretty girl Analeaise. You loved her, didn't you Dagen?'

'What?' Dagen gasped slowing down to talk to them. 'You know her? You know me?'

'NO!' I shouted, moving in front of the spirits, forcing them back. Reaching behind me, I grabbed Dagen by the wrist and pulled him away. 'Do not get involved.'

'He knows me,' Dagen said, struggling to break free. 'I do know him. Stephan Berlik. I do know your son, Phillipe.'

The spirit moved swiftly as though the air itself and somehow prised apart Dagen and me.

Some spirits gathered around me and pushed me away from Dagen. 'No, get off me!' I yelled, but they paid more attention to Dagen. 'Dagen, come here, don't listen to them! They are lying! They want to take your immortal soul! Dagen listen to me!' I screamed at him, unable to use any magic I quickly felt what it was like to be a mere human.

The spirits quickly descended upon Dagen and without warning he was taken from me by a strange mist that engulfed him. The spirits of the dead soldiers had vanished into thin air.

'No!' I yelled in frustration. 'This can't be happening. Please dear Atlas no. DAGEN!'

CHAPTER FOURTEEN

THIS BARREN GREY WASTELAND WAS LOOKING MORE AND MORE LIKE AN old film of the Australian outback. The various dead grey prickle bushes were strewn haphazardly around the arid landscape. Being mindful of them, I didn't happen to notice that there were small sand traps dotted around. Twice, when I wasn't looking, I found myself sucked into one and had to wait until I reached the bottom before being belched out by my force of sheer will.

Covered head to toe in sand and chaffing annoyingly in places I'd rather not mention, I continued on my trek to Atlas knows where. The landscape began to change as the sandy spots became less so and more dead bushes erupted out of the ground. Gazing ahead, I saw scorched trees burnt to a cinder long ago. Unable to live the trees became petrified and remained oddly shaped black crystals, covering a small area beneath a dried-up moat.

Walking to the nearest crystallised tree, I tested to see how strong it was before I began to climb it. Shaking it a little, I found it sturdy enough to hold me. Jumping neatly from crystal limb to crystal limb I ascended and smiled at the sight before me as I reached the highest part.

The dried-up moat wasn't all that this place held. A haze was lifting before me and there as grand and prominent within the landscape was a very large ruined castle. It appeared to be floating on a cloud of constant swirling dust. 'Why is that dust moving?'

'Morgana made it so,' came a voice from below. I yelped in fright and fell from my branch, smashing through the black crystal limbs as though they were soft coral.

Hitting the ground hard and winding myself, I rolled over gasping for air. A shadow loomed over me and I came face to face with a two-foot troll-like creature. It had abnormally large, hairy feet with rather knobbly knees. On its squat face was a prominent chin and nose with a large pulsating black mole situated on the end and it had two glassy little black eyes. The creature wore a loose-fitting grey tunic and ragged bottoms. It looked well-fed, if anything from its rotund belly, though there were a load of cut marks up and down its legs. Just one look at him and there were many questions as to why this creature was here.

After catching my breath, I rolled over to face him properly and stared at him. He stood his ground but seemed as though he would rather run away from me. He waited for me to ask who he was, but I was more interested in his reply. 'Morgana made the dust move?' I asked.

He nodded then pointed back towards the dust-filled moat. 'It's magical. Stops things getting to the castle. I've managed to get many a thing in that invisible water. Don't they half drowns!' he cackled. 'Can't bleedin' swim that's why!'

Shaking my head of dust and shards of a black petrified tree, I stood up and finally took him in. 'You're a gob—no,' I stopped myself as his eyes squinted at me carefully. 'You're a hobgoblin aren't you?'

'Oh aye she gets it in one!' he clapped happily. 'Cousins to the goblins,' he said with disdain, 'yet more intelligent and nicer. Though don't tells anyone, it's meant to be secret. I'll lose out me moneys for kiddies birthday parties.'

'Um sure,' I nodded.

'But my lady, let me introduce meself. I am Portberry Conk-Shine Dinglewood, or for short, Dinglewood, at your service,' he said with a bow.

'Thera,' I said feeling a little put out that I only had one name. 'It's a pleasure to meet you Dinglewood. May I ask how did you come to be in Avalon?'

'Ah,' he nodded. Placing his hands behind his back and walking in front of me as though a teacher to schoolchildren. After a moment or two, he stopped in his tracks and turned to look at me. 'I had a slight problem. That's about it.' He smiled.

'Pardon? A slight problem?'

'You wants information, you pays up,' rubbing his dirty gnarled fingers.

'With what? There's nothing here,' I gestured around.

Rubbing his hands greedily, he inched towards me, almost drooling in delight and then pointed to my chest. 'Those!' he laughed madly.

'Excuse me?' I shouted, slapping his hand away. 'I'm not paying you that way. Who do you take me for?'

Cowering from me, he bowed apologetically looking upset and confused. 'Begging your pardon, my lady, I means no harm. I only mean your magics. My magics was taken from me long ago, how I'd love to get out of this place, yet you need magics to do so, or so I was told.'

Well, that stopped me from asking him if he knew how to get out of here. Unlike the many myths who willingly come to Avalon, he didn't and he wanted to leave. Maybe it was a punishment? Maybe it was by mistake? I was unsure. Taking the little bag out from under my dress, Dinglewood clapped happily and jumped up to try and grab it.

'Ah, ah!' Shaking my finger at him. 'You can sense magic I see, yet you don't know what is in here.'

Motioning me to show him the bag, I lowered my hand but kept a firm grip on it. Waving his hands in front of it, he smiled greedily. 'So much power from little leaves. Give me one! I want one now!'

'No!' I snapped, quickly lifting the bag as he reached out to snatch it. Shoving it back down my dress, I put my hands on my hips and glared down at him. 'That was impolite. Don't snatch, you're not a child.' I spat. 'Besides, I must go. I have a friend to find. He was taken to that barren wasteland behind me.' I motioned with my thumb.

'I knows where he's gone,' Dinglewood said happily. 'Soldiers takes newcomers to Morgana's for extractions.'

'Extractions? Extracting what exactly?' I asked him suspiciously, though I wish I hadn't.

'Magics!' he squealed, spitting on the ground in disgust. 'She steals magics then leaves poor shallow myths trapped in this world. Tis what happened to me! Bleedin' hag that she is. Punished I was by my kith and kin, and that dragon is a nasty fat gecko.'

'The soldier's though, they take souls, don't they?' I frowned but he shook his head, vigorously, which confused me. With his index finger, Dinglewood beckoned me towards him.

Whispering he said, 'The wrong end of sticks.' Looking askance to see if he was being overheard he added, 'the soldier's, they are the souls that Morgana took from their bodies. They cannot pass on unless Morgana releases them from Avalon and she won't, she needs them.' Suddenly realising what he did, he clamped his hand to his mouth and then shoved out his hand. 'Pay up with magics! You are sneakingly sneaking your way into making me tell!'

'No, you are willingly telling me yourself,' I smiled sweetly. 'Listen, I have my friend to find so I shall be heading in that way,' I pointed towards the dusty moat. 'But you take care of yourself.'

'Oh, my lady!' he jumped, grabbing my dress. 'Lets me come with you? I can be of helps.'

'Only if you know the time or when the next full moon is,' I asked slyly.

'I do!' he smiled proudly. 'But if you want to know you need to pay with magics...' he left his sentence hanging dangerously in the air. The little terror knew I needed to know the time and he was withholding the information. In truth, I didn't want to give him anything of my Amber Tree. No one was meant to know of its existence. Legends don't create anything. Strictly speaking, we're not allowed.

'Well?' he asked, snapping me out of my thoughts. 'You pay me with magics?'

I didn't like the thought of passing over an unknown source of magic to a hobgoblin but considering his magic lacked in every respect, I guess there was no harm in giving him one leaf.

Scowling, I brought out my bag and delved into it, withdrawing a shiny grey leaf.

'Here,' shoving the leaf into his hairy outstretched hands, 'and don't ask for another. That leaf is very powerful, do you understand?'

Sniffing the leaf as though trying to taste pure magic, his greedy eyes shot off in different directions to see if anyone was watching us. Like a magpie, he stared at the leaf for a while before stuffing it quickly into his jacket pocket then grabbing my hand, yanked me down to his level and escorted me through the black crystal forest.

Walking with him, I found out how poor Dinglewood ended up in Avalon. He had a nasty row with his cousins the goblins, who tricked the dragon into opening the gate and threw him inside three decades ago. Though Dinglewood tried hard to find a way back, he was captured by the soldiers, taken to Morgana who stripped him of his magic and cast him into the wasteland of Avalon.

'Course it didn't always look like this,' he stated, looking around the burnt crystallised forest. 'Once there was colour, once there was wind and water and sunshine, a real paradise for the fallen. After Merlin cast Avalon aways from the human world many centuries ago, it remained untouched. Over time though, myths and legends cames to regard Avalon as being a lost paradise. It meant to be for those who had connections to the legend. But, not so long ago, Arthur, Guinevere, Lancelot and Morgana cames here. In truth, I think they fled here. You see, some humans were tracking down myths and using their powers to create more myths.'

'I know of those humans,' I told him. 'They are called the T.A.T.'

'That's them!' Dinglewood squealed. 'Anyways, frictions arose between the four. Morgana became corrupted by greed and power as Avalon was the place of her birth, she tried to claim it as her own. She's kept whole armies here in Avalon. Never letting them leaves, she won't ever let them go, ever.' Shaking his head in despair he muttered, 'Poor buggers.'

'And where is Arthur in all of this? Surely he should stand up to Morgana after what she's done to the place.'

'Gone,' he replied with a shaky voice. 'Morgana has been even more ruthless.'

I slowed down as I wondered how Arthur and others could have left. Yes, they were mythologically related to this place, but there must be an opening to the outside world somewhere. 'So,' I began, catching up to Dinglewood, 'the time, you know it? And of course the next full moon?'

I saw his face turn slightly in my direction but he remained quiet.

'Um, I gave you "magics" you give me information, remember?' I said in a harsh tone.

Stopping the little hobgoblin turned around and smiled smarmily with crooked teeth. 'I don't knows the actual time but I knows someone who does.'

Concealing my annoyance, I asked politely. 'Well lead the way to this person who knows the time because I don't have much time and I need to find my friend.'

Bowing low and with a cheeky smile, Dinglewood led me out of the forest and towards what looked like a small clearing, surrounded by large thick petrified tree stumps wherein situated in the middle, were old Celtic style burial mounds; some of them occupied.

'Hoffer,' Dinglewood called, 'Hoffer you here?' his voice rebounded against the tree like cracks from a gunshot. With some grumblings, a large capstone that was the entrance to one of the mounds closest to us, moved slowly out of the way, revealing a very skinny old man, with next to nothing on his back apart from a ripped cloth around his midriff.

'Who speaks my name is such a hurry?' the old man cried, as with a bent back, he emerged from the mound and came towards us. 'Oh, it's you Portberry, why are you here at this unholy hour?'

Smiling, Dinglewood nudged me. 'Told you he knew the time.'

'The time? We all know the time if we ask for it,' he grumbled, spitting on the floor. Scratching his backside, he straightened out his spine with a resounding crack then chuckled. 'Ah, that's better. Now, who's this?' About to open my mouth to introduce myself, the old man shook his head and waved his finger at me, 'No don't tell me I can figure it out myself.'

Stooping slightly he ambled towards me and started from the bottom up, taking in my shoes, dress and chest, which annoyed me greatly. I heard Dinglewood snigger when he reached that point. Then eventually to my neck and face. 'Hmm interesting,' he said, grabbing my hand and yanking me towards him. Turning my hand over to look at my palm, he traced a line with his finger and smiled. 'Yes very interesting.'

'Do you know who she is?' Dinglewood asked, though he knew my name, I wondered if this old man, called Hoffer, knew who I was.

Hoffer let go of my hand and stared at Dinglewood. 'Not a clue. Never seen her before in my life. So,' he turned to me, wiping his nose with the back of his hand, 'who are you and what are you doing here?'

I kept from rolling my eyes but addressed him all the same. 'My name is Thera, I'm looking for a friend,' I started. 'He was taken by some soldier's to the castle-'

'To the dungeons in the castle!' Hoffer corrected me. 'But why were you here with a friend? Most people here have no friends. I don't and I don't need one.' He said matter-of-factly. 'Nope. I find myself talking to myself and that's much more fun, plus I always win my arguments.' He grinned. 'No you don't!' he said in a voice that sounded quite girly, 'Well yes I do!' he replied in a deep manly voice. 'No, you don't! Yes, I do!'

'Oy!' Dinglewood shouted breaking the crazed argument Hoffer was having with himself. 'What am I to you then?' Dinglewood barked. 'Aren't I your friend?'

'You, wee one, are a pain in the arse,' Hoffer roared. 'Little snit always asking me for favours then wanting magics. It's magic you fool! You should learn how to speak properly then maybe those poor old beggars in the wasteland may give you some respect.'

'They don't respect you?' I hid a smile.

Looking downcast, Dinglewood shook his head. 'No miss, they c-call me a goblin!' he wailed.

'Oh for the love of Peter Finklemeister!' Hoffer yelled. 'Pull yourself together and you-' he rounded on me, 'you need to know the time right? Its five hours past the twenty-sixth hour, time moves back'ards in this place and in double time,' he snorted again and spat on the floor. 'You need to get out on the stroke of the thirteenth hour, which is the next new full moon. You have until then to find your friend in seven and a half hours of normal time.'

I was unsure of how he came to that number.

'Are you confused?' he asked me smiling.

'Yes.'

'Good! I believe if you get confused at least once a day, it saves room for being less confused if you don't know what you're confused about in the first place. And yes I am a little mad,' he laughed loudly.

'You know the time now my lady Thera,' Dinglewood squeaked, grabbing my dress to get my attention. 'Let's go and get your friend.'

'Thera,' Hoffer choked, spinning around to stare at me properly. 'The Water Nymph?'

I nodded though I watched him cautiously. 'I did tell you. I guess you didn't listen.' His movements were erratic and also quite disgusting. Though Hoffer admitted he was mad, I was unsure if he was.

'Ah-ha! Your reputation precedes you. The Lady of the Lake spoke of you often. Thought she was a nice girl, turns out she's extremely crabby,' he said in thought.

'You know of her?'

Scoffing, he waved his hands at me and headed back into his burial mound. Moments later, he came out with a ring attached to a thick wristband that was inlaid with a few pale grey jewels.

'I was a magician back in those days. My magic was stolen, so I remain here powerless and continuing in this boredom of crap with that annoying imp who can't speak properly,' he shouted pointing a finger.

'Why don't you come with us?' I asked him. 'It may do you good to leave this place? And who knows, my friend may be able to stop Morgana and put the magic back into this place.'

Hoffer burst out laughing in a manic way, wiping his tears from his eyes. 'Ah, that's the funniest thing I've heard in decades. Aha!' He sighed then coughing, shooed me away. 'Be gone with you and your foolish words. No one can defeat Morgana apart from the only little thief who stole Merlin's magic. Oh, what's-his-face?' He looked at me as though I knew. 'Oh you know, straw-haired little brat, his name sounds boring and childish?'

Dinglewood shrugged his shoulders.

'Began with a 'D' I think...'

A memory of Dagen, his confession on stealing the magician's magic. 'No way. You don't mean Dagen do you?' I asked my brow furrowed in confusion.

'Dagen that's his name. Yes, did you know him?' Hoffer asked, though looked forlornly at his ring and wristband.

'Dagen's here in this domain,' I told him, 'the soldier's took him. He's the friend I'm trying to find. We came here together to find the Book of the Mage to unlock his powers. He confessed to stealing Merlin's magic,' I rambled, trying to fill him in quickly.

'Oh,' Hoffer said in shock. 'That little bugger! Right, let's go!'

Hoffer wasted no time in preparing to leave. Quickly grabbing odds and sods from his little burial mound, he pushed the decorated capstone back in its place and hobbling with a gnarled pole, huffed and grunted as he headed off, beckoning us to follow him.

'Are you going to tell me why you're coming with me, or rather us,' I added as Dinglewood looked upset that I hadn't considered him.

'No.' The old man spat on the floor then abruptly stopped. 'That way is safer,' he said taking a right and with his pole, headed off.

Catching up, I walked beside him, eyeing him now and again for tale-tell signs of whether he was going to tell me anything. I still had the horrible oppressive atmosphere hanging over me, even if he did have a safer way to go. 'You knew Dagen,' I began but he waved his hand at me for silence.

'Hoffer,' Dinglewood squeaked, 'perhaps it may be best to explain. I hates being confused sometimes and your acting oddly, more so than usual.'

'Speak properly you little cretin,' Hoffer growled, scratching his backside again.

'You remind me of bridge troll I met a long time ago,' I said, smiling a little.

'Eh?' Hoffer asked, seeming mildly interested. 'A troll? Met one once, stupid blighter was terrible at jokes.'

'Maybe we met the same one,' I suggested. 'He was stationed by a bridge in-'

'Don't want to know and I don't care,' Hoffer said impatiently. Pointing ahead of us where there was a pale light that flickered now and again. 'Fire, we'd best be prepared.'

'Fire? But the fire is alive, how can that be?'

'Morgana is looking for us. It's magic fire and she is the only one who has magic apart from you,' he eyed me suspiciously. 'You are a threat to her and a danger to us.'

'Then why are you coming with me?' I said testily, 'You know I am capable of getting to the castle on my own.'

'Ha,' he barked, shaking his head and laughing in spite. 'When you entered you were on the cliffs yes?'

'Yes.'

He picked his teeth with jagged, dirty nails then spat it on the floor. 'And since then you thought that because you saw the castle in front of you that is where you need to go? Well, you have no guide, meaning you had no invitation to come here so you have been walking about in circles. You are not seeing the castle you are seeing a mirror image, which changes every abnormal back'ards hour. It's like humans following a rainbow; they are never able to catch it. Since I was "put" here many years ago, I know this place and that light,' he nodded towards it, 'is a good sign as well as bad. It means Morgana is putting blocks in our path to slow us down long enough for you to be stuck here and for Dagen to...'

'To what?' I demanded. 'Finish the sentence.'

'To-,' Hoffer scrunched up his face as though he was having an internal argument with himself. 'Never you mind!'

'You said that Dagen was the only one to stop Morgana right? So what happens if Dagen and I are stuck here?' I probed.

'Ah!' he shouted and grabbed his head yanking some hair out. 'You'll disappear like a raindrop in a desert. Being in here I've felt the world shift into a darkness that has never been felt before. That darkness breached this world when Arthur and the others left.' He poked Dinglewood with his pole. The hobgoblin squeaked. 'I bet this pus filled little earwig told you Arthur left of his own accord?' I nodded. 'NOPE!' he spat then picking his nose, flicked his bogey on the hard ground. 'He was taken from us by someone. I am sure it will be back again to claim Dagen, especially if he gains the power of the Book of the Mage.'

'So, we would need to get out of here as soon as he learns magic?' I asked, pondering on the possible outcomes of us escaping and returning this place to normality.

Hoffer shook his head, 'Too bleedin' right! You honestly think you can get out of here in a short amount of time?'

'How do you get out if you're not invited in? I mean you could leave easily I would imagine…' I thought aloud but Dinglewood tutted at me.

'How rude of you my lady! You don't leaves without saying goodbye,' he said, tugging on my dress. 'You would end up staying here forever if that happened.'

Frowning at his words, I was about to question what he meant, when Hoffer placed a finger to his lips, shushing us. As we had talked about Dagen, Morgana and escaping, we had neared the light, and it was now apparent that Hoffer was correct. The flickering light was instead a floating orb of flame that blinked occasionally.

Within the orb was an eye that swivelled around, staring at things that it found interesting. Ducking low, Hoffer motioned us to hide behind a thick petrified tree. 'Morgana's Spies,' he wheezed. 'Fire turned against us and turned to her for aide to "live" in this domain. The imps are at work here.'

'How do we get past it?' I whispered, carefully peering around the dead black tree to see the eye continuing to swivel.

'Well, I don't know,' he sniped. 'I just know we're on the right path.'

My eye twitched in annoyance. 'You are unhelpful aren't you?' I tried to shout but controlled my volume.

Dinglewood pulled on my dress. 'I'm helpful.' I ignored him.

'Not now, Dinglewood,' I chided but suddenly I heard the break of twigs. Spinning around on the balls of my feet I noticed that he was gone.

'You fool!' I heard Hoffer growl.

Seeing what he was looking at, I saw Dinglewood calmly walk up to the eye. Immediately it turned to stare at Dinglewood, then, strangely enough, ignored it and looked elsewhere. Scratching his chin, Dinglewood picked up some dirt when the eye was paying attention to a tree right beside where Hoffer and I were hiding and threw it over the eye. 'Dirt snuffs out a fire,' he smiled. Igniting a few pieces of flammable grit, the eye engorged rapidly and then quickly shrank to the size of a pea and disappeared in a tiny puff of dark grey smoke. 'Easy is peasy,' Dinglewood laughed, clapping his hands to get rid of the excess dirt.

'Oh well done you clever little hobgoblin,' I called out joyfully, as Hoffer and I came out of hiding. 'Whatever made you think of that?'

'No water, use dirt,' he laughed looking smug.

'Yeah, yeah,' Hoffer growled as he continued to trudge on. 'Let's go, we haven't got time to waste.'

Passing through the black stumps of the petrified trees, they began to thin out again. From what Hoffer had said, I was almost prepared to have wandered back to his little burial mound, but instead, we came to a deep bank. The bank of the moat.

'We've made it!' Dinglewood squealed as he jumped up and down but then stopped, his smile wiped clean from his face 'oh yeah, thing's drown in there.'

'Be careful,' Hoffer warned, as I edged closer towards it to get a better look.

The embankment was approximately three metres in height, a perfect circle around the castle that loomed tall and imposing above us. The castle was situated at least half a mile away. Though from where we were, I couldn't see an entrance.

The dust that swirled around the moat so effortlessly sparkled with magic. Though pretty, the noise it created sounded like a savage sandstorm from an old dried desert, filled with peril and disaster. You could even taste its bitterness in the air.

Approaching the others their faces looked hopeless, which made my heart heavy. 'Dagen,' I whispered, feeling guilty that whatever happened to him, it was my fault. 'I'm so sorry.'

With no clue on how to cross the dust-filled moat, we all sat down on the ground, a little ways from the noise of the sandstorm and tried to think of a plan. 'You got us this far,' I told Hoffer, 'do you not know of a way across?'

Sighing, he crossed his legs and strangely picked at the dirt, making a small mound. 'I do but-' he began, looking conflicted with his thoughts '-it means being captured and your magic taken away. I cannot allow that to happen.'

'Soldiers are coming,' Dinglewood said suddenly, scrabbling up and pointing to our right. 'What do we do?' his voice, panicky as he looked between Hoffer and me.

'Is there no other way?' I asked him, standing up and preparing myself for the flowing words of the soldier's to send me into a stupor.

Upset, he quickly pulled out the ring, wristband attachment and gave it to me. 'I had hoped to use it for the three of us to escape but you and Dagen need it more.'

'They are here,' Dinglewood cried as he ducked behind me.

'Wait,' I asked, as he grabbed his pole and began to head off. 'How do I use it? What is it for?'

'You'll know when the time comes, good luck...' he called back as he disappeared from view.

Placing the ring and wristband on I expected something to happen, yet nothing did. The ring had a tiny crack in the middle of its gem perhaps it was already broken.

Poor Dinglewood fretted beside me, unknowing what to do. 'I will go with you my lady,' he squealed in fright. 'I said I would.'

Moving like the shells of men that they were, the soldiers came towards us, ghosting across the ground, making no noise. 'Help us,' they called out. 'Help us be who we were.'

'Dinglewood,' I whispered, getting his attention. 'Do not listen to them. Do you understand, plug your ears.'

He nodded once. 'They frighten me, they hurt my heart,' he whimpered.

Dressed in the uniforms they died in, the pale men surrounded us, reaching out with pasty thin hands and grabbed onto me. 'Help us,' they whispered as they began to drag me.

'My lady!' Dinglewood squealed. Reaching out for him, I grabbed onto his hand and pulled him with me.

'Hold onto me,' I muttered as the ghosts forced us to head towards the dusty sandstorm. Lifting Dinglewood, he clamped his legs around my waist like a child and clung onto me for dear life. I noticed that the soldiers paid him no mind.

A strange dark mist passed over us as we neared the embankment. The oppressive air above me felt so tight around my throat I felt like I couldn't breathe. Blackness quickly engulfed us as the ghosts pushed me.

The mist suddenly cleared and I found myself standing on hard cold paving slabs staring at the inside of the castle walls. It appeared to be some sort of throne room, yet only the throne was present. There were no tables, no windows, just her. The ghosts were gone too, which made thinking easier.

Dinglewood jumped off and hid behind me. 'It's her,' he whimpered.

'Welcome,' a sultry voice cooed from behind.

With long dark straight hair that fell past her shoulders, a sleek shiny dress that caught the light from a blazing fire beside her, Morgana's lips curled back into a menacing grin.

'Well,' she asked, her cooing voice suddenly became hard and wooden, 'aren't you going to say "thank you for inviting me?"' she asked, her eyes ablaze.

I shook my head, 'You know full well that I wasn't invited and if I was, I'd never come here.'

Making a tittering laugh, she moved gracefully to the large throne and sat down, her eyes never leaving me. 'Your words sting. It sounds as though you do not like this place.'

Scoffing, I shook my head and looked right at her. 'What have you done with my friend?'

Raising one perfectly shaped eyebrow she asked, 'Oh the boy? Why would I tell you?'

Rolling my eyes, I gingerly took a step towards her. 'Oh, because without his help this domain will be forever colourless.' I smiled. 'So yes, I need to know where he is so we can get out of here and stop that particular evil who took Arthur.'

'You know it?' she asked, her voice changed again, this time sounding frightened.

'My dear lady Morgana, I'm trying to stop it.'

Smirking she turned around and snapping her fingers a chalice appeared in her hand. 'You have courage. I admire that, especially in my presence.'

'That's nice' I humoured her. 'But your powers don't work on me.'

'Let's try out that theory shall we?' she hissed like a snake then struck out a pointy finger at me. A strange lightning bolt fizzled out of her hand and hit me square in the chest, yet I felt nothing. 'How! How is that possible?'

'I'm a legend,' I smiled sweetly. 'Legends cannot harm other legends. Just tell me where Dagen is and then we can leave you in peace.'

'Dagen?' she whispered. 'No, it cannot be.'

'Oh blast,' I sighed, letting the cat out of the bag. 'Um,' I glanced at the windowless arch behind her, 'Holy Atlas is that the dragon from the gates?' I suddenly shouted pointing behind her.

Like an idiot, she looked and like a crazed mad person, I span around, picked up Dinglewood and bolted for an exit.

Knowing that her magic was useless against me, Morgana shrieked curse words and threw stuff at me. Her chalice with the remains of her drink flew over my head, smashing against the wall beside me and then a tray was frisbeed in my direction where I had to duck to miss it.

'COME BACK HERE!' she screamed.

'A door,' Dinglewood pointed ahead. As I ran to the door and yanked it open, impenetrable darkness suddenly found me.

'MORONS!' she cackled madly from behind me. 'Have a fun time being forgotten!' I heard her scream then I felt something heavy hit the back of my head, making me unbalance. Pitching forwards into darkness, Dinglewood let go of me and joined in my screams as we fell into an old oubliette.

CHAPTER FIFTEEN

I HEARD AN EAR-PIERCING SCREAM OF "NO!" BESIDE ME AS WE FELL IN darkness. Cold air whooshed into my face, the feeling of butterflies dashed around my stomach and threatened to enter my mouth; it was the terrible feeling of lost gravity. Within seconds, I came to the quick realisation that at the bottom of this oubliette, Dinglewood and I were going to meet some very pointy friends.

Wishing to stop before the outcome of our falling came to a very sticky end, I had hoped that we'd fall flat on our faces, instead of impaling ourselves on probable sharp spikes below. In my eyes, the former would be more acceptable and less bloody. But my thoughts of that particular outcome abruptly stopped as I felt a certain tightening around my wrist and finger. I yelped out in shock as it felt like something or someone had grabbed my dress, stopping me before I was skewered.

Dinglewood's scream vanished and was replaced with a sigh of relief. 'My lady,' he whispered.

'Just shush for a second, I need to think.' I told him. I felt around me carefully, trying to see how far to the ground, we were, or more importantly how close to the spikes we were. 'I wish there was some light.'

No sooner had I said that I felt a small vibration that came from the wristband. Suddenly the ring shone bright white light that pierced every dark space around us. Hoffer's magical items came through and when needed.

'Oh my,' I gasped, seeing a very sharp spike an inch from my throat. 'That would have hurt.'

Glancing at Dinglewood I couldn't help but titter as he was suspended in midair. Even if he had continued to fall, he would have missed the spikes completely. He should be grateful he was so small.

'Your ring, it glows,' Dinglewood spoke softly, pointing at it.

I uttered one word. 'Hoffer,' and the little hobgoblin beamed.

'Tis but wishing magicks! You have one wish left.'

'We can figure that out later. First, we need to get down from this um, situation we are in.'

Dinglewood tried to swim in midair but he hardly moved. Scratching his head in thought, he reached out and managed to grab onto the tip of a spike and pull himself towards it. Hearing a strange snapping noise, as though someone had broken a twig, Dinglewood slid down the spike, like a strange pole. Copying Dinglewood, I reached out for a spike that was underneath me and took a deep breath. Grabbing it firmly, I pulled as hard as I could onto the spike and felt a strange sensation, and then the sound of a twig snapped.

'Ah!' Sliding down the cold metal, I sucked in as one grazed my bottom. Landing gracefully near to Dinglewood I took in the oubliette. 'Help me find some sort of fracture in the wall.'

'My goddess,' Dinglewood yelped, clutching his hands to his mouth. Looking a little paler than usual, I hastened towards him but he shook his head and looked down. 'They're h-human b-bones,' he whimpered.

'Just ignore them,' I said firmly, raising my hand to shed more light on our situation. The round walls looked caked in slime and lichen. Old cobwebs, that somehow withstood the test of time, laced around the walls; attaching themselves to the skulls, bones and occasional shield of the oubliette's victims.

'There is a cracked brick there, my lady,' Dinglewood pointed, peeking through his fingers.

Gingerly, I trod over the bones to reach him, unfortunately; I couldn't help breaking ribcages and skulls that got in my way. As I reached to where he had pointed, I saw that it was instead a natural fracture in the wall. Putting my hand on it, I smiled smarmily. This fracture showed weakness caused by water. Stroking the damp wall, I sensed the castle was full to the brim with magic. Though Morgana's domain was devoid of everything, her castle was not.

With the sharp end of the spike, I plunged it into the fracture with great force.

CRACK!

The entire oubliette suddenly shook. A large crack sped up the wall in a jagged way. 'Huh, I've made this oubliette unstable, how interesting.'

Moving forward, I grabbed at the broken wall and finding some purchase, began to pull away the loose parts. After making a small hole, big enough for Dinglewood to get through, I placed the still shining ring inside and saw an old staircase that curled steeply down to the right. A sudden smell of mildew and a rotting stench filled my nostrils. 'This hasn't been used in years,' I said aloud, motioning for Dinglewood to see. Clutching something to his chest, I thought it was a small shield from one of the impaled fallen. Ignoring it I pointed through the hole. 'I promise it's nothing scary.' Shaking from fright, he crept towards me peering inside. 'See, just an old stairwell.' I said in a positive tone. 'Want to help me make the hole bigger, so we can both get out?'

Taking a deep breath, he nodded and crawled through the hole and began to kick from the other side. 'You need to put your shield down,' I said to him.

'Oh just an old book my lady,' Frowning he placed it on the step below. 'A religious one it looks like,' he said casually.

Ignoring it, we continued tearing the wall away until it was big enough to get through. As I emerged onto the other side, Dinglewood hid behind me and grabbed hold of my dress. I smiled as he was beginning to remind me of Jane. He followed me as I began to descend.

With each few small rock-cut steps that turned so sharply making me dizzy, they abruptly stopped. I faced a low archway with a statue of a gargoyle in the middle. It's sunken chiselled out eyes and poking tongue made it either look insane, silly or quite frightening. Of course, this wasn't a real gargoyle. Gargoyles have horns, a tail or wings but look like normal humans. This was a medieval impression.

Beyond the archway, however, was a long corridor with two flaming torches on the opposite side of the walls; both placed in old cast-iron sockets that were nailed to the brick wall.

'Someone's been down here,' I whispered to him as he clutched tightly to me. 'Stay close.'

Entering the corridor, I noticed several thick English oak doors with heavy metal bolts fastened across them with a carved square hole with four metal bars. I had finally found the dungeons.

'Dagen!' I suddenly yelled out, unable to contain myself. 'Dagen are you here?'

'Yes!' called a frightened familiar voice from the very end of the corridor from a door to the right. Ignoring Dinglewood, I bolted to it. 'Thera is that you?' he asked, his voice sounding more like himself.

'Yes it's me,' I said as I reached the door and lifted the heavy bolt. Opening it, I saw Dagen's happy face, but it quickly changed as he folded his arms and stared at me.

'Took you long enough!' he smirked. 'What's with the shining ring?'

Hitting him on the shoulder, I reached out and hugged him. 'Never mind that. You idiot, you made me worry and that means you made me care about you!'

Letting me hug him, but not hugging me back, I pulled away and smacked him on the arm again.

'Ow, what was that for?' he yelled.

'For not listening to me! And also, don't tell Etrician I've hugged you-' but I stopped talking as I saw Dagen's eyes fall to the floor.

'What is that thing?'

'I is not a thing!' Dinglewood shouted, shaking his fist with one hand while still holding on to that religious book he found. 'Little snivelling wretch will address me as Dinglewood or Master since I did help find you.'

'Uh-huh,' Dagen said, stifling a yawn. 'I've gathered this is a rescue operation?' I nodded as he came out of his cell and looked around. 'Well that's nice of you, so shouldn't we be escaping now as the second apart of the rescuing operation?'

'Good call,' I smiled. As we headed back towards the archway, Dinglewood went up first and scurried off ahead but I wasn't worried about him. He was so small that no one would recognise him as a possible threat. Dagen however, was top of Morgana's list.

As we passed the hole in the wall, I saw a bit of brick fall away and spilt onto the steps below it. As Dagen continued to ascend the twirling steps, I peeked inside the wall. 'Dinglewood?' I asked but heard no response.

'I am up here my lady!' he called from above me.

As I climbed a few more steps, I suddenly heard something moving from inside the oubliette. I quickly caught up to Dagen. 'Hurry,' I whispered to him, 'we're being followed.'

Dagen didn't question it and began to stride up the steps as quickly as he could. We emerged out of the stairwell and went through a large door that led into a grand tapestry decorated corridor.

'This way!' Dinglewood called, jumping up and down in joy pointing to a corridor that led off to the right. He opened the book glanced at it and hurried off.

'Where is he taking us?' Dagen asked as we followed him without question.

'No idea but he knows something we don't.'

He shrugged. 'He's finding us a way out, I hope. That's good enough for me.'

'No,' I told him in a confident voice. 'We already have one,' indicating the ring and wristband. 'You have to have the Book of the Mage or at least read it. That's initially why we came here.'

'Why are you two gassing?' Dinglewood shouted, as he came back for us, his hands empty 'big book in the library! Tis over here!'

'How do you know?' I asked, folding my arms.

'Because it is my right to know, my lady,' he said, his tone of voice not sounding as enthusiastic as before. 'I've seen things and heard things in this castle and I knows I'm right. The library is around there. Now come on!'

Dagen made to move, but I grabbed him and shook my head. 'No,' I said firmly. 'No, I'm not going with you Dinglewood.'

'My lady, I wants you to be safe,' he said.

'Does safe mean the same as incarcerated to you? Does safe mean stripping away my magic just for your benefit? To be free?' I demanded.

'What's going on?' Dagen asked.

'Dinglewood used to be in the castle.' I narrowed my eyes at him. 'You worked for Morgana didn't you?'

Big thick fat salty tears began to pool from his little beetle black eyes, 'I'm sorry!' he bawled. 'It's to keep Mistress happy—always happy.'

'The book!' I gasped as everything clicked into place. I thought Dinglewood yelled "No," as we fell into the oubliette. But it wasn't, it was Morgana. The something heavy that smacked me in the back of the head was the book! 'The stupid woman threw the Book of the Mage at me...' Dinglewood found it in the oubliette and when he ran off, most likely gave the book back to Morgana!

'Dinglewood, how could you?'

'I'm sorry!' he wailed again.

A door to my right suddenly burst open and we came face to face with Morgana, clutching the book to her chest. 'Not sorry enough, you petulant grovelling worm.' Such amazing power pulsated from her and she stared down at us as though we were nothing.

'Oh, I feel strange,' Dagen gasped and without warning the book in her hands began to shake violently, as though it wanted to be released from her grip.

'No. It's mine.' she shrieked snapping herself out of her stupor, clasping onto it; almost digging her sharp pointy nails into the leather-bound cover. 'You cannot have it.'

Dagen's eyes were wide in shock, but they began to turn green, actual green. It was bizarre that I couldn't see any other colour or any other object that had a colour apart from Dagen's eyes. There were like an emerald flame, burning brightly and ferociously.

Lifting his hands towards the book, it suddenly leapt from Morgana's and flew to him. The book radiated a strange eerie colour that resembled a luminescent grey and then suddenly and abruptly dropped to the floor; Dagen's eyes returned to normal.

'Let's get out of here,' he said, grabbing my arm and yanked me away.

'Wish us back!' the hobgoblin squealed as he ran after us.

'NO!' Morgana screamed and with it, the castle around us began to shake.

'She's going to destroy the castle with us in it!' Dagen bellowed. 'If you've got a wish, for Atlas' sake, WISH IT!'

Morgana pelted after us, her heels clicking loudly and threateningly. Alongside her, a scurrying little hobgoblin wailed and boohooed that he had let his Mistress down.

'I wish we were at Giant's Causeway,' I whispered, clutching onto Dagen.

Behind me, I heard Morgana scream out as though in agony and then, something clutched my dress.

Bright colours of real grey, real blue and real black burst into my vision. The sweet smell of saltwater hit my taste buds making me salivate slightly. The loud crash of the angry waves of the Irish Sea that beat roughly against the basalt columns was music to my ears.

'I'M FREE!' I heard Dinglewood yell in triumph behind me. 'I'M FREE!'

Dagen and I were flat on our faces, panting from running for our lives. Turning over, I scrambled to a standing position and beckoning the sea, engulfed the little traitor in a ball of water, similar to Darren's, though, unfortunately, I had to leave his head clear for him to breathe.

'Oh my lady, please don't!' Dinglewood yelped.

'This is me very angry hobgoblin!' I spat, feeling my blood begin to boil.

'Oh, that's what it was,' Dagen laughed slightly as he stood up beside me. 'I thought it looked like a goblin.'

Suddenly looking red in the face Dinglewood shouted, 'How dare you call me a goblin! We are creatures to be feared the most in the whole magical world! We will not take your words lightly myth of Arthur!'

'Thera!' came the shocked voices of the group from somewhere behind me.

'Be prepared for a long sleep, Thera Mother of Sea Nymphs!' Dinglewood shouted maniacally. 'No one can escape once you've been marked!' There was an explosion of magic and I felt like I had been punched very hard in the stomach. Unable to maintain the ball, I dropped the water and flew back into the columns of basalt behind me.

Hearing panicked voices as the group hurried towards me, I watched Dinglewood turn himself into a cloud and float away on the breeze. I doubt I would ever see him again but was angry that I had been duped so easily and I was angry that he had managed to punch so hard. His magic was beyond that of a normal hobgoblin.

Etrician pulled me into a hug and checked to see if I was alright. 'I'm fine,' I lied, giving him a small smile. 'The hobgoblin must have retained his powers when we hitched a ride out of Avalon. 'Dagen is he?'

'He got hit too,' I heard Jane whisper beside me. 'Though you took the full brunt of it. He's fine though and conscious, but he keeps saying we're not enough to stop it.'

The others left me alone as Etrician asked me what had happened in Avalon. I explained everything to him, right from the beginning of meeting the dragon to Dagen's eyes that flashed green when he held the Book of the Mage and also what I felt when Dinglewood hit me with his magic.

'Dagen dropped the book though,' I frowned. 'I have an inkling of what happened, but I don't want to bother him.' Sighing tiredly, I rubbed my eyes and stared at Etrician. 'So, tell me, how are the others doing?'

With a half-smile, he looked over my shoulder. 'They are doing fine to a certain extent, but do you know how long you were gone?'

'I shouldn't think I was gone long, Avalon's time is…well in Hannah's words, was whacked,' I chuckled to myself.

'You were gone for five months,' he said, a blank look on his face.

An icy feeling suddenly spread through me until I saw a small smirk in the bottom right-hand side of his lip. 'You evil,' I laughed hitting him on the shoulder, 'dumb-' smacked him again, 'ARSE!'

Laughing, he rubbed his beaten arm. 'Sorry, I couldn't resist.'

'So,' I smiled, nudging his side playfully, 'how many hours?' but he shook his head '...days?'

'Day and a half,' he said soothingly, brushing some stray hair from my face, 'but Hannah and Darren have been practising their "Martian Arts" as they call it. Kicking and punching, ducking and rolling and flying in the air,' he laughed. 'It's been entertaining at least to see the fools practice.'

'What about the others?' I asked ignoring the "fools" comment, as I stretched out on the flat basalt columns, gazing at the others in front who were huddled around Dagen for some reason.

'Under my tutelage, Renita has improved greatly. She can call the rocks to her and they obey her easily. I've been teaching her how to use more of the ground at her command, but it's difficult as she says it goes against the wishes of her father. Jane needs a bit of encouragement,' he added, 'I think she can do well but she has to focus more on how she needs to get somewhere. If she improved she would be able to cast anyone anywhere but I haven't told her and I don't think she requires to know that at this time.'

'That's a bit wrong, don't you think?' I asked him frowning in puzzlement as to why he would withhold important information from her. 'Surely she should know what she is capable of. I mean, in regards to casting anyone anywhere she could put someone in the Underworld if she wanted.'

'I know,' Etrician said a little shortly. 'But it's best that we keep the information from her until she can handle it. She could abuse her powers.'

I burst out laughing. 'Jane, abuse her powers? Are you serious? Come now Etrician, Jane is too timid to abuse her powers. I think if she found out what she was capable of she wouldn't even dare try to phade again in case she accidentally sent one of us away to an unknown location on the planet.'

'Be that as it may, I think we should refrain from telling her, at least for a while,' he suggested with a shrug.

'Sure if you think so. So what of Tyr?' I asked, moving the conversation along.

Looking grateful that I'd dropped that particular topic, Etrician continued. 'Tyr, well I think he is doing alright by himself but he should practice with you. He's of the sky and I'm of earth, the complete opposite. At least with you two, you have water in common.'

Nodding in agreement, I rested for a bit and let the sound of the nearby waves crash over me, taking away this oncoming fear that loomed ever closer. I needed to think and to understand. All my hopes rested with the two people I was most anxious to talk to and to ask for help. Though Hannah and Darren had transformed through their bracelets, it wasn't permanent. However, if they did become myths once more, with the use of their bracelets, then Darren was going to be a problem. If he was a girl it wouldn't be an issue.

Mermaids who had the privilege of coming on land, behaved themselves but, a merman on land surrounded by all these women, Atlas help me. It didn't matter if he was smitten with that girl Saskia, he wouldn't be able to help his urges.

Closing my eyes, I fell into a light sleep though troubling images sprung to my mind. Dagen being tortured, Dinglewood laughing at me and Hoffer hobbling away saying, 'I didn't think it would be him.' All the while, I tried so hard to understand the Staff of Zeus. The mark on me, the little girl in the field who held the staff, and the Cabinet of Idols. All of this led up to something, but what? What was the missing piece? What would fit everything together?

Naturally jolting myself awake, I looked up the see dark rain clouds moving inland but I quickly noticed that no one was with me. Stifling a yawn, I stood up and surveyed the lower tiers of the amphitheatre. Etrician, Hannah and Tyr were in a group practising, while the others huddled around Dagen still. Suppressing an annoyed tut that was trying to escape my lips, I headed towards them.

'Have a nice nap?' Jane skipped towards me, a broad smile slapped on her face.

Rubbing the sleep from my eyes I stretched and felt I'd pulled a muscle. 'I've had better,' I told her truthfully. 'So Dagen, any improvements?' I asked as Renita and Darren parted out of the way to reveal Dagen. At first glance, I was unsure of my eyesight. Dagen had become, cooler, as the humans would say. His straw-coloured hair was slicked back; he seemed a lot muscular and had maybe grown a few inches. What stunned me the most was his eyes. They had turned the brightest shade of green that I had ever seen in my life. It looked like the colour of fresh spring grass.

'Isn't he gorgeous?' Jane drooled, batting her eyelids at him.

'Er,' I began, trying to formulate a good enough retort. 'Well, he's certainly improved in looks,' I said, folding my arms and staring at him. 'I mean, now at least you're tolerable to look at.'

Scowling like a mad shark that just got smacked on the nose, he pointed a finger at the ground, a few feet away from us, and shot out a quick stream of green light. BANG!

Chipped basalt rained down on us as Dagen blew a small crater in the ground. 'Well that was uncalled for,' I told him in a droll voice, unfazed by his actions as I brushed the debris from me. 'Is that all your capable of now? Showing off?'

Holding his right arm out, he smirked. 'Arm wrestle, you and me!'

Snorting at his idiotic behaviour, the others rolled their eyes. 'Are you serious?' I asked. 'Has testosterone gone to your head? Or has some dormant power of pure idiocy taken over your brain?'

'Well actually he was always stupid,' Renita intervened looking smug. 'Now he's pent-up and stupid.'

'No, he's powerful,' Jane cooed. Renita nudged her in the side and stuttering a little she added quietly, 'and stupid I guess.'

'Too chicken, ey?' Dagen scoffed, folding his arms, looking at me as though I was incompetent.

Normally in situations like these, I wouldn't have fallen for the obvious goading trick, especially if it was Santorini who pulled them on me. It was always, 'I bet you can't do this,' or 'I dare you to do that,' or 'I bet you're scared that you won't do this.' After ignoring him for so long, I grew tired of it and so took up his challenges. But that's what brothers and sisters do. We fight.

Dagen, however, was not my brother he was not even close. However, I wondered if by taking up his challenge, would it be childish of me to stoop to the level of an inexperienced myth? Or if I didn't, would I seem fickle and weak?

About to turn away, I heard him poke fun at me and that annoyed me greatly. Spinning around, I grabbed his arms and yanked him close to me, my mouth pressed right by his left ear. 'Don't cross me, Dagen. If you want to show yourself up in front of everyone by playing the high and mighty card because you know how to use your stolen powers then by all means. But mark my words, you cannot hurt me in any way shape or form and if you even think about hurting either of the others I will give you such a reckoning you shall feel it until the ends of the earth.' Letting go of his arms, I stood there and watched his face turn pale. Giving me a quick understanding nod, I turned and left him with the others and headed toward Etrician, Tyr and Hannah.

'Got annoyed with him too?' Etrician asked as I heard Renita and Jane ask Dagen what I had just told him. I nodded stiffly and sat on a small pillar of basalt and watched Tyr and Hannah perform some practice moves. 'What did he ask you to do?'

'Arm wrestle him,' I glared in annoyance continuing to think about it. 'What is wrong with him?'

Chuckling, Etrician came over to sit with me. 'He asked me to throw boulders at him to improve his aim.'

'What?'

He laughed. 'I was quite tempted just to pummel him with heavy metamorphic rock but I just walked off. It hurts his ego more if you ignore him.'

'Yes, but haven't we been ignoring him since he came with us?' Tyr stated, as in-sync, Hannah and Tyr made a complicated little move where they jumped into the air then twisted; landing gracefully on the ground.

'I hate bolshie people,' Hannah added. 'Saskia is very similar to Dagen, but she's way bitchier, which I think is worse actually.'

'How so?' Etrician asked.

Taking a breather, Hannah and Tyr sat down next to us. Wiping the sweat from her brow, she stretched her legs out and rubbed her knees. 'If you challenged Dagen and won he'd sulk and leave it at that. With Saskia, if you beat her, she'd continue trying to impress you and will continue challenging you until you gave in.' Laughing lightly she shook her head, 'Tara is the only person who doesn't stand for Saskia's crap. Though they won't admit it, Saskia admires Tara and I think Tara likes Saskia for challenging her authority. It keeps them sane.'

'So this Tara, she is the leader of your group?' Etrician asked, a light breeze of salty air whipped past us and I inhaled deeply. It smelt as though a storm was coming, though I took no heed of it.

Hannah pulled a perplexed face. 'Well, she was when we were myths but now that Nathaniel is the owner of the house, he's taken charge and it's annoying Tara.' She laughed. 'It's not that it's getting to her head in a sense of her being second in command or whatever, but like the rest of us, we miss being what we were.' Absentmindedly picking up a small rock, she twirled it around in her fingers. 'It's a sore topic in the house. If you mention wings or flying Tara starts slamming doors and shouting at people. If you mention water both Darren and I, we would go into a sulky mood and become quiet. Macie is constantly worrying about everyone and refuses to watch fantasy films in case there's a griffon in it and Lionel now despises dogs. Oh and Sam won't eat chicken or eggs. Saskia hogs the T.V. remote or PlayStation and constantly wants to argue and winds people up. And poor Henry is trying to overlook it and see a positive side to us being human again but we just ignore him and think he's become a pansy.'

Etrician and I stared at one another, dumbfounded. Clearly humans had problems. 'You do realise that when you were in that house that you were being watched?' I asked her. 'The whole house is on magical lockdown by the Ancients.'

She flicked the stone away and sighed. 'Yes, I did realise that. We knew there were fairies outside in the hedgerow and you mentioned centaur magic. I mean, as soon as I left the house I felt free, as though something was keeping me there. I just felt so sorry for Tara when Amjee sent us a letter the day after Boxing Day.'

'What happened?' Tyr asked softly, bringing his knees to his chin.

Staring at her, I could see that she was trying to stop herself from crying, but it wasn't going to work. Snapping her head down to the ground and with shaky hands, she wiped her eyes. 'Amjee told Tara and Nathaniel that their father was going to be cremated in London where his body was sent back to the T.A.T. Both of them were on the phone trying to contact Amjee and to ask to be let out of the house to attend, but they were told they were not allowed. From what Nathaniel has told me, Tara had it rough growing up. Though her parents loved Tara, they had a funny way of showing it and tried, in their way, to keep her from people like Maynard. It's taken Tara all these years to realise that her parents were wrong and that she was in danger of being taken from them and turned into what she became.'

'Parents do strange things to hold onto their children,' I whispered, my voice catching. Clearing my throat, I saw Tyr and Etrician look at me cautiously, but I avoided their gaze. They didn't need to be told what I had witnessed.

'How is Tara now though?' Tyr asked her, breaking an uncomfortable silence.

Hannah shrugged. 'She doesn't talk about it.'

A few moments later, Dagen, Renita, Jane and Darren turned up. 'So now what?' Darren asked us. 'I'm hungry,' he grumbled.

As the others began to squabble over food or the lack thereof, I got up and headed towards the edge by the pillars and peered over into the harsh iron sea that constantly called for me to join.

Santorini wouldn't stand for the belligerence of the myths towards me. He would have sorted them out no problem. But spending time with these myths and humans, I felt myself understanding them and maybe in some way, becoming like them. They weren't in charge of such troubling elements as the world's oceans, they were carefree.

With each passing moment, I felt the push of the tide as I pulled away from it. Although, as I stared at the churning waters I saw the pull and it continued pulling. Startled, I looked out to sea and saw the waters receding at an alarming rate. 'No, it's impossible,' I whispered in fright. Spinning around I called to Etrician. 'Was there an earthquake?' I yelled, unable to control the panic in my voice. Hearing my alarmed tone of voice, the others sprang to action and hurriedly came to me, their faces concerned and worried. 'Was there an earthquake, Etrician?' I asked again, my head whipped round to look at the still receding tide. 'Out there, the mountains under the Atlantic, they sprout lava now and again.'

'No,' Etrician said listlessly.

'Thera,' Hannah's panicked voice came smashing into my skull, making me more agitated. 'The tide is going out.'

'I know!' I shouted at her. 'But why?'

'Well call it back!' Darren yelled at me, grabbing onto my shoulder and shaking me from my fear.

Placing my shaking hands out, I willed the waters to come back, but they ignored me. Repeating myself over and over again, but it was all for nought. With a pang of pain from the lack of response, I fell to the floor in horror. 'I can't,' I whispered, thick tears falling fast down my cheeks. 'I can't call it back. It-it won't come back to me. I've lost its fealty.'

'What? That cannot be.' Etrician's horrified gasp felt like daggers at my heart.

'I don't understand,' Renita whispered and placing a warm hand on my shoulder I shook it off. Something was wrong; my mother would never do this to me. Never betray me to fools.

'COME BACK!' I suddenly screeched to the waters that fell away from my reach. Mustering up all the energy I had, I jumped down into the wet sands beneath me and ran full pelt into the sea bank that was left by the retreating tide, leaving deep soggy footprints behind me.

'Thera!' Etrician and Tyr called as I heard them squelch after me but I ignored them. I had to know, I had to find out why my home was abandoning me. Was it because both Santorini and I had left and it didn't feel like it needed or wanted me anymore?

Racing after the waters, I felt more and more nervous, agitated and sick. This wasn't looking good. For starters, no tide is allowed to ignore me, the waters come to me whenever I call them. It may mean that I had lost my fealty from the sea and that meant that someone else was controlling it. The only other being capable of controlling the waters, apart from Santorini who wasn't here, was my mother.

'THERA STOP!' Etrician shouted at me, his voice boomed through my skull. Suddenly the sand beneath me caved and I tripped up, falling flat on my face.

Panting, I laid there as the cold saltwater lapped at my face, trying to comprehend everything that was happening to me. In a daze, I felt warm hands turn me over and saw two vexed faces staring down at me. Etrician and Tyr helped me up and carried me back to shore.

After placing me down on the broken pillars, Etrician sat me up and made me look into his eyes. 'Thera, can you hear me?' he asked, his voice sounded so far off, it was like I was trapped in my own nightmare, a nightmare that I couldn't wake up from. 'Thera, can you hear me?' he asked again, a little louder.

'Yes,' I muttered feebly.

There was a moment of relief that swept around the group, but Etrician's eyes became dark and frightening. Trying to focus on them, my mind over kept replaying the same vision over again. The tide did not come back. It did not obey me.

'Thera tell me, how high is it going to be?' he asked, all seriousness flooding into his voice made me aware of the situation. 'How long do we have until the wave hits?'

Glancing over his shoulder, I saw how far the waters had left the shore. Fear like I had never felt for the human inhabitants for any island or country washed over me like a cascading torrent of water. My entire body turned icy cold. 'By the volume of water being pulled in such a short time... Fifteen minutes.' I answered him slowly, as I made myself sit up, all the while staring at the impending doom before us.

'How high is it going to be?' Etrician asked me, holding my right hand and squeezing it as though trying to give me the courage to face my fears.

Judging by the rapidly retreating waters, I came to a quick conclusion. Turning to the others I looked at their worried faces and said, 'Sixty feet, seventy tops. In fifteen minutes a thunderous wall of water will crash against the coast of Northern Ireland and there's nothing I can do to stop it.'

Chapter Sixteen

'There must be something we can do,' Jane said in terror as Etrician helped me up. I felt unsteady on my feet, emotionally unbalanced by the notion I was beginning to face—the oceans weren't under my control anymore.

'I need my brother,' I whispered, fear rippling through my entire being. 'I need him; I can't do this on my own.'

'Yes, yes you can,' Etrician said grabbing my shoulders. 'The causeway can act as a partial-'

'It'll be too late.' I spoke so softly it even unnerved me. 'I've seen it, I've done it,' I spat bitterly, thinking about Atlantis.

Hannah snapped her fingers. 'What about a trench?' She glanced at Renita and Etrician. 'What if you two made a deep hole or something, then the water can flow into it? And we have a second defence and build up the pillars.'

Etrician had his eyes closed, thinking. 'The pillars are made of breakable basalt. They won't be strong enough,' Etrician muttered in thought. 'But I can change that. Dagen,' he said snapping his eyes to him, 'can you do anything to help?'

He nodded. 'I know a few barrier spells I could put up to stop it, but they won't be long enough to cover the entire northern coast.'

'We need more help,' Tyr said folding his arms in thought.

'Airmed,' I said out loud, unsure of why I was even thinking of her, but her name popped into my head, 'Dian and Airmed. Quick Jane hurry!'

Jane sprung into action and pelted off back up towards their house.

'Mind yourselves!' Etrician shouted as he raised his hands slowly. Stumbling, we nearly fell to the floor as the pillars around the causeway began to tremble fiercely. The shiny surface of the basalt cracked like fragile glass, splintering in a root-like manner; running from the beach heading inland. Erratic in motion, the pillars by the sea pushed up from the earth, forcing Darren, Hannah and myself to roll out of the way. When the trembling stopped, I was amazed to see that Etrician had pushed them up at least fifty feet in the air.

'Renita, let's go!' Etrician called and he jumped over the pillared wall that had practically blocked out the wisps of sun. Using one pillar that was still on ground-level, she pushed it up with her powers and vaulted over the wall.

'My turn.' Tyr then practically flew up to the very top of the newly enlarged pillars and surveyed ahead. 'I'll warn you when it's about to hit!' He called.

Dagen positioned himself just behind the pillars casting his spells and Etrician and Renita went out into the soggy sands to make a long deep trench.

'What has happened that the waters turn from me?' I asked no one. Did the Moirae see this in my future? Why didn't I feel my powers wane? Was it venturing into Avalon that I lost my powers? Did Morgana take them from me without my noticing? Confused, upset and worried, I could only think of Santorini and wonder what he would say to me. 'I miss you, brother,' I said softly, closing my eyes and thinking of him.

'You'll see him again,' Hannah said gently, as she took my hand. 'We'll try and sort this out together. Right, Darren?' I heard him give a small grunt in response. 'He says yes,' Hannah interpreted.

'I'm sorry,' I said to her. 'I'm sorry to both of you. This was a situation I never wanted to be in and now that I'm in it, I'm not sure what to do. In my years being created nothing has prepared me for this.'

'I see it!' Tyr shouted. 'It's coming!' Glancing up, I saw that he had crouched down, grabbing onto the top of his pillar for balance.

'Thera!' I heard Jane scream behind me. She kept stumbling from loss of balance, but still tried to reach us. 'Thera something's gone wrong,' she cried, as she reached me, slumping down next to me she could no longer stand.

'What is it?'

Panting, she wiped the tears from her eyes. 'Dian is gone. I got there and the barrier was gone, the house was broken into. Airmed would not wake,' she said continuing to cry, 'the blue and yellow flower was beside her half-eaten. Will it kill her?'

I shook my head, not from answering her, but from the situation that she presented me with. 'What has happened in such a short space of time?' I asked confused.

Jane shook her head, visibly frightened.

The earth shook slightly as Renita and Etrician finished their task. Seconds later, they joined us, covered in wet, salty sand. 'We've done what we can, it's just up to Tyr and Dagen now,' Etrician told us, but his face suddenly fell as he saw the look on our faces. 'What now?'

Jane was so upset she was barely coherent. 'Dian's gone, Airmed had eaten that stupid flower and she's-' she began, and burst into tears.

'Hey!' Tyr shouted down to us. 'Now is not the time. It's coming!'

The group span around and saw Dagen standing there, steady as a rock, mumbling his spells. I felt the blast of sea air as it hit the pillars. The wall of water was approaching me and for the second time in my existence as a Water Nymph, I felt sick with worry. All those humans on the island had no idea what was happening to their coast.

'Tyr,' I called up to him, 'call the winds to blow it back if you must.' Looking up I saw him give me a thumbs up and stared dead ahead. 'If it's not controlled by me then it won't act like a normal tsunami,' I said to anyone who could hear.

'What's that supposed to mean?' Darren demanded, flicking his head in my direction. 'How can water act differently?'

Unable to explain, Tyr's worried voice sent a terrifying chill down my spine. 'Hey get ready,' Tyr shouted, as I saw him prepare, protectively raising his hands.

'Brace yourselves!' I called.

Tyr suddenly shouted then jumped off the pillars. 'We need to go, now!'

'No,' I gasped, realising what I was seeing, Tyr was giving up. 'We can't abandon our posts.'

Tyr shook his head violently. 'No, it's not that its-'

'OH THERA!' came a terrorising echoing call from the pillars behind me.

The wall of water approached threatening to bash Etrician's pillars into sharp black shards, but then abruptly stopped. Halting in its tracks, unnatural and controlled. Stepping out of the water, and still magically dry was The Minister and three of his lackeys.

The group suddenly placed themselves around me; almost protecting me as The Minister, along with his men in smart black suits, slowly descended from on high.

We all stared at The Minister with murderous eyes. Though each of us was unsure of which the greater threat was; a magical wall of building water or The Minister.

'Dinglewood,' I whispered, his name fleetingly popped into my mind. 'He must have been the one who told The Minister where we were. None of this can be a coincidence.'

'How did they get here so quickly?' Hannah asked.

'A human who has control of myths and magic, you figure it out,' I seethed. The last time I saw The Minister, he said that I would see his way eventually. Was it to do with everything that has been happening? Did he know my future?

'Thera, Thera, Thera,' The Minister drawled confidently. 'You get around a bit, don't you? You should invest in travel miles–you'd save a fortune.'

Frowning at his strange words, I took the opportunity to look at his men. One of them positioned quite close to the Minister, had his sleeve rolled up, his palm flat and ready to fire magic on order. On closer inspection, the man's right hand looked like he was branded with a symbol. My eyes flicked to the other two men, they each had the same reddish-tinged scar on their hands.

'Curious as to how I'm here?' he smiled evilly.

'Dinglewood,' I said with a smile but his eyes showed the hint of confusion. Maybe it wasn't the powerful hobgoblin who called him.

Scoffing, The Minister shrugged off my response and folded his arms. 'You know, we need to stop meeting like this.'

'We need to stop meeting altogether,' I sniped back.

'Oh, I love it when they play hard to get,' he sighed in a raunchy way as he glanced at his men. 'Do you know Thera how it pains me that we can never have a decent conversation?'

'Is it because you keep trying to shoot me or capture me every time we meet?' I asked, as I very slowly began to back up.

The Minister clicked his fingers and the men had their palms pointed at us, aimed at my heart. 'Ah, ah Thera. Don't run away when I'm trying to talk to you, it's rude.' I heard Jane gasp and suddenly everyone stopped moving. The Minister smiled widely. 'That's better. Now then, I have a riddle for you.'

'Never been good with riddles,' I said to him, trying to think of ways to get out of this situation but I couldn't. Though their magic couldn't kill me, they would do serious harm to the others and I couldn't let that happen.

He shrugged and continued nevertheless. 'You'll like this one. What happens to a Water Nymph who cannot use her powers?'

Standing there in shock, I could almost see the evil aura around him. It fluctuated in black and a crimson red. He was a very evil human and although humans were capable of malevolent things, I couldn't believe that one human would go so such lengths to destroy the myths and legends of the world. Humanity needed them to survive. I only wished that they knew this.

'Don't know the answer?' he asked in a smarmy way, nearly goading me into rushing at him.

I felt someone grab my right hand and squeezed sympathetically. 'It's alright Thera,' they whispered. 'You'll be fine, we are stronger together.' The hand felt cool but there was something else to that. I felt an undiluted immense power that coursed through my entire body like a raging flood, continuously thrusting raw magical energy into me.

Gasping in shock, the hand let go of me. 'Santorini?' I whispered. My eyes flung open and quickly locked onto The Minister. His face and his own steely cold eyes showed that he believed he had won and that his words had cut me deeply.

I knew what he wanted. He wanted me to throw myself at him and beg him to return my powers, to give up and make a deal with him to spare the others. But that was not the case; it was far from it. 'I will never lose my powers,' my voice rose in confidence. 'As long as I am connected to my brother, whether he be in this world or the next, we control the Oceans no matter what you have done with them!' A menacing frown instantly etched on his hard brow. Motioning to his men, they raised their arms, but ignoring them, I shook my head. 'You can't beat me. I am a legend!' I shouted, raising my arms high into the air and reached out with the power I was given to take back the control of the seas that was somehow taken from me.

I felt the tug of the waves coupled with the ancient magic that was my birthright. Somehow, I was gaining my control. As though I was playing tug of war with someone, I heard a very familiar loud CRACK! The Centaur magic had been broken.

'NO!' The Minister bellowed as the wall of water began to crash down. Reaching out, I stopped the wave in its tracks, but I wasn't quick enough to stop everyone from being dowsed in sea spray. I grinned at The Minister and held the wave threateningly over him and his men in black. I was going to give them a choice: run or die.

'Are you so callous?' he screamed at me, with fear in his voice.

'Are you?' I yelled back. 'You, who were so high and mighty only a minute ago were willing to shoot me? You, who is so willing to capture me and help destroy the world? Is there no sense of faith and compassion for the human race that you would turn your back on all that you know and bring down human civilization by destroying their faith and creations?'

The Minister's startled eyes watched the rolling wall of water gurgled and gushed closer. 'I have no choice!' he spat, spittle flying out of his mouth.

'There's always a choice!' I shouted back. 'There is the choice of doing what is right and what is wrong! Can you not see the difference? Can you not see the bigger picture?' Backing away with his frightened-looking men, he shook his head.

I scoffed. 'Your employer neglected to tell you? Or don't they know?'

'She doesn't know,' he quivered, his gaze torn between myself and the water that was inching ever closer. 'Rhea's just a child, barely ten.'

'What?' Hannah and Darren demanded. They each shared a look, panic passing through them like a ghost. They pushed past me. Disbelief swept across their faces. Hannah slid onto the salty wet glassy floor, shaking her head and muttering, 'No, it just can't be. She's not allowed back here.'

Momentarily distracted The Minister grabbed the arm of one of his lackeys and swiftly turned his palm onto me. Angry, I motioned for spout of water to pelt the Minister and his henchmen. Landing twenty meters away, I froze the water around them, holding them to the earth.

'Thera, get rid of the wave please,' Etrician begged, his face looking worried as the wall of water was still inching towards us.

With a small smile, I lowered my arms and the wall of water collapsed behind the pillars. Dagen was prepared, however, and stopped several crashing tides with his magical barrier as the waves were powerful and destructive.

Etrician and Renita brought the pillars back down to their regular size and everyone breathed a sigh of relief as the sea returned to normal. 'You haven't killed them?' Jane asked as we all looked out towards the roaring waves, the wind had picked up again as the weather was turning bad. Dark ominous clouds encroached from ahead.

Sighing, I shook my head. 'No, they are alive. They just can't move. Legends don't kill humans, if we can help it.'

Tyr thumbed behind him. 'What do you want to do about this one?' The group gathered around one of The Minister's lackeys, who I had purposefully left behind. He was going to give us answers to a lot of questions whether he liked it or not.

Still facing the ocean, the others waited for me to answer Tyr's question. Lifting my right hand, I looked at it and smiled. The power that I had received in that brief moment wasn't from any of the others; it was too pure, too ancient and too familiar. 'Santorini,' I whispered, happiness and sadness spread through me all at once. I don't know how he did it, but I was glad that he was watching over me. Etrician caught my eye and nodded with a smile.

I faced the others. 'We are going to take him with us to see the only family of immortals that exist on this planet.'

Darren thought on what I said. 'But there's no such thing as vampires.'

Raising an eyebrow, Etrician bent down and scooped up the human and threw him over his shoulder. 'Who said anything about vampires?' I asked. 'Not all immortals are known as vampires, although the villagers in Switzerland don't know that.'

Striding over to Jane she took hold of my hand and smiled at me. 'Where to miss Water Nymph?'

'Ewig Castle, Switzerland,' I smiled. 'We're off to see the Von Reeds.'

Jane had phaded us into a dark, yet, glistening snowy Switzerland. Tyr and Etrician were looking after our prisoner, who Darren had named Silent Cyrus. As for some unknown reason, even though he was free from The Minister, he wouldn't talk.

Darren and Hannah were muttering together behind me, their tones sounded worried. Though I had pressed them to tell me, they too remained quiet. However, I did hear the name Rhea mentioned a few times. They mentioned her name along with Maynard. If it was the same girl, it posed a problem.

Crunching along the sparkling, frozen ground, the group made its way down the windy path towards the looming Castle Von Reed. Its large curtain wall and turrets stood out against the darkened skyline behind it, giving off an austere presence. It was as though it commanded attention and respect. Of course, it wasn't called Castle Von Reed, not by the locals anyway; it was called a different name. But the last I heard, Hadriana had let the castle out to the tourists during the spring and summer months. We were lucky the castle was tourist-free, or we'd have a problem. Nevertheless, though they let out the castle to visitors, I informed the others that when they met Hadriana and her sister Eleanor, they must address them as Lady Hadriana and Lady Eleanor, or they'd offend them.

Hadriana was never one for being subtle and heavily expressed to me on many occasions the servants never addressed her properly. Etrician and I, however, were on the same "royal" standing as them, though we still did bow and curtsey. It was common etiquette after all.

Though there was one thing that Hadriana and Eleanor knew, they owed their lives to me and nothing that they could say or do could get them out of the binding contract they made all those years ago.

Approaching the entrance, the snow-capped sheltered bridge loomed ever closer, but before I got there, I smiled and stopped.

'What is it?' Renita asked her breath hung in the frosty air.

Indicating with my head, I mouthed the word, 'troll.' Hadriana was one of the few people who needed protection during the time the castle was closed to the public.

'Want to deal with this my beloved?' I turned to Etrician.

'Stay put,' Etrician said to the mute human, who looked unimpressed at the sight before him.

Tyr took over and held him tighter as Etrician moved past me, heading towards the bridge. Clearing his throat, he approached the edge and as expected, a large troll jumped out from underneath and blocked his path.

This troll had a rather bulbous nose and seemed to be wearing smart clothing. I suspected it was Hadriana's doing. She always ensured her servants, and protectors dressed smartly. The troll was about ten feet tall, with a rotund belly and matching thick neck. Wearing long dark brown trousers, a cream long-sleeved shirt and a heavy-looking necklace with the crest of the Von Reeds, the troll appeared well looked after.

'No one shall pass unless you can answer this riddle,' he spoke in a posh manner, his eyes looking nervously around him like he was being watched.

Sighing, Etrician said, 'Here me Troll of Bridges, I am Etrician, son of Gaia. You may let us pass and-'

'Nope, can't do that,' the troll smiled, looking proud of himself. 'My Mistress said you especially cannot get past me.'

Jane glanced at me. 'She knew we were coming?'

I nodded slightly. 'Hmm, maybe.'

Standing to his full height, Etrician puffed his chest out. 'You will let us pass or I shall assign you back to the Hebrides!'

The troll chuckled. 'My Mistress said you might say that. She said to tell you, you,' he nodded at me, 'and your friends aren't welcome here. She's busy and wants time to herself.'

'Got you,' I smiled. Striding towards the troll with my head held high I asked, 'How can an immortal want time to herself?' Looking bamboozled by the question, I leaned back and scanned the curtain wall. There was a figure near one of the arrow windows, looking down at us. 'Oy Hadriana!' I screeched at the top of my lungs. 'You open this door right now; I need to speak to you!'

'So much for your etiquette,' Dagen sniped behind me.

Glancing askance, the others had joined us by the foot of the bridge, but kept a wary eye on the troll.

'Now see here! You are not allowed to talk to my Mistress like that,' he said frowning, his voice sounding peeved.

'Your Mistress owes her life to me,' I told him, glaring. 'She cannot refuse me. And also, you cannot refuse a command or threat from Etrician.'

'Yes thank you Thera,' Etrician groaned sounding embarrassed. 'I wish for you to step aside and let us pass,' Etrician asked the troll a little more forcefully. 'Do you understand?'

Nevertheless, the troll refused to move and folding its arms shook his head. 'Mistress said no,' he said stubbornly.

Before I opened my mouth to protest, there was a loud thunk of metal grinding against the wood. Up ahead a hefty thick wooden door opened, spilling soft orange light across the bridge's planks. A figure stepped into the light, showing an elongated shadow that stretched towards my feet.

'It's alright,' said a strong posh German accent of a woman. 'Let them pass.'

The troll grunted in disproval and unwillingly stepped aside. Our feet clonked on the bridge as we headed towards the opened door, the figure leant against the lintel puffing on a cigarette clamped into a long sleek, black holder.

'Lady Hadriana,' I smiled inclining my head. Giving me a small nod, she silently motioned at the others. 'These are guests of mine, all myths apart from these two,' I said pointing to Hannah and Darren speaking in English for their benefit.

Cottoning on, she continued our conversation in English. 'Who's the mutt?' she asked, looking at The Minister's flunky.

Standing by I motioned for the others to bring him forward. 'I was hoping you could help me with him,' I said to her politely. 'Been in a bit of a spot lately, I need your help.'

She scoffed and flicked her ash on the cold paving stoned floor. 'My help, from you?'

'Don't sound too surprised,' I said scathingly.

'With you, how can I ever be?' she said silkily, her eyes flicked to Etrician. 'Don't I know you from somewhere?'

'Etrician,' he said looking annoyed. 'We've met before, several times.'

'Huh, all right then whatever,' she said taking a drag. 'So, I suppose you'll be wanting to come in?'

'How kind,' I drawled, as she moved away from the doorway and headed down the massive hallway; her arse shaking to and fro with her grey silk dress. 'Still playing the part of a millionaire?' I asked her, as I saw a small ticket counter to the right of the entranceway.

Scoffing, she immediately turned around and glared at me. 'Got to live somehow don't I?' She inhaled again. 'Those tourists who come here every spring and summer to gawp at the architecture of the 9th century.' She laughed dryly. 'It was a poxy century by my standards, could have been a lot more interesting. In any case, just because I'm immortal don't mean I can't eat caviar and lavish on designer dresses, fine tobacco from Cuba and import illegal goods,' she added with a smile. 'I guess that's why your here, for my double dealings? Checking up are you?'

'Not the Black Market?' Hannah asked scandalised. 'Thera, I don't want to be involved with anyone who-'

Like a trained hawk, Hadriana glared at her. 'Who asked you!' She screeched. 'It's not the human Black Market you nit, it's the Magic Market, for myths and legends and I happen to be the Go-To-Girl,' she laughed. 'But first,' she said clapping her hands in the air, 'you lot piss-off while I have a word with Thera. Mummy and I have things to talk about,' she said to us, but I could hear the disdain in her voice.

'Will you be all right?' Etrician asked, as the little butler, Offo, suddenly appeared from nowhere in his usual black and white ensemble and began to usher the others away.

Nodding at Etrician, he gave me a swift kiss to the forehead and followed the others. Turning on my heels, I trailed behind Hadriana's swishy movements through the castle.

'I must say your appearance wasn't at all a surprise,' she said turning around to look at me. 'But then again the timing of it is somewhat interesting.'

'How so?' I asked passing a hallway that was lined with old metal suits of armour, each holding a shield of the Von Reed crest and a long pointy spear.

'Well as I hear on the magical grapevine, there is a bit of trouble going on with a pack of humans.' Hadriana led me towards a large set of double doors that must have reached up about forty feet and effortlessly pushed them open. An impressive drawing room with old leather chairs, a grand piano, and tapestries adorned the room; a roaring open fire blazed in front, giving off only a small amount of heat in the room.

Heading towards one of the large glass cabinets, she pulled on the doors and brought out a decanter filled with a dark red liquid and two crystal glasses. 'Care for some wine from 16th century France?'

'What year?' I asked her, as she poured herself one glass.

'1657, a good year for France allying with England,' she tittered, pouring out a glass for myself.

Moving to her, she passed me the glass then gestured for me to take a seat. 'I find it interesting that you call them 'packs' now. Are you so high and mighty that you have removed yourself from your human lineage?'

Sighing in boredom, she raised her glass to me. 'When one is near to her one-thousandth birthday, you get the feeling that you have already been removed from humanity. I've seen it all Thera and though I tolerate humans, I am finding their ilk more annoying by the century.'

'And Eleanor?'

Scoffing, she withdrew another cigarette from an embossed silver container and lit it. 'She lives in her head and rarely ventures into the world that is presented to her. She has done well mind you, especially when it comes to education. It's pathetic the way the world treats intelligent women, though we all expect great things from her.'

'Helping you, or human society?' I asked, sipping my wine.

'A little of both,' she shrugged. 'Mind you, she doesn't like my dealings in the magical black market, she finds it distasteful.' Snorting she took a sip of her wine and placed it gently onto a wide rectangular glass table in front of her.

'Distasteful is an interesting word choice,' I smiled, placing my glass down. 'I suppose she's tried to stop you dealing?'

Hadriana smirked and gave me a quick nod. 'Every year at one point she'll get into a hissy fit and scream at me for endangering our family.' She sneered and drew on her cigarette, 'what family?' she said sadly. 'How I wish my parents were alive. I still visit their grave every year. Eleanor may come with me, but she finds it disturbing. Why grieve over your parents who have been dead a millennium, when you can grieve over the fact that you have to live forever.'

Keeping my temper, I wondered when this topic would be brought up again. 'I gave you a choice,' I said coldly. 'I told you the consequences and you said you'd understand them. Why is it,' I began, stopping her from interrupting, 'that when we meet we always have this conversation about you being immortal? Can you just for once accept the fact you messed up and come to terms with it? I always think that the Gothic era started because of you.'

Throwing her head back, Hadriana roared with laughter. 'You'd be surprised how much influence I had with those simple architects. Though now, I am surrounded by everything I witnessed right from the very off and I don't want to leave. But no, you're right of course, we do always have this conversation every time we meet. And when we do meet it is on a rare occasion and it is always about something you want from me and always without charge…naturally.'

'Naturally,' I agreed.

'So mother,' she said sarcastically, 'what can I help you with?'

I reached out for my glass and sipped the wine. I wasn't a keen wine drinker, but Hadriana's wines were always the finest and rarest in the world. 'Many things, but first I want to know why some centaurs are jumping the fence.' Hadriana had just reached out to grab her glass when she stopped and looked at me in concern. 'Yes, you heard me. Not twenty minutes ago we were in Ireland. An incident occurred and would you believe it, powerful centaur magic was placed on me. The magic was so strong it stopped me from using my powers to control the Ocean, and that my dear girl is not allowed to happen. Centaurs do not have that kind of power.' I explained hearing that loud crack when I broke their spell. Though I neglected to tell her about Santorini's help.

Finally taking her glass, she leaned back on the leather sofa and stared at me in worry. 'I have heard something, though centaurs, yes that is troublesome.'

'Tell me,' I asked.

Leaning back, she brought her feet up onto the seat and kicked her shoes off. Hadriana would never be so relaxed in front of other people, but she was with me. 'Some myths are getting additional power. I'm not sure how they are getting it but it's changing them from neutral to bad. Is this the first time you've come up against a powerful myth?'

Shaking my head, her eyes grew wide with panic. 'No. I met a hobgoblin in Avalon. That power was beyond anything I had ever felt. I daresay it was on par with an Ancient's magic.'

'Ancient's power? Holy crap, it would make sense but that cannot be!' she gasped and sat up. 'I have heard of a new Ancient of late but how is this possible?'

Taking another sip, I delved into the theories, assumptions, and facts we had come across. By the time I had finished, poor Hadriana looked paler than normal and was growing exceedingly anxious.

Staring at the carpet in shock, she quickly downed the rest of her drink. 'There is something evil stirring in the world of the Ancients. I have heard of it over the past few decades but in truth, nothing came to the surface until I rumours about a group of humans from London.'

'The T.A.T,' I informed her, she nodded. 'Hannah and Darren are part of that group. You may find it interesting to talk to them.'

Hadriana was never shocked but that trinket of information practically blew her away. 'Yes. I want to find out how they possessed mythological abilities. Only a few witnessed it. I was surprised when a lady called Amjee contacted me. I had known her parents through dealings of the O.M.C. but she asked for my help to protect the humans.'

I smiled at her. 'You sent them some fairies.'

She nodded. 'Amjee had explained that the humans would have Ancient protection, but they needed something extra. Only recently, I was told that their spell was broken. Was that your doing?'

'Guilty,' I raised my hand. 'Though that was the second time we had bumped into what people are called The Minister and I have to tell you, I didn't like what I saw from him. Something is going on and I want some answers out of him,' draining the rest of my glass, Hadriana took it from me and got up, her dress swishing elegantly, it looked like rippling water.

'Thera my dear, are you sure you're not just being nosey?' she laughed airily. 'One nymph cannot expect to know every little detail that's going off on land. You'd drive yourself mad.'

'And one immortal cannot expect to survive delving into things she ought not to without gaining bad habits and baiting demons,' I snapped back. 'I know your customers, not all, but I know a few who came back from the other plane to ask for your items.'

Slamming her fist on the cabinet making the glasses and decanter clink through the vibrations, she turned around and glared at me. 'So what? I get paid enough to survive and that's good enough for my family.'

Standing up I glared at her. 'No, you get protection Hadriana and it's recently as well. Trolls and centaurs are at your beck and call. Who are you working for where you need protection? You're not going to die, you can get stabbed, poisoned, set alight, hacked into bits, drowned, encased in concrete but you won't ever die.'

'There are worse things in this world than dying,' she said with deep sorrow in her voice, 'and you know,' she said pointing at me with a shaky finger, 'what they are. I know your predicament with Santorini. I know he left you. Dynessa told me the day the portal closed.'

'You still keep my Water Nymph in your lake?' I asked, bemused. 'Did she tell you that I was being hunted?' Looking hurt gave a short nod. 'And still, you deal with demons in this madness!' I shouted at her. 'Why do you not think?' I yelled at her.

'If they threaten to take my sister then yes, I will do what is necessary,' she shouted angrily. 'I know you would do the same thing.'

Her words struck me funny and before I knew it, I was bent over laughing. 'Hadriana, you do make me laugh.'

'I see nothing funny about that,' her voice sounded snippy and annoyed.

'My brother left me two weeks ago,' I said, wiping my tears as my laughter died down. 'I constantly think about him and yet I am trying to help the world first. That is my job that is my duty. I cannot let the Staff of Zeus be played with by a ten-year-old girl, destroying myths with the flick of her wrist.'

Putting her shoes back on and she whispered what she knew, 'There is more to it than just flicking your wrist. You have to want to kill, want to destroy. It's a failsafe the Ancients placed upon the staff should it ever fall to earth. It was a secret to know about the failsafe, though now that the staff has fallen to the earth, it would make sense with your theory that this Ancient called Maynard took the staff and brought it to earth. And you've said you've been struck with the staff?' I nodded, remaining silent. 'So, then I'm guessing you have the mark of Zeus on your back then?'

'Yes,' I whispered in fright. 'You know what it means?'

Laughing she turned around and looked at me. 'You dear Thera are screwed. The staff does destroy myths, but it depends solely on the magic the myth has. Any myth with low-class magic would be gone in an instant, like a centaur or a unicorn, puff!' She snapped her fingers. 'But any myth with higher-class magic takes a few days to die, but before they do, they are marked by those who shot them. As we know, the Ancients can't control or destroy legends because it's not in their jurisdiction. If any other magical being were hit with the staff the person or creature that shot them would mark them. This encompasses the mark of enslavement-'

I felt icy and despair took over me as though the earth was opening a deep chasm, threatening to pull me in. 'The Minister shot me,' I told her, unable to comprehend why I didn't figure out this information. 'So that means he can control me?'

'Though that child in Greece is destroying myths left, right and centre, you are safe that she possesses it and The Minister does not.'

'Dian!' I gasped. 'I bet he poisoned Airmed. I couldn't understand it when Jane told me but... the child, this Rhea made him do it.'

'If he had a mark on him from the staff, then yes,' she replied sadly. 'And he would have been controlled by this Rhea.' It made me feel sick. 'Such a sad thing to hear. You know, Dian and I go way back,' she said with a smile.

'How do you mean?'

'Come, I'll show you.' She beckoned with her finger and glided gracefully out of the room.

After twenty minutes of turning down long tapestry filled corridors and old portraits of aristocrats from the past, we travelled underground into a cloister-looking cellar. Most of the cellar was packed with dozens upon dozens of dusty crates of wine from centuries ago as well as information boards for the tourists. But Hadriana passed all of these without the slightest interested glance and took me towards an old church door.

Dipping her hand into her cleavage, she brought out a heavy bronze key and placed it into the lock. Turning it with a soft click, the door unlocked and she pushed it open. 'Here is where the magic is,' she said, clapping twice. Instantly bright lights flooded the room and to my amazement, I saw why Hadriana was known as the Merchant of the Magical Black Market. She was the go-to girl that was for sure.

Partitioned from the cathedral cellar, its high arched ceilings glittered with old cobwebs that delicately traced the hand-carved stone; hanging from the ceiling like some strange witches cavern.

All around stone pedestals stood topped with items and encased by domed glass. With a passing glance, some of the items looked of intrinsic worth, while others seemed out of place.

Hadriana moved to the side to let me pass as I ventured into the hall of magical items. Before me, I noticed one particular stone pillar where a simple ostrich egg sat upon a royal blue velvet cushion. But on closer inspection, it was decorated with symbols from a tribe in Africa.

'The answer to the age-old question. Which came first the chicken or the egg?' Hadriana said as she came to my side. 'The answer is the egg, though no one even comprehended that it was magical. It was just a simple reptilian-like creature who laid an egg, but an African witch cursed the creature after it ate her son. The curse was that it could never reproduce any more of its kind, so the creature died out. This is one of the first eggs it laid after it was cursed. I was unsure at first, but I kept the egg knowing that there would be a way to find out. Sure enough, technology came into existence. I x-rayed it and the egg proved true. Inside there is an unborn baby bird.'

'How, how did you procure this?' I gasped as I read the symbolic inscription, claiming that the egg was over ten thousand years old. 'It is before my time, before yours!'

Tapping a finger to her nose, she silkily turned around and locked the door behind us. Moving quickly, yet carefully, I went to the next pillar where perched on top of another royal blue cushion was a bangle with a snakehead eating its tail. But nearing it, the head rose and spat at me in anger.

'For the love of Atlas!' I yelped, taking a step back. 'That's not...'

'Yes, the original Ouroboros,' Hadriana smiled with pride. 'Literally cost me my entire right arm after I acquired it. One of my favourites, I could never part with it.'

'How ironic of you.' She moved away from it to gaze at her other possessions. 'For someone who would have gone to heaven and hell to become immortal and who was granted that wish, now hates it, yet, she finds herself loving the idea of a never-ending cycle.'

'Didn't you hear? I love irony,' she tittered. 'I take much pleasure in my life by obtaining ironic things. It's the controversial things in life that make me smile.'

'Indeed,' I agreed following her past some dusty filled cabinets that lined the craggy walls.

Taking a fair few minutes, I glanced at some of the objects that unfortunately caught my eye. One was a biosphere with a strange white and blue frog inside it. A small note was stuck to the top reading, "Brian." 'Hello Brian,' I smiled, moving close to it.

Hadriana stopped and turned to me. 'Watch it, if you ask him a question, he'll deduct years off your life.'

'I'm immortal,' I said scathingly.

'Then I won't answer your questions,' the frog croaked.

'He's an immortal frog that can tell your future. Though the reason why he's immortal is that people ask him questions about their life and he steals from them.'

'Again with the immortal objects and… animals in your collection.'

She smiled and swiftly moved away. 'Ironic though there is something that is bothering me from what you said previously about myths gaining power,' she said in thought, turning around and staring at me as though slightly confused. 'This hobgoblin you mentioned earlier, was his name Dinglewood by any chance?'

My head snapped to her, my heartbeat unsteadily. 'Yes, it was,' I told her. 'How did you know?'

She tossed her long dark hair behind her, 'I know Dinglewood and I know that he has no connections with this Minister that you speak of. You are fishing in the wrong pond.'

CHAPTER SEVENTEEN

FROWNING AT HADRIANA'S WORDS, I WAITED UNTIL SHE SPOKE AGAIN. Moving around I passed what looked like a fallen star in a jar that had a thick coating of dust. The label was faded but I could just read Astria.

I was bamboozled how she even knew Dinglewood and found it impossible to even comprehend those two even meeting. They were the complete opposite.

'I'm amazed at how little you know, Thera,' she cooed, a sarcastic smug smile on her face. 'Dinglewood was ordered to Avalon not by this Minister which you speak so ill of, but by someone else, someone who has recently come into a big business.' Her smile became smarmy and she looked immediately annoyed. 'I can't explain further, it's on a need-to-know basis. But Dinglewood isn't evil; he's just slightly misguided at times.'

She motioned me to follow her out of the collections room. She locked the heavy door and placed the key down her cleavage. Beckoning me with a finger, I followed her back into the cellar, heading towards the stairs to take us back up into the main part of the castle.

'I cannot believe it,' I said to her, all evidence to the contrary as the past few hours raced around my head. 'The centaurs are meant to be neutral. Why tear down the protection barrier at Dian's? And why put up a magical barrier against me? I just can't fathom what they are doing and why. What's their motive? What's their reason for siding with anyone?'

'My dear, the centaurs know about what looms head, we all do. They, like the rest of us, are choosing sides carefully.' Shrugging, she led me back into a draughty grey-bricked corridor then across to one of the tapestry, suit of armour corridors. 'I am taking you back to the others,' she explained, 'I want to meet them. It's only polite if I'm going to let you all stay here for a few days.'

'A few days? You're too kind,' I smiled.

'Just stay out of Eleanor's way. She's in one of her decade lasting sulky moods,' she warned.

'Duly noted.'

As we approached the colossal entranceway that coated the walls with beautiful canvasses on various scenes from the past of heroic battles in rolling fields, adventures on craggy peaks, a massive crystal chandelier dangled in spectacular shining wonderment from the arched ceiling above us. I had to hand it to Hadriana, she sure had a lovely home. It was just a shame there was no love in it.

The family butler, Offo, came out of a room, which had large embossed gold leaf painted double doors. Upon closing them, he headed straight to Hadriana. Stopping short a few meters, he bowed and waited to be asked to speak.

'Yes, Offo?'

'A Master Garrick called while you were entertaining Lady Thera. I have led him into the drawing-room,' bowing again, he stood to attention.

'Good, tell him I shall be there soon. I shall see to Thera and her guests first,' she told him.

He bowed again. 'As you wish.'

Hadriana strutted off, wiggling her arse as she went. Hiding a smile I asked, 'Is Garrick a client? Or a close personal friend?'

As she headed to the room that Offo came out of, she grabbed onto the door handles but stopped. Silkily turning round she smiled, 'He was a client but now he's a very close personal friend,' she winked then pulled the doors open. 'Welcome to my home,' Hadriana laughed, throwing her arms up into the air in an overzealous greeting. The room went immediately quiet; everyone sat in comfortable-looking chairs. Their eyes swept to Hadriana in bemusement. 'It's lovely to have you here in my castle and I wish you all, a pleasant stay. But how silly of me,' she giggled, 'where are my manners? I am Lady Hadriana Von Reed, the head of the household and proprietor of the Magical Market. I specialise in anything mythical, magical and ancient, wouldn't you agree Thera?' she asked turning to me.

'I noticed you misinformed them in your introduction,' I whispered. 'Isn't it Magical Black Market?'

'Shush!'

Hannah smiled as she stood up and made a strange little curtsey. 'My name is Hannah Smith. It's lovely to meet you.'

'You're the half myth half human aren't you?' Hadriana asked in a quick tone. 'From that T.A.T. group?' She never missed a trick that woman.

Looking a little putout Hannah forced a smile and nodded. 'I'm too a myth!'

'Not quite Hannah,' Darren muttered.

'The other human?' Hadriana asked me, I nodded. 'I see. Thera has told me about you and the T.A.T., though of course I already knew, Amjee and I are quite good friends.'

'You know Amjee?' Hannah asked in shock.

Tittering, Hadriana moved over to a cabinet. Opening it up she silently asked if I would like more wine, I politely declined with a small shake of my head. 'How do you think you got those bracelets?' she asked pointing to them.

'Chris Cringle gave them to us,' Darren said.

'Yes, but how do you think he got them? That isn't part of his magic. He gives out toys to humans, not magical objects to part-human part-myths. And I thought you humans were intelligent,' she jeered.

'So Amjee contacted you to help us?' Hannah questioned lightly.

'Correct,' she replied, pouring herself a glass of wine and instantly downing it. 'God it's so annoying I can't get drunk, no matter how much I try,' she turned to me.

'Part of the deal I'm afraid,' I shrugged.

'Hmm, indeed,' she frowned. Turning back to the others, she wiggled her way to an old sofa and sat down. 'Amjee contacted me just after your base was destroyed. She told me that there was more in store for the little ex-T.A.T group even though they would end up being humans again. Naturally, I have a lot of items in my collection but I was clueless about how to help you. I contacted Chris who knew what to give you. So, that's my story that will clear a few things up. It's thanks to me that you can be myths again.'

'Do you know how they work?' Darren asked her. 'We can only be myths when we're in the water...other than that we're human all the time.'

She nodded slightly and smiled. 'That's right. The Aqua Stone only works in saltwater. It's pointless you turning back into a myth while on dry land unless you're like Thera.'

'I am.' Our attention instantly turned to Hannah. 'I am like Thera. Only Darren's a–'

Darren flushed red. 'Don't say it,' he grimaced.

'A Merman,' she said loudly. 'But I'm a Water Nymph.'

Hadriana glanced at me and I nodded in agreement. 'Don't you mean were a Water Nymph?' She asked looking down her nose. 'I'm sorry hunny but you look human to me right now. See these guys?' she indicated to the rest of us, 'they look mythical or legendary. They have the power, the strength, the speed the capability to control magic; you two do not.'

Angry, Hannah retorted, 'Well you don't look mythical either.'

'Oh Atlas,' I cringed looking away, 'she shouldn't have said that.'

Glancing at Hadriana, her eye twitched then quickly locked onto me and glared. She was very angry... again. 'Want to explain... mother dearest?'

'Please don't call me that,' I sighed, waiting for an explosion of shouting to ensue any minute. 'It's disrespectful.'

'Why not? After all, you're the one who created me!' She screeched, leaning forwards on the sofa, her talon-like hands digging into the armrest, her evil glaring eyes boring into my skull.

'Here we go again,' I groaned. 'Hadriana, listen to me very carefully because I am so sick to death-'

'YOU CAN'T DIE YOU'RE IMMORTAL!' she bellowed making everyone jump. Hadriana went suddenly from dainty and dignified to raging lunatic in seconds. Santorini always believed it was an effect from drinking from the spring, but I just thought Hadriana was nuts in the first place.

'Hadriana, please be quiet,' I said calmly and carefully. 'Your shouting alone can wake the dead.'

'AT LEAST THEY CAN DIE!' she yelled again, Etrician suddenly doubled up in a silent fit of giggles.

'Oh, for the love of Atlas! Hadriana, I didn't create you. You found the fountain and I told you the consequences! I'm sorry that your parents wouldn't drink and I'm sorry you've lived such a long life, never growing old, never being able to experience death like the seven billion humans on the planet. But I gave you a choice and you and your family, including your butler, made that choice!' I yelled, instantly getting annoyed that we were having this argument, yet again.

'What are you two talking about?' Tyr asked, edging away from Hadriana who looked like a volcano ready to blow.

'Hadriana's father was a sailor and a very good one during his time. He was ambitious enough to sail as far as his Knarr, or for those who are unsure of its other term, Viking merchant ship was able to travel.' Tyr smiled at Hadriana and gave her a quick wink.

'I'm Tyr. Grandson of Odin,' he smiled. Hadriana rolled her eyes, remaining mute.

I coughed to get everyone's attention. 'His family somehow managed to find themselves close to the un-chartable moving island called Bonica. Then after a mild storm, created to force them to turn the other direction away from the island, Vikings being Viking's, he decided to head straight into it and ended up shipwrecked on the island. A lot of the family and friends died in the wreck, Hadriana, her sister Eleanor, their father's friend Offo and her parents, all survived the tragedy. Then, when they explored the island, they stumbled on the Fountain of Youth.'

Darren practically laughed. 'You mean, it exists?'

'Shush,' Renita and Jane said together.

'Santorini and I got anxious and decided to show ourselves to the humans. We thought it appropriate to at least explain what would happen to them if they did decide to drink from the fountain. Though when we got there, we noticed that the humans were severely ill so we gave them the choice of living forever or dying on the island.'

'My parents,' Hadriana scoffed, slumping in the seat and staring at her empty glass beside her, 'my parents were fools. They didn't want to live forever. They told us that they had reached the end of their time and wished to depart this world. Cowards,' she said harshly.

Gasping I stood my ground. 'No, Hadriana. They were not cowards, they had respect for life.'

She waved my words away. 'My parents took their own lives, a disgrace and dishonour to the Gods they held so dear. Yet, it shocked me to the core. They may think that watching their children dying is harrowing enough, but they never understood what it was like the other way around. Offo, Eleanor and I decided then and there to live forever, to have a life, to experience all that it has to offer. So we drank the water and lived.'

'The only problem is that Hadriana regrets drinking from the fountain,' I told the others, the room had gone deathly quiet. 'And she blames me.'

'You didn't tell me the consequences.'

With an exasperated sigh, I moved towards her. 'Oh, how was I meant to know that no drug would affect you, no drink would get you drunk? You are living a life that it is yours. You have joined the immortal world and have benefited exponentially from it whether you want to acknowledge this or not. If you want to continue to feel miserable for living forever well then that's your prerogative. Though do not complain that you are the only one who thinks it's miserable.'

'Your knowledge on mythical or magical items is insurmountable in comparison to a lot of myths who hoard items,' Etrician added. 'Though Vikings weren't the first to hoard their findings, they sure did a good job of it.'

A small flicker of a smile showed through the corner of her mouth. Leaning back, she sighed and nodded. 'It's true. I am a good hoarder.' Hadriana's smile faded as something caught her eye. Quickly sitting up, she pointed to Tyr's silver hand. 'Dian did that, didn't he?'

The room became silent again, all eyes looking between Hadriana and Tyr. 'You said you knew Dian,' I pressed her, leaning against the sofa casually.

'I do, I deal with him,' she told us, as she moved to Tyr to examine his hand. Turning it over, he flexed it to show her its movement. 'That's extraordinary. And for your information, I deal in mythical drugs like Banshee's blood, powdered Unicorn hoof scrapings, Demeter's grain from the first harvest of the year, Everlasting Onion from Ogygia. That set me back a few trips, that's for sure.'

'Trips?' Etrician asked her, puzzled.

Tapping her finger to her nose, she answered, 'All in good time. Now, I need to have a word with a friend who's popped over for a little chat.' She rose and went to the double doors. 'I'll send Offo in to take your dinner requests, I'll be back soon.' She strode out of the room, quickly closing the door after her.

Hannah and Darren immediately got up and went to the far end of the room, talking in hushed tones. I left them alone. Etrician left his seat to come and talk to me, his face contorted in puzzlement. 'Are you mulling over what she said about these trips?'

I nodded. 'She is free to come and go as she pleases. But some of the things she's mentioned have been lost throughout the centuries.'

Etrician scratched his stubbly chin and couldn't come up with anything. Eventually shrugging, he looked at the others who were also deep in whispered conversation. 'Well, I think she isn't telling us everything.'

'Agreed,' I nodded. 'Perhaps we should keep this to ourselves until after dinner? I have a funny feeling we'll be up into the wee hours of the morning.'

Minutes later and Offo waddled into the room. 'My Lady wishes to know what dishes are to be served for you tonight,' he said with a plastered grin. Quickly bringing out a notepad and a pen, he clicked the top and waited for orders.

'CHEESEBURGER'

'BEEF CUTLET'

'LOBSTER'

'PEPPERONI PIZZA'

'ROAST LAMB'

Everyone shouted together, making it impossible to decipher who ordered which food. Sniffing in a pompous manner, Offo toddled off to each person and took their order. Though what started as a simple meal of a first course, turned out to be a seven-course meal when Offo got round to Dagen.

'And I want spinach, and carrots, parsnips, lashings of potatoes, turnips, peas, mushrooms and rich brown gravy and at least half a roasted lamb,' he droned on. 'Then for my fish course, I want halibut with a nice lemon cream sauce.'

'Dagen shut it will you, you fat git,' Darren chided. 'You can't eat all that, it'll go to waste.'

Puffing out his chest pompously he said, 'I'll have you know that I was dared to eat half a lamb as a bet once…idiot didn't think I could do it, but I did. And I won my money back off him!'

Hannah and Jane burst out laughing. 'What was his name?'

Dagen shrugged in an uncaring fashion. 'Some idiot called Hobin Rood or whatever.'

Hannah gasped. 'Oh my God, you don't mean…'

'Ah-hem,' Offo coughed. 'Will that be all sir? Should I scratch off your fish course and leave you room for dessert instead?'

'Oo a trifle, I've watched humans make them, they look very nice,' he smiled.

'Very good sir. And for you Lady Thera?' Offo turned to me, his pen poised over the paper.

'Um.' I paused, trying to think about it, 'can I have a traditional Lutefisk dinner, please?'

Offo smiled, 'Of course. I believe Hadriana will also be joining you in that selection.' After finding everyone else's choices, he left us alone.

'What's Lutefisk?' Jane asked me, as Etrician and I sat on a sofa together. About to open my mouth to respond it was instead Tyr who answered.

'It's a Nordic dish of white fish, potatoes and other foodstuffs; it's a very old dish. The Vikings used to eat it.'

Dagen leaned towards me and whispered, 'You trying to get on Hadriana's good side?'

'Be quiet boy,' Etrician ordered, putting Dagen in his place. But Dagen just shrugged his shoulders, and turned his attention to Darren and Hannah who were still huddled in the corner whispering away. Though they rise from their conversation at the mention of food, they had immediately returned to it afterwards. What was it that they were discussing that they couldn't tell us?

Shaking my head of those childish thoughts, I rested my head on Etrician's shoulder and closed my eyes. As my mind drifted in and out of consciousness, I picked up the odd lines in Hannah and Darren's conversation. At one point, I distinctly heard Hannah say, '...we need to tell her about Rhea soon... with the staff she can destroy everyone we know...' Unable to wake myself up, I slipped into blissful unconsciousness.

'Thera.' Etrician's voice faded in and out of my mind. 'Thera, wake up.' I felt a warm hand shake my shoulder, my eyes fluttered open to see Etrician smiling lovingly at me.

'What?' I asked thickly.

'Dinner's ready.' He replied. Tapping my legs, I looked down to see them draped over his lap. Confused, I sat up to see the others moving towards the door.

'Dinner?' Stretching, I hefted my legs off his and tried to rid myself of the groggy feeling.

'Yes, we're at Hadriana's remember?'

'Oh right,' I nodded, rubbing my eyes. 'How long was I asleep for?' I was having more and more naps, which was rather unusual.

'A few hours, though I'm quite surprised you didn't wake up sooner,' he chuckled, standing up and offering me a hand. With a confused look, I took it but held onto it. 'Dagen and Darren argued about magic. Dagen was close to threatening Darren with turning him into a goat.'

'A goat?' I laughed as Etrician guided me out of the room. 'Why not a frog, or a mouse or something relatable to his powers? A goat just isn't helpful.'

Shrugging his shoulders, we followed the others down the elegant black marble-floored hallway. With the large intricately decorated oak double doors of angels and creeping ivy, Offo opened it wide for our admittance. Stepping into the dining room, I smiled it hadn't changed at all.

The four 18 carat gold and Austrian crystal chandeliers hung gracefully from the painted domed ceiling. Tapestries in royal vibrant colours depicting great, noble Knights from far away counties draped along the walls. In the middle of the room, a twenty-seated 17th-century cherry wood table, was covered by the delicately made ivory tablecloth, gleamed with polished silverware and groaned with an assortment of delicious smelling food. 'Wow, fancy,' Hannah laughed, as she Renita and Jane went to their seats; a cursive name card was placed by their plates.

'You'd expect to be seated first before they bring out the food,' Dagen sniffed, walking to his seat.

Rolling his eyes, Tyr scanned for his name card. 'Please don't sit me next to Dagen,' he moaned.

Glancing at the name cards, I was surprised to see two extra placements. Eleanor and a Mr G Moncur. The name didn't sound familiar, though, with Hadriana, she went through men like water. Living as old as she did, I was afraid to ask who her new partner was. After a certain amount of time, she'd have to love them and leave them. She could never get too close; the emotional heartbreak when she'd outlive them would be too painful for her.

Taking our seats, Tyr looked a little happy that he had Etrician in the middle separating him and Dagen. Darren, however, was not happy being sat right next to him.

Directly opposite Etrician, I silently inclined my head towards the boys, pleading with my eyes for them to behave. Etrician flicked his eyes to his left to see them tense up as they sat in silence waiting for our host. Jane who was placed at the very end of the table leaned forward to look at the name card in front of the empty seat that was at the head of the table. 'Eleanor... who's she again?'

'She's me,' came a strong-willed voice from my right. Our heads whipped round to see her strutting into the room with a very annoyed yet determined look on her face. Wearing the equivalent of an early 20th-century attire of an Egyptologist, with a tight light beige shirt, taut brown trousers, and long, brown leather boots, Eleanor appeared as though she'd just come back from excavating a tomb.

Etrician and I immediately stood up and inclined our heads in acknowledgement of her presence. The others did not. 'So rude,' she spat, her eyes boring into the others, flashing red with anger.

Striding to me, she stopped, giving me a small smile. 'Nice to see your still around, Lady Thera. To what do my sister and I owe the pleasure of your company?'

'Dropped by for a visit,' I smiled.

'With your rude friends?' she spat, glancing at them. 'I don't like being lied to. Why are you here?'

Folding my arms, I took a deep breath. 'I didn't realise I needed a good excuse for visiting my children,' I mocked.

Her eyes slanted then flicked her head towards Etrician. 'Why are you here? I have no connection with you apart from Thera and even then it's a very pathetic reason to invade my home.'

'You speak to me like that?' Etrician raised his voice angrily. 'I may be in your home, but you have no right to talk down to me like that.'

Rolling her eyes, she glanced around the room to the others. 'Are you the three ugly sisters?' she sniped at the girls. Renita's chin immediately wobbled and she looked away, not wanting to show her tears. 'And you three,' she looked at the boys. 'I can only see one good-looking one between you. Fight it out for me before dinner. I like some entertainment,' she laughed in spite.

'Eleanor,' I warned. 'Please don't be nasty. Your sister tells me you're in a mood, one that lasts for a decade? You think that conducive?'

Turning to me, she shrugged. 'I've got nothing better to do. But then you'd know that wouldn't you?'

'Is she another one who regrets?' Hannah piped up, leaning across her food staring at her.

Looking past me, Eleanor's evil slanted eyes locked onto Hannah. 'Pumpkin hair,' she snapped, 'are you addressing me?'

Hannah nodded. 'There is no need to be in a decade long mood. I'm sure no one else has done something so childish.'

Wincing, I closed my eyes and waited for the onslaught. It was wrong of Hannah to make that assumption—because we are immortal, we do go through periods where we are annoyed or vengeful against the world or happy. By Hannah voicing it aloud, Eleanor would instantly know that she wasn't a myth.

'Childish?' she shouted, instantly rounding on her. 'Do you know how old I am?'

'Oh, Atlas here we go,' I grumbled. Even Etrician groaned.

'I've been alive for hundreds of years! You sit there and call me childish? You, who is no doubt a disgusting human who looks barely twenty has the audacity to call me childish after living as long as I have?'

'Hey now wait a minute,' Darren shouted, standing up so he could speak to her on her level. 'There's no need to be so nasty. Give her a break. She is just saying it is pointless being so unhappy all the time when you can live as long as you have. There are so many things to see and do-'

'Been there done that, got bored!' she said. 'I think you're human too. Shame… I initially classed you as the good looking one but now you're all ugly.'

'Hey!' I yelled at her, banging my hand on the table, she flinched at the sound. 'Calm down. There's no need to insult us.'

Snorting at me, she moved right into my face. 'You have no right to order me around,' she snarled. 'This is my home!'

Before she could say anything more, I heard loud stomps of high-heeled shoes approaching us. 'Our home dear sister,' Hadriana's voice boomed around us as she strode into the room, 'must be welcoming for all. That means it does not give you the right to insult our guests, it is not how we act. So I suggest you take your seat and be quiet.' Hadriana stormed right to her, almost breathing down her neck. I could feel the tension between them; it felt almost hostile and alien. Something was going on between them. With a short apologetic nod, Eleanor moved around me and took her seat. Though the tension was still swirling around us, Hadriana casually brushed it aside. 'Three hundred-year-old P.M.T. it's a bitch.'

With some small tittering from everyone, there was a collective sigh of relief as the argument quickly diffused and with a gesture from Hadriana; everyone began to eat their meals. But, there was one place that was still empty.

'Oh, I'm sorry, Mr Moncur will join us later.' Hadriana informed us as she caught me staring.

During the meal, I did notice the astringent glares the sisters were shooting at each other from across the table. Etrician too seemed to notice it, but he was trying his best to steer any eye contact or conversation away from their direction. It was a private matter and somehow the group was placed right in the middle of it.

'So, how long do you plan to stay here?' Eleanor asked us.

Etrician looked at me as though to say, "Do we tell her?" though thankfully, it was Hadriana who answered.

'As long as they wish.' Hadriana cut in. 'But knowing Thera there is an adventure to be had on the other side of the world somewhere.'

Glancing at Hadriana, I saw a cheeky smile in the corner of her mouth. 'You're the one who wanted to see who could travel to the South Pole and back the quickest. Never underestimate a Water Nymph,' I smiled. Just as I was about to explain the game we had, I heard shoes approaching the dining room. Instantly all heads looked up to see who was coming towards us.

At first, I thought it was Offo coming to collect the plates or to bring round our dessert, but when the person came into the room, I was wrong.

Wearing a smart dinner jacket, with pressed black trousers and a red striped tie, he stood beholding at the scene in front of him. My mouth instantly fell open in shock; my eyes grew wide in panic and horror, my heart pumped loudly in my chest, threatening to burst. With his salt and pepper hair, steely light blue eyes and two-day-old stubble, The Minister stood there looking at us, just as we sat looking at him.

Like a Mexican stand-off, though without guns, we were frozen to our seats. Hadriana was the only one who moved and seemed perturbed with the look on our faces.

Blinking, I quickly collected myself and standing up pointing at him shouted, 'GET HIM!' Suddenly turning around, he pelted out of the dining room, Etrician, Dagen and I close behind.

'NO STOP!' Hadriana screamed as we chased after the man who was responsible for so much pain and torture in such a short time. I almost felt sick that I was chasing him in such a pathetic human-like manner.

'Get out of the way!' Dagen suddenly yelled. Turning around, I saw him take a stance, his arms raised, palms facing upright. Etrician suddenly pushed me out of the way, just before Dagen shouted his spell. 'BLOCK!' he shouted.

A powerful burst of green energy erupted out of his hands and flew towards The Minister who was heading for the exit. The green light formed a large impenetrable shield where he promptly smacked into headfirst. Falling back, Dagen threw more green light at him. Flying through the air, it picked him up and snaked around his legs forcing them together and pinning him to the shield behind.

Continuing to wind up The Minister's body, the light restricted his arms to his sides and sneaked up to his mouth where it was instantly closed shut.

Etrician let me go. I heard others scarper out of the room and gasped as they saw The Minister in a vice-like hold through Dagen's magic.

'Hadriana,' I boomed, 'explain yourself!' There was no formality between us now. There was no room for etiquette, no room for being polite.

'Let him go and I will,' she said in a shaky voice.

'No!' I bellowed, feeling my blood boil. 'Tell me what is going on. Of all places in the world to go, of all the times that we turn up, a man who we have feared for our very lives is within your home? Hadriana,' I spat menacingly, eyeing her, 'you tell me what is going on right this minute!'

Eleanor nonchalantly peered round the door as though it was all too trivial for her. Seeming bored, she leant against the doorframe and watched the scene unfold.

Hadriana, walked tentatively towards me, her eyes darting between the Minister and me.

'He's being controlled,' Hadriana told me, putting her hands up.

Shaking my head, I could not believe it. It was too easy for her to say that. We'd only been discussing it a few hours ago and now she was using this as an excuse for his behaviour towards us?

'I promise you.' She implored. 'He's being controlled by one single entity that neither you nor I can break. Now and again, he returns to his normal self, as Mr Moncur. That man that you brought with you, the one with a mark on his hand, he belongs to Mr Monsur's alter-ego, The Minister as you call him. The marked man is, in fact, a Jinn, you know they can shapeshift. The Minister has two of them. It's how he can find you and track you down. It wasn't Dinglewood.'

'You knew this before we arrived?' I asked, shaking my head in disbelief.

Hadriana placed herself between us. 'Please listen. This man bound in magic is Garrick Moncur, he's human. He's known about myths for near five decades. He worked for the T.A.T. he knows Amjee and me from a long time ago. When the Staff of Zeus fell into the wrong hands a few weeks ago, Garrick was in retirement when he got captured and was forced to hunt you down for the Cabinet of Idols. When he is his alter ego, this Minister, he doesn't remember me or Amjee or anyone. He's being controlled.'

'What do you know about the Cabinet of Idols, Hadriana? Out with it!' I yelled.

Flinching, she sighed and looked at the floor. 'The Cabinet of Idols is made up of powerful legends that are needed to unlock a terrible entity. This entity was created when mankind decided that to every beginning... there is a permanent end.' Burying her head in her hands she began to cry.

Ice gripped my heart and I staggered away from her. Realisation dawned on me, I wished my mother could destroy me here and now. I would not do it. I would not be the cause. 'No,' I gasped, slumping to the floor in terror. 'No, I won't do it... I won't... I'll-'

'You'll have no choice,' she said in a watery voice. 'You've been marked by the staff already. The Jinn told me that Garrick's alter ego zapped you with the staff on the pier a few weeks ago. When The Minister gets hold of the two humans in their magical forms,' she nodded to Hannah and Darren, 'the prison will unlock and the entity will use your combined magic and destroy the humans.'

'As there'll be no humans in this world, the Ancients will adhere to their old rules. Myths and legends will head into oblivion as they will become superfluous,' Etrician finished.

Everyone was too shocked to speak. So this was the grand design of this Cabinet of Idols? To bring forth the apocalypse, by creating such immense power, to open the gates to The End of Days. But, why though? What is to gain from all of this? What could be achieved if only Ancients existed on the planet?

'This is all Rhea's fault, isn't it?' Hannah whispered. 'She has the staff.'

'Rhea is controlling that man.' Darren said looking to The Minister who was still pinned to Dagen's shield.

'Who is Rhea?' Renita asked as all eyes focussed on Darren and Hannah.

'Rhea was the third siren in our group.' Hannah began. 'But she turned against us. She and Tara fought in London. Tara tried to stop her from transforming fully. If she did, she would have started a war because of the imbalance the T.A.T. was creating. But before Rhea was defeated, she was taken away by the Ancients.'

'So, this Rhea girl, what does that mean for us?' Etrician asked Hannah and Darren.

'We're screwed,' Hannah said simply. 'I hate to say it, but that girl was a total biotch. She's a siren but it looks like she didn't fully transform or else-'

'She doesn't remember…' came a feeble voice from behind us. Turning to look, Dagen's magic was beginning to wane; Garrick's mouth was free to move. 'She doesn't remember who she was. One of the Jinn told me-'

'What's a Jinn?' Darren asked Hannah quietly.

'A genie,' Etrician quickly replied. 'Does that help us though, if she doesn't remember who she was?'

Hannah shrugged. 'Maybe. It means that we still have a fighting chance to get her back to our side.'

Etrician scowled. 'Garrick, tell us now. The Ancients who took Rhea, was one of them, new? Had he just become an Ancient?'

Garrick nodded. 'Yes. He's my employer.' Garrick sighed. 'He took Rhea and gave her the staff. His name is Maynard.'

CHAPTER EIGHTEEN

THE FEELING OF SHOCK WAS AN UNDERSTATEMENT. IT WAS JUST AS WE feared. All of us felt like we'd been kicked very hard in the stomach, multiple times. It all seemed so pointless now. There was no escape. The Fates were correct. I couldn't escape my destiny. Though Garrick had told us Rhea had no previous knowledge of who or what she used to be, I was growing increasingly worried why one particular Ancient was usurping the rest. Maynard was the newest Ancient and he was going to destroy us all.

Hadriana pleaded to let Garrick go. We did so for Hadriana's sake, but as he headed to the dining room with Hadriana in his wake, I caught him and grabbing his arm; I squeezed tightly and dragged him to me.

'Please don't hurt me,' he whimpered, 'I couldn't stop myself from hurting you. I don't mean to, it's the staff. She makes me, she orders me. I have no choice.'

'You said that to me the last time we met,' I spat. 'You retain some of your sanity when you are being controlled it seems. I take it you are controlled by the staff as well?' He nodded once. 'How is it done? It is supposed to kill myths!'

'No,' he shook his head. 'Zeus created it to control all legends. Legends are more powerful than myths,' he explained. 'He found a way to control them, as Ancients cannot do this.'

A spark of understanding flashed in my mind, making me smile. 'And the Ancients took the staff away because it was dangerous, towards them!'

'Yes!' He exclaimed. 'The staff was used on me within the very day of it leaving the magical plane. The T.A.T. created me in a way, as they did with Hannah and Darren. I have magical blood in me, legend blood. Therefore,' he said sadly, 'I can be controlled by it.'

I released him and he rubbed his arm. 'It's all starting to come together.'

'When I retired, I went into hiding, gave myself a different name so that Maynard couldn't find me. But he did. He's an Ancient now. Of course, he found me.' Something crossed over my eyes and he stared at me. 'You've just thought of something.'

'The Cabinet of Idols, is it purely meant to be for legends? Hannah and Darren...' I let the sentence hang in the air. He knew what was going on and he needed to tell me.

Garrick placed a tender hand on my shoulder and his eyes didn't betray him. He was gapingly apologetic for what he was about to say. It was a side I never saw and I wished that The Minister had retained Garrick's heart and understanding. 'Maynard wants them because Tara ordered both to become myths and they retained their powers longer than the others, not only that, she was an Ancient when she did this. Because of this, Hannah and Darren and anyone else who was forced to become a myth under Tara's command, are somehow much more powerful than regular myths.'

'But that's impossible. I thought she was a Siren?'

Garrick shook his head. 'I don't understand it either, but Maynard is afraid that Tara and the others will get their powers back. He wishes to destroy Tara's group by taking Hannah and Darren away from her,' he said bitterly.

'About the mark's, is there a way to undo the spell?'

He shook his head. 'No. There's nothing I can do for your mark. I'm sorry.' Clutching his arm, he gazed at me with terror in his eyes. 'I did not mean to harm you but there is nothing I can do when I'm being controlled. Just know this Rhea wants you alive. I cannot tell you when Rhea will give me the staff to control you. It's only a matter of time though.'

'If she has the staff, why is she not controlling you now?'

'She is asleep. I have four hours until I have to go back with the Jinn.'

'So Rhea is being manipulated by this Ancient called Maynard?' I asked, pondering on the new information.

'Yes.'

'But how is it that you are telling me all of this? Won't Maynard find out that you've told me and foiled his plans? Doesn't he know that you're here? I mean he's an Ancient and their powers are limitless.'

Garrick smiled in a boyish manner. 'No, Hadriana found their weakness. Hadriana's castle is the most protected place on the planet. The Ancients know that Hadriana and her family exist and that she deals in the Magical Black Market, but they leave her to it. As far as they are concerned, she is just a boring immortal human. When I leave this castle all of the conversations that I have had with her or you will be suppressed by old magic that even the Ancients are unaware of. It's something that Hadriana found. But don't ask me as I don't know what it is. Even Hadriana can be selfish to keep her prized secrets.'

That piqued my attention, but I didn't question him further on it. I'd just have to question Hadriana when the time came. 'So when you leave, Rhea will control you again and you will continue to hunt me until you catch me.' It was a statement and his eyes betrayed him.

Silence fell between us but Garrick decided to stay. He saw that I wasn't finished talking with him. 'When you were The Minister, I asked you about Dinglewood.' I suddenly asked, making him flinch, which surprised me. Even though he looked like The Minister right down to every strand of salt and pepper hair, his posture and how he spoke to me was entirely different, ashamed and almost, humble. 'It seemed as though you didn't know him?'

'No, I don't and as far as I am aware, he is not a part of Rhea's or Maynard's plans. Why?' he asked with curious eyes.

'Because for some unknown reason he has power and by that, I mean Ancient-type power. I can't explain it, but I thought he got it from you.'

'No,' he shook his head. 'Maynard and Rhea take power, they don't give it.'

There was a long strange silence between us. Feeling that our conversation had dropped, Garrick inclined his head, mumbled an apology then walked off. My head was splitting from information and I just wanted to crawl into bed and sleep for a hundred years. Though I could potentially do that, it wasn't conducive to the situation the group and myself were in.

Sighing heavily, I headed up the grand red-carpeted staircase that had an ivory capped banister which had gilded embossed flowers. Caressing the gilded banister as I slowly ascended the stairs, I felt like a princess. In my mind's eye, I saw dozens of people dressed in regal clothing. The men in handsome suits and the women in gorgeous silk and lace gowns that trailed behind them, rippling as though water. Classical music of placid soft strings and a sweet sobering piano melody gently flowed to my ears. Closing my eyes, I felt like I was there... all those years ago.

I reached the top step and jerked out of my daydream. With a small sigh, I spun around to see the grand hallway and staircase devoid of life, of fun and entertainment. All that was in this large castle now was hollow feelings, secrets, cobwebs, and a sordid collection of magical items.

Meandering my way down the long spooky corridors, I came to a halt as I saw Renita flit out of her room and dart into the one opposite. Frowning with curiosity, I followed her and knocked on her door.

'Renita, it's Thera,' I spoke softly.

After a few moments, the door opened and Renita stood looking at me with a sunken face. 'Can I help?'

'Are you,' I began but suddenly changed tact. It wasn't a good idea for me to keep asking if she was alright, we both knew she wasn't and I would be a horrible friend if I reminded her of her fate. 'Are you safe?'

'Yes,' she frowned, confused. 'Why?'

'Well, with the Minister and all, I just wanted to check,' I explained lamely then moved away.

'I don't look right do I?' she whispered from behind me, her voice shook me with distress. She was still upset about what she was going through and though I had kept my promise and hadn't said anything to the others, the process would start soon enough. I wanted to remember Renita, even though I knew I wouldn't in the end. At least, I could give her some comfort that she was a good friend and she was wanted and loved.

I reached out and hugged her, pulling her close to me. Standing there, Renita's small frame shook. With quaking hands, she placed them around me and sobbed uncontrollably into my hair. I wished there was something I could do, someplace where she would be safe and cared for... but nothing came to mind... unless...

Stroking her hair, I guided her back into the room and closed the door so the others wouldn't be able to hear. She went to her bed and sat heavily on it, staring at her hands.

Placing a lock of her raven hair behind her ear, I tilted my head at an angle to look at her properly. 'Do you know why Garrick told us that information tonight?'

'Because he's an idiot and he has signed our death warrant,' she laughed dryly.

'No. Garrick was free to tell us everything that has happened because of Hadriana. There are some things in this world that even I don't understand. Hadriana has nothing better to do than travel the world and seek out rare magical items. By travelling the world I mean in a more paradoxical sense of course.'

'I don't understand,' she whispered.

I sat beside her. 'Garrick told me that Hadriana has acquired some very old magic, magic that slipped through the Ancients radar. Anyway, all beings that are under this roof are safe from the Ancients.' She still didn't seem to understand. 'Renita, if you are out in the open with us, the Ancients can find you and continue the process of-'

'Of permanently destroying my essence and self-worth in this world,' she spat bitterly.

Ignoring her adolescent comment, I continued. 'If you stay here Renita you're safe from them. You'll get to live here forever if you wish to. I would need to speak to Hadriana to see if my theory is correct but... if it is, would you remain here, with Hadriana, Eleanor and Offo?'

She stared at her hands. 'I don't know them,' she said sadly. 'Hadriana is kind but Eleanor is a feculent childish toad.'

Laughing, I kissed her on the forehead, stood up and made for the door. 'The choice is yours and you have a while to decide before we leave for Greece.'

'Is that your next move? To go to Greece?' she asked in a frightened tone. 'But that's where Rhea is, where Maynard is. They'll know you are coming a mile off. And what if you get controlled by them and turn on us? We won't be able to defend ourselves because our magic doesn't work on you.'

Putting a finger to my lips, she was instantly quiet. 'We'll cross to that bridge when we come to it. Right now, I just want everyone to get a good night's sleep and tomorrow after breakfast we can have a large group discussion about what to do next. But, we will need to go to Greece at some point and the longer we prolong it, the messier it is going to be for the world and I cannot allow that to happen.'

'But...' she sighed, looking up at me with glistening blue eyes, 'your fate is sealed too. Garrick said that Rhea wants to control you and we already know that if they collect you and your brother it will unleash the world's greatest evil. Even thinking about it now, it's difficult to comprehend.'

I smiled. 'Don't worry about it. I'm not,' I lied. 'Anyway, you get some sleep. I'll see you in the morning.'

Leaving her alone I felt a tremendous sadness erupt in my heart. She was going through so much I couldn't possibly comprehend and at the end of it all, I would never be able to help her as I wouldn't remember I even knew her. Though she and I had different destinies, they were both depressingly sad. I didn't want to be responsible for the death of the world but as soon as

I got marked by the staff, it was the start of the countdown. The only question was, on what date would zero fall.

The following morning and feeling well-rested, I followed the sounds of laughter flowing from the drawing-room and instantly picked out Hannah, Etrician, Tyr and Darren.

I was met by Offo when I opened the door. He bowed as I entered. 'Good morning Lady Thera. May I offer you something to eat or drink for breakfast?'

'Water,' I smiled, 'but can you add some salt to it.'

'Adriatic Sea salt as you wish,' he smiled. 'And would you care for something to eat?'

'Halibut,' Hadriana laughed from her comfy chair by the large roaring fire.

I shook my head. 'No. I'll just stick to salt water, for now, thank you Offo.'

'Very good,' he bowed then headed out of the room.

'No food? What's wrong, you lost your appetite?' Hadriana asked laughing at me.

'You know I don't eat much. That dinner from last night will probably last me for a fair few decades.'

I took a seat next to Hannah who wore a lovely pair of flared brown cords that looked like they came from the 1960s and a white pirate-looking puffy shirt with a leather waistcoat. She smiled as I joined her.

'Garrick told me everything last night,' I spoke quietly to Hannah and Hadriana. Hannah's eyes widened in curiosity, while Hadriana's creased in shrewdness. 'He told me how the staff works, he said it's only a matter of time before Rhea gives the staff to him to control me. But Maynard needs legends and you and Darren, to open this prison.'

She gasped. 'Why us? We're myths. If the Cabinet of Idols is purely for legends...'

'Tell me about Tara?' I asked. 'She became a Siren, right? But she ordered you and Darren to become full myths, correct?'

Hannah nodded. 'Yes. However, Tara had said once that she gained so much knowledge from being a full Siren; she said she got ancient knowledge. But,' she bit her lip, 'Tara always thought she was more than a Siren.'

Hadriana flicked her eyes at me and I tried to find the right words. 'It's because Tara commanded you to become myths that you gained more power than a normal merman or water nymph and that's why you are marked for the Cabinet. Garrick said that Tara had Ancient powers.' Hadriana instantly furrowed her brows. 'He doesn't understand it either,' I said to her, 'it doesn't make any sense, but we have to believe things will make sense along the way.'

She blew out a frustrated breath of air. 'Maynard wants the most powerful beings to open a prison,' she said to us. 'You and your brother are extremely powerful, making you an asset to his collection.'

Irritated at how flippant she was, I said, 'And you're all right from Maynard because of the protection that you have, that anti-Ancient magic.'

As soon as I spoke, the room went quiet. Darren and Tyr stared at me in confusion, Hannah had her mouth open and Hadriana appeared furious. 'Why did that idiot tell you?'

'Don't know,' I shrugged. 'But it leads onto some very interesting questions doesn't it?' I asked her curiously. 'For example, where did you get the magic from? If it's so old that the Ancients themselves have overlooked it, it must go back very, very far. So, Hadriana the immortal one who is so old and wise, care to explain how you have managed to travel back in time thousands of years? And by thousands of years, I'm going back at least seventeen.'

'Not seventeen, try forty.'

Astonished eyes locked onto Hadriana. In shock, no one dared breathe. Flicking a smile in my direction, Hadriana's head looked up as Offo tottered in with a glass of water and handed it to me. Downing the refreshing icy cold saltwater quickly, I passed him the glass and he walked off, closing the door behind him, but suddenly the door flew open as Dagen strode into the room.

'Did anyone have the most terrible night's sleep, or was it just me?' he asked, as he headed to Darren and Tyr.

Ignoring him, I continued with the conversation with Hadriana. I was still gobsmacked. 'F-forty thousand years?' I gasped. 'But that's impossible.'

She shook her head. 'It's not impossible. I can't be exact, but humans began to invent ideas that were based purely on belief. The power of belief has gone back more than what we have originally understood. When you made me immortal, you told me about myths and their origins. It seemed far too simple. First, there came Ancients, and then Ancients created myths and myths created legends. It seemed too easy to create that developing concept starting with humans knowing why they exist.' She reached forward and took a handful of peanuts that were on the table in front.

'This planet has been surrounded by potent magic,' she continued, 'yet humans don't actively seek it.' She popped a few nuts in and crunched them with ease. 'I mean, sure, you get New Age witches and wizards who prance around Stonehenge every six months, but they don't know the real reason why Stonehenge was built. And it's not for religion or ancestors as they originally believe.'

'It's the ley lines isn't it?' Dagen asked, joining in. 'The collective magical lines that pull myths to them. Stonehenge was like a magic hub. The bluestones from Wales are the best for magical currents.'

'Like an electricity plant,' Hannah added.

'Aha!' Hadriana shouted making us jump. 'But why are they there? Ley lines have been in the ground since the earth began. It had nothing to do with myths until humans or Ancients used them. But, what I do know is this: though ley lines have been here since the beginning, they were in specific places for a reason. From my research, I am reaching an understanding that the ley lines were in place for humans to create magic. This is because ley lines are everywhere on the planet. Being on every continent and every country is giving a more diverse scope of mythology around the world, leading to every culture. It forms a large web, which links together. Our planet has always been magical, it's if we choose to ignore it, believe it, or use it that has separated all humans into what we are today.'

'Holy cow,' Darren gasped. 'This is amazing. I... I never thought of the ley lines having anything to do with the Ancients.'

Hadriana shook her head. 'No, not the Ancients. You're getting confused. This theory of the ley lines goes back much farther. Before the Ancients, there was one very powerful, knowledgeable group of early humans. These early humans used the earth's ley lines to guide themselves from one place to another. It's a sort of sixth sense that humans had but lost years ago, like humans seeing the future or whatever.'

'Can we do that?' Hannah asked.

'Shut up, I'm trying to listen,' spat Dagen.

Taking a deep breath to calm down, Hadriana continued. 'Anyway, this group of early humans were wise, by that I mean like robins they could "see" or sense the ley lines and discovered that water and plants that grew on the ley lines made them stronger, that led to abilities. They were the first users of magic. Not in a way of producing energy like Dagen, but they used heightened magical plants and clean magical water to help them.'

'Can you get on with this, I'm growing impatient.' I huffed, finding it annoying that Hadriana sometimes went off on a tangent about things which seemed interesting to her, so you'd get an hour's worth of lecture before she got to the point. Reaching this far, I just wanted a straight answer.

'Witch Hazel,' she said quickly. 'Witch Hazel, the bush or small shrub or tree; that is old anti-Ancient magic. It's anti-Ancient magic because it was created by legends. I have four planted around the castle and have more or less dowsed the perimeter of the entire building in the stuff. It's created a protective shield over me and I bet your Amber Tree would be something similar.'

'So you've just gone around the corner to get some Witch Hazel that you buy at a chemist for like a few quid?' Hannah asked her. 'That's kinda stupid.'

'Whoa, shut up for a second Hannah,' I said putting my hand out to stop her. 'My tree, it's one of a kind,' I told Hadriana, 'my brother and I made it–'

'Exactly! The Ancient's don't know about it. Its magical properties are limitless,' she said excitedly.

Sighing, I closed my eyes and placed my head in my hands. This was another bout of information overload and it was giving me another niggling headache. 'Alright, let's just assume all this is true how did you find out all of this, forty-thousand years ago? You are not Death in any way shape or form.'

Smiling, she got up. 'Once everyone is up, I'll take you all to my collections room. Just do NOT touch or speak to anything!'

When everyone was dressed and fed, Hadriana took us down to her coveted underground magical storage area and thrusting the door open dramatically bellowed, 'Welcome to my splendiferous collections,' she laughed. 'Don't touch anything!' she slammed the door behind us.

'Oh, what's that?' Jane asked as she approached the age-old answer of what came first, the chicken or the egg.

'If there aren't any labels, then ask Thera, she's been told what a lot of these are,' Hadriana said lazily as she strode to the back of the room.

'Oh when you come to a frog, don't talk to it, especially you two;' I pointed at Hannah and Darren. 'It steals years off your life and you're mortal at the moment.' Giving each other scared looks; they stuck together and peeled off from the rest of the group.

'Everyone, over here!' she shouted, her voice echoed in the large item filled room.

We found Hadriana right at the left-hand corner. 'Oh,' I simply said as I came to some troughs that were filled with various plants. Partitioned by colour, the plants looked healthy and well cared for. With heat lamps that hung from the ceiling and watering cans placed by the sides, I could tell that Hadriana looked after them.

'Right we've got mini saplings of Witch Hazel,' she pointed. 'You can thank Dian for that. He introduced it to me many years ago. Forget-Me-Not's, which I am using alongside Nepenthe. I'm trying to see if it can completely block out all bad memories. Not quite there yet,' she shrugged. 'Over here we have Anemone, a lovely little white flower that stops bleeding and helps rejuvenate tissue. Also, I have Love in the Mist, a lovely little flower that can create real blind love. Monkshood, Snapdragon, Wolfsbane,' she pointed to each in turn.

'That's Zinnia elegans,' I added, indicating the bright magenta flower with the yellow middle. 'It has magical properties?'

'Yes,' she sighed. 'Dian managed to brew a potion to make you young or old. Take it cold and it makes you older. Take it warm and it makes you younger.'

Folding my arms, I stared at her, 'I am very impressed Hadriana. Truly I am.' I pointed to the pipes surrounding the plants. 'You also have an interesting irrigation system.'

'Yup. Waters pumped through the tubes on the inside and it's filtered and purified. There are a few magical spells on it also. I took a leaf out of Dian's book,' she smiled. 'So, can everyone gather around please?' she called out to the rest of the group who were about to wander around the room. Clearly, plants bored them.

Taking a deep breath, Hadriana turned, grabbed a jar of sand and a small metal box that had a distinct pattern of feathers on it, and held the items up for all to see.

'These little beauties help me go back into the past or forward to the future. This,' she said holding up the little metal box that was about the size of her hand, 'is the only one in existence and as such it doesn't really have a name, so I made one up. Copying Casket.'

'Oh that sounds SO original,' Dagen mocked. 'And let me guess, it copies things?'

With her left eye twitching, Hadriana stared at him her eyes quickly narrowing. 'Atlas, I hate you,' she sighed then looked away from him.

'What?' he protested, with the look of mild hurt on his face. 'If it's called a Copying Casket it's kind of obvious you copy stuff in it.'

'Yes you annoying little boy, but you spoil my fun of telling you the story of why it's called a Copying Casket. Damn, don't you ever just bite your tongue and give people a break? It's a wonder you're still here. If I was Thera I would have thrown you in a maelstrom already.'

I nodded. 'The thought had crossed my mind.' Feeling Dagen's eyes shoot towards me, I shrugged my shoulders. 'You're an idiot, you annoy everyone, get over it. And you,' I shouted to Hadriana, 'get on with it.'

'This,' she held up the jar of sand, 'is special sand from Father Times Hour Glass. You just sprinkle some on the ground, say a date and it goes by the numbers of the year, not months or days, jump onto the spot you've sprinkled the sand onto and BOOM, you're in the past, or future.'

'So the numbers, you would say "The Year 1942 Day 127" which would be…um…' mumbling he looked up to count, 'May the 7th and you're there?' Darren asked.

'Yes. However, what I have discovered is that you can't give a time. Therefore, the time that you leave the present is the same time you travel into the past or the future. Also, the place where you travel from is going to be the same place you arrive in the past or future.'

'Well this is all very fascinating, but how on the great Atlas did you manage to get even one iota of sand?' I demanded. 'Father Time's Hour Glass is… well even I can't describe it. It's like trying to smack the Moirae in the face; it cannot be done, period. And even seeing Father Time let alone procuring one grain of sand, is impossible.'

'Ah, ah, nothing is impossible if you are immortal,' she laughed. 'You should know that.'

'There are limitations, Hadriana,' Etrician told her seriously. 'We cannot do certain things, especially mess with time if we have the ability. You haven't been given the authority or the responsibility of time travel.'

'Now just a minute,' she shouted, rounding on him, 'I have the right to do what I want. It's not my fault I'm like this.'

Rolling my eyes, I looked the other way, just in time to see Hannah bent over clutching her stomach. 'Hannah!'

'Something's wrong,' she whispered.

Everyone took a step back in horror. Hannah's entire body was beginning to fade, as though she didn't exist.

CHAPTER NINETEEN

'Hannah,' Jane whispered in a frightened voice. 'What's happening to her?' she asked Hadriana. 'Is that what one of your flowers is meant to do?'

With wide shocked eyes, she looked up and shook her head vigorously. 'No. None of my plants does this. Hannah is fading from life itself.'

Renita suddenly burst into uncontrollable sobs, drawing attention to herself.

'What's wrong with you?' Dagen asked her with a frown.

'Etrician, Hadriana, find out what's going on with Hannah.' I ordered them. 'Come on, you don't need to see this,' I went to Renita and taking her by the shoulders, steered her out of the room. Closing the door behind me Renita let it out. It was such a horrible thing for her to see and it brought everything back.

'I don't want to be forgotten,' she wailed, 'I want to stay here with you and Jane and Tyr.' I noticed that she left Dagen out.

'If you want me to talk to Hadriana about what I said the other night…'

'No,' she sniffed, 'no please don't. I-I'll talk to her.' She hiccoughed softly as she took a few steadying breaths to calm herself. 'I think Jane is rubbing off on me. I'm becoming so timid because of what I know I just…' taking another deep breath she shook her head. 'I'll be alright. It's Hannah we have to worry about.'

Drying her eyes, we were just about to turn towards the door when it suddenly banged open; Darren's concerned frightened eyes met ours. 'Hannah is fading from her timeline, if we don't sort it out, she won't exist. It'll affect everything we've done and everyone we've met.'

Pushing past him, Renita and I headed to the back of the room where we left them. Still huddled around Hannah, their concerned worried faces made my stomach do a back-flip as Hannah's body flickered from solid colours to a faded transparent. 'Damn.' My eyes found Hadriana's who was strangely looking at me. 'How?'

Sighing she shrugged. 'I don't know. Someone has messed around with her ancestors but it could be anywhere in time.'

'Is there anything we can use to find out?' Darren asked her, as he knelt beside Hannah and placed a comforting arm around her. Hannah's pained face and laboured breathing were worrying me. She was trying so hard to hold onto her existence, just as Renita was trying to do.

Kneeling beside him, I placed my hand on his quaking shoulder. 'Darren, look at me,' I said softly. His watery blue eyes showed he was frightened for her, but there was also something else that he wouldn't admit to; he cared for her. 'You know Hannah better than all of us. Is there anything about her past that you know about?'

Taking a deep breath to collect his thoughts he nodded, 'Yes. One of her family members used to be in the O.M.C. Miss Ann Smith. She worked alongside Mr Raleigh. He was the one who created a small book on mythological creatures. He left Tara a clue to find out about the Ancients. Do you think someone has killed Ann?' he asked, his eyes flashing back from myself and Hadriana.

Frowning, Hadriana shrugged, 'It's possible. If someone has gone into the past to mess with the future, they don't necessarily need to make that big of a change. Just one small move can affect everything in the future. Though, any myth or legend must always obtain permission from an Ancient first if they want to go into the past.'

'So that means that it's a myth or a legend?' Darren asked her. 'Regardless, Maynard the Ancient would have granted them permission.'

'Most likely, but humans can also go into the past through magic,' she explained.

'Darren,' Tyr asked him, as he moved forward into my periphery. 'When did the O.M.C start?'

Closing his eyes Darren tried to remember... 'It's in the damn library in London, in that hotel that Amjee works in. It has everything about the O.M.C and the T.A.T.'

Hadriana's eyes flashed. She walked to a small panel and pushed a small red button. 'Offo, get me Amjee on the phone, now.'

'Yes, my lady,' came Offo's clear voice, as though he was in the room with us. Hadriana's hand moved to a lever and pulled. Part of the wall moved and with a small thunk, it became a door and slid open revealing another smaller room full of TV screens and other random devices I couldn't name.

Moving inside, Hadriana sat in a large black leather chair; her hand poised over a silver telephone. 'Transferring the call,' Offo's voice sounded.

The telephone beeped a few times and Hadriana's hand shot out like a rattlesnake. 'Yes hello I would like to speak to Amjee Khan please,' she spoke in a business-like manner. 'Hadriana Von Reed. Yes, I'll hold.' Spinning in her chair, she glanced at Hannah's flickering body, a crease of confusion etched on her brow. 'Amjee,' she said, a small smile appearing on her face. 'I have a favour, I have Darren and Hannah with me h-' she paused while I heard screeching down the phone, though I couldn't make out the words. 'Yes I know but this is important.' More screeching sounded over the phone, Hadriana's smile faded into an annoyed look. 'I don't know, hang on,' putting her hand over the bottom end of the telephone, she glanced at me. 'What's this about them being in a house in Bristol?'

Darren shot her an annoyed look and held out his hand, 'Give it to me, please,' he asked.

Sighing, she passed over the phone. Grabbing it tightly, Darren shoved it against his ear. 'Amjee its Darren listen to me, Hannah's timeline is vanishing... we had to leave the house, please don't ask why.' He pleaded. 'I need to know some information about the O.M.C from the library, is it still accessible?' Darren was quiet as Amjee began talking to him. I noticed that she wasn't screaming at him as she did at Hadriana. 'I need to know about Ann Smith and when it all started,' he replied to a question. 'The group started in 1825 in Devon.' Pausing as he looked down at Hannah, he nodded at Amjee's questions. 'Where in Devon?... Anstey's Cove in Torquay,' he said looking up at Hadriana, but I caught his eyes and nodded in understanding. 'What was the exact date?'

'If we don't find the exact date, then what?' I asked Hadriana, who swivelled in the chair, biting her nails in thought. She shrugged nonchalantly but remained quiet. 'Is there a way to find out if time has altered in one year?' She stopped swivelling her chair and looked at me with cautious hazel eyes and closed them in response.

Darren passed the telephone to Hadriana. 'She doesn't know the date and she knows very little about Ann but she said she will have a look and get back to us.'

Taking the silver telephone off him, she placed it back down, then quickly standing up slammed her hand down on the red button. 'Offo get me Wong Tai Sin, Airmed if she's still available and…Aeon.'

'No,' Etrician gasped in shock. 'You have connections to him?'

Hadriana ignored him and waited for Offo to respond. 'Yes, my lady.'

'Tell them it's important if they won't come here on their magic, send them Hermes Boots. Just get them here now.'

'Yes my lady,' Offo replied quickly.

'Right everyone upstairs,' Hadriana barked. 'Darren, take Hannah into the drawing-room, the fire is still alight. Thera, Etrician stay here, I need to talk to you,' she ordered.

Jane and Tyr helped Darren carry Hannah out of the collections room while Dagen and Renita gave us concerned looks. 'We'll be up soon,' I told them. Looking troubled, Renita nodded and unwillingly followed Dagen out.

'Right, we need to get things sorted and fast.' Hadriana began when she heard the door close. 'I'm not counting on Amjee to get the exact dates and though I didn't want to say anything in front of the others, there is a way to find out the date but I need your help.'

'Why us?' Etrician asked, but I had a sneaking suspicion that it had something to do with our powers. The others, Tyr and Dagen especially, who have a lot of power could not control it yet. Last night when Dagen had Garrick pinned up against his shield; I noticed his powers were waning. That alone told me he wasn't ready yet.

'Your powers,' she sighed, looking at each of us.

I shook my head in dismay. 'I knew it.'

'It's not that bad,' she snapped at me. 'Your powers are legendary and don't let that get to your already fat head,' she pointed at me. In response, I frowned, but she continued to explain. 'Mythical powers and legendary powers are different,' she smiled, 'and I feel such a genius to have figured it out. All legends that have powers, draw their energy from ley lines.'

Folding his arms Etrician stared at her. 'I already knew this.'

'Come with me,' she beckoned, quickly heading towards the exit.

Trailing behind her, she walked briskly out of the room and let us by. Promptly slamming the door shut behind us, she hastened back into the domed cellar. Bending down, she grabbed hold of the corner of a long Chinese threadbare rug. Pulling it back, she threw it away in a cloud of dust, revealing a five-pointed star that was painted in red paint on the flagstones. Looking closely, each point had an ancient symbol of the elements. The fifth element, which would usually symbolise the soul, instead symbolised time. 'Welcome to the convergence of a ley line that runs right through the castle. Very convenient that it's in the cellar, don't you think?'

'A pentagram?' I asked scathingly. 'That's going to do what exactly?'

'Help find out which point in time in the year 1825 has been messed with-' stopping herself mid-sentence she scrunched up her face. 'Damn, I hate being unprepared.'

'What do you need?' I asked as she brushed away the dust that had collected on the star.

Flicking her hair out of the way she said, 'I need a bit of Hannah, toenail clipping, a bit of old skin from a blister-'

'A strand of hair I think would suffice,' I grimaced. 'I'll get it, you stay here.' Giving Etrician a warning look, I smiled sweetly and left. A few minutes later, I barged into the warm applewood smelling dining room to find everyone crowded around Hannah by the fire, looking upset.

'Wong Tai Sin is on his way,' Jane told me as I made my way to them. Creating a makeshift bed of cushions from the dining room's sofas and chairs, they placed Hannah in the middle, close to the fire. Dagen, Tyr, Renita and Jane were stood around her staring at her with furrowed eyebrows, neither one of them wanting to get close to Hannah. Darren, it seemed never left her side.

Stroking her hair and smiling at her, he tried so hard not to get upset, but I could tell he was deeply troubled. The others parted as I went next to Darren. 'I need some of Hannah's hair,' I explained as I reached out to her head, but like a whip, he snatched my wrist and stopped me.

'Don't touch her,' he growled. 'Leave her alone.'

Taking a long slow breath, I said softly, 'Hadriana believes that Amjee won't find the exact date in time, we need to act fast and we need one strand of Hannah's hair.'

Holding her tightly, Darren looked down at Hannah and plucked a single strand from her head. Passing it to me, I took it in my thumb and forefinger. 'Thank you,' I told him calmly.

Turning on my heel, I headed straight to the door then stopped short. Sighing I faced the others who had watched me leave. Glancing at Tyr and Dagen I decided that they should come with me. Dagen would know about pentacles and Tyr had godly powers—either one of them might be useful.

'Tyr, Dagen come with me. The rest of you stay here, Renita, explain to Wong Tai Sin about Hannah.'

Minutes later, the three of us were back in the cellar room. Hadriana screwed her up face up in annoyance as she saw the others. 'Um, no offence but get lost,' she shouted at Dagen and Tyr as they followed me in.

'I invited them,' I explained.

'Don't care,' waving a finger at me, 'you two, get lost, now.'

'I have the hair,' I told her, holding up the nearly invisible strand of hair. 'Where do you want it?'

'Around their necks, if they don't leave,' she spat putting her hands on her hips. 'They don't have the right power.'

'Didn't want them for their power as such,' I lied, 'I want them to come with us.'

'Wait, I don't want to go,' Dagen interjected putting his hand up. 'I'm not helping a human.'

Etrician glowered at him, 'We help humans, it's what we do. You cannot turn your back on them. Without the T.A.T. without the group, a lot of myths will not exist. Tara and her friends risked their lives to save us. Without Hannah's family—'

'Hey,' Dagen shouted over him, pointing a finger, 'I didn't sign up for this alright? Santorini asked me and I said yes, but hell knows how I got into this mess. Let Darren help her, he'd jump off a cliff to help her if you asked.'

'Oy blond wizard, shut it,' Hadriana screeched. 'Thera give me the damn hair, Etrician go and get the other human, Wind Boy are you coming with us or what?'

'Yes,' Tyr said bemused.

In a huff, Dagen stormed away, Etrician hot on his heels. Walking calmly to Hadriana, I gave her the hair. Taking it from me carefully, she went over to the star and placed it in the centre of the floor. I gasped as the entire pentagram suddenly lit up in a dazzling soft blue light.

'Right, Thera I need you to stand on the West point of the pentagram please,' she said pointing to it.

Doing as she asked, I suddenly felt a strange power envelope my body, making me tingle all over. 'This was something I felt when I was in Glastonbury Torre,' I explained.

She nodded. 'Ley line central there, just like it is here, although, with a pentagram, I'm focussing the energy.'

A few moments later Etrician returned with Darren. 'He wants to go.'

'Good,' Hadriana smiled vaguely.

'The girls are staying with Hannah,' he informed me.

She pointed at Etrician, 'Stand on the point opposite Thera. Darren and Tyr, stand behind me, when Thera and Etrician have opened the gate, we need to jump in alright?'

'Huh?' Tyr and Darren asked, but Hadriana ignored them.

Etrician laughed standing on the point. 'I've only felt a couple of consolidated ley lines before, but this is something else.'

'Thera, Etrician stand with your arms out, palms facing each other,' she demonstrated.

Doing as she asked, I suddenly felt my arms get heavy as though I were holding weights, not allowing me to move. 'My arms are locked,' I gasped trying to pull away from them. 'Are yours?' I asked Etrician. With an uncomfortable expression on his face, he nodded.

'Good, it's working,' she said, beckoning Darren and Tyr to her. 'Stand behind me,' she ordered, as they didn't move from the spot. 'Thera, Etrician concentrate on the year 1825. Try and remember something during that year.'

'What? Are you crazy?' I raged. 'I don't want to be reminded of a flood Santorini and I caused in Jutland!' It was a horrible thing to happen but our hands were tied.

'She's right. I had to make an earthquake that same year, flattening an entire town. Both are not something we are proud of, nor want to remember-'

Suddenly the lines on the pentagram fizzled and turned from this soft blue to a deep blood red colour. 'Thank you,' Hadriana smiled. 'I love it when I get my way.'

'You conniving wretch!' I shouted.

Ignoring me, she retrieved her jar of sand; grabbing a handful, she sprinkled it onto the centre of the pentagram, where Hannah's hair was. Instantly the centre blew out a large burst of energy, almost winding me. Gasping for breath, I watched intently as the sand lifted from the ground and formed a strange sand storm within the centre of the pentagram. The shiny particles of rock caught the glow from the red light beneath it and refracted projecting a crackled image, similar to that of an old broken mirror.

The image showed the entrance to a cave. To the left was a full-moon hanging just over the horizon of sparkling waters. The stars were already out. Then two strangers in dark clothing hobbled to the cave and bent down to the ground. Then a large heavy looking implement swung over their heads and smacked down onto the ground below. The light then suddenly dimmed and the image had gone.

'What was that all about?' Tyr asked, but no one responded to him. We hadn't a clue.

'I think that was Anstey's Cove,' Darren told us. 'I think they were smashing up the mermaid skeleton, which would have been bad because that's when people began to take an interest in the O.M.C theory.'

'Brilliant! Of course!' I gasped, smiling. 'Anstey's Cove. The beach was only accessible during low tides. However, there was a small cave. It was only reachable during low tides that synced with the moon. It was in March. I'm certain.'

'Got a specific date in March?' Hadriana asked. But I shook my head. 'Fine then. Are we ready to go, because we have seconds before the gate closes and I'd rather get this over and done with.' Hadriana told us, as the grains of sand began to fall gently to the centre of the star.

'Where are we going?' Darren asked her, poking around to look at the falling sand. 'And what's the date?

'To the past-and, the date is 1825, sixty. JUMP!' she suddenly yelled as the sand swirled up again.

Feeling my arms unlock, I waited until Hadriana, Darren and Tyr jumped into the swirling sand. Giving Etrician a worried look, he shrugged and together we jumped in after them.

Impenetrable darkness encapsulated us as we zoomed backwards in time. It was a stomach-wrenching experience and to be frank, I felt sick. Having no sense of direction, my body feeling I was pulled in every direction, I yelped as something or someone grabbed my ankle. Then without warning, a bright golden light smothered me, crawling up from beneath me it rapidly spread. I felt a strange tightness from both sides, engulfing my torso, arms and legs, but didn't think anything of it.

Then before I knew it, I was standing on grass. My eyes adjusted to a balmy partially cloudy day. It was considerably warmer with the taste of sea-salt and a hint of dampness in the air. Breathing in the freshness, I had forgotten how clean it was compared to the 21st century. Looking down I gasped at the state of my attire. I had new clothes. A high-waist bluebell coloured dress that draped down to the ground with a bow at the back that was patterned with thin vertical black stripes and puffy long sleeves. My feet were scrunched into a pair of high knee black boots with a small heel.

I was in a park that sounded so quiet and sedate, no honking cars, no buses or vans or anything that resembled large annoying mechanical machines. Large horse chestnut trees were dotted around the edge of the park; the tips of the leaves were budding showing spring was around the corner. Also in spite of the time I was in, I was quite aware this wasn't Switzerland.

In the distance on the other side of the park, a few people walked on a small muddy footpath that ran around the edge. A man dressed in a fawn-coloured suit with a cane and tweed hat was guiding a slender woman with a pale blue bonnet and a long lemon high-waist dress with little frills on the sleeves. I smiled at the loving serenity of the past. How I missed it.

I spotted the others looking bewildered at their attire. Tyr and Darren wore similar clothes as the man on the opposite side of the park; however, both of them wore grey suits with a travelling coat and a black silk top hat. They wore the epitome of gentlemen's fashion.

Hadriana looked beautiful and I did envy her. She was wearing a cream high-waist dress with forget-me-not blue flowers at the hem and along the sleeves. A lovely detailed shawl wa draped around her shoulders and she carried a matching parasol. Her long chocolate brown locks were neatly curled up on top of her head.

'What the?' I heard Etrician gasp from behind me. Turning around I gasped in fright at the sight of him. Etrician was dressed just as smartly as the others were, but he looked so out of place and he hated dressing smart.

'What have you done to him?' I yelled at her in anger. 'Why is he dressed like that?'

Shocked at the sight of Etrician, she shook her head. 'It's the magic of the sand, don't look at me. When Grandfather Time travels in time, the sand helps you blend into the past or the future.'

Frowning, I headed over to him and gently touched his smart grey jacket. 'This isn't you,' I said to him softly. 'You look smart and you are clean-shaven for once.'

With a puzzled face, he touched his cheek. 'Smooth as a baby's bottom,' he chuckled. Grabbing my chin gently he then lifted it so our eyes met. He smiled, 'I won't look like this for long.' Embracing me, I hugged him tightly but then quickly, I pulled away. 'What's wrong?'

'You don't even smell like the earth,' I sighed in displeasure.

'Will you two stop it,' Hadriana snapped. 'You're not meant to act like that in public. A polite smile, a waving of a fan to hide your blushed face, a quaint flirtatious giggle and that's it. No holding hands, just the offering of an arm, certainly no bum grabbing, no grinding or any cheap twenty-first-century pick-up lines. It's 1825, the first of March,' Hadriana smiled, trying to brush the creases out of her skirt. 'And we need to go to Anstey's Cove to check out this skeleton. So,' she said softly, her tone of voice changing so dramatically I was unsure of what she was going to say next. 'One of you offer your arm or you will look rude,' she said hissing to Darren and Tyr.

'And for your information, I know how to act in this century. You think I was born yesterday?' I shouted. 'Why does EVERYONE think they know things better than I do and I'm OLDER then they are?' I complained.

'Well, I'm older than you and I know more things than you,' Etrician chuckled.

'Shut up,' I said trying to suppress a smile as I slapped him teasingly on the arm.

'I'll do it,' Tyr smiled, giving her a small bow. 'Darren isn't old enough to know the basics of etiquette.'

'Sod off,' Darren spat. 'I'd do it if Saskia was here,' I heard him mumble.

Something then clicked in my brain. 'Hang on a minute,' I shouted, moving to stand in her way as she and Tyr were about to make a move. 'How did we get to England? You said that the sand doesn't transport us to different places, so shouldn't we be standing in your castle cellar?'

Smiling at me in a conniving way, Hadriana shoved her hand down her top and pulled out a bottle of what looked like gold dust.

'Oh yeah because shoving your hand down your cleavage isn't a slutty thing to do in this century unless you're a prostitute,' Darren spat at her. 'Some etiquette that is.'

Ignoring him, she held the bottle out to me, 'a little Stardust.'

'How do you get these things?' I gasped, grabbing the bottle to inspect it. 'It's next to impossible getting hold of Stardust. Oh, dear Atlas!' I smiled in jubilation. Only once in my life had I seen Maat bless a falling star. I was in Egypt having a debate with Hapi as he wasn't doing his job when one night a large bright shooting star flew over the Nile and was caught by Maat before it struck the ground. Blessing it, the star turned into dust and was placed in a lapis lazuli and ivory coffer. Maat explained to me that Ancients used stardust, but that sometimes she kept some for herself to make wishes for the people of Egypt, which was dangerous. For something, so pure and magical used in such a silly way, was beyond my comprehension. However, in spite of all that, it was such a rare occasion to see I felt truly honoured.

'I don't get it,' Darren said.

'Stardust is used for making dreams or wishes come true,' Tyr explained to him. 'It's extremely rare and those who possess it must use it with caution. It's enormously dangerous.'

'How so?'

Feeling a snap of annoyance at his naivety, I turned to him holding up the bottle. 'Anything you want, anything you desire, any dream that you've had could all come true with a sprinkling of this. When you've reached the point where you've got everything you've wanted, you'll search for more things to get and then after that, it'll become like an infectious disease. I want, I want, I want. If everyone on the planet had everything they wanted, it would be a very sad lonely world. Myths, legends, what we stand for will be non-existent and the world will fall into chaos. This little bottle of dust is nearly on par with the destructive herculean power of the Staff of Zeus. So Darren, in answer to your question that is why it is extremely dangerous, also it answers my question as to how we got here, Hadriana wished us here to England.' Giving her back the bottle, she placed it down her top and took Tyr's offering arm.

With a frightened look on his face Darren muttered, 'Damn, I'm sorry I asked.'

'Best you know now than later,' Tyr smiled clapping him on the back.

With Etrician holding his arm out for me, I placed it lightly on top and he guided me along the dirt path with Darren, Hadriana and Tyr trailing along behind us. Clearing the park, we came to a road and I smiled at the lack of concrete. In the dirt, there were wheel tracks of horse-drawn carriages and hoof prints that scattered in different directions. Debris of small rocks, leaves, and the occasional stick littered the ground, but there was no point in avoiding them or swerving them as you would in a car. So many things that I had forgotten being in this century that made me think how unfortunate I was living in the twenty-first century. I missed the old days. I missed the times when the oceans were clean of oil spills when nuclear warships weren't firing torpedos at one another. When whales weren't choking on plastic waste.

On land, it had changed so much I could hardly keep up. For example, automobiles were rare, the lack of fumes was refreshing, the tarmac was nonexistent, cobbled streets were in abundance and nature was thriving. People in the twenty-first century took things for granted. With constant electricity, warmth and digital entertainment, it is a wonder how they still managed to converse with each other.

As we rounded a corner of the road, we came to a large wooded area that seemed to stretch down to the coast. The water was calling me and I was eager to join it. Looking askance at Darren I saw him reach out and touch his sleeve where underneath was the Aqua Stone bracelet. He must feel something too.

Tyr pointed to a small wooden sign that read, "Anstey's Cove," at the top of a steep path that snaked down to the beach. 'Come on,' he took hold of Hadriana's hand, which was not very proper, and led her down the path where large trees failed to stop the dimming March sunlight piercing through the canopy above.

A cacophony of birds sang and twittered around the pine-smelling copse, and as we neared, I heard the sound of waves crashing onto sea-beaten rocks. 'We're near,' I laughed, as I sprinted onwards, Darren hot on my trail. My heart pounded in my chest as I neared the ocean, I felt the thunderous continuous beat of the thrashing tide against the sand. The new whipped up spray delivered a fresh scent of saltwater to my nostrils and I instantly felt at home.

Coming to a stop just by some ragged red coloured cliffs, I stared out at the ocean and felt elated.

Breathing heavily from running, Darren came to my side and stared out at the ocean with me. His eyes were ablaze with wonder and awe, he longed for the sea just as much as I did. Like a child wanting and longing for something for so long, I grabbed his hand to jump into the cascading waters below, but before I managed a single step, a warm hand gripped my arm stopping me.

'Are you insane,' Etrician shouted, as he yanked me back. 'It's still daylight and if people see a woman in a blue dress fall into the ocean it could raise a lot of questions, not to mention it'll damage the timeline.'

Pulling away from his grip, I rubbed my pained forearm and moved away from him. He was right of course. 'Fine. I get it. So the cave, it has to be around here somewhere,' I said to them, trying to veer onto a good conversational topic.

Hadriana nodded and swiftly moved away, with us following her. The four of us came to a manmade walkway that wound its way like a white unnatural coastal path on the edge of the beach. Pounded by roaring tides, throwing driftwood further onto the pebbly sands, carrying seaweed along with it, I noticed that the tide was on its way out.

Behind me, Darren looked out towards the sea and sighed, but he had a frown on his face. 'What's wrong?' I asked, slowing my pace so he could catch up to me.

'Something's bothering me,' he said, not looking at me. 'I remember that the mermaid skeleton was found by a group of... adventurers or something like that.'

'Pioneers? Treasure hunters?' I added as adventurers weren't the right word for people wandering into a cave.

'Treasure hunters,' he smiled snapping his fingers. 'They were treasure hunters, but by going into the past, what if they weren't a group of men who discovered it? What if they were, well us?'

His question made me stop and he smacked into me. 'That's a very good point,' my mind reeling with new information to process. What if he was right? What if these treasure hunters weren't humans, what if they were us from the past? 'Curse it all,' I groaned, getting an instant headache, 'I hate time travel.'

Rubbing my forehead, I shielded my face from the sun that now blared out from the trees to the west as it was beginning to set. Frowning at a darkened red crack in the cliff straight ahead of me, I stared at it for a few more seconds before realising what I was seeing. 'Oh my Atlas, it's the cave!'

Not wanting to get her dress wet, Hadriana insisted that we all waited until the tide was out enough to go searching inside it. Etrician had joined us at this point as we all sat on little metal benches that looked out towards the sea.

'I just want to jump in,' Darren said motioning with his hands in a diving position, 'then just keep swimming. I'll swim to somewhere warm.' I nodded but Etrician was right. We'd bring attention to ourselves and mess up the timeline. 'I just keep thinking, will I be myself again, will I be able to become who I was before?'

Sighing, I didn't answer his question but instead said, 'If that time comes, make sure that it's your choice and yours alone. Don't let anyone hold you back I mean. If Saskia–'

'Ah,' he said sadly looking away from me. 'She knows how I feel about her, but I don't get why she loathes me so much. I've tried to do everything for her but still, she turns me down at every corner. We've been through hell and back, all of us have and everyone has found someone apart from Saskia and me.'

'And you think it's natural for you two to pair up since everyone else has?' I asked him, with a raised eyebrow.

'Well no. But, I do care for her, like a lot, but she just doesn't like me in the way that I like her. It sucks.'

It was dusk by the time the tide had receded enough for the five of us to enter the cave. Hadriana complained that there were too many tide pools as she frequently stepped in them. 'I wanted to keep my dress dry.'

Rolling my eyes, I told her I could dry it for her but she ignored me.

'So, these treasure hunters why would they come to a cave down here in the first place?' Darren voiced aloud. 'Surely piracy was over with by then.'

'They were-' Etrician began.

'Who said they were treasure hunters?' Hadriana asked me with a curious look.

'I did,' Darren piped up. 'I remember reading about it in the library in London. The ones who found the mermaid skeleton, they were treasure hunters, which makes me think that they may have been us.'

Hadriana's head whipped in his direction, a look of pure terror on her face. 'We cannot change the past. It's already messed up. It can't be us. If the skeleton is there then we must keep coming back every night to see if it's this point in Hannah's timeline and the O.M.C.'s timeline that is altered. If not, we have to think of something else.'

'Why is it that I'm getting the feeling that you have been back in the past more than I can count?' I asked her.

Shrugging in response she replied, 'If you want objects of good market value, you need to get them when they have come into existence. If I hadn't had come across the power of the ley lines, I would be poor and my business pathetic.'

I sauntered onwards. Arriving at the entrance of the cave first, I stepped carefully inside the puddle filled floor. The cave was more like a large fissure where the water had forced it open bit by bit over thousands of years. Barnacles and limpets had clung to the lower half of the soaking wet walls. The stench of drying out seaweed made me feel right at home.

'Etrician, I need some of your fluorescent rocks, please,' I asked.

'Excuse me please Darren.' After some shuffling of feet, Etrician brushed my arm and slapped a hand onto the wall beside me. Bright green rocks began to sprout beneath his hands, illuminating the cave. Peering inside, Hadriana stood beside me and together, we continued into the small fissure.

I wondered how a mermaid got to this part of Britain. They knew that they had to stay away from humans, but to be this careless and die in a cave... that was the strangest thing. Mermaids and mermen don't die in this plane. They are immortal.

As we moved closer, it was becoming increasingly difficult for the others to follow us, 'You're going to have to get out,' I informed them. 'There's hardly enough room for two of us, let alone five.' With a few sighs of annoyance, the others backed out of the cave.

The fissure, I noticed, only cut in so deep into the rock; it seemed the sea was still carving out the cave. Before I took another step, Hadriana pointed to the ground beneath me. 'Look,' Tainted with age and covered in molluscs were the weathered bones of the bottom half of a large fish. Bending low, Hadriana moved out of the way so the green light shone on the bones. My eyes raked the bones and I sighed. It was definitely part of the merfolk, but as I glanced at the skeleton of the upper body, something struck me ill. With the skull laying on its side pointing to its right, the right arm was across its body and there, on the joints of the wrist was a silver bracelet, with an Aqua Stone, set in the middle.

Cringing I looked away as Hadriana suddenly saw what I had seen. 'I had wondered if it was a hoax but I guess not.' A dark morbid silence enveloped us and I was troubled by what I was seeing and also how it had happened. 'Are you going to tell-'

'No,' I gasped as I reached out and gently took the bracelet off the skeleton. 'I'm not going to say a word and neither should you. No one needs to know and definitely not Darren. How would you feel if you saw your skeleton?'

CHAPTER TWENTY

TRUDGING OUT OF THE CAVE, HADRIANA AND I HAD MADE A PACT NOT to say a word about the bracelet that was concealed in my dress. Etrician gave me a strange look as I exited the fissure and headed towards the others who were sitting on some nearby limpet covered rocks.

'I'm guessing it's in there, the mermaid skeleton?' Darren asked. With a quick response, we both nodded. 'Right, so now what?' he asked as we joined them. 'Are we going to head back to the future?' he abruptly stopped himself and burst out laughing. 'I love that film.'

'Er no-' Hadriana frowned at him. 'I think its best that we check into an Inn for a few days and see if we can find these people who destroy the skeleton.'

'What if they destroy it without our noticing?' Tyr asked her. 'What's your backup plan then?'

She flashed her dazzling teeth. 'Not to worry, I have an old nag to help me out. Just don't tell her I said that.'

Inwardly groaning that she had a centaur friend running around Torbay somewhere, we headed back towards the road, Etrician purposefully lagging to talk to me.

'You are in deep thought,' Etrician whispered, stating the obvious.

I nodded, glancing at the back of Darren's head as he Tyr and Hadriana were having an argument about which hotel to stay in for the night. Darren was adamant for a four-star hotel with an en-suite bathroom while Hadriana was screeching at him that en-suite didn't exist and hotels were non-existent; that their real names were called Inns.

Feeling that it was safe to tell Etrician, I hung back a little more. 'The skeleton... it was visible.'

'So it is a mermaid then?'

Looking at him, I shook my head. 'Merman.'

'How can you tell?' he asked.

'He was wearing a bracelet, a bracelet with an Aqua Stone set in it.' With wide eyes, he stared Darren, unsure of what to say. 'And before you ask, no mermaid or merman would wear one of those, there's no need. Hannah and Darren are the only ones who have one. That skeleton in the cave is Darren in his future, but he's ended up in the past. I don't understand it and I don't like it. Someone or something is going to mess with time.'

The darkness had completely engulfed us now. As the waxing moon began to rise into the sky, its feeble rays only cast a small amount of light for us to see where we were going.

'There's something else you need to tell me,' he urged. 'I am your confidant as well as your lover. Do not keep me in the dark. You know about this,' he said gently touching the mark on my back. 'Tell me please, I wish to help.'

'I know my fate. Garrick told me last night. They will capture me eventually and I will be controlled.'

'No, I won't allow it.'

I put a gentle finger to his lips. 'Do not deny this for your peace of mind. It will happen. It's just a case of when. There is one thing you can do for me.'

He didn't say anything.

Staring into his deep eyes, the next words that would spill out of my mouth would hurt him more than destroying a thousand acres of arable land with oaks thousands of years old. 'Banish me.'

'No,' he said quickly, definitely shaking his head. 'No, never no, don't even ask me NO!' he shouted, suddenly reaching out and grabbing my shoulders, shaking me as though he was trying to rid my mind of my request. 'Don't even think about it, Thera! Don't you dare think to even ask me!'

'Please,' I begged, tears leaking out of my eyes. 'Please do this for me, I can't...' I gasped, trying to get the words out, 'I can't live with myself knowing what will happen if they use Santorini and me together, if they collect us together, it's the end anyway. Forget the fact that we can open up this prison to release this entity. We can do incalculable damage to the world, we could wipe out entire cultures; I cannot have that on my conscience.'

'I can't banish you down there, it's not like the abyss for you,' he said biting his bottom lip and pinching his eyes to stop himself from crying. 'You won't get any leniency because you're a legend. Once you're banished, that's it forever.'

'I know, I know, but at least I won't be able to hurt anyone,' I told him, as I clasped his hands, bringing them to my lips to kiss. 'Please Etrician. Please do this for me.'

Grabbing my waist, he pulled me close to him, staring intently into my eyes; full of deep sorrow. 'I could never hurt you. I cannot do what you ask of me. I'm sorry, I'm so sorry.'

'Can you two hurry up!' Hadriana's voice boomed from ahead.

Hadriana didn't ask what we were talking about and I was grateful. Catching up to her, the others watched a man in a dark scruffy-looking overcoat shuffle towards us holding a long metal pole with a small light on the end of it. Lighting the few street oil lamps that dotted the edge of the road, he tipped his hat as we walked past.

'They only light these lamps for the houses here, but we need to find some tavern or inn.' Tyr pointed out. 'Though Thera, if you want to take watch over the cave, you should go.'

'What?' Hadriana and Etrician yelled, staring between myself and Tyr.

The Norse God shrugged. 'She needs to go home. She's safe in this century. I think she should take Darren with her.'

'Have you got sand in your head?' Hadriana reprimanded him. 'Thera cannot babysit a merman who will be inclined to entice women to their deaths. I think it is utterly preposterous you even contemplating for her going back to the sea,' Hadriana shrieked like a hawk.

'I LIVE THERE!' I shouted at her, but I neglected to tell them my true feelings. More than anything, I wanted to see my brother. Turning on my heel I headed back towards the cave. 'Go and find your bed Hadriana and bleedin' lie in it! Come back tomorrow night, I'll be there,' I shouted behind me.

Hearing footsteps behind me, I turned and saw Darren's beaming face bounding towards me. 'I'm coming with you, sod the others.'

Reaching the beach, I inhaled the smell of the salty air that gently caressed my face and I felt instantly content. As I walked along the pebbly seaweed strewn beach, I heard Darren crunch in my wake, but as I neared the water's edge I stopped and looked towards the fissure. I still had the bracelet that I took from the skeleton. If I went into the water with it, there was a high possibility that it would glow.

Thinking of a quick excuse to check the cave, I hurried back at an awkward trot. Carefully stepping inside, I felt for a niche in the walls to put the bracelet and my shoes away. Hurrying back to Darren, I saw him sitting on the beach, inches from the water's edge, staring forlornly at the white horses that splashed effortlessly onto the soft red sand.

'I won't be me again, will I?' he asked, not looking at me. Not understanding what he was talking about, I stood there motionless waiting for him to elaborate. With a heavy sigh, he continued. 'I remember that moment in Ireland... I didn't want to listen to you, I didn't want to come back on land. What if it happens again?'

I sat on the damp sand next to him. 'I can't have you running amok in the past, especially other mermaids that may catch your eye.'

Chuckling, he shook his head. 'I only have my eyes on someone I can't have. Sea and sky don't mix. It doesn't matter if she has any affiliations with the water too. We're the complete opposite.'

'No, you're wrong,' I corrected him. 'Sea and land are complete opposites and I should know. Etrician and I have our disagreements.'

'You've been together a long time, haven't you?' he asked softly, as the waves thrummed against the sand.

I nodded and stared at the sand below. 'For many, many years, but we've also separated for many, many years. We have our arguments like normal humans, but the time span is a little excessive. The longest I've been with him was nearly a thousand years. Meeting him in Norway was completely out of the blue. I didn't expect him to show up, I didn't even know if he knew what we were doing. He's been helping me through this.'

Darren remained quiet and for some unknown reason, I decided to tell him my true feelings.

'I'm frightened.' I said simply. 'I'm frightened of losing myself to the staff, losing my abilities to evil beings. I don't know why Maynard would want to do this, I cannot fathom his motives. But if this Cabinet of Idols has us included, then the world will cease to be. There is one thing that Etrician can do to stop me. I need to be put in a place where no one can use me or my powers. I asked him, but he refused.' I smiled sadly. 'He doesn't want to cause me pain.'

A deafening silence formed between us. My mind reeled in conversations I'd had with myths and legends in the past; trying to remember if they were powerful enough to stop me. But I could think of none that were in this plane, they'd all left.

'What about being commanded?' Darren asked me softly. 'Like a Siren's command. Would that work on you?'

I hadn't thought of it before. Yes Sirens were myths and they did possess incalculable power, so it was no wonder why they made one the leader of their group. But could Tara help me? After a few minutes thought of believing it myself that she could do it, I was stumped by the awful reality that Tara was now human and vulnerable.

'Neither Tara nor Saskia can help me,' I sighed, as I stood up staring at the calm ocean where ripples from the moon reflected dancing rays of light across my eyes. 'They are human and they must stay in the house.'

Darren brushed the sand from his clothes, which I thought was odd considering he was going to follow me into the ocean. 'What about sirens in the others plane?' he asked, moving to stand in front of me, getting my complete attention. 'The plane could be opened up now as we're in the past.'

With the sudden realisation dawning on my face, my heart thrummed madly in my chest. Beaming with happiness, I grabbed Darren and hugged him. 'Thank you! You're right, it is open now! Come, we must go there now, we must find out,' I told him, grabbing his hand and dragging him to the sea.

The cold salty waves splashed up my legs as we waded into the water, I felt instantly better, as though all my worries and cares were flowing out of me, instantly replaced by calm contentment. With the sea at our midriffs, my forget-me-knot blue skirt puffed out with air behind me, making me look like a strangely patterned buoy. Letting go of Darren, I saw his vexed face as the bracelet on his wrist suddenly beamed blue. The light quickly encased his body and with the following sound of a great tear of his trousers, Darren flopped into the sea, unable to stand anymore. Taking his soggy clothes, I took them back to the cave and placed them near my shoes.

Bringing up the cold waters to engulf us I carried us out into the sea, so Darren could get his bearings. Within seconds, I heard the ocean's myths gabble in my mind, but I had to shut them off. The Thera of this century was still very much alive and very much a part of the ocean. If she was aware of me being here, I was in trouble.

'*This is so cool,*' Darren yelled in my head, as he swam around me in circles, flicking his tail in my face.

'*Modulate your tone in your mind please,*' I cringed as I swam next to him. '*Come here, I have something to show you.*'

With arrogance in his voice, very similar to Dagen's, he replied, '*I can't understand how I would be able to see anything in the dark. Is it a trick question with you?*'

Seconds later Darren was close enough for me to reach out and grab him. Yelping in fright, I ignored him and placed my right palm on his forehead. '*This is what I want to show you,*' I told him, as I sent memories to his mind. '*Merfolk can live a long time, they are immortal because of what they can do. They survive by stealing love, which is eternal.*'

'*What?*' Darren gasped, sounding bemused and scared by my words. '*Stealing love, how do they steal love?*'

Producing memories I had from years ago, I showed Darren the circumstances that happened to various humans when they were exposed to mermaids. '*Mermaids have two songs, song of luring and song of misery. The song of luring entices both genders of humans to them. Once they are in the ocean, the merfolk work as a team to steal love directly from the heart.*' At that point, I showed Darren a mermaid and a merman placing their slippery webbed hands on the chest of an unconscious human male. A strange pink light seemed to leave the unknown man and flow directly into their hands. As they did so, a frown appeared on his face as all the love he had for friends, family or even the occasional tipple of rum before bed, was stolen from his heart.

At that juncture, I lifted my palm off Darren's head. He had seen enough to not ask questions about himself and what he would do if he ever remained in this form. Darren could probably figure out as much as his understanding would allow him, but sooner or later the questions would start and I would be the only one he turned to.

'*Damn,*' he gasped pointlessly in his mind. '*Are we... are merfolk created without hearts?*'

'*No, they are created without the capability of loving. So they steal it.*' I explained though I found it interesting that though in his present form, he didn't consider himself a merman. Puzzled, I took his hand. '*You've met Poseidon before have you not?*'

'*Y-yes,*' he stammered, sounding uncertain. '*But he didn't acknowledge me, he was talking to Hannah most of the-*'

'*Good, let's pay him a visit,*' as I used my magic to phade us through the water.

Yelling in fright at the sudden, abrupt motion of a whirlpool as I closed the distance of four thousand miles of water the feeling quickly vanished as we arrived to witness the brilliant luminous from the grand palace of the Ocean.

With its dozens of beautifully decorated turrets, sparkling crystal domes where balls and parties were thrown in jubilation, that usually lead to anti-social behaviour, Darren and I swam down to the enormous front gates.

The Ocean Palace was the only sanctuary at the bottom of the M.A.R, or the Mid-Atlantic Range, the longest and tallest underwater mountains in the entire planet. Santorini and I created the palace for myths who wished to stay in this plane. Big enough to house hundreds of water-related myths from various cultures throughout time; it was also directly over the main portal to the other plane, which connected the three most important tectonic plates, the Eurasian Plate, the African Plate and the North American Plate.

The two merman guards at the front of the guard tower saluted me as I approached them, but as I swam past, they blocked Darren with their spears. 'It's alright boys, he's with me.'

Begrudgingly letting him through, Darren gave them shifty eyes as he passed and quickly caught up to swim right beside me, his brown tail whipping fluently.

The dazzling azure coloured gates began to creek open as we advanced to them. Passing through Darren moved behind me as Water Nymphs, merfolk and a few myths swam by, acknowledging me with a curt nod.

Swimming right up to me and looking rather bemused that I was here, was a Water Nymph called Gatrayer. An attractive auburn-haired nymph, with a timid disposition who looked after the Western Mediterranean shores, I recalled asking her to stay at the Ocean Palace for a few years to get to know the other water-related myths. '*What brings you here mistress?*' she nodded curtly.

'*I need to see Poseidon,*' I said.

'*You bring a…*' she began as she took in the sight of Darren then frowned at him. Looking at him up and down, she gave me a puzzled look but didn't question it. Not introducing him, I bid her goodbye and left without another word.

'*Well cheers,*' Darren said testily behind me, '*that was rude.*'

'*I can't introduce you to myths in this century you fool. Think of the consequences,*' I snapped back. '*No merman has got such a common name as*

Darren and I'm not in the mood to create lies at the moment in time. They only lead to more lies and that would be troublesome.'

'*Sorry I was such an annoyance to you,*' he said in an upset tone.

'*You're not an annoyance Darren; you're cumbersome, in the nicest possible way. I cannot introduce you to any Tom, Dick and Harry that swims by.*'

Heading down the large glorious entranceway that glittered in the faux light from magical shaved pearls that were embedded in every inch of the walls, we came to a set of glistening large double doors that were guarded by two more mermen.

Nodding at the sight of me, they moved out of the way to open the doors but gave Darren a cautious look. Reaching out to grab Darren's hand, I pulled him forward. '*Stay close,*' I warned him. Doing as I asked, Darren kept right behind me, keeping a wary eye on the other myths that were swimming around.

Entering into the vestibule of the vast maze of corridors laid out in every direction to kitchens, bedrooms, shops and other necessities Santorini and I provided, I motioned for Darren to swim with me to the left. '*We need to head up,*' I told him.

'*Why couldn't we have swum to the top outside, instead of entering the palace and getting funny looks from everyone?*' Darren asked as Lir, Sinann and Boann went past us, giving strange looks in our direction, proving Darren's point perfectly.

'*Well for one because it's rude and secondly, if you even attempted to swim to the turrets at the top, you would get frozen by magic. Santorini and I ensured that protocols were in place when anyone stayed or visited this place. We don't want intruders.*'

Winding our way up to the tower where Poseidon resided, I inwardly groaned at the prospect of meeting the most pompous myth I ever had the unfortunate pleasure of knowing. With his stupid tuft of a beard, his bushy eyebrows, steely grey eyes and rotund belly, the Greek God of the seas was so frustratingly annoying to talk to.

Approaching four heavily armed guards, all mermen with very beefy looking torsos, one brave merman swam in front of me, giving Darren a cautious glance. '*My Lady,*' he inclined his head towards me.

'*We wish to see Poseidon.*' Raising my eyebrow, I remained silent.

'*Very well, my lady.*'

Without another word, they let Darren and I pass and opened the doors. *'My lord. Lady Thera and her guest wish to have an audience with you,'* one of the guards bellowed in my head.

I quickly whipped out my hand to form an impenetrable bubble of water around Darren. The magic that Poseidon insisted while staying here, was that he was to live in the air and not water. So, Santorini and I developed a magical barrier that kept the air in one room and the water in the other.

Dripping water on his expensive-looking blue and white rug, I smiled and looked up to see the pompous old trout being fed red grapes by a maid, who giggled each time she plucked a juicy grape and popped it into his mouth. I scowled. I hated the way Poseidon treated women, especially his wife, but then again it made sense that Amphitrite left him for the other plane hundreds of years ago.

The only thing I had to give Poseidon credit for was his taste in decor. His entire room was decorated in thousands of coloured shells and magical gleaming pearls that formed patterns on the azure walls and ceiling. The room wasn't exactly bare of furniture, but it wasn't packed with rubbish.

In one corner, he had a gleaming silver trident that I called his three-pronged fork that was attached to the front of a beautiful tall plinth inlaid with flecks of oyster shell. On top of the plinth was the glittering Aqua stone.

Forcing myself to avert my gaze, I looked for the one thing that I came here for. Glancing up, I saw a large silver bowl suspended from the ceiling about thirty feet off the floor. Four heavy polished chains attached around the rim, holding it in place and joining to some hefty metal rigging at the top. The chains then became one thick and much heavier chain and ran across the ceiling, meeting at a joist by the crease in the wall. It then ran down to a decorated silver lever. I noticed too, that under the silver bowl were four grooves in the floor which the bowl could easily rest on and not tip over.

'Oy Thera, what have you done to me?' Darren asked angrily in my mind as he swam around in his bubble of water, trying to poke through but finding that the edge of the water was as hard as a brick.

I flicked my eyes to him. *'I can't have you flopping around like a dying fish on his carpet, can I? It doesn't matter that you can breathe out of the water, but if that bracelet changes you back, it's going to be very difficult to explain, so I suggest you be quiet and put your hands behind your back!'*

'Enough now darling one,' Poseidon said in a drawling voice to his maid. Smacking his lips, he sat up and grabbed a napkin from a table beside him.

'Oh yes it's you,' he said giving me a half-smile. 'What do you want at this hour?'

'Evening Poseidon,' I said trying to keep up my mannerism from the early 19th century. Strolling towards him, I crossed my arms and stared at him. 'Been up to much lately? Or is the other plane too boring for you?'

'Why would I tell you such privy information? It's not like you control the other plane Thera. Even you are not that worthy,' he smiled smugly.

Controlling my temper, I gave him a curt nod. 'No, but I am worthy in this plane and I have a right to know why you are here. You are doing nothing apart from lounging around in my palace.'

'Tsk, tsk,' he said shaking his head. 'Why do you always insist that everything is yours, dear Thera? It is your brother's too. Don't think yourself too important, or it'll go straight to your head. And we don't want that, do we?'

Ignoring the last piercing comment, I gestured to Darren. 'I need to use the portal if it's not in use.'

He frowned. 'For you? Dear Thera you but only need to ask me and I shall provide,' he smiled, standing up in a regal manner, a log royal purple and turquoise robe flowing down to the ground. 'And I feel honoured that you had to come to me to use my portal. Why I have never felt the need to be at your beck and call, and yet, here you ask of me.'

'The portal is not yours,' I snarled, 'it was entrusted to you to look after, to watch over when you are here in this plane-'

Sighing loudly, he interrupted what could have been a lengthy argument. 'But of course, I am doing as you wish, you asked me and only me and of course, I willingly agreed. But, why do you need the portal? There is nothing that you need from over there, is there?'

I took a deep calming breath. 'Just, get the portal up and running will you please? I need information from one of the Sirens.' I felt that I had gone too far in telling him that, but really, there was no other option. 'Please send them a message for one of them to come through.'

Clapping in amusement he sardonically smiled at me. 'Of course. But, the Sirens? Whatever can they offer you?'

'Nothing that you need to worry about.' I lied.

Strutting over to a silver lever that seemed like a blemish on the azure tiles that decorated the entire room, he turned around to shoo us back.

Pushing Darren back against the wall, we waited for him to open the portal. 'We aren't going into the other plane,' I told Darren privately as

Poseidon grabbed the lever and with a loud thunk, the bowl slowly descended to the ground.

'*Why not?*'

'Well, strictly speaking, legends like Santorini and myself don't go into the other plane. There's no need. We're going to bring a Siren into this plane, briefly, to speak with her. There are several portals around the globe. But, we need to use this one. It's less conspicuous and it is maintained properly, not like the main one in America.'

The bowl had now reached the ground and gently touched down on the grooves on the floor with a dull thunk. '*How? Where's the main one in America?*' Darren asked quickly.

I began to push the bubble towards the bowl where you could see its clear contents as a reflection on the other side. It was sunny. Briefly pausing, I looked at him. 'If it's not monitored properly, well, ever heard of an incident in Roswell, New Mexico in 1947?'

Frowning Darren hurriedly asked, '*But that was a U.F.O wasn't it, or something like that or a secret government conspiracy?*'

I shrugged. 'If you mean U.F.O being a Pegasus that flew out of the portal and ran amok, then yes, that's right. But no, not little green men from outer space.'

'*Holy cow-*'

A flash of bright light emitted from the bowl, stopping Darren mid-sentence. 'There,' Poseidon boomed across the room, slapping his hands together, quickly cutting off Darren's flabbergasted thought. 'Portal is now open and your message has been sent. Now, how long do you want the portal open for?' Striding over to the large gleaming silver bowl that measured at least fifteen feet in diameter; he touched its rim tenderly, avidly gazing inside.

'I need to have a word with someone. So, if you don't mind leaving for a few minutes, it would be appreciated.'

His eyes narrowed. Pulling out a drawer, Poseidon withdrew a little golden hourglass. 'A few minutes? Ha! My time is precious, Thera. I'll give you five minutes.'

'You'll give me until I've finished!'

Turning the hourglass over, Poseidon turned his nose up at me and withdrew from the room. Closing the door, I sat down in a chair.

'*Hey look!*' Darren pointed to the active portal, without warning, a flash of black burst out of the bowl, forming a strange hazy mist. The Siren swooped around the room, flapping her enormous wings and slowly descending, landed gently on the ground. '*Wow, she looks so much like Tara,*' Darren voiced.

'Hello, my name is Urius. I am one of the sirens who live by the southern cliffs. How may I help you? Your message said you wanted to ask some questions?' she asked, her piercing blue eyes landed on my own, as though she was trying to see into my soul. 'You aren't a myth, are you? But you are a Water Nymph.'

'Perceptive,' I smiled. 'I am a legend. My name is Thera, daughter of the Ocean herself. My questions are rather important.'

'Continue.'

I nodded soberly. 'Can your magic command me?' I asked her.

A great frown appeared on her brow and she stood up to full height. 'I do not command legends. It is not in my nature to go against the wishes of the Ancients.'

'But if you could, if you were asked, would you?' I asked, a tone of desperation in my voice, which she quickly noticed.

Staring at me, her eyes suddenly went wide and she knelt and placed a comforting hand on my shoulder. 'I have seen a glimpse of your future and you bare a heavy burden Thera but you know this, do you not?'

Replying, I simply nodded.

Urius sighed heavily then stared at Darren, the large siren shook her head sadly.

'Please, can your voice command a legend? I know, deep down, that if you tried, if you truly tried, the sirens of old, the leaders of battles, could command a legend. You could command me.' I begged her.

Deep remorseful eyes met my own and she stood, looking down on me with such regret my heart almost wept. 'Thera, Mother of Water Nymphs, please do not ask, for I fear I cannot help you.'

'But I will end up killing millions of people!' I shouted at her. 'I have to be stopped, someone has to stop me. If you know, if you've seen my future even if it's just a fleeting moment, you must be able to see what will happen.'

With angst written all over her face, as though she was having a massive battle of her own conscience within her, she took a deep breath. 'It's not your specific future that I see. I see a connection to you that's all. Thera, even if I tried, I do not think my voice can command you.'

I gazed at Urius, there was something else I needed to ask her. 'Please then what is this great burden you speak of?'

'Renita,' she said with a frown. 'Your burden is Renita.'

The shock of her name suddenly hit home and I felt such pain that I hadn't thought about her. I had promised that I would try and remember her, try and stop the Ancients erasing her from everyone's minds. Until that point, I was solely focussed on one thing and though I was torn in so many directions on what to think about, what to plan and how to respond, it didn't occur to me to remember everything all at once. Although the next words that Darren thought made this trip, seem idiotic and worthless.

'Excuse me, but who is Renita?'

Chapter Twenty-One

'What did you say?' I whispered, but Darren just shrugged. He really didn't know her. 'He is forgetting, isn't he?' I turned to Urius, her crystal eyes staring intently at me. 'One by one, they'll forget her.'

Her sad eyes closed with such empathy it was difficult not to make me cry. 'Your burden is weighty Thera, daughter of the Ocean. I give you this advice though you did not ask for it. Try not to forget who you are along your journey.'

Without another word, Urius bent down, and with a large flap of her wings, took off into air and dove headfirst into the swirling misty portal.

Poseidon came back into the room seconds after the portal closed. He eyed me suspiciously. 'Want to explain?'

'No. Thank you for assisting us.'

'Then why don't you explain that as word has it, you are currently in the South Pacific at the moment, with your brother of course. Sorting out some problems with an underwater island.'

'*Oh crap,*' Darren said in my mind.

'Clearly, you have been misinformed,' I said, trying to sound indignant. 'I'm clearly standing right in front of you.' Snapping my fingers, I moved Darren out of the room and popped his bubble. Darren tried to catch my eye as we swam through the palace. A lot of myths ogled me as I went past and whispers erupted all around.

The merman guards let us pass and finally making it out without any consequences, I phaded us back towards Anstey's Cove.

Darren and I were sitting on red rocks, his tail in the water, splashing softly. I refrained from looking around where the cave was. I needed to get my shoes back and the Aqua stone bracelet. 'Darren,' I began, wanting to try and find out what he thought about the group. 'How do you feel about Jane?'

'What do you mean? Has she said anything to you?' Chuckling at his slight paranoia, I shook my head.

'What do you think of her?'

He relaxed a little. 'Oh. Jane's just a blond-haired wimp.'

'Well, that's not nice.' I chided. 'And what do you think of the others?'

'Dagen's an arse, but that's self-explanatory. Hadriana is a vamp if ever there was one and I don't mean vampires, I mean one of those people who-'

My hand came up to stop him. 'Yes I know what you mean.'

He shrugged. 'Tyr is a decent bloke, I like him. He's down to earth even though he's a God of the Sky, and Hannah, is well, she's one of my best friends.'

An icy wind blew through me as I noticed he didn't mention Renita. 'And what about Renita? Black haired girl with beautiful eyes? The daughter of Pygmalion, who can create life from the earth?'

Darren frowned at me for a second then shrugged. 'She's attractive, I guess, but rather quiet, she tends to fade into the background.'

Inwardly sighing that he had at least clung onto some part of his memory to remember her, I responded with a weak smile. 'Renita is a very, kind, sweet girl. Don't forget her, Darren; keep a memory of her with you at all times. We all need to keep a good memory of each other to make us remember what we were like.'

'What do you mean?'

'I fear that in the dark times that are looming ever closer, we will forget ourselves. So, it's up to each of us, as friends, to remind one another of who we really are. We are all here together for a reason, to stop Rhea and Maynard from collecting legends and myths. Though I am a target, I have to be stopped, Darren.'

An uncomfortable silence descended between us and I decided to call it quits. The tide was still out which was a bad sign for Darren. 'You stay around here,' I ordered him, moving towards the beach. 'No one can see you if you stay around here and I mean in this small area. If you go out to Torquay way, you'll be seen by night fishermen and drunken sailors. There's no need for extra publicity, and you can't mess up history. Understand?'

'Yes sir,' he said, giving me a sarcastic salute.

Rolling my eyes, I made my way back to the beach. Being as quiet as I could, I went around the long ago fallen barnacle ridden rocks and peeked into the cave. Unable to see anything, I stepped inside and felt my way in the darkness. Remembering where I put my shoes, I poked around the hollow and pulled them out with the bracelet inside. Having a fleeting instinct to check, I bent down to feel for the skeleton. 'Oh no,' I gasped as I began to frantically pat around for the skull or ribcage... but I felt nothing. 'The skeleton is gone!'

With my heart beating like a hammer inside my chest. Scrambling out of the cave, I lifted my foot and stamped on the beach, hoping to send some sort of signal to Etrician, but after waiting a minute or two, he didn't come.

'Damn.' I raced back to the water's edge and picked up a small ball of seawater. 'I need to find Etrician,' I said and threw it into the air. The sphere turned and then shot inland.

Sitting on a rock, I waited for the others. It must have been at least ten minutes later when the four of them raced towards me, pelting down the leaf-strewn hill at top speed. Panting, they were unable to speak. 'I was away for maybe an hour at the most. I came back to check on the skeleton. It's gone.'

'Are you freaking kidding me?' Hadriana screeched in such a high loud pitched my ears crackled.

Darren bobbed in the sea talking to Tyr who sat on a rock as Etrician and Hadriana had headed into the cave to double-check. A strange green light emitted from it and muttering came from within.

Hurrying to them, I suddenly stopped as I noticed various sets of footprints in the sand that led to and from the cave. Bending down, I counted at least a dozen. One of them was mine, two belonged to Hadriana and Etrician and the others must be the men who destroyed the skeleton.

Unable to do much, I sluggishly walked to the cave and then stopped. Waiting for the onslaught of Hadriana. However, a few minutes later, they came out looking upset. Hadriana looked completely deflated and sat on a winkle covered rock, staring at the sand. Glancing up, Etrician sighed, placing his hands on his hips and looked at me.

'We need a plan,' he said quietly, as Tyr had seen us gathered outside of the cave, and was making his way towards us climbing over the slippery rocks as quickly and carefully as he could. I noticed that his jacket was gone and frowning I looked into the distance and saw Darren make his way towards the beach, holding what I could only assume was Tyr's jacket high out of the water.

After a few minutes and looking like a bedraggled rat, Darren joined us and sat on a rock near Hadriana. 'It's gone then,' he said, thumbing towards the cave. 'Bugger. So now what?'

'It's gone, and there are bone fragments.' Etrician replied. 'We need a plan; we need to know what to do next. Anyone have any ideas?'

Shivering slightly, Darren put his hand up, 'history cannot change. If no one knows about the mermaid skeleton, then the O.M.C won't start and neither will the T.A.T. It's probably why Hannah is disappearing. Ann Smith and Mr D.C Raleigh wrote the little red book. '

Tyr coughed and intervened, 'I have a question to put to you, I've been thinking about it before, but what if we're meant to leave it alone?'

'What?' Darren barked.

'No, hear me out,' trying to get comfortable on his jagged rocky seat, he leaned forward, 'I've been under the impression that this war between humans and myths began because of humans using the D.N.A of myths and putting it into humans and unbalancing the world. But if there is no O.M.C. if there is no T.A.T. then they'll be no war, they'll be no Maynard to become an Ancient, Rhea won't exist for what she is, Thera, you won't be marked. All of this will not exist like it is.'

Silence pressed down upon us quickly and painfully. Tyr was right in every sense of the word. Santorini and I wouldn't be separated, the T.A.T. group wouldn't be afflicted they would have gone on with their normal lives. The myths wouldn't be angry at humans for creating more myths in an obscure manner. But, something stumped Tyr's theory. 'Madagascar' I told him. 'The writings on the walls, it spoke of Maynard, history has to be as it is. It's all well and good wanting to stop all of this, but we can't, it has to happen and play out as instructed. I think that the Minister is behind this.'

There was a collective gasp, all apart from Hadriana who was angry. 'Don't blame him for this. The Minister is under Maynard's orders; they need Hannah and Darren for the Cabinet. So that theory doesn't work, try something else.'

I snapped my fingers. 'Hannah said that originally the OM.C wanted to destroy all evidence of mythological creatures. Perhaps by us coming here, we were seen and led them right to the cave, and they destroyed it because they saw us find it when instead they would have taken the skeleton?'

We all stared at one another for some other explanation, and no one said anything.

'So then we need a plan. If Darren said that the mermaid has to be discovered, who discovers it?' We all turned to Darren for the answers.

'As far as I remember, the mermaid was found by a group of treasure hunters and Father McEnery got involved, who was around this area near the quarry at the top of the hill where there are some caves. But if there are treasure hunters and the skeleton has gone then...we're screwed. The only thing I can think of is if we find another skeleton and we become the treasure hunters ourselves, and we tell the press,' he said simply.

Tyr sighed, 'we won't find another mermaid skeleton Darren they don't exist. Mermaids and mermen they are immortal, once they've spent a certain amount of years here, they leave for the other plane.'

'But... how is there a skeleton of a mermaid in the cave?' he asked, frowning in confusion at us.

Feeling my face flush, Etrician saved me. 'It is an anomaly that sometimes, mythology cannot explain. But the point is Tyr is right, there will be no more skeletons, and even if there is, it would be impossible to find one.'

Biting her nails in thought, Hadriana flicked her locks out of her face and folded her arms. 'I have an idea, but she won't like it.'

'Uh oh,' the four of us said together.

Tutting, she rolled her eyes. 'It's not like that, it's just... she will do it because she owes me a favour, but don't expect her to be nice about it.'

'Hadriana what are you babbling on about?' I asked in a snappy tone.

'Trinia, she's a chestnut centaur who lives on Dartmoor not too far from here. Etrician could probably reach her in seconds,' she glanced at him for a reply, without saying a word he nodded once. 'She can use her magic to show the illusions of the skeleton, and she can continue that illusion for as long as she wants. She's also one of the rare few who can withstand being in the presence of humans.' Our eyes glanced at Darren.

'Oh, cheers! Thanks for singling me out, not that I already feel like an utter gimp swimming around Poseidon's palace!' he shouted.

'Oh crap,' I sighed as suddenly Etrician, and Hadriana began to yell at me.

'You went to the Ocean Palace?' Etrician demanded. 'What possessed you to go there?'

Hadriana took a threatening step towards me. 'We asked you to watch the cave! You can so easily screw up the timeline, you idiot!'

'Yes I know, just shut up the pair of you!' I yelled at them, my voice clipping the nearby cliffs, which rebounded around the small forest above us. Sighing, I rubbed my eyes, shaking my head. 'I know it was a stupid thing to do. I just wanted information from someone, and I'll leave it at that. Don't ask and don't pester Darren either. Do I make myself clear?'

Opening my eyes, Hadriana and Etrician both shared a curious frown, but they nodded gently. Whipping my head to Tyr, he put his hands up in defence. 'Hey don't look at me, I don't gossip and don't look for it.'

'Good. Etrician, please go and find this centaur called Trinia and take Hadriana with you.'

'It's going to take all night to bloody find her!' Hadriana shrieked. 'Dartmoor has over one-hundred and twenty tors!'

That made me smile. 'Good. Darren, Tyr and I are going back to the inn. I want a good night's sleep. Tyr and I will go and see the good Father. Darren can stay at the inn to greet you when you get back. Any questions?'

Hadriana immediately shot her hand in the air. 'Yes, why am I going with your boyfriend? Why can't you go with him? I need my beauty sleep too.'

'For three excellent reasons. Firstly, you are a pain in the arse tonight, so I want you out of my sight; secondly, you know where this Trinia centaur lives and thirdly, it doesn't matter how many hours of beauty sleep you get you'll always be unsightly. Now, both of you go please.'

Comically, Hadriana's jaw dropped, and her eyes went wide. 'How dare you?' she screeched.

'I dare, now bog off!' I scolded her.

Etrician smirked and grabbing Hadriana around the wrist, pulled her into a nearby rock and vanished into it.

'Okay that right there,' Darren sniggered, 'that was utter genius. I'd love to see that on replay.'

Rolling my eyes, I mumbled an incoherent, 'whatever' and finding Darren's rolled up clothes, stomped back up to the inn with the boys.

Just as dawn was about to creep over the hills in the east the following morning, I was up. Dressed and sitting at a table downstairs with a cup of mead in my hand, waiting for Hadriana to turn up. A sleepy-looking Tyr was in the corner by the fireplace, yawning over his mug of elderflower cordial. Darren was still asleep in bed.

As I stared out of the murky window that gave a view of the dirt road that led down to the entrance to the beach, I stifled a yawn and asked, 'Do you think this is all a big mistake?'

Yawning at me, Tyr rubbed his eyes. 'What? What's a mistake?'

'Being here in the past, trying to sort this all out? I couldn't help but pour over our words from last night, about knowing that none of this has to happen. I can't help but think if we hadn't seen what we saw in Madagascar, would we still be in this situation? Would we have let Hannah fade out of existence if it would be to save the myths and the world?'

Blinking to get the sleep from his eyes, Tyr downed the rest of his drink and shrugged. 'I don't know why you are asking me that question when you already know the answer. If you want my opinion, you're not that callous Thera. You have an amazingly big heart. I've seen how you care for Hannah and Renita and Jane and even Darren and myself. Though I can't really vouch for Dagen and even though we all hate the guy, we do look out for him. I suppose in the time we've known each other, we've sort of become a strange family. Although, I'm not sure if we should add Hadriana into the mix.'

'Um that would be a resounding no,' I laughed.

'But I'm serious. You and Etrician are the parents, and the rest of us are your abnormal children with Dagen as our pet.'

I burst out laughing. 'Ah dear, I suppose you're right.' Sobering up slightly as I thought about the combination of Hannah and Renita, I sighed. Seeing movement outside, I moved to get a better look and saw Hadriana, Etrician and a beautiful chestnut-haired girl walk up the path.

Tyr saw what I was looking at, raising his eyebrow. 'Wow, she's terrific looking for a centaur.'

'They all are,' I chuckled. 'Centaurs hide behind their enchantments. They waylay you with their beauty. Go and get Darren, will you, please?'

Scampering up the stairs, Tyr left to get Darren as I made my way to the front door, pulling it open just as Hadriana was about to enter. 'Morning,' I smiled sardonically, looking past her to see Trinia who had disguised herself as a beautiful human. 'Greetings to you Trinia.'

Her wide earth-brown eyes locked onto mine instantly. Tilting her head as though I puzzled her, she inclined her head. 'Greetings to you Water Nymph. Hadriana has told me little about you, yet I feel I have met you before.'

I shook my head, 'I doubt it. I spend so much time in the waters I barely visit the mainland. Though when I do, I always end up making waves,' I smiled, sharing a secret memory with Etrician.

He giggled behind her, but Trinia didn't look happy. 'Your musings are atypical for a Water Nymph, perhaps an outside influence of humans?' About to open my mouth to reply, she continued as though what I would say would be uninteresting to her. 'Though, that does not matter. Perhaps I should listen to the human in question? Hadriana has explained to me what the skeleton looks like; I can only presume that you would also have an accurate account.'

'I can produce for you a picture, providing, of course, you do not show the human male,' I warned her. 'It's imperative that the details of what you see, you keep to yourself.'

Inclining her head in understanding, she smiled. 'As you wish.'

Thundering behind me, Tyr and a fully clothed Darren raced down the stairs and came to an immediate stop by the door.

'Wowza,' Darren smiled lustfully as he stared at Trinia. 'Aren't you just drop-dead gorgeous.'

Shifting her eyes to mine, she asked, 'The human male?'

I closed my eyes and nodded softly. 'Trinia this is Darren, Darren, this is Trinia. He shall accompany you while Tyr and I speak with the good Father. I shall bring him with us, as is the history of the detailed accounts of the O.M.C.' Turning to Tyr I raised an inquisitive eyebrow. 'You ready?'

'Yes, miss,' he smiled.

'Good, Etrician keep an eye on fish-boy will you please? You know what they can be like?' I sighed, as Darren ignored me and seemed to drool at the site of Trinia who by the looks of it, found him quite repulsive. 'The poor boy.'

Laughing, he nodded. 'I'm quite surprised he hasn't been that way with you?'

Blushing, I teasingly hit in on the arm. 'Please, not in front of the others.'

'Oh don't make me vomit,' Hadriana groaned.

Giving her a smarmy smile, I walked off with Tyr following behind me.

Leaving the little thatched inn, the small group headed down the quiet country road and came to the bottom by the playing field, all looking at one another in a silent gesture of good luck. The field was devoid of humans. Apart from the few birds that pecked at the ground for worms or some house cats that slunk in the undergrowth, waiting for a mindless bird to hop by to pounce on, it was a very peaceful early morning.

With dawn now fully expanding over the eastern skies, clouds patched the dazzling azure and blew a brisk breeze of salty-air in our direction. Inhaling deeply, I felt peaceful once more.

Tyr and I headed towards the quarry some thirty minutes later. 'I don't think he's going to be down in the caves. I mean, it's not like he's down there all the time is it? The good Father has other duties to attend to.' Tyr thought aloud. We came onto the main road from the previous night and was astonished to see how close we were to the quarry. It was literally right in front of us, blocked by huge stones that we did not notice.

People serenely passed by in normal-day plain clothes, the men sporting shiny leather walking boots while the women held onto their arms wearing bonnets to keep the sun off their faces. Children were playing with large wooden hoops which they slapped with sticks to keep them moving, jumping in between them for fun. A few horse and carriages passed us with snooty occupants inside; the large shire horses already looked fatigued and worn out just from pulling the carriage up the hill.

'All right, fair point if he's not there, then where is he going to be?' I asked, theatrically looking around me. 'In a house, down in the harbour, in a local village?'

'Um, in a church?' he suggested, shrugging.

Feeling a little deflated at the obvious answer, I then folded my arms and nudged him.

'Which church, there are dozens around here, and we do not have all day to check every single church and asking if a Father McEnery practices here.'

'Father McEnery?' a couple asked as they passed behind us. 'Are you looking for him?'

'Er,' Tyr asked a little confused.

I smiled sweetly and I nodded, trying to uphold a polite conversation. 'Why, yes, we are. We are new to this area and have come to...' I started, unsure of how to continue this little white lie '...ask for Father McEnery's help,' I finished, laughing airily. 'Would you perchance know where he may be?'

'Torre Abbey,' the gentleman smiled, pointing up the hill. 'It is about a mile. At the top of the road, take a left. Then go down the hill and past the harbour and Torre Abbey sands is on the right. Though Miss, it would be best if you asked for a carriage down there.'

Giving him a small curtsey, I reached out for Tyr's arm and together, we began to walk up the hill. 'This is going to be a long day, isn't it?' he moaned.

'Hush. I want to check the caves out, see if anyone is in there, just in case.'

Sighing but not arguing with me, Tyr obliged.

The edge of the quarry was rather steep and appeared extremely dangerous. A few men were dotted around below and took no notice of us as we approached. Staring up at a man-made carved hole in the rock, I laughed. 'Etrician would go bonkers if he saw that.'

'Can I help you?' came a quick unexpected voice from behind me. Yelping in shock, I turned to see a scruffy man in overalls, covered in grit and grime. 'Sorry, Miss, I did not mean to frighten you, but you really shouldn't be around here.'

'Yes, I understand. However, could you tell me, have you seen Father McEnery around? I have heard he likes to visit here.'

'He's probably down at Torre Abbey. It is a good walk though, Miss,' he said, scratching his head, where I thought I saw a flea jump off his brow and back into his hair.

'Yes I had heard it was a bit of a walk, well thank you. Come then,' I said to Tyr, pointing back to where we came.

'Excuse me, Miss. Couldn't I perhaps offer you a ride?'

Beaming in delight, Tyr and I thanked him and took him up on his offer. Not half an hour later, the quickened pace of his single skinny bay horse and a poorly patched up wooden cart, wound its way through the streets of the heart of Torquay where the people busied themselves with their daily business.

On the right-hand side were rolling hills that only had a few large houses dotted within the landscape. Although I noticed there was one outsized grey building surrounded by several acres of land with substantial oak trees hiding most of the building from view. The beach was just a short distance from one of the buildings.

The kind man, who introduced himself as Tom Hawkins, dropped us off just by the entrance and headed back into town. The hooves of the horse clip-clopped into the distance and with it, my heart suddenly sank. I didn't particularly fancy walking up that hill.

Entering the turreted part of the building, I approached a man in a dark suit who was standing by the door looking rather important and seemed a little miffed.

'Excuse me I was wondering if you could possibly point me in the direction of Father McEnery? I must speak to him.'

'The Chaplain is busy. Come back later,' he sniffed, looking away from me.

Letting go of Tyr's arm, I heard him sigh impatiently beside me. 'No, I will not come back later. I would like to speak with him now, it is of the utmost importance, do you not understand?'

Sniffing he scrutinised me. 'Begging your pardon, but the Cary family requires his service today. If you would like to wait, you are welcome to stay within the grounds until this evening.'

Taking a threatening step towards him, I snarled, 'You go and tell Father McEreny that I have found an abomination to God and he needs to bless the evil away. Do you understand me now, sir! He must come right this minute. I do not want to go to press with this; it is too dangerous. I need the good Father's guidance.'

Raising his eyebrows, the man took a step back, a little wary of me and nodded. 'V-very well, please wait here.'

As he walked off, his feet clipped on the marble flooring and hurrying into a room off to the side. Grabbing my arm, Tyr pulled me to the side and whispered hurriedly in my ear. 'I think that was one of the family's butlers you just threatened.'

'So?' I asked, 'we don't have time to mess around.'

Pacing around the entranceway, Tyr and I studied some of the local paintings that hung regally in the vestibule; all signed by the painters and all in large gold plated frames. A few people in rather upper-class looking attire, walked casually around, giving Tyr and me odd stares as we lingered there in silence.

Growing impatient and thinking of ways to curse that idiotic servant, a door creaked open, and there stood a priest, whom I instantly took to be Father McEnery.

'That is the lady there,' I heard the servant say, inclining his balding head in my direction.

'Thank you,' the Father said in a solid Irish accent and walked quickly towards us. Tyr stood to attention and bowed, greeting him. 'How do you do?' the Father asked.

Sensing Tyr's eyes on me, I had to ensure that I was to play the part perfectly. I had to prove naive and scared at what I discovered in Anstey's Cove, and I had to plead with him to come with us. 'Father, my name is Martha Stewart,' I lied, already feeling horrible that I was lying to a priest. 'My friends and I were down at the beach in Anstey's Cove just last night. My friends think themselves treasure hunters, but indeed Father they found an abomination!'

Frowning, he turned to Tyr, who confirmed it with a quick nod. 'Tis true sir. We found something which I am afraid to say goes against the Lords' work. It is as my good friend here says an abomination.'

Offering to walk with him, the two of us led him out of the building and back outside into the breezy March morning. 'Pray, my children, tell me what you found.'

'A skeleton Father, a skeleton that is part human and part…fish.' I whispered. 'It is a mermaid, sir if ever we found one.'

At first, the Father shook his head and repeatedly said, 'No, you are mistaken my child,' but our pleading words somehow forced him to at least agree to see the abomination for himself, just to put our minds at ease.

Thankfully borrowing a carriage from the Cary family, Tyr and I sat comfortably as it bounced along the roads, heading back up towards the top of the hill. However, as comfortable as we were Father McEnery asked and re-asked us what we had seen, but we kept to a short story and not elaborating on it; there was not much else to tell the poor man.

Reaching the road that led down the Anstey's Cove, the three of us got out and trotted down the steep lane, trying to search for the others who were hopefully still on the beach.

The winds began to pick up, and the waves crashed onto the beach. I could make out the cave, and the waters were closing in. I whispered to Tyr to halt the winds while I calmed the waters and pushed the tide out just for an hour or so.

Meeting the others on the beach, they each introduced themselves with false names. While Hadriana and I hung back, as it was unladylike to accompany men on such an egregious revelation, she hurriedly explained to me what Trinia had done.

'She has created an almost perfect replica of the skeleton, minus the bracelet,' she said, frowning as we watched the men head into the cave. 'As per the history of the O.M.C's account of the skeleton, Darren has informed us that it will be removed from the cave and housed within the confines of the Torquay Natural History Society building. Trinia has promised to stay with the skeleton until it pans out when it has been ordered to be destroyed.'

'Good,' I nodded nervously, still staring at the cave and hearing nothing but the roaring ocean waves that were smashing against the beach. 'They don't have long before the tide comes in. I can't keep it at bay for long.'

Not a few minutes later, Tyr, Darren, Etrician and Father McEnery came out of the cave, the poor Father looking rather grave. He shook Etrician and Darren's hands, turned on his heel and trotted towards us.

'Good morning, ladies,' he bowed quickly then headed back up the small lane.

Watching him go, the others approached us with smiles on their faces. 'He is going to write an account and send it to the Bishop of Exeter,' Etrician told us.

'Just as the O.M.C. reported,' Darren confirmed.

Then without warning, Etrician's face suddenly turned dangerous and frightened all at once. Grabbing Hadriana and myself abruptly, he forced us to the floor. 'GET DOWN!' he shouted to the others, just as crackles of electricity shot right over our heads. Spinning around on the pebbly floor, I whipped my head around to see four men dressed in black clothing holding up their palms, pointing directly at us. Their hands still smoking.

Enraged that they had shot at us, Etrician dug up the beach in front of him and threw a gigantic rock in their direction. Soaring high into the sky, the men began to panic and were unsure of which way to run. But, unexpectedly, as though the men were not in charge of their own fate, there was a blinding flash of blue light and the men were gone, seconds before the rock crashed to the ground, severely fracturing the floor beneath.

Yelling in frustration, Etrician darted off to the place the men had been seconds before.

'What was that all about?' Darren asked as he and Tyr helped Hadriana and me to our feet.

'They have magic that shoots electricity. They're from the future, or our present, I mean, not this present but-'

'Yes, Tyr, we know what you mean.' I frowned, watching Etrician kick the broken parts of the rock back towards the cliffs over the top of our heads. 'HEY, WATCH IT!' I shouted at him. 'Getting angry isn't going to help!'

'Then what did you want me to do, huh?' he shouted back. 'Stand there and let them shoot us?' Heading towards us, the others looked quite frightened being caught out like that, and so was I. I didn't expect them to still be around, I thought they would have screwed up the past then left, but then again, if you wanted to ensure that you kept to your plans, you should see it through.

'That was them, wasn't it?' Hadriana sighed heavily. 'Those are the Minister's lackeys.'

'Oh, so you are calling him the Minister too, are you? Not Garrick then?' I snapped at her, though she didn't deserve my nastiness and shooting her a fervent look, I nodded. 'Yes, it was them, but I doubt that he would be here. If you noticed, those men didn't know what to do, they were summoned back by the looks of it. Probably going to try again in the not too distant future I would imagine.'

'How is it that they managed to get back into the past?' Darren asked when Etrician clomped back towards us, still in a foul mood.

'Maynard sent them back, no doubt. He is an Ancient.' I explained.

Tyr stared at Hadriana, but her mind was on something else. 'Thera, do you think it's safe for us to go, or should we stay here a little while longer?' he asked.

I shook my head. 'No, we need to safely move on to the next date. The centaur can mislead the good Father and anyone else until the deed is done. Darren, any suggestions?'

'1859, though still in the same area and it's guesswork on the date and month. I believe Charles Darwin visited the caves and hears about the skeleton at the Torquay Museum.'

Hadriana pulled out of her reverie. 'Trinia knows she has to maintain the illusion, but she will need guidance in the future.' Hadriana told us, as she brushed the sand from her dress. 'Oh, I give up with this stupid thing. Right, I can help with the exact date and month, because I was there when Charles gave his talk.' She smiled, 'I love it when a plan comes together.'

CHAPTER TWENTY-TWO

HADRIANA CARRIED US TO THE 22ND OF JULY OF THE SAME YEAR. Although, I was slightly uncomfortable, with a new bodice that was constricting both movements and breathing. Still situated on the beach in Anstey's Cove, there seemed fewer people around as it was a slightly cloudy, windy day.

Moving from the beach, the five of us began to hike up the annoyingly steep hill, leaving me out of breath. Having barely any grip on my soles, I clung onto the railings as though my life depended on it. Several times, I slipped on the leafy ground, hearing Darren giggle behind me.

Reaching the top Hadriana put her hands on her hips and glanced back at me. 'Well let's go, I'm starving,' Hadriana said as she strode off towards the little inn at the top.

'No, hold it,' I yelled. 'We cannot go back to the same inn.'

Turning around with a scrunched up face, which totally made my unsightly retort ring true she asked, 'What are you talking about?'

I placed my hands on my hips and glowered at her. 'You idiot, we need to go somewhere else. We've already been to that inn; we need to go somewhere closer to Trinia, which invariably will be the Torquay Natural History Society. Tyr and I passed it as we headed down to Torre Abbey.'

Tutting, she flicked a few strands of hair from her face, 'Fine whatever.'

Walking across the playing field, the group gasped as we saw how much the quarry had changed. The caves had been heavily excavated as spoil heap after spoil heap were piled one on top of another. Bones from wolves, rodents, and ancient hyenas were scattered around, sticking out of the dirt as though a strange old graveyard. Large pieces of either stalagmite or stalagmite strewn haphazardly onto the mound, seemingly they were of no consequence at all. They appeared to have been blasted out of the tunnels so excavators could get further into the chambers.

'What... what have they done?' Etrician whispered in pure rage, I was unsure of what he was going to do. 'Don't they know how old that cave system was? I... I can feel the earth screaming, as though pouring salt onto an open wound.'

Moving in front of him to block the view, I softly touched his face. 'Etrician look at me, please,' I begged. His eyes showed so much torment it was hard for me to rip him away. 'I know how you feel, but this is neither the time nor the place to get involved. What's done is done. It had to happen in this part of history and someday in the future people will look back and see the damage they have done and learn from it. That is the lesson that humans will learn they will be more tentative. But, we cannot stay here; we are of no use to the earth right now. We have the planet to save for the future.'

Closing his eyes, a single tear of pain and sadness rolled down and splashed onto my right hand. Sighing in agony, he reached up to grab my hands; cupping them in his, he kissed them softly. 'You are right.'

'I'm so sorry you have had to see this. The humans are ignorant, it's their flaw.'

Hadriana put a supportive hand on Etrician. 'Let's go then,'

In silence, we began our trek back up to the top of the hill. Etrician lagged behind as the others ploughed on ahead. He kept looking back at the quarry, disturbed at what the humans had done. 'I really am sorry,' I whispered gently. 'Humans are destructive, but a mistake will always lead to an understanding.'

A quick soft, gentle wind picked up, carrying the wonderful odours of the past around me. I smelt bread, fish, the sea, and a waft of the cornflowers that carpeted the grassy embankments of the houses we passed. Wives and husbands took strolls along the road. Those indoors rested by bay windows of their large houses with a book in their hands staring calmly out of the window. Children were running around playing with their Cup and Ball's or else gathered in a circle on the floor playing marbles or Spinning Tops. It was a lovely, quiet summer morning.

'I have something to tell you,' Etrician said quietly, out of earshot of the others. 'Are you forgetting yourself?'

The word forgetting immediately reminded me of Renita, and I held onto a memory of her. After a few seconds, Etrician gently shook my arm, waiting for a reply. 'How do you mean?'

'You are a legend, Thera.'

Frowning at him stating the obvious, I tutted and looked away. 'Yes, I know that.'

'I don't think you do.' His words were cutting and almost cold. It felt like I'd been thrown into a vat of arctic water. 'Thera, listen to me. Your world is of the sea, your life is immortal. You cannot drown; you have no need for oxygen. Does that not tell you anything?'

I only had to think about it for a moment before I quickly understood. 'I've been out of breath.' I realised it when I was walking up the hill. I had clung onto the railings, but I was pulling myself up.

'Exactly. There is no need for it. You only started doing it when you met Darren and Hannah. They are humans; they need oxygen. You are either sympathising with them by copying them or... well I don't know what else it could be, but you need to stop it. It's worrying me. I mean, it's all right to get a little fatigued now and again, if you ran a thousand miles without stopping, but really Thera, walking up a small hill?'

'Atlas your right,' I cringed from embarrassment. 'I don't know why I'm doing it, it never occurred to me.'

Etrician nodded and smiled. 'As long as you are aware of it, that's all that matters.'

Finally rounding a corner after a twenty-minute walk downhill, I pointed to the large grey stone building on the right. 'It's there, that's the Torquay Natural History Society, soon to be the Torquay Museum.'

Crossing the road, we headed inside through the archway. But were stopped by a short man with a handlebar moustache, 'I'm sorry, but the building is closed to the public today.'

We hadn't really had a plan. In all honesty, we didn't think of one, and we had now come face to face with a dilemma.

Hadriana stood up to her full height and said in a very posh voice, 'We are here to speak to one of the members of the society.' The human wasn't having any of it and tried to usher us out, but Hadriana didn't budge. 'It's a matter of importance, my good sir.'

Huffing, he stopped. 'Do you have an appointment?'

Raising an eyebrow, she replied snootily, 'We have no need of one. Now, be a good fellow and find a member for me.'

Embarrassed, I groaned and looked away.

'How dare you speak to me like that!' he said outraged, his white moustache flicking in anger from side to side.

Etrician cleared his throat and stepped in front of Hadriana. 'Forgive us, sir, but we do need to speak with a member right away.'

The man nodded, and glared at Hadriana, 'Very well, Mr?'

'Rogers,' Etrician lied, bowing a little, then offering his hand.

'Hmm. Well, Mr Rogers, please ensure this woman keeps her mouth closed when addressing others. I believe the saying should be amended to Women and Children should be seen and not heard!'

As the man left, I clipped Hadriana around the head. 'Ow, what was that for?'

'Could you be any ruder?' I told her. 'Women didn't speak like that. Not even royalty. Besides, why do we need a member of the society? Surely, we need to go and speak to Trinia?'

Glancing around to ensure that no one else could overhear she whispered, 'Charles Darwin is in Torquay on holiday. He is coming here in a few hours to do a speech on his paper, which by the end of the year, will be the most influential book known to the human world, "The Origin of Species by Means of Natural Selection." It is during this time, we need to get Charles to look at the skeleton. Right, Darren?' He nodded. 'Perfect. Once that happens, history will be back on track. But there is a slight problem.'

Realising what she was getting at, I explained to Tyr and Darren who looked baffled. 'Your past self can't see you now in this timeline.'

'Exactly. I was here when Charles gave his speech. In about four hours, I will be arriving by carriage. Half an hour later, Charles will give his speech. Afterwards, he will get booed at, and he will leave in a hurry, but you mustn't let him go. Grab him on the way down the first flight of stairs and then take him to one of the storage areas on the right,' she pointed, but it was difficult to see.

Moments later, the man came back with a bald, older gentleman, who had long white sideburns that spread to his cheeks where they were trimmed off neatly. Wearing a rather smart grey suit with a green velvet smoking jacket, the man nodded and bowed slightly.

'Mr Rogers, who wished to see you, sir,' he introduced him, then left us alone, heading back into the side room and slamming the door behind him.

'Good morning,' Hadriana smiled and offered her hand, looking ruffled at not being addressed. 'Lady Von Reed.'

He took it gently then dropped her hand as though it was too cold. 'Mr Theeks.'

She smiled. 'I am aware that Mr Charles Darwin will give a speech today at this lovely establishment and I was wondering if there are any seats available?'

With a quick smile, he looked up at Etrician, ignoring Hadriana. 'You gentlemen want to participate in this afternoon's lecture?'

'Indeed,' Etrician replied.

'Very well, I shall mark you down for three seats, but may I suggest...' he said taking a deep breath and glancing at Hadriana, 'it never is a good idea letting a woman speak for you. Makes us look unimportant,' he chortled, clapping Etrician on the shoulder. 'You women wait here.' He ordered us, as the others followed the white furry-cheeked man.

Then it suddenly occurred to me how Hadriana witnessed the speech given by Charles Darwin. Clearly, only men were allowed to see the lecture.

Nudging her, she frowned at me. 'So what did you call yourself?' I asked, trying to stifle a huge grin.

'I beg your pardon?' she asked testily, turning her back on the men who were now having a good old laugh.

Giggling I leaned close to whisper in her ear. 'I know you dressed up as a man or magically changed yourself to look like a man. So what was your name? Fredrick, Bernard, oh... Peter!'

Pulling away, Hadriana's cheeks went bright red. 'Oh, trust you to figure it out,' she sniped.

Stifling a laugh, I shrugged. 'If that man hadn't have said anything I wouldn't have guessed it, but anyway, tell me, tell me, tell me!' I was too excited for my own good.

Sighing, she looked away from me and mumbled '... Richard.'

'Sorry, say that again, a little louder?' I asked, putting my finger to my ear and leaning towards her.

'Richard Richardson,' she yapped. 'It wasn't a name I wanted to give myself I could have any God-given name, but that one popped into my head. I was a bit flustered.' Sighing, she folded her arms in a sulky manner and turned her back on me. 'You know even grown-up men are cruel.'

Trying so hard not to laugh, I said in a very polite conversational tone, 'You weren't called Dicky Dick were you?'

Abruptly a door opened to the left, and the man appeared with a face of thunder. 'Ladies, please keep your voices down I am trying to work!'

Moving out of the way, Hadriana and I wandered around the ground floor. The men had gone into the library and were still chatting away. 'We need to find Trinia.' Nodding, Hadriana headed up the stairs, and instinctively took a left and headed along a small corridor. Another short flight of stairs connected at the top and doubled back towards a landing and two doors on either side.

'Trinia,' Hadriana whispered as she carefully led me along the corridor. 'Trinia!'

Hearing a lock click, Hadriana jumped a mile as a door unlocked of its own accord. I ran forwards and pulled it open. Before my eyes were dozens of shelves of various artefacts, all from local stuffed animals, to bones, old weapons and gasping in amazement, I saw what looked like a very long coffin situated at the very back of the room. 'Come on,' I urged Hadriana.

Hurrying to the back of the room, I pressed my hands on the coffin and instantly saw the wood shimmer, as though it was a mirage. 'Trinia,' I laughed, 'it's the Water Nymph.'

'Oh!' said a soft voice from behind. Turning to look, Trinia as her beautiful human self appeared out of what looked like a large stack of books. Hadriana smiled warmly at her as Trinia came towards us. 'I have done what you asked,' she said, pointing to the coffin behind me. 'I have stood by these past years at your request. So, I am guessing that you have returned as the skeleton will be destroyed soon.'

'We hope so,' I told her. 'Charles Darwin will help get the skeleton destroyed; he just needs to see it later on today. Darren, Tyr and Etrician will be here when Mr Darwin arrives for his speech. But Hadriana and I are not permitted into the lecture.'

Giving me a small smile, Trinia nodded. 'I understand. I have not had any trouble keeping up the illusion, and I will continue to stay here until I am needed no more.'

Hadriana smiled gratefully. 'Thank you for all you have done, Trinia.'

Leaving the centaur, Hadriana and I headed back down the stairs just in time to see the men come out of the library shaking hands with Mr Furry Cheeks, as I secretly nicknamed him.

'Good morning to you and I shall see you soon,' he said, waving goodbye as he headed off into another room.

'Have fun?' I asked them as we went back into the bright sunny outside. Walking down the steps, we crossed the road and went into the park opposite, sitting down on a bench.

'It's going to be very entertaining,' Etrician told us. 'Mr Darwin has his notes on his soon-to-be book but Mr Theeks, the bald gentlemen, explained to us that a lot of people do not want Mr Darwin to speak at this lecture. In fact, he said that there were a group of people the other day who wanted to try and boycott it.'

'Do you think they are The Minister's lackeys?' Hadriana asked him.

Tyr nodded in response. 'We do, therefore you two need to keep an eye out for them. Mr Theeks showed us the list of people who are attending. There are twenty gentlemen in total, the three of us included.'

'Ha gentlemen, since when, is Darren known as a gentleman?' Hadriana scoffed derisively.

'Hey! I look like one dunn'I?' he shouted.

'My point exactly' she smirked. 'But anyway, you were saying?'

Ensuring that he got everyone's undivided attention, Tyr continued. 'If these men turn up, you have to stop them from getting into the building. We can't have any adverse effects on the timeline, keep them away, and we'll get Mr Darwin to see the skeleton.'

'Once he sees it'll be destroyed by some Bishop in Exeter or something like that,' Darren added. 'Mr Raleigh hears about this "mermaid abomination" and thus starts it all off, continuing the timeline unhindered.'

'I'm glad you guys figured that out,' I smiled at them. 'We saw Trinia. The skeleton is being kept, in a coffin on a room up the stairs and to the left. Just guide him to it and tell him about Father MacEnry being told of the skeleton. Charles is going to be very annoyed when he sees the skeleton, so just play along with him.'

As the hours passed, Hadriana and Darren went off to get something to eat and drink, while the three of us stayed in the park, going through every bit of the plan at hand. It had to be flawless, no mistakes.

Hadriana and Darren came back just in time as I spotted Mr Darwin walk up the steps to the building, behind him was a slender, curly-haired boy with a devilishly handsome face. Before I even turned around to grin at Hadriana after spotting her disguise, she smacked me in the stomach as a warning to keep my mouth shut.

'See you later,' Darren said as he and Tyr made their way across the road.

Etrician turned around and kissed me lightly on the cheek. I inhaled his smell of petrichor, and it made me happy. 'I'll be back soon, everything will be all right.'

Watching them enter the building, I suddenly got this horrible feeling of dread. It was something I had felt before many times, but this was different, it was an oppressive feeling that loomed over you, leaving nothing but despair.

Frowning in confusion, I sat down on the bench and watched the entrance like a hawk, my nerves utterly rattled for no apparent reason. Was I missing something? Did I overlook something abundantly clear to me? Confiding my dreading fears to Hadriana, she nodded in agreement.

'I feel the same thing, though I think it's because we're not there to witness it, we're not there to help out if something goes wrong inside the building.'

'What can you remember about it?'

She hesitated then replied slowly, 'Thera, I can't remember. I have a damn good memory, but I only remember leaving the building in the later afternoon. I can't recall the lecture at all.'

'Oh, Atlas,' I whimpered. 'Something's going to go wrong. We have to get in there.'

Suddenly jumping up from my seat, I was about to run when Hadriana grabbed my arm, stopping me. 'No, not yet. Give it some time. I know you want to rush in there and beat the lackeys up, but they might not even be in there. Trinia is looking after the "skeleton", so we know it's safe, so be patient.'

Yanking her grip off me, I began to pace around. 'I hate not doing anything.'

'You don't even know what's going to happen. Just wait a few hours, please. And sit down, people are staring at you.'

Not caring about whether people were staring at me, but not wanting to seem odd, I gently sat down and took a deep relaxing breath. 'It's going to be fine…'

Promising Hadriana, I sat on the bench for a good two hours; staring at the entrance and seeing no one go in or come out. My impatience got the better of me, and I quickly stood up. 'I have had enough,' I told her. 'I'm going to see if they've finished. Are you coming with me?' I asked, looking at her.

Giving me a short nod, we headed towards the building, quickly crossing the street as carriages rattled past, and their occupants thrashing madly in the back from the uneven ground.

'May I help you?' Asked the man whom Hadriana had a spat with earlier on; eyeing her he sighed and took a step back. Standing by the door with his pocket watch laid neatly on his jacket, I gathered that the man was also impatient and was clockwatching.

'Yes, I would like to know when the lecture is over.' Hadriana asked him, a little more kindly than from before.

Frowning at her, he picked up his pocket watch. 'I am not sure when it will finish. Mr Pengelly assured me it would perhaps last about one hour and three quarters, but I have heard nothing from the room, no applause, no talking. It's quite silent in there.'

I wanted to punch him. What an idiot! 'Excuse me,' I said quickly, the feeling of panic suddenly burst out of me. 'ETRICIAN!'

'Miss come back, you're not allowed to go up there!'

'Like hell I am!' I heard Hadriana thunder up the stairs behind me. Glancing right, I saw a little sign with an arrow pointing towards an oak panelled door which read "Conference Room." I ran to it and pulled as hard as I could and ripped the door off its hinges.

Gasping in shock, Hadriana came up behind me. 'Oh my God, what the hell has happened?'

Everyone was slumped in their seats, as though they had gone to sleep. 'Etrician!' He was on the floor, his body protecting Tyr and Darren underneath. Running to him, I pulled him off. With glazed eyes, he found mine.

'And here I thought that women weren't allowed in the lecture.' He wheezed and gingerly sat up, rubbing his back. 'They hit me with something on my back.' Feeling sick I lifted up his shift, I saw a small dent that had healed up. Thankfully, he wasn't hit by the staff.

Hadriana came to my side and roused Tyr. 'I'm fine, but my head is pounding,' he mumbled. Hadriana lifted Darren gently. His head rolled back, and his mouth hung open. He was out cold. 'This strange gas erupted from four different points in the room. No one stood a chance.'

'Darwin,' I whispered, looking to the podium in front. Poor Charles Darwin was spread-eagled on the floor, his papers scattered around him. 'Hadriana, get Darwin. I'll see to the others,' I told her.

'Wait a minute,' Hadriana said, 'this doesn't make sense.' She began to back away from everyone. 'Where are The Minister's men?' she asked. 'Thera, come out of the room. We need to leave the building.'

Her voice shook in fright. 'What?' I repeated in shock.

Etrician slowly got up but was very unsteady on his feet. 'What are you talking about, leave the room? Are you nuts?' He questioned her. 'We have to help everyone. This isn't how it's supposed to be.'

Tyr sat up and blew a gust of wind around the room, dispersing the invisible knock out gas. Etrician went to Darwin and roused him awake. Likewise, Tyr did with the others. Helping Darren up, I slapped him across the face a few times, and he soon opened his eyes.

'Whattimeisitmum?' he slurred. 'Damn my head.'

Before I even managed to say anything to him, large bangs were coming from outside in the hallway. It was the sound of electricity. Grabbing his hands, I dragged Darren to the back of the room, beckoning the others to come with me. Tyr and Hadriana knelt down beside me, and Etrician picked up Mr Darwin and carried him over to us.

'We need to get to the little storeroom where Trinia was waiting.' I said to the others.

'I'll go out first,' Etrician said, passing Mr Darwin over to Tyr. The old man was beginning to wake up. His crumpled face grimaced from his headache.

Hadriana then gasped. 'No, wait! These people are just waking up, they need to forget they were knocked out and be convinced that Mr Darwin's lecture has finished and the questions were over with, and they can leave.' She brought out a little pouch containing her Star Dust. 'Oh, I am good.' Pouring a little in her hands, she said, 'I wish that everyone in this room woke up without a headache and believed they had had a good lecture with Mr Charles Darwin and had finished their questions and are about to leave the room in good spirits.' She blew on the dust and smiling, nodded for us to go.

Etrician was the first out of the door. My heart was pounding as Hadriana, Darren and Tyr were gathered around Mr Darwin, pretending to show him something interesting. A few seconds later, Etrician poked his head around the door. 'All is clear,' he smiled.

'Clear about what?' Mr Darwin asked.

'There is something we wish for you to see,' Hadriana spoke to him. 'Forgive my gender, sir; I am just a humble woman trying to understand the truth.'

He nodded but looked a little disgruntled. 'I do have places to go and things to do.'

'This will take but just a moment,' Tyr pressed him.

Tyr, Darren and Hadriana stayed with Mr Darwin, sauntering as I headed past them trying to catch up with Etrician. As I passed the top of the staircase, out of the corner of my eye, I saw a young girl walk hesitantly into the entranceway. Dressed in a plain concrete-grey dress and a white blouse, she headed towards the room on the right and knocked thrice.

'Who is it?' came a voice from within the room.

'It's Miss Smith, Miss Ann Smith.'

'Come in.'

I stopped walking and turned to see that Tyr, Darren and Hadriana had heard the same thing I did.

'I do believe we have just met our target,' Hadriana told me, surprise in her voice.

'First things first, ey?' I whispered. Hurrying along the corridor, I got to the storage room first and heard Etrician bang on the door, asking Trinia to open up.

The heavy white painted door swung open to admit us and Trinia stood there ashen. 'They transported into the building by unknown magic about an hour after you saw me last,' she explained in hurried whispers. Her eyes widened as Mr Darwin, Tyr, Darren and Hadriana all came into the room. Instantly Trinia turned herself into a handsome looking man with the same auburn hair, but considerably shorter and with a matching moustache.

'Good afternoon, Mr Darwin,' she said, offering him her hand.

Mr Darwin took it, and Etrician quickly closed the door behind us.

'This is what we wanted to show you, sir,' Etrician nodded at Trinia, who went to the "coffin" and opening the lid revealed the mermaid skeleton.

The naturalist's mouth fell open in astonishment. 'This, this is a hoax, surely! It cannot be real.'

No one said anything. A moment later, the door swung open, and a man with a prominent nose, dark brown eyes and black balding hair and black side-burns that went down to his cheeks appeared in the doorway looking aghast. 'What in heaven's name are you doing here, Mr Darwin?'

'Mr Pengelly, why are you harbouring such an abhorrent disfigured hoax?'

'Hoax?' He questioned. 'Sir, I assure you this was found in a local cave. We still need to test its authenticity.'

'Authenticity!' He raised a hand to his head in astonishment. 'Are you a mad man? Mythological creatures do not exist. My studies on the age of man render things like this, moot. No, Mr Pengelly, as accomplished as you are, I hope you can understand when I say that I will personally see that this hoax gets destroyed! The damage it will cause,' he said more to himself. He bowed a little to us all then left without a backwards glance. 'I bid you all good day.'

The six of us quietly left the room without saying a word; however, a broad grin showed on our faces.

Darren laughed as we were about to head outside. 'Darwin is outraged! Well, guys, mission accomplished!'

'Yup,' Hadriana smiled. 'And plus,' Hadriana stopped just outside the office and pointed to the door. 'Hannah's ancestor is in there, and she's alive.'

We heard mumbling, but nothing else came of it. Sneaking out of the building, we crossed the road and sat on the benches, relishing in what we had done.

'We've done our job here and Ann, by the looks of it, is safe so,' Tyr asked. 'So we go back now, don't we?'

Abruptly we stopped laughing and turned to Hadriana for a response. 'I'm not sure. I had thought about it, but if Ann has appeared now, then the actions of today may affect her future.' She bit her fingernails in thought. With a little shake of her head added, 'It's best to continue with the dates that start the O.M.C. That's what the Minister is trying to accomplish. To destroy the beginnings of the O.M.C and invariably the T.A.T.'

Chapter Twenty-Three

With no rest for the wicked, we bunched together and listened to Darren ramble on about other mythological creatures that had turned up in the transcripts at the London hotel's library. One unusual incident that happened in the same year of 1859 was a finding of a griffon's head on Burray Island in the Orkney's in Scotland. The only problem was that, once again, we had no exact date.'

'I suppose I could go back into the present and contact Amjee again,' Hadriana suggested as we still sat on the bench opposite the entrance to Torquay's Natural History Society building watching the men leave.

'Oh that's fantastic, and if something happens to you, we'll be stuck in the past,' I said scathingly.

'Well,' Darren began, 'we don't know if what we've done has even helped Hannah. Plus if we go to the island, it'll be damn cold up there.'

'I'll fix that,' I smiled as I rooted around for my little pouch with the Amber Tree leaves in them, but I was unable to find them. 'Huh, I guess I left my pouch at your castle,' I told Hadriana as I continued to search.

Hadriana raised an eyebrow and asked, 'What do the leaves do? You've hardly mentioned your tree to me, though I know it's the only one of its kind.'

I explained. 'It has limitless powers as far as Santorini, and I are concerned. We've never truly tested its power. I've used it on Dagen, Jane, Tyr and Renita, but I-'

'Who's Renita?' Hadriana asked with a frown on her face. Etrician looked rather blank as well, and my heart sighed.

'Renita,' I said slowly so they could all hear, 'daughter of Pygmalion, dark-haired girl, brilliant blue eyes, animates sculptures from the earth?'

'Oh I think I know who you're talking about,' she said still frowning.

Renita didn't have much time left, and that meant that I didn't have much time left either. I wanted to be with Renita right until the very end. No one should be alone at the end.

With panic rising inside me, my head snapped to Hadriana. 'Go then, go back to the present, get the date and see if Hannah is alright then come right back to us.'

Smiling, Hadriana dug her hand into her dress and pulled out the jar containing the Sand of Time. Throwing a handful of it on the ground, then quickly mumbling, said the date for the day after we left and then vanished in a whirl of dust.

Not fifteen minutes later Hadriana came back in a whirlwind of dust. Shielding our eyes in time as the sand pitted my hands and face.

'I'm back!' Hadriana chimed with a smile waving a piece of paper in her hand, but with a gaunt expression, she explained, 'I have good news and bad news.'

'Good news first, please,' Tyr asked her.

Looking at me for conformation, I nodded slowly. 'All right good news it is. I found out the date for when this fossilised griffin head was found.' My head glanced up to her, and she gave me a warning look. 'I wrote this down from Amjee: "On Burray Island, part of the Orkney Islands north of Scotland, a fossilised skull was found of what appeared to be a strange animal which was part lion part bird. Upon further investigation, the locals had informed Mr Answorthy, of the University of St Andrews." Then blah, blah, blah, "After Mr Answorthy had visited the site (X-71P12), he gathered intellectuals around the country. Thus, the O.M.C. had officially begun."'

Another fossilised mythical creature. I glanced at Darren's placid face. He had no idea what was going on, not able to piece the information together, but Hadriana, Etrician and I had. Trying to ignore that fact for a second, I continued to listen to what Hadriana had to say.

'Not only that, the mermaid remains were destroyed in September of this year. The O.M.C started the same year on the 16th of October,' she concluded with a smile.

'Wait, what's the bad news?' Etrician asked the look of apprehension on his face.

Putting her hands on her hips, she shook her head. 'It's the reason why we have to keep stopping The Minister's men. Hannah is still fading.'

Darren swore under his breath. 'We haven't found the right time yet,' she told him.

The others looked downtrodden, and I understood how they felt. Everything we had done was for nought. They were a step ahead of us, and I wished I knew their motives. Something then came to mind. It was a stretch, although what other excuse could there be?

'The actions these men in suits are committing in the past are extreme,' I voiced aloud, 'and the more I think about it, the more I believe that Maynard really is behind it all. He's using the Minister's lackeys to destroy the O.M.C. Maynard doesn't care about the past anymore. Or what happens to the timeline. He just wants the guild's end.'

Darren groaned. 'Yes, but he'd need Hannah and I to be myths, right, for the Cabinet of Idols?'

'You said that it was already in your blood? That your parents had myth blood in them, right?' he nodded. 'So, take Tara and Saskia out of the mix, who are Sirens and can command with their voice, and take me and Etrician's interference and understanding of this mythological war that nearly happened a few weeks back, and Maynard has got a straight run to his goal.' It began to dawn on the others what I said. 'That would include Tyr, Dagen, Renita and Jane and even Hadriana. None of them would get in the way because Santorini and I would be captured and wouldn't need their help. We wouldn't know anything about his plans, and as immortal and as an Ancient, he can wipe out one timeline even if it affects me while continuing to exist as he is.'

'So,' Etrician began, 'he is trying to get rid of everyone who pertains to the start of the O.M.C. So, what about Darren and Hannah?'

Hadriana answered. 'Maynard's an Ancient. He can turn them into myths and throw them in the Cabinet of Idols and voila, Apocalypse Now.' Frightened into silence, Hadriana jumped us several months into the future and used her stardust to travel up the country to the cold north of the Orkneys, specifically Burray Island.

The landscape was mainly flat, compared to the towering peaks some miles south. Although, you could see oddly angled field boundaries where the farmers put up low walls for the sheep and wheat, and other crops were grown in the adjacent fields.

Glancing through the dim light as night was fast approaching, in the distance you could see small lights from the neighbouring islands around, though the population in the Orkney's were extremely slim.

Dark rain clouds threatened to burst above us as we stood by the little lane, unsure of where to go or what to do next. Thankfully, Hadriana once again stepped in to give us information.

'It happens tomorrow, the finding of the skull I mean,' Hadriana said as howling cold winds immediately found our ears. 'I checked with Amjee, she said there's the little village of Burray. There is a small pub we could stay until tomorrow.'

'And where are we exactly?' Darren shouted over the winds.

'Right on the site where the fossil was found,' she replied.

Looking around there was nothing out of the ordinary, nothing that would amount to the finding of a mythical creature's head. It was just a plain, little island in the north of Scotland and, it worried me. Discovering the merman in a cave by treasure hunters sounds understandable for its time, but just randomly finding a fossilised griffin's skull shortly after. It was liable for falsity. There had to be a connection somewhere, something had to happen for someone to find the skull.

Not wanting to wait around any longer, the five of us began to walk into the cold southerly winds, barely seeing the few lights of the village that clumped together in the distance.

Walking with the others, they weren't looking exactly happy. Etrician walked on in front, leading the way, with Tyr and Hadriana side-by-side behind him, both of their heads were down as the wind blew over Etrician and smacked into their faces. Darren was beside me and grumbled from the cold as we trudged on and though I caught no words, I hazarded a guess he was more concerned about Hannah then his frozen appendages. His eyes were focussed on Tyr's jacket as he followed closely behind, blinking only when the occasion called for it.

'Hey,' I said, tapping him on the shoulder. 'It's going to be all right. We'll sort this out.'

Showing me his worried face, he nodded and then focussed on Tyr's jacket, not saying a single word.

A short walk later, we approached the tiny village of Burray. It consisted of approximately twenty houses and ten farmhouses. Crossing the dirt road, we saw the inn, aptly named The Sands, which was strategically positioned very close by the beach, ideal for fishermen.

Fierce dark waves crashed heavily onto the nearby beach, sea spray and even tiny particles of sand spat into my face as we neared. Threatening to strike the building violently, I checked to see if no one was looking and calmed the waters. 'Shh,' I cooed. 'There's no need for you to get riled tonight.' The seventh wave gave a feeble attempt to creep ever higher up the beach but caved under my powers, and the waters instantly calmed to a soothing rhythmic caress.

With a few dim lights on inside the quaint inn, it appeared as if it saw little business but not wanting to spend the night in the fields, the five of us filed inside. Warmth and the surprising smell of salty-wood wafted into our faces from a blazing log fire situated at the back of the room. Similar to the inn back in Anstey's Cove, brass mugs and plates were nailed around the walls, as well as glass cases of fossilised fish.

One particular wall, adjacent to the fire, was solely dedicated to these ancient creatures as well as old underwater plants and insects. Dozens of glass cases were haphazardly pinned to the walls, and on closer inspection, as we made our way to the little bar in the corner of the long low ceilinged room, they had Latin names.

'Fascinating,' a man in a green tweed jacket gasped in a slight soft Scottish accent, as he stared at one of the fossilised fish on the wall in front. 'This is just...unbelievable.'

Ignoring him, Tyr, Darren and Etrician walked to the empty counter by the bar and knocked a few times. Moments later, a man who resembled a grizzly bear came out, with a bushy brown beard and matching thick eyebrows. Cleaning a glass, he placed it on the counter and curtly nodded. 'Aye, canny help?'

Darren was just about to open his mouth when I stepped forward and spoke in Scottish Gaelic. 'My friends and I were wondering if you have a spare room for the night? We are just travelling around the islands, island hopping as it were.'

With a shocked face, the man tilted back his head and roared with laughter. Replying in his mother tongue, he said, 'Of course. We don't really let out rooms to any folk, but since your island hopping and all, I don't think the misses will mind. We'll work out a fee now?'

Nudging Hadriana, I mouthed 'money' and digging into her skirt brought out a small purse and tipped out its contents on the counter. 'Is this enough?'

Slack-jawed, he nodded and scooped the money into his paw-like hands, pocketing it with a feverish expression. 'I'll sort out your rooms, have a free drink,' he boomed and poured out a pint of ale for us each.

As the man headed off, we took our pints and sat at a rickety black polished table by the log fire. Looking around, there were only four other customers. One man, in particular, was practically going gaga over the stone dead fish.

'You like fossils, do you, sir?' Tyr asked him, taking his pint and heading towards him.

Looking up, the man's happiness practically shone onto Tyr, illuminating them both. 'Oh, I cannot get enough of them. They are so interesting; I wish to learn as much about the earth as I possibly can, and these tiny little remnants of the past can help. Only recently did I fully understand that the world is much older than it is,' he said enthusiastically. 'I am a man of science, and I must understand what I see in front of me, if not, then I am not a true man of earth sciences.'

'Pah,' an old man grunted from our left. 'Science has done nothing to us apart from generating stupid questions no one wants to know the answer to!' he spat. 'I don't care about old fish that's been covered in ashes.'

'It's not ashes sir,' the man told him, a slight teacher-esque edge to his voice. 'They have been fossilized, turned into rock from years of pressure from other rocks. The calcium in the bones of these fish has been displaced. There are hundreds and thousands of fossils all over the islands. Do you know, fossils have been found all over the world already, yet we hardly know anything about them?'

'A load of tripe,' he grumbled, taking a swig from his pint.

Frowning from the old man's lack of enthusiasm, he pointed out to a fish near Tyr and began to explain to him how fish died in such a large quantity.

'Hot water, they were burnt to death,' he explained with a half-grim half-enthused face. 'Hoards of them died instantly, probably due to volcanic eruption in the waters or perhaps volcanoes on the surface that spilt out and fell into the ocean.'

'Oh De Ja Vu,' I muttered scathingly, remembering my own birth.

Etrician laughed and shook his head.

'Well sir,' Tyr said, blown away by his knowledge. 'You seem to be quite learned.'

The man laughed and nodded. 'I read a lot. I am the Keeper of Rare Books from the University of St Andrews. John is my name, Mr John Answorthy at your service.'

'Pleasure to meet you-'

'Mr Answorthy!' Darren choked through his ale. Darren immediately stood up and went over to Tyr and our target.

Hadriana's eyes nearly popped out of her sockets. 'Idiot boy should not get involved with this. We're meant to be on the periphery of the past damn it.'

'Hadriana,' I whispered hurriedly, grabbing onto her arm. 'Have we changed the past already?'

Staring into her eyes, they showed the essence of fright and understanding. 'The kids, before they are placed into the hands of the T.A.T. they go to this hotel in London where Amjee works, yes?'

Etrician and I moved closer to hear her, 'Yes, go on.'

'They have a library where all the transcripts of the O.M.C and the T.A.T. are housed dating back to this very period. All the missions they have been on, the myths they have seen, taken, fought against, everything. But, what Amjee seems to believe is that we are writing history.' She shook my arm. 'Thera, we are starting the beginning of the O.M.C.'

Etrician sighed and leant back in his creaking chair. 'Darren was right. We had to become the treasure hunters in the first place because Darren had already read about us when he was in the library,' Etrician said in a whisper, trying to understand it all.

Copying Etrician, I sat back in my chair and let out a long breath, trying to make sense of it all. 'So then, we are meant to meet this Mr Answorthy here, tonight and get acquainted with him and then… what?'

'Thera, Etrician,' Darren called from the other table, where they were raptly discussing fossilization. 'Want to go and search for fossils tomorrow? Mr Answorthy wants to show us.'

Etrician lightly chuckled and slapped his hand on the table, 'I think that's just answered your question. We have to persuade the locals to contact Mr Answorthy to look at the site when the griffin head had been found.'

'Or,' I began, thinking about it, 'we are the locals, and we find the griffin and inform Mr Answorthy?'

'It's fun writing history, isn't it?' Hadriana laughed as she raised her glass, 'slàinte mhath.'

Heading to bed that night, Hadriana and I shared a room while the guys shared another. It was a small room with beams running along the corners of the ceiling that stretched out and pressed against the walls, as though they could cave in at any moment. Attached to the black beams were dusty cobwebs and small dead spiders, giving the room a very unkempt look.

Hadriana's face was a picture when we got inside and was she being extremely girly about the entire situation. 'No clean towels, no soap, no hot water, I don't know how these people can stand it.'

'Please don't forget that you are not in a hotel!' I quipped as I took off my dress and climbed into the bed with my undergarments on. 'Just go to sleep, and you can annoy me more in the morning after you've eaten something.'

Sighing, she threw her clothes down and jumped into the other small camp bed opposite me. Rolling over she looked at me in the dark. The window behind me was clean enough to let a beam of moonlight shine into the room, illuminating Hadriana's pasty face. 'Thera,' she began softly. 'I know you find me annoying and after all the things I've said and done to you over the years, I do respect you.'

Snorting, I kicked back the duvet that felt heavy on me and laid on my back, staring up at the ceiling where a few strands of spider webs caught the moonlight and glistened as they danced gently in the draughty room. 'Hadriana, I know you respect me, but sometimes you have a funny way of showing it. I understand the situation you're in and that you've separated yourself from humans but… you need them as much as they need you and-' I added as she was about to say something and interrupt me, 'you still need to eat and sleep like a human. Just because your immortal doesn't mean you are a myth. I've told you this many times before, you haven't earned the right to be given a job. You don't have magical powers or abilities. You take them or borrow them, but they aren't yours in the first place.'

'But what if I did, what if the Ancients granted me the power of…'

'Sweetheart, don't even start with the Ancients. They are not in my good books right now, and they certainly don't want anything to do with you, and I say that in a very caring way. If they got involved with you, there'd be hell to pay on your behalf. You have collected some very mysterious and potentially fatal items, and the way you've procured them is subject to investigation from their point. Still, they are a little busy at the moment.'

'But what if I had powers of invisibility or I could read minds, which category would I be placed in?'

Looking over at her, I saw her propped up in bed, staring at me for answers. A shadow passed over the window and darkened the room in seconds. Glancing to my left, I saw massive dark clouds with fluffy white tops quickly pass by as the high winds pushed it onwards. Not looking at her, I said, 'You wouldn't be allowed to stay in this plane if you had those gifts. They don't help anyone in any given situation any more. Back in the olden days when myths were called from on high to help mere mortals, they used their powers to move mountains, divert rivers or rain during a drought. But those days are over and for a good reason. The Ancients were naive enough to let both good and evil myths onto this plane. And they are meant to be intelligent!' I glanced back in her direction and saw her stare forlornly at her hands. 'If you had powers and your sister didn't, you would never see her again.'

'I know…' she said in a harsh sombre tone, then turned her back on me and went to sleep.

The following morning after some helping of rather nasty gruel for breakfast, the five of us were waiting outside of the inn for Mr Answorthy. Etrician and Darren had walked around the entire village looking for any suspicious signs of The Minister's men, but there wasn't any. Either way, Etrician and I were on high alert.

As we sat by the sea wall, still waiting for Mr Answorthy, I asked Hadriana about her chat with Amjee. 'These transcripts in the library, was there any mention of explosions or people dying?'

However, she shook her head. 'Nope, I asked her the same question. Amjee wouldn't lie to me, she can't, she owes me big time…actually she owes me for a lot of things that I've lost track of. What would it matter if there were? It's not like you can prevent it. We've already obliterated the paradigm of messing around with time and future just by seeing Hannah fading from existence, so what's one little explosion or a missing person have to do with anything.'

About to yell at her for her flippant disregard for history and someone's life, she flicked her hair in my face and stomped off. Balling my hands into fists, I smashed them down onto the sea wall, breaking the rocks underneath. 'Oops.'

'What has she done to annoy you this time?' Etrician asked as he came over to see the damage I had done to the wall.

'Just being flippant and callous I suppose,' I sighed, watching Etrician place his hands on the broken rock and then as he pulled back, the cracks were sealed, and they looked as though I never got angry and broke them in half.

'Thank you,' I smiled.

'I missed you last night,' he replied, sitting next to me. 'My feet were cold, and you're rather warm in bed.'

'Shush.'

In earshot, Darren and Tyr turned round to smirk at us. Ignoring them, I looked out at the sparkling sea that caught the early morning rays of the sun as it ascended into the sky. Before I opened my mouth to say how picturesque it was, I heard a loud cough from behind me.

'Look who I found wandering around staring at the ground,' Hadriana smiled mockingly, pointing to Mr Answorthy who looked rather bashful.

He bowed, 'Sorry I'm late, but I saw some flakes of rock that are known to contain fossils,' he said with just as much enthusiasm as the night before.

'I bet you wish he was your son, don't you?' I asked Etrician jokingly as our group followed Mr Answorthy down the road. 'He'd be a perfect son. Compassionate about rocks, obsessed with fossils, enthusiastic about the earth and helped start the O.M.C., he'd be the best son alive.'

Chuckling, Etrician shook his head. 'He does make me smile, but his enthusiasm for science has put me off mentally adopting him. Science and myth do not really mix as you are fully aware, and we have to persuade him otherwise. I don't think he'll be as bad as Darwin, though.'

Shrugging I saw Mr Answorthy abruptly stop and stoop to the ground, almost pressing his nose to the floor. 'Aha! See here, Darren,' he pointed to a rock partially covered in grass. 'Some fern has been fossilized. Oh, I wish I had brought my kit.'

'Kit?' Darren asked as we crowded round to see this old fossilized fern in a rock.

'My extracting kit,' he explained. 'Just some tools to chip away the fossils and take them back to the university. My own private collections have grown astronomically,' he laughed. 'I am trying to find enough funding to help me with my project of exotic creatures.'

Etrician and I shared a look but remained quiet.

For the rest of the morning, a very fervent Mr Answorthy guided us around the islands, showing us the various places where he believed fossils of ammonites, trilobites and mysterious ancient plants used to live. Hadriana looked extraordinarily bored and annoyed by Mr Answorthy droning on about his findings. At the same time, Darren and Tyr seemed to have a rather fun time asking him all sorts of questions. Etrician and I, however, kept out of it. It wasn't that we found him annoying, but Etrician knew rocks inside and out. He didn't need an amateur human telling him how to suck eggs.

Deciding he would like to at least, record his findings of the morning, Mr Answorthy headed back to the village of Burray, accompanied by the rest of us, as Hadriana and Darren wanted something to eat.

Huddled by the fire and digging into some hot broth of lentils, carrots, onions, potatoes, mutton and thick gravy, Mr Answorthy, Hadriana and Darren were discussing his university and the work he did. Dunking his bread into the steaming broth, it splashed onto his pale shirt as he stuffed the soggy bread into his mouth. 'I watch over the collections of rare books,' he said through a mouthful of food. 'Someone has to do it.'

'What rare books, sir?' Darren asked him, as his spoonful of broth was poised over his bowl, waiting for an answer before he ate.

Mr Answorthy swallowed his food, and dabbed his broth splattered chin. 'Mythology,' he beamed.

Tyr, Etrician and I sat up in our seats, listening intently to what Mr Answorthy had to say.

'Unicorns, dragons and all other manner of creatures are only a few that are in my possession. Not quite sure how I've managed to procure such a collection of waffle, but I must admit they are an interesting chuckle.'

'I told you,' Etrician whispered in my ear.

Sighing, my attention to the topic of conversation became lax. Catching Hadriana's eye, I glanced at the door, and she nodded.

'Why don't we leave you to your thoughts Mr Answorthy?' Hadriana told him silkily, as she finished the rest of her broth and stood up, burping slightly. 'Ooh, please excuse me,' she smiled.

'Of course. Shall I expect you and your friends' company later? I do hope so, as I travel back to the university very early in the morning.'

With a curt nod, she replied, 'Of course you shall. We live on the island,' she added, remembering that the transcripts mentioned the local people on the island contacted Mr Answorthy. 'We too set off later on tonight as we have other things to do. But we shall be back to say goodbye.'

Leaving him to his thoughts, theories and work the five of us set off to find the griffin skull.

'Etrician?' I asked as I saw him stride off into the darkness. Gazing back at me, in the light of a lantern that Hadriana had flippantly wished from her stardust, he had a wide grin on his face. Lifting his arm, he pointed about twenty yards in front.

'It's there, about ten inches deep, but it's not just the skull, it's the entire body. The rest of it is deeper in the ground. We're only meant to find the skull, not the rest of the body.'

'Wow. That's so cool seeing through the earth,' Darren laughed, running to where Etrician pointed. Kneeling down, he placed his hands on the ground as though trying to feel the lump of the skull, but naturally, it was too deep to tell.

Moving closer to it, Etrician swept his hand in front of him and quickly removed the topsoil; bits of grit and little worms wiggled around on the floor, not expecting to be exposed to the cold surface winds so abruptly. Although on closer inspection, the removal of the soil revealed the stained coloured fossil of a griffin's head. Seeing the cranium with the large perforated edged beak with a sharp tip at the end, my heart sighed. Yet another mythical creature had found itself in the deep past and had died. The Ancients were not doing their job.

Thanks to Etrician's expertise, he helped excavate the skull only and placed it on the ground so all of us could see. 'So,' he began, staring at it, 'do we hurry back to find Mr Answorthy or what?'

'Or what, what?' Darren asked quizzically. 'We can't just stand here staring at it, we need to take it to him…'

'Or get him to see it for himself,' Tyr added with a small shrug. 'What do you two think?'

Glancing at me, Hadriana shrugged, 'I think it's a good idea to go and get him and show him the site. It would look more professional in the transcripts and also more like an accident that we found it, so Darren and Tyr,' she said turning to them with a dazzling smile, 'run along and get Mr Answorthy like good little boys. We'll stay here and talk behind your back while you're gone.'

Shaking my head at her with a disgruntled look, Darren and Tyr headed off.

'Did you have to say that? It was rather uncalled for,' I huffed.

'What? They need to do as they're told, and they need to learn some respect as well,' she replied in a waspish tone.

'If I was your mother I'd slap your behind for that impudent tongue!' I shouted.

Smiling at me with evil slit eyes, Hadriana sweetly said, 'Then I'm glad you're not, Thera dear.'

Turning my back on her, I stomped over to sit on a small half buried lichen-covered boulder, grumbling incoherently to myself. Behind me, I heard Etrician sigh, though he didn't comment. He hated when Hadriana and I fought, but that was our relationship. Some days we'd get along fine and others we wanted to kill each other, like today.

In some respects, I acted like a mother to her. Not in a cuddly over-possessive way, but in a concerned way. I wanted her to at least learn some humility and that she's wasn't the centre of attention. Hadriana was aware that she could very easily hurt people's feelings. Whether or not she does it to wind me up, I'm not sure, but she knew not to push me too far.

Within half an hour of arriving, Mr Answorthy was being guided by a very enthusiastic Darren. 'It's over here,' he said breathlessly, pointing to the fossilized cranium of a mythological half-bird half-lion. 'It's unlike anything we've ever seen,' Darren explained as we all moved towards it. 'It looks like a bird but, the connection to the spine through its neck... that isn't bird-like sir.'

Bending to investigate, Mr Answorthy pulled out some spectacles and placed them gently on the end of his nose; frowning at the odd artefact and pondering in thought as Hadriana held the lantern aloft. Lightly touching the skull, he pulled back and looked at his dirty fingers then reached it again to scratch it. 'I... I cannot say what it is but, it...' he dug a little deeper and saw the neck bones and palled. 'No. It can't be. It's not,' he said definitely, shaking his head. 'I won't believe, no sorry gentlemen, but it is a hoax.'

'A hoax?' we all chimed, looking in confusion our acting skills playing the part perfectly.

'A hoax of what sir? A giant bird?' Darren asked in puzzlement.

Standing up and brushing the dirt from his trousers, he sarcastically chuckled, 'a giant bird indeed. That...thing is not a bird, but I refuse to believe that it is real. Who told you to dig this? Who placed it here? Is this some joke that Frank put you up too, ey?'

Etrician stepped forwards, with a concerned look on his face and spoke slowly and plainly to him. 'No, we do not know Frank. We merely found this after you so enthusiastically taught us about fossils. The only problem was that after we found it, we were unsure of what it is. How you described the technique to tell what is bone from rock, I saw you testing the skull by scratching it, so we all know that it is a fossil. And begging your pardon sir, you cannot fake a fossil, it is unheard of. So, may I enquire as to what you think it is if you do not believe it is a giant bird?'

Picking a handkerchief from a breast pocket, he dabbed his forehead from perspiration then shoved it haphazardly back, a smear of muck visibly seen. Sighing and wiping his mouth, Mr Answorthy was fretting about telling us what he believed, and by the looks of it, he didn't really want to voice his opinion.

'You know what it is, do you not?' I demanded.

Immediately stopping in his tracks, his eyes grew wide with shock at my outburst. Frowning at me, 'Look, I am a scientist, and I cannot accept this... this THING! It's monstrous, barbaric even. It does not make sense. Half-birds half... half... lions,' he finally said, 'do NOT exist.'

'It is a real fossil,' Hadriana urged. 'You know it is. But the question is, what are you going to do?'

'Do?'

'Yes,' she said, putting her hands on her hips in a motherly way, her eyes boring into him. 'You work for a very prestigious university Mr Answorthy. You have these rare books in your charge for a reason. You were meant to witness this auspicious event for a reason. Take charge and find out the truth of our world, know its secrets, its mythologies. You know I'm willing to bet that there are others like you who believe there is more to life, others that want to see the world for what it truly is.'

Shaking his head and mumbling, Mr Answorthy walked around the site a few paces, giving the skull a wide birth. Sighing, he looked up at us, 'What do you want me to do? Form a secret guild? Start an organisation? All because you've presumably found a griffin skull!' He barked out a laugh.

'Yes,' the five of us chimed in together, making him jump a little.

'Mythical creatures obviously originated somewhere,' I smiled at him. 'Find out for yourself.'

Motioning to the others, we left Mr Answorthy alone to contemplate his next step. Heading away from the site so that no human would see, we gathered around Hadriana.

'Well let's hope that did the trick,' she said, looking over her shoulder to see if anyone was behind us. 'Right guys, sorry but there's one more stop just to be sure.'

Believing it was safe to do so, she threw the sand into the air, said the date, which became the 7th of March 1884, and in a whirlwind that swept around us, we travelled forward in time and crossing the country sped away to the busy capital, London.

'No way. The British Museum!' Darren gasped as the sand fluttered away from us, trickling gently to the soggy ground below. Standing in a small alleyway, adjacent to the large, soon to be historic building, motorised vehicles passed by in front, chugging along the bricked roads honking at the pedestrians who busied themselves with their day. Though there were still horse-driven carriages around, it seemed that the looming new century was putting a new perspective on London.

'I hated London in the 1880s,' Hadriana grumbled as we stepped out of the smelly alley, dressed in new Victorian clothing. Both Hadriana and I wore large moss green dresses with puffy sleeves; our heads decorated with black slanting hats with white ostrich feathers pinned on the top. There was just one problem with what I was wearing. After a few steps, I stopped and reached out for Etrician's arm for support.

'What's wrong?' he asked in a frightened tone, as I gripped onto him.

'Bloody... tight... corset,' I gasped.

Etrician pulled me close to him and whispered with a sarcastic tone, 'You're not human, stop acting like one.'

Immediately I stopped and pulled myself together. Staring into his eyes, Etrician gave me a warning look and nodded. 'Let's get going then,' I said to the others.

Hurryingly crossing the busy London Street, we headed over to the British Museum, though I was unsure of why we were here. When asking Hadriana why she had brought us here, her reply was, 'Amjee told me to.'

Not questioning it, we pressed on through the gates where one man sat in a booth reading a newspaper and paying no attention to who walked in or out of the premises. Hurrying up the stairs and under the large archway, we were about to enter the building, when a thin red-haired man stopped us before the rather flimsy looking doors. 'I'm sorry, but no ladies allowed.'

'Another reason why I hate this decade,' Hadriana spat, making the man jump.

'I say!' he frowned at her, affronted. 'There is a gentleman's meeting commencing. The museum will be open to everyone tomorrow.'

'Oh,' she said sheepishly. 'Um, we just wanted to talk to Mr Raleigh.' We all stared at her in confusion. Why did Amjee want us to seek him out?

'He is not back yet,' the man told us. 'He is not due to return to the country for another few months.'

'Where is he sir?' Tyr charmingly asked him as a deep frown etched on Hadriana's brow.

'Bombay. He is there on business, writing up reports and forms and all that nonsense for the museum. I don't know why he bothers. We are perfectly capable of finding out all the information from our correspondents overseas, but he insists that he must go there himself.'

'Is his assistant with him?' Darren asked him. 'Miss Ann Smith?'

Frowning the man shook his head, 'No my boy, I'm afraid not. I'm sorry to say that Miss Smith died a few years ago in a terrible train crash in a tunnel heading back to London. They say it was instantaneous.' Seeing the shocked look on our faces, the man gave us a curt nod. 'I am sorry to provide such bad news, but if you'll excuse me, I have to ask you to leave.'

Gently shooing us away, the five of us trudged down the stairs with mortified expressions on our faces. We were too late to save Hannah, or were we? Yes, we could go back in time, but when in time and where in the country did the accident happen? We needed information, and Mr Raleigh was the only one who could provide it.

'Hey, what about the newspapers?' Darren asked as the notion had flittered across my mind.

'That's a point,' Etrician said as we passed by the booth again, the man still reading his paper. Grabbing my arm gently, Etricina nodded to the man. 'Excuse me, sir?'

'Museum's closed today, try tomorra' mornin' sir.' Not looking up from his paper, which I knew Etrician would find extremely rude, he tried again.

'I just want to ask about a train crash that happened a few years ago,' he said to him loudly, hoping to distract the man from reading. 'We have just found out a friend died and we do not know much about it, apart from the fact it was heading to London.'

Finally putting his paper down, the stubbly chinned man with a bad comb-over frowned at him. 'The Edinburg Line Crash? Is that what ya on abawt?'

Etrician nodded.

'Oh yea, nasty business tha'. 'Appened two year ago in the summa. 17th of June I recall. A lot of people died, still don't know how it 'appened. Many say it could 'av been prevented. Yet, what 'appened, 'appened. Ya can't change the past.'

'Want to bet?' Hadriana asked as the five of us moved away.

Chapter Twenty-Four

FINDING SOME OLD DISUSED VEGETABLE CRATES THAT WERE PROPPED UP against the dirty, polluted walls, we sat down and discussed the issue at hand. Firstly, we were now aware that Ann Smith was dead. Her death seemed to be the focal point for Maynard. Initially, we thought he'd try and obliterate everything that started the guild, such as the fossilised evidence. However, we were wrong. Without Ann Smith, the O.M.C clearly never started, and so he had a clear shot to his goal. Secondly, her death clearly was in such an extreme way, and most likely dozens of others too had perished, it had drastically altered the timeline, perhaps to the point that it was unfixable.

As I sat there half listening to Darren rant about how we needed to move and get this sorted, I couldn't help but feel that Maynard's total disregard for the past and its repercussions made him even more dangerous. He was an Ancient; surely, the other Ancients would have stopped him by now? They must know… they must-

'Come on!' Darren insisted. 'We're wasting time!'

'Darren, shut up!' I shouted. 'We have all the bloody time in the world. We need to think this through.'

'Right, so we know that she's died-' Hadriana began.

'Correct,' Tyr said.

'We know that it was two years ago on the 17th of June-' Etrician added.

'Again, correct.'

'And we know that Mr Raleigh knows but,' I added quickly before Tyr could distract me with his mental checking list, 'how on Atlas have the other Ancients let Maynard get away with it all?'

'Hannah doesn't exist!' Darren yelled at me. 'That entire incident has changed the O.M.C. Clearly, the Ancients don't care. They didn't seem to care when they stripped us of our powers and made us housebound in Bristol!'

'No, Darren. Ann Smith, as I recall, is Hannah's great-aunt. Not her great-grandmother. We don't know the full repercussions of Ann dying. So shut up and listen.' I chided. 'Mr Raleigh was the one who wrote that book you mentioned? That has all the information about mythological creatures?' He nodded. 'But Mr Raleigh is still alive. He'd be affected by this upheaval of Ann dying. Although, I think there's something else to this and I think we need to go to India and find out.'

'India!' Darren screeched, causing passers-by to glance in our direction. 'Why do we have to go there? We need to stop a train in England!'

'No, we need to learn from the future about the past,' I said to him wisely. 'Then we can go into the past and stop the train.'

Groaning, he slapped his forehead. 'I've had enough of this time travel malarkey.'

Making me titter, I motioned for Hadriana to get the stardust out. 'We're not going to the past. We're just in need of a ride to Asia.'

'So it's India now?' she asked as we moved further into the alley so that people wouldn't notice us.

'Looks like it,' Etrician smiled. 'I haven't been there in a while actually. It would be nice to check up on at least one of the centaur herds there.'

I shook my head. 'Nope. We need to talk to Mr Raleigh and only him. No pit stops.'

'So, we are in need to travel to Bombay to speak to Mr Raleigh then? Though we have no idea where he is...?'

'Nope,' we said together.

Sighing, she brought out the stardust. 'I have never used so much of this stuff in my entire and expansive life. And I daresay I'll be using it a lot more being with you lot.'

'Less cheek, more magic,' I quipped. 'India is four and a half hours in front, it's already half-past two now,' I informed them.

Without further ado, Hadriana softly whispered a wish and sprinkled the stardust around us. In moments, the landscape melted away like an oil painting left out in the rain. Afternoon daylight suddenly became evening twilight. The cold, damp climate of London suddenly changed to become humid, with the air full of exotic spices mixed in with a hint of coal.

Standing in front of an open space, old building work was visible, from piles of neatly cut brick to large thick planks of wood. The five of us were utterly bemused by the scene in front of us, looked around for any sign of Mr Raleigh.

'He can't be that difficult to spot...' Darren said peering through the dimmed light as a few local people taking leisurely strolls in front while gave us strange looks as they passed. 'He's white.'

Suddenly a loud pitched whistle came from behind, making us all jump, but I quickly understood why I had smelt coal. We were standing right in front of what appeared to be a new train station. White plumes of smoke billowed out of a train's funnel. Its shiny black coat of paint caught the last rays of the dying sun that fell behind the buildings in front of the station.

As people headed to and fro, we managed to find someone and ask if they knew of a Mr Raleigh and thankfully, they did.

'Yes sir he's up in the office,' a tall Indian smiled, pointing to a set of double doors on the right-hand side. 'Just follow them up to the third floor and turn left. Mr Raleigh is on the second door to your right.'

Giving us a slight bow, we hastened off and followed his directions with Tyr leading the way. Then as we reached the third floor, Tyr turned left and hurried down the painted wood-panelled corridor and knocked on the door.

Catching up with him, the pane of frosted glass in the door flickered with a pale light from within. After no answer, Tyr knocked again, a little louder. 'Mr Raleigh.'

My heart lifted as I heard the scrape of a chair. A figure walked towards it and turning the door handle, it squeakily opened inwards, a breeze of pipe tobacco filtered out through the corridor as well as the distinct smell of melted tallow wax.

With bloodshot eyes and the smell of whiskey on his breath, Mr Raleigh appeared unkempt. His unshaven face, half un-tucked white shirt, stained brown trousers, and messy hair met us with a lagging smile. 'Can I help?'

'Um, I hope so,' I groaned. Mr Raleigh's eyes drunkenly fluttered as he tried to focus on me. 'May we come in, please? We would like a word with you.'

'Of course.' Opening the door wider, he stumbled back into the office, knocking into a chair then reaching out, gripped onto the cluttered table full of papers, quills, empty ink bottles and empty whiskey bottles. Plonking himself in his seat, he gestured to the two unoccupied chairs by the side of the table, 'Hafa seat,' he slurred and grabbed some papers that were on the chairs.

Tyr and Etrician pulled the chairs out for Hadriana and me to sit on. As we sat down, I took a few seconds to take in the room. On first glance, it was as though I had walked into an old student's room. Tottering towers of books were stacked haphazardly along the back of the wall to my right, around them were more empty whiskey bottles, and screwed up bits of paper. A pair of grey socks with holes in them were draped over a stack of important looking documents that had, what seemed to be, a tea stain which ran all the way through them, discolouring them a light yellow and crinkling them up on the one stained side. Two jackets had been thrown to the floor; one of them had a ripped front breast pocket, the other was stained by what looked like red wine.

'Mr Raleigh, what have you done to yourself?' I asked as I had seen enough of his office.

'I may be inebriated miss, but introductions first,' he hiccoughed. 'Mr Raleigh that I am and you be you whoever you are.' Slipping down in his chair a little, he glowered at the lack of control he had on his body and sat up, flopping onto the table.

'My name is Thera, this is Hadriana Von Reed, Etrician, Tyr and Darren,' I said, pointing to everyone but he didn't seem to take a blind bit of notice.

'Darren?' he smirked, 'That's the first real name that's been uttered.' Looking up, his eyes fluttered again then smiling like an idiotic child said, 'care for a dash of whiskey?'

'Don't tempt me,' Hadriana groaned.

'Look, we came here to ask you about what happened to your assistant Ann Smith.'

Frowning in pain, he shook his head, 'Don't want to talk about it,' he mumbled, looking away. 'I miss her,' he sighed. 'I miss her so much.'

'You cared for her?' Etrician asked him, the room became instantly sober.

'She was such a good organiser,' he said, waving his arms around, gesturing to his office. 'She could tidy up things like no other woman could.'

'Oh for the love of Atlas!' Hadriana was furious. 'You blithering idiot, is that all she was to you? Someone who could organise all your crap?'

'Excuse me miss Hadri–what's your name,' he spluttered, 'but don't you dare talk about my files like that in front of me. They have feelings too! Besides, why are you bothering me at this hour about my former assistant?'

'We just want some answers about the accident,' Darren asked him.

Sighing, he shrugged his shoulders dramatically. 'Well, what can I say? She boarded a train to London to visit her sister, who was within a few days of giving birth, and it crashed. Though, why is it important to you? In fact, why have you come to see me? You could have asked anyone, seen it in the papers... Who are you?' Frowning at us, he pushed his chair back and stood up, swaying a little. 'Who are you, people? No one comes all the way to India to ask about my assistant... an assistant that no one really knew was connected to me.'

'Uh oh,' Tyr mumbled behind me.

'Who are you!' he demanded, suddenly shouting.

'Please don't get upset,' Etrician said firmly. 'We... we were just–'

'What do you know?' he demanded from us again. 'You know something about the group, don't you?'

'The O.M.C, yes we do sir,' I confirmed for him. 'We are not a part of it, but we know it well, Darren here...' but Hadriana slapped her hand over my mouth.

'Shut up! We're not supposed to tell him anything.'

Grabbing her hand and pushing her away from me, I rounded on her. 'The timeline is already screwed up by Ann dying! If we go back and change that, this conversation with him won't happen.'

'She's got a point,' Tyr told her. 'She needs to be alive, so Mr Raleigh being here in this drunken state won't remember a thing because the conversation wouldn't exist.'

Throwing her hands in the air, she yelled, 'for the love of ATLAS why don't people listen to me! Now we're going to have to explain to him, or he's going to kill us!'

'What?' I asked, but following Hadriana's eye line, I saw what she was talking about. Mr Raleigh had produced a pistol and was pointing it at us... though it wavered as he was having trouble focussing.

'Well, not us,' she gestured to Etrician, myself, Tyr and her, 'just Darren.' She clapped him on the back. 'Not fun being mortal, is it?'

'What the hell is going on?' Mr Raleigh spat. 'What are you doing here? Who are you?'

'Mr Raleigh, we are from the future,' Hadriana told him pleasantly as though they were having a polite, normal conversation. 'Also, we are all immortal, so you can't kill us, well apart from him,' she thumbed to Darren. 'The point is, we know about the O.M.C. because it transgressed and became something bad, so bad in fact that it nearly brought about a war between the Ancients and mythological creatures.' The poor man sat heavily in his chair, his mouth open in shock, the pistol dropped, pointing to the floor. 'We've come back into the past because one of our members is related to your assistant, Miss Ann Smith. She's fading away as her timeline is being affected. We believe Ann was killed by a group of people who wish to destroy the O.M.C.'

'Well, they succeeded!' he spat, then put his head in his hands. 'I can't finish the work that Ann helped me with. It's too painful.' He snorted and wiping his mouth looked at us. 'And you,' he pointed a wavering finger, 'you say you are all immortal?'

'Myself and Etrician here are legends,' I explained. 'We were created from myths. Tyr is a myth, the God of the Winds from Norse mythology. And Hadriana was human until she drank from the Fountain of Youth, she's now immortal. Darren here,' I pointed at him, 'is a temporary merman. The O.M.C turned into the T.A.T. which stands for Tattoo of Arcane Technology. They harness the blood of myths that the O.M.C collected from around the world, and place them into unwilling hosts and turn them into myths.'

'If-if all you are telling me is true, then why kill my assistant?' he blurted out. He placed the pistol on the table in front, but it was still cocked. 'Ann was so kind, so pure,' he said and began to weep.

Hadriana and I caught each other's eyes. Something that Mr Raleigh said piqued my interest. 'Sir, I would like to ask about the circumstances why Ann had to travel for the birth of her sister's baby.'

Frowning, he dropped his head sombrely, as though a man defeated with the reality of the situation. 'Ann was her midwife. Her sister didn't want anyone else. I found out that her sister lost the baby. I had always thought that if Ann had been present, the baby would have survived.'

'Of course,' I sighed, piecing it all together. 'Hannah's great-grandmother isn't alive because she didn't survive childbirth.'

'I bag your pardon?' Mr Raleigh slurred again.

'It's beg your pardon, you drunken buffoon,' Hadriana sighed under her breath.

Without any words, Mr Raleigh shuffled away from his chair and turned to the stained jacket on the floor. Kneeling down, he shoved his hand inside it and pulled out four tiny golden eggs that were the shape of my thumbnail. Still, on his knees, he turned around and showed them to us, 'If you are who you say you are, then you'll know what these are.' Smiling greedily at them, smoothing them as though a child would to a baby chick, his eyes glanced up at us, sharp and keen as a hawk. It was as though he wasn't drunk at all.

'Those are fairy eggs,' Tyr told him gently, 'and it looks like they are about to hatch.'

'Why do you say that?' he asked him curiously. 'I've had these for months, and they haven't hatched, they've just turned colour. First, they were bronze, then they turned silver a few weeks ago and now they're gold.'

'That's the development of fairy eggs Mr Raleigh,' Etrician told him, 'you have to put them back where you found them. The Mage would be very sad to know her children have been taken.'

'A Mage? So it's true, they do have a hierarchical society.' He smiled, as he carefully placed the eggs on the table then grabbing some paper and a quill, began taking notes. 'But I didn't steal them. I found them here in India, saved them actually,' he added feverishly, scribbling away. 'I was on a field trip around the Sunderban forest with a few colleagues when I inadvertently got lost. Well, I ended up tripping over a hidden rock, stumbled down this embankment and smacked into a tree and was knocked out. But when I came too, I saw this queer little bird hopping towards what looked like pennies. However, after closely inspecting them, I saw they were fairy eggs and snatched them away before the bird could eat them.'

Sighing I rubbed my aching temple. This really wasn't happening, was it? My headache seared, causing me to wince. Staring at Mr Raleigh, I stood up. 'Sir, we need to go now. You've told us all you know, I think, and I believe that you need to go home and get some rest. Hadriana, if you'll do the honours, the sooner we're in the past to fix this, the sooner none of this happens, and I can get rid of my headache.'

I heard Etrician mutter, 'Legends don't get headaches,' but I ignored him.

'You're, you're leaving?' Mr Raleigh stammered as he stopped writing. 'But I... I have so many questions,' he smiled, sobering up quite quickly. 'I wish to know what becomes of the group. You said that it transgresses into the T.A.T., but why, what will happen to it?'

Hadriana stood up beside me and grabbed her little jar of sand. Moving the chairs out of the way, the others gathered around.

'Please don't go! I have so many more questions to ask you,' he pleaded, moving towards the door as if that was going to stop us.

'And they are best left alone for now,' I said testily. 'Thank you for your help, Mr Raleigh. It's been interesting meeting you. Once the timeline has been restored, you won't remember this conversation, so goodbye,' I added unsurely.

Hadriana got out her sand and sprinkled it around us, just as Mr Raleigh shouted out, 'No please!' He voice wavered as though warped as we were taken back through time, two years ago, 1882 to the 16th of June, the day before the tragedy.

Edinburgh in June was cold, miserable and wet. Normally it was idyllic with lush green rolling hills speckled with various coloured wildflowers. It was a glorious city that housed fantastic architecture and history. And dotted with ruins from the past which you could enjoy visiting during a hot summer with a lovely breeze flowing from the North Sea. But not this year. This day on the 16th of June, 1882, was terrible.

Throwing it down with rain and finding ourselves transported on a hill that looked over Edinburgh city, the five of us ran for cover, slipping and sliding down the sodden grass.

'Ah crap,' Darren yelled as I heard a soft thud and looking back, saw him rolling down the hill, his swear words cut off as he was hit in the stomach every time he turned.

Unable to help it, I burst into a fit of laughter as Darren's wet hair flipped in his face as he rolled down the hill and out of sight. Throwing myself on the ground, I did the same thing, my head spinning as the world was turned around and around.

'THERA! WHAT ON PROMETHEUS' LIVER ARE YOU DOING?' I heard Etrician yell.

'IT'S QUICKER,' I tried to call back as my stomach pelted by the ground when I rolled onto it.

Hearing a crunch below me, Darren swore, and then I too quickly found out where the crunching sound came from. Smacking hard into an old wooden fence and half breaking it, I began laughing uncontrollably; wiping the tears from my eyes. 'Wow.' My eyes were unable to focus on anything as my head was still spinning. 'That was fun, and I've got rid of my headache at least.'

Hearing Darren giggling from beside me, he stood up and offered his hand for me. 'I never thought you were that fun.'

Taking his muddy hand, he helped me up. 'Well our clothes are ruined, but I don't particularly care,' I shrugged, as I looked down at my olive green and now, brown dirt dress. 'Who says I wasn't fun? You can't be boring all the time, or what's the point in life?'

Darren's smile faltered a little, but suddenly our attention was drawn to our right as in the distance, Etrician, Tyr and Hadriana came quickly yet carefully towards us.

'Are you all right?' Etrician asked as he hurried to me, grabbing me by the arms and checking to see if I was injured.

Laughing, I shrugged free from his grip. 'I'm fine, though that was awfully fun.'

Giggling like an idiot, Tyr peered around an angry-looking Hadriana. 'As Hannah says, that was epic. Darren falling over and rolling uncontrollably down the hill is one thing, but you literally hurtling yourself on the ground and rolling after him, I haven't laughed that hard in… centuries.'

'Yes it was all very amusing,' Hadriana said snarkily, momentarily dulling the mood, but I couldn't help but see the small glint in her eyes and burst out laughing again. 'But I am now drenched, so can we go please?'

'Come on,' I said, chuckling as we stepped around the wooden fence and carefully walked down the rest of the hill. Just as we reached the road, Etrician took the mud out of our clothes so that we wouldn't draw attention to ourselves, though we saw very few people around.

In the distance, you could see the town peek out of the haze of the rain. So picking up the road, we headed in a westerly direction; minding the neatly packaged balls of hot fresh manure.

'Why did you do that?' Etrician asked me as we lead the others down the road. 'My heart was beating a mile a minute, seeing what you did.'

Frowning curiously at him, I reached up and placed my hand on his forehead. 'No, you don't have a temperature.'

'Get off,' he growled. 'You had me worried sick.'

'Well, aren't you acting human? You Koalemos, it was just a bit of fun. Can't I have fun before I…' I cut myself short as Etrician's face saddened. Shaking my head, I smiled at him. 'Never mind. Anyway, we have to find out which train goes down to London. That's the first step. It's going to be difficult though, like looking for a needle in a haystack.' The problem I saw was even if we found her, the train was still going to crash and we had no idea how the accident happened. We had to be extra attentive to everything around us.

As we walked around the hill, we soon came to a road off to the right. After a unanimous vote, we took the path saying Holyrood Road.

'Oh so that's Holyrood Park,' Etrician chuckled as he looked back towards the big hill we had rolled down. 'I know where we are now.'

'When have you been to Edinburgh?' I asked him, as we headed down the road and following it, rounded to the left, a few horse-driven carriages clattered towards us.

'Well, I was visiting Ben Nevis to sort out a mountain troll problem some decades ago. I decided to check out the major cities as I was in the country. I spent a good few weeks going around the sites, so I know my way around pretty well.'

'Oh goody,' Hadriana said sarcastically, as I heard her shivering and chattering teeth behind me.

Suppressing an evil grin, Darren and Tyr were having a laugh about the many hills they could roll down, while Hadriana complained about being cold and wet and wanted nothing better than to find a hotel with a big log fire all to herself. Etrician and I were perfectly happy wandering around the city linking arms and looking at all of the sites the fantastic city had to offer.

'Hey does anyone want to just head into a pub and chill out for a bit?' Darren asked, as the heavens turned the taps off and streaks of brilliant sunlight burst through the grey, gloomy rain clouds above refracting the light, making a robust multicoloured rainbow. I hazarded a guess that a leprechaun would be taunting the eye with its mystical pot of gold.

Rolling my eyes I said, 'No, and please refrain from using 21st-century slang. If someone was to overhear you, we have no idea what the implications would be. We cannot interfere in anything, no interaction with anyone. We are here to inspect and save, that's it.'

'You were fun not half an hour ago, and now you've turned into my Mum,' he grumbled.

'Well, it's about time someone did act like a mother!' I shouted. 'I am getting fed-up of Hadriana's complaining, just be quiet, we're not staying in a comfortable hotel, we have no time,' I sniped.

With shocked wide eyes, she hitched up her dress and walked off. 'I'm going to get some answers. Mummy and Daddy and the annoying child and pet can stay here!'

Etrician laughed and nudged Darren, 'She meant you as the pet.'

'No, Hadriana!' I called, but she had crossed the street and headed into a nearby public house.

'Oh for the love of Atlas!' I groaned. Darren and Tyr were about to follow Hadriana when I reached out and grabbed their shirt collars. 'Nope.

You two are staying here. The less interaction the better.' Not wanting to destroy the timeline anymore we waited outside.

'You know, this is the last time that we'll be in the past,' Etrician said sadly. 'I've quite enjoyed it, to be honest.'

'Yes but we have to go back, we don't belong in this world... well, era.'

'No, I think you got it in one,' a slight crease on his forehead. 'We don't belong in this world, not anymore. Yes I know they'll always be earthquakes and tsunami's but doing this and not my actual job feels so much better, don't you agree?'

'I don't like getting involved,' I told him sternly. 'I like doing my job, but I've had no choice but to do this because of Santorini. I like staying in the water, I like sorting out the myths, and I liked the feeling of being content. If I had the chance, I would stay as foam on the waves forever.'

'You don't mean that,' he frowned sadly. 'You can't want to give up that easily.'

Etrician's eyes found me, but I looked away from him, too embarrassed to hold his gaze. Lately, I've been pushing myself, to not give up without a fight, to be strong and keep going. However, my fate was inevitable. 'The last time I did was when I... was when we...' sighing I glanced at his pained face, and he nodded, understanding what I was thinking.

'I never meant to hurt you, I didn't want to. It was, it just got complicated between us,' Etrician replied. 'And you couldn't visit me as much.' Indicating it was my fault. Instantly I felt my blood boil. I didn't wish to discuss it, let alone dwell on it. There were more important things to think about.

Moments later, a smug-looking Hadriana came out of the public house. Flicking her hair behind her, she said, 'Princes Street Station is the only one where its trains go to London, thank you very much to me.'

Etrician and I tutted.

'And we have a lift to the station.' Traipsing behind her, a man with a flat blue cap and covered in a black overcoat went around the corner, gesturing for us to follow. As we did so, we saw him hop up onto a horse-drawn carriage. Trotting down the pebbled road in her heels, which clicked on the street surface, Hadriana called, 'Angus, you are a darling.'

He nodded as we hurried towards him. Climbing into the carriage, I heard him mutter in Gaelic, 'Bloody English.'

Biting back a laugh, I smirked and got inside.

As the black leather-covered carriage trundled along the cobbled road to Princes Street railway station, the wafting smell of horse permeated the inside. It wasn't an overbearing smell, in fact, I found it rather calming, reminding me of a better time without exhaust fumes.

Darren and Tyr chatted away about Dagen missing out on all the fun, while Hadriana made small talk to Etrician on where she was in 1882.

I ignored them all making myself stare out of the carriage. I wasn't in a particularly chatty mood. Etrician had brought up the past, which I didn't want to think about, as I should be more concerned about the future and wondered, if after we saved Hannah's history, what Maynard or the Minister would do next. We had been thwarting their plans, but I felt we were kicking a hornet's nest and we'd only discover their wrath when we returned to our future.

'All right I give up, what is wrong with you?' Hadriana asked in a bored tone, five minutes into our journey. Making no real attempt to add to the situation, I shrugged.

'Oh, you are such a child,' she sniped. 'Think you are better than us, keeping secrets are we? Aren't we important enough to know what you are planning?'

Hadriana irked me; she didn't need to know everything. Some things that I wished to keep to myself and not discuss with her. That child can be so disrespectful it was almost disgusting of her to act in such an un-ladylike manner. Crossing my legs and shaking my foot to stem myself from exploding in a fit of rage, I folded my arms and gripped them tightly, solely focussing on getting to the station and stopping this awful accident from occurring.

'Um... Thera,' Darren said softly from beside me, 'you're making it really hot in here. I think I see steam coming from the top of your head.'

Grinding my teeth, I ignored him. He wasn't my concern, none of them were...

'Thera,' Hadriana's eyes peeked through my steam. I saw her apprehensive look on her face. 'If you don't calm down, you will burn through your clothes.'

The heat I was generating from my boiling blood was actually drying my wet dress. Taking a deep breath, I exhaled out steam, creating a small sauna in the carriage.

Feeling my body cool down, I opened the carriage door to let the steam out, then when the majority of it was gone, I closed it. I felt the group's worried faces stare at me.

'Aren't you going to tell me what's going on?' Hadriana asked me. She glanced at Etrician, who refused to look at her. 'Well?' she demanded.

'No Hadriana,' I replied quickly. 'Please, leave it alone.'

Tyr lent forward in his seat and said softly, 'You upset her too much. Can't you be nice for once?'

Hadriana blinked in confusion and turned to each of us for answers, but everyone just ignored her. It was nice for Tyr to defend me, but on the other hand, it shouldn't be necessary.

An hour and a half later, the carriage came to a rumbling stop. 'We're here,' Angus called from up top. Immediately getting out of the carriage, I took a deep breath and tried to calm down. I had to focus on the task ahead. The history that Etrician and I had was in the past. It became difficult for the two of us to spend some time together that much was true. But I was naive to think we'd be together forever, he was of the land, and I was of the sea. No matter which way I looked at it, Etrician and I were totally opposite and regardless of the saying that opposites attract, how can they if we could only see each other once or twice every few years?

While Hadriana paid Angus, I took in the surroundings of the station. It was a new high red-bricked building with tall arched windows, fitted all the way continuously around the bottom half of the building that covered one sizeable first floor. There were three levels above those with windows for each room or office. Above those was an interesting feature of a pyramid type collection of windows, giving off a very Victorian gothic feel to the building. It was a grand train station.

With a small whip of the reigns, the carriage rattled along the road heading off to its next destination. The five of us stood there, bewildered, unsure of what to do next. By the looks of the station, there was no train in sight. And as there were very few people around, I got the impression there wouldn't be a train for a while, possibly not until the following day.

'This is where my money comes into good use again,' Hadriana remarked. 'As you can see, there is a hotel an actual hotel not far from here and forgive me, but I would like to stay in it. Whether the rest of you want to go with me is up to you.'

Sighing heavily, I took a deep lungful of air and smiled. Tainted with the freshness of dusk, the air smelled of gardenia and wet grass which were carried from the hills. Overhead the rain clouds were now swirling away from the high winds, revealing a gorgeous dimming sun of deep orange. 'Let me just check what times the trains are running tomorrow,' Darren said, as he headed off towards the double doors in front, only one of which was open. A few minutes later, he came out with his face looking grim. 'I've got some bad news,' he said as he scratched his head. 'Man at the ticket desk said there are two trains that run tomorrow to London. One runs in the early morning at half five, and the other at half ten.'

'Oh well that's just brilliant,' Hadriana shrieked. 'This is just typical of us. We travel across the world, across time itself and we find out there are two bloody trains!'

'Enough!' I shouted at her. 'Stating the obvious isn't going to help. We shall split up, that's all we can do.'

'Oh an uneven three and two, who gets the human?' she said in a shirty manner.

Darren's eyes became slits as he shot her a look, 'Says you. You're human too you old hag!'

'Oh no,' I cringed as I began to walk away with Tyr and Etrician as Darren and Hadriana began to have a very loud argument. 'Whenever you've finished, we'll be over there in the Green Bow,' I called to them as I spotted what looked like a hotel close by the station. Looking newly refurbished with a fresh coat of paint, we were greeted by a door attendant.

'Good evening Miss,' he said in a rather thick Scottish accent.

'Good evening. There are five in our party. The other two will be along shortly.'

'Aye, very good Miss,' he nodded then opened the door for us.

'Let's get a drink and wait for the others, huh?' Tyr suggested. 'They should finish their arguing soon enough.'

The three of us sat at a quaint table in the corner of the lounge. Tyr had a clear view of the front doors and nudged us when he spotted Hadriana and Darren trounce into the entrance hall looking thoroughly vexed. Waving at them, they nodded and walked to us, completely ignoring one another.

'Sorted out your differences?' I asked Hadriana. Out of the corner of my eye, Darren headed straight for the bar. He'd seen a woman with mocha-coloured hair. She hadn't noticed Darren as she sipped on a glass of wine, staring down at her hands. The woman seemed deeply troubled.

'Hmph.' Hadriana sat down opposite me, folding her arms and staring at my glass of white wine, following the bubbles that rose to the top of the liquid. 'Ungrateful little snit.'

Smirking, I sipped the rest of my drink, carefully monitoring Darren, who was now having an in-depth conversation with the attractive woman at the end of the bar.

After a few minutes, I heard Darren say, 'I'll see you tomorrow then.' Standing up, he made his way towards us and plonked half of his beer on the table, keeping quiet as the woman got up and shining a smile in his direction headed to a set of stairs that led to the hotel's rooms.

'Who was that?' Tyr asked him as Darren smiled proudly.

'That my friend, would you believe it, was Ann Smith,' he said excitedly.

We all craned our necks to see her disappear up the stairs. 'No way!' Tyr laughed. 'The luck you have!'

'Well done!' Etrician clapped him on the back.

Darren grinned proudly. 'Thank you. Anyway, she is boarding the half five train tomorrow morning as she is heading down to London to visit her sister who is going to give birth any day now.' Downing the rest of his drink, he slapped his lips and beamed at us. 'You are very welcome.'

Chapter Twenty-Five

'Come on, get up,' Hadriana tiredly knocked on my door. 'Thera please we're going to be late, and I want breakfast.'

Rolling over in my slightly uncomfortable four-poster bed, I glanced at the door by the far end of the room that Hadriana had paid for. I saw her shadow under the door. Glancing around the rather large expensive hotel room, I noticed it was still horribly dark. How Hadriana managed to get up before half five was beyond me. Closing my eyes, I grabbed a pillow and threw it over my head, burying deeper into blackness.

'I know you're awake.' Her hot temper got the better of her as she smacked the door. 'Get up you lazy sod!'

Taking a deep breath, I rubbed my eyes and sat up. I didn't use to feel so tired and sluggish, but all this time, travelling and running around wasn't helping matters. Stifling a yawn, I threw the bedclothes off me and put my clothes on. Still, with tired eyes, I slipped into my shoes and headed out the door, gently closing it behind me. Tottering down the dimmed hallway, I heard moans and groans of other people in the hotel who had been woken up by Hadriana banging on my bedroom door.

Still annoyingly dark out, we all met outside of the hotel. 'Sleep well?' Darren asked, rather cheerfully as he smiled at us. 'I did. I had a dream about Ann last night, and I've come to the conclusion that what Hannah doesn't know won't hurt her. It's not Hannah's direct descendant, it's her great, great aunt, so I'm allowed to kiss... but not tell.'

'You are a rather pathetic specimen of a human being, aren't you?' Hadriana said in a haughty tone as she came out of the hotel, placing some strands of flyaway hair behind her ears. 'Anyway, I thought you were chasing after this Saskia girl, the other Siren?'

Darren shrugged his shoulders. 'Ann talks to me, Saskia insults me, there's a difference right there for you.'

'But Darren,' I said sadly, 'you know, you can't be with the girl, don't press your feelings on her or she'll get upset that you will have to leave and never see her again.'

'Plus,' she said, turning to Darren with her hands on her hips, 'how would you feel if you saw her gravestone for God's sake. It wouldn't be pleasant. It's happened to me a few times with some old boyfriends.'

Darren gave her a cold look, 'Well, thanks for putting it so bluntly.'

'You're welcome,' she smiled sweetly. 'Now then, we have a train to catch.'

As Hadriana strode off in the direction of the train station, Darren mumbled obscenities. Hearing Tyr and Etrician give a sympathetic sigh beside me, I too felt sorry for Darren. He seemed like he was becoming increasingly desperate to find a girlfriend though it might be more of his merman instincts than genuine human feelings.

As we entered the high domed ceiling, with red painted steel arches that stretched from one side of the large room to the other, Hadriana had somehow managed to procure some travel papers. On returning, she waved them in front of us. Timing her, I noticed it only took her fifteen minutes or so; however, I did see that her lipstick was a little smudged on her upper lip. When I asked her about it, she explained that she had gone ahead of us and had slipped into the ticket office to have a "word" with the train guard, though she smiled evilly and gave me a playful wink.

'Oh, please tell me you didn't?' I asked as she slipped the papers down the front of her dress.

'Did what?' she asked me innocently as we headed to the platform. The train was due to arrive in a few minutes.

'Well you didn't just wipe your mouth on the back of your hand, did you?' I said in a huffy tone. 'Please tell me you didn't?'

She laughed. 'Alright, I didn't.'

'Oh my Gods!' I groaned, 'why, why must you act like this? Do you always do it? In fact, don't answer that,' I added quickly, not wanting to pry into her personal and private affairs.

'What? If a girl can't get what she wants, give something in return,' she laughed playfully. 'And you have one dirty mind, my dear Thera. I only gave him a little kiss.'

'Ha,' Darren barked out a laugh from behind.

'What?' she snapped, demanding to know what he meant.

'A little kiss?' He drawled. 'Yeah, I don't think so, more of a groping, grinding snog. That's your style, isn't it?'

'What are you implying? And so what if I did, what's it got to do with you fish-boy?' she said, grinding her teeth, her eyes turned into slits.

'You,' he said standing up to his full height, folding his arms as though showing he wasn't scared of her, 'are the most God awful garden tool I have EVER met!'

While looking confused as to what he said, Darren grabbed her by the waist and pulled her to him. For a split second, I thought he was going to kiss her, and then it was my utter mistake as he reached down her dress and pulled the papers from in-between her cleavage.

'Utter garden tool!' Forming an 'L' shape with his finger and thumb, he placed it against his forehead, then gave her the middle finger and walked off.

Staring after him with our mouths open in shock and confusion, it quickly dawned on me what he meant by garden tool, and I burst out laughing.

Etrician and Tyr's confused faces turned to look at me, and I mouthed the word, 'hoe.' Clocking on, they tried to stifle their laughter as Hadriana's face turned a deep puce. 'We need to get going-' I tried to say amidst my giggling.

'I'm going to punch him so hard his children's children won't be able to procreate!' Seething, she stormed off after Darren, her teeth grinding together, her hands balled into fists.

Passing through a set of red and black painted doors on the right-hand side by the small ticket office, I noticed one of the men had a glazed look on his face with a red smudge on his lips.

We came out onto the platform where a shiny black train slowly and loudly rumbled along the tracks billowing white smoke out of the funnel against the velvet blue sky. Crawling towards us, hissing steam poured from the sides, spreading like a strange white powdery mist alongside the concrete.

Glancing around for Darren, I spotted him talking to a mocha-haired woman who I instantly realised was Ann Smith, dressed in a long purple dress. Looking past us, she nodded in our direction, and Darren turned around. From the sound of steam engine, I couldn't hear what he said to her.

After a few moments, there was a high-pitched whistle from behind. 'All aboard please, ladies and gentlemen.' A portly man with a pocket watch in one hand and a whistle in his mouth ordered some of the train staff to help carry passengers luggage into the carriages. Having none, we went to Darren to get back the travel papers to find out which compartment was ours.

'Compartment C13,' he said when we approached him. Shoving the papers in our hands, he took his own before helping Ann with her luggage then accompanied her onto the train, completely ignoring us.

'Come on,' Tyr called, as he followed Darren and Ann on the train. Sighing, the rest of us followed.

Boarding the train, we saw Darren and Ann head into a carriage further along the train on the right, checking the letter and number, our group was along on the left. Finding our rather spacious compartment, I smiled at a small crystal vase with a single red rose that was placed delicately in the middle of a table. It was only until the train departed from the station after the whistle blew from the conductor that Darren turned up.

'Well I have some news,' he said, sliding the door shut as he sat next to me, coincidently his seat was the furthest away from Hadriana who was still seething from what he had said to her in the station not fifteen minutes previously. 'She's being followed.'

'Yes, by you. Little slug.' Hadriana barked, but it was a pathetic retort.

Ignoring her, he met my eyes, 'She's seen four men in strange black clothing, just before we arrived. I think that means that whoever is in charge of them is figuring us out.'

'So they get there a day before us,' Etrician finished. 'Smart.'

'But what does that mean for us?' Tyr asked, though, from the tone of his voice, he had already figured it out.

Looking at Etrician and Darren, they both shared the same worried expression, 'We are too late,' I voiced. 'They are clearly staying by her to witness the accident and ensure her death. In about eight hours the train is supposed to have a crash in a tunnel. That means that they have already rigged the train to cause the accident in the tunnel.'

There was silence in the carriage for a few moments as everyone tried to collect their thoughts. There was no point in going back into the past again to stop the men from rigging the train. The only thing we could hope for now was that whatever the crash with the train might be, we could hopefully prevent it, and if not ensure that Ann lived through it.

'We need to stay near her,' I piped up, shattering the silence. 'Tyr, go and check the carriages near her, Etrician, I need you to find a way to check under the train. Use your magic if you must.'

'What am I looking for?' he asked with a frown.

'Anything magical, something or anything that may prove fatal to the journey,' I looked at their eyes, meeting their calculated stares. 'This accident never happened in the past, we must prevent it at all costs-'

'Except exposing yourselves for who you truly are,' Hadriana spoke in a sleazy manner. 'At all costs? I don't think so Thera-'

'This accident cannot happen, you fool!' I shouted at her. 'Ann must live; these people on this train must live! Maynard has no concern for human life. He has no idea of the consequences of killing over one hundred people on a train! It will do incalculable damage to the timeline, and that cannot happen. At all costs Hadriana, bind yourself to the cause you so willingly put yourself into, or else I shall relive the duties I entrusted to you from the very get-go and be rid of you and your family! Do I make myself clear?'

Flabbergasted, that I had spoken to her like that, she nodded, muttering a small, 'Yes.'

'Good. Tyr go and check the other carriages towards the front of the train... now,' I barked. Nodding at my instruction, Tyr got up and left. 'Darren stay with Ann, inform her there is a suspicious character onboard the train. Give her a good excuse to stay in her carriage and leave her sliding door open, don't ask why,' I added as he frowned but didn't ask. 'Etrician go and check under the carriages, please. Look for anything suspicious.'

'Fine,' getting up he strolled out of the compartment, not looking back.

'You,' I turned to Hadriana, 'go along the carriages and check to see if the men are on board or not. They may be here, just in period clothes like us. If you see anyone who looks like them, make an excuse to open the door but not close it properly.'

'So what, are you going to sit here and do nothing while you bark out orders for the rest of us? Who put you in charge?' she asked haughtily as she got up and went to the sliding door.

Looking away from her, I reached out for the vase and held it up, staring at the colourless liquid. 'No one put me in charge, and I'm not going to sit here and do nothing, I'm going to ghost the train.'

Hadriana had opened the door a little, but closed it, looking confused. 'Huh?'

Taking the flower out, I held it on my hand and showed it to her. 'Water is everywhere. It's in humans, it's in this flower, and it's in the air. With a little extra water, I am going to ghost the train, or as Santorini and I called it "Ghosting."' Closing my fingers over the flower, I inhaled and magically sucked the water out of the rose, instantly turning it dry and lifeless, as if it had been pressed in a book for months. Looking sideways at Hadriana, a small worried crease etched on her brow.

'What does "Ghosting" mean exactly?'

'Turning oneself into evaporated water,' I smiled, pouring the water from the vase onto the table, I placed my hand over it and immediately it began to boil; steam gently rising into the air.

'The steam in the carriage from before... you can make your entire body into steam?' her voice sounded as though I was telling her an odd joke, but it wasn't.

I took a deep breath and placed my hand into the steam, within moments my hand disappeared; more steam billowed out, the particles swirling around my head. 'I need you to pull the blinds on the doors and leave it open ajar.' I informed her. 'Once I have looked around the carriages I can come back here and reform.'

'That's a really odd ability,' she said with a slight smirk on her face. 'But why are you asking me to leave the doors open?'

I shrugged. 'It's easier for me. I can go under the door, but my evaporated body still has to abide by the laws of the earth. Hot air and steam rises, and when cooled, it forms back into water. Frankly, I'd rather not end up as a puddle on the floor.'

'Um, alright.' Unsure of how to respond, she grabbed hold of the blinds and pulled them down, attaching them to a small clip at the base of the door.

'Wish me luck,' I said, pushing the rest of my body through the steam, my body literally disintegrating into millions of invisible particles. This particular ability was similar to sea foam. It was relaxing yet dangerous. You could quickly lose yourself to the serenity of becoming so content with riding the waves; I had lost many a Water Nymph who chose that life for eternity.

It was a strange sensation to be vapour and how Santorini and I even found out we had the ability was one of the scariest things either one of us had seen and done. Annoying each other as siblings do, we became so hot-tempered we turned the surrounding water into steam, and after Santorini abruptly forced me into it, I suddenly became it. Interesting as it may seem, it was frightening. I had no eyes to see, nobody to move and no ears to hear, yet I could feel the vibrations of sounds that moved in the ocean.

Taking a very long time to figure out how to reform myself again, we tried it on land and found it was similar though dangerous in other ways. For one, we knew that steam rose, so there was the possibility of continuously floating up into the air and being unable to contain our evaporated bodies, and the winds would carry us off until we were unable to reform again. Also, sounds were distinctively better to "hear" through the vibrations of the air, and it was even better in still air or for want of a better word, dead air, for example inside a closed room, or inside a train.

In this evaporated state, I was "listening" for the librations of sound in the air. Still, not only that, humans had the uncanny ability to send out waves of fear or anxiety or love or discomfort. The humans gave themselves away, purely by the fact that they could not control what they were thinking.

Extending my thoughts out, almost feeling as though my mind was expanding through the air, I "felt" the edge of the door and slipped through the few millimetres of air. As soon as I was aware I was in the long corridor, I extended out in both directions and instantly checked every single door that was ajar. Still, all I was aware of was mixed signals of annoyance, contentment, apprehension. None of the messages I was sensing matched to the dark, intense ones that I should be able to feel from these four men.

Continuing to stretch out, I "felt" people walk below, the brisk air carried towards me, swirling around but it wasn't enough to throw me off my concentration. Sightless, deaf but not dumb, I continued to check the doors, hoping and praying that Hadriana had at least grown suspicious of someone when suddenly I "felt" something that could have frozen my heart if I had one. Hatred, loathing and a slight taste of recklessness was sitting in one compartment with two other bodies. Their thoughts were all very similar. But four people were following Ann… so where was the other one?

Heading back to the compartment that was void of all emotion and vibrations of anything of the sort, I reformed myself and waited patiently for the others to return. Tyr came back first after an hour and nodded as he sat down opposite. 'I've seen three compartments with men inside them. Only one has a group of four inside, and they have pressed suits and looked a little out of place.'

'What about the groups of three?' I asked him.

'There are two groups to the left-hand side of the train. And another a little further towards the front of the train on the right. Why are you asking about three men, I thought we were looking for four?' Tyr asked, confused.

Before I could answer, Hadriana popped in, quickly closing the door behind. 'Well, did you sense them or whatever you did?'

I turned to Tyr. 'There are three men who have the darkest of thoughts running through their minds. I know we are on the lookout for four men, but I definitely think that three men are involved in this. I would stake my eternal life over it.'

'We need to wait for Etrician to-' but Tyr's sentence was cut short by a strange tapping sound, as though rock on glass. Looking past Hadriana who was still by the door, she slid it open, but there was no one outside. Making me jump, the tapping came again, only this time a little louder.

Turning my head towards the only other glass that was prominent in the room, I saw a floating almond-shaped pebble flying alongside the train. 'Etrician!' I gasped. Lunging forwards, I yanked the window open. As quick as it could, the small almond pebble, along with a wheelbarrow full of medium-sized rocks of different shapes and colours, came pelting into the compartment with a loud clattering sound.

Tyr yelled in shock and jumped onto the seats as the rocks fell to the floor then began to collect together forming feet at first, then legs, midriff, upper torso, arms neck and head.

'Well that was interesting,' Etrician smiled as he returned to normal.

'What did you find?' Tyr asked Etrician as he sat down, staring at the empty vase and dried up flower on the table. He then held up the vase and looked at me.

'Ghosted?' I nodded in reply. 'Fair enough and yes, Tyr, I did find something. An acid bomb, right at the front of the train.'

'What?' we all asked.

'It looks like it would act like a normal old 19th-century bomb with a fuse, but the explosion would be minimal. It's just enough to make a canister of highly corrosive acid melt through the brakes at the front of the train, making it unable to stop. The canister is being protected by magic,' he added, staring at Hadriana's puzzled face.

'That means,' I pondered, 'it'll hit another train along the way or-'

'Will go too fast for the track switchers and end up someplace it ought not to be,' Etrician finished my sentence. 'That's what I was thinking too, and we can't find out either way.'

Hadriana made a little cough so she could have our attention. 'Excuse me,' she said to Etrician, 'but you couldn't take the bomb off the train because…'

'Because a Jinn is guarding it like its life depended on it.'

Tyr gave a small unenthusiastic smile and looked at me. 'That explains your missing man then Thera. The fourth man is under the train.'

'Great, we can't use stardust on a Jinn,' I complained.

'Why not?' Tyr asked.

'Both grant wishes. It wouldn't work.' Tyr didn't understand. 'It's like getting Zeus to defeat Thor. It wouldn't work,' I explained. 'Both use lightening. They'd cancel each other out.'

'Dad would beat Zeus any day,' Tyr muttered.

In the distance, we heard a lady call along the corridor, asking if anyone would care for anything to eat. Hadriana bought some food and drink and sat and munched through it on her own while the rest of us thought of plans to get the train safely to London. Afternoon, Hadriana had a kip while Etrician and I took a stroll along the corridors to stretch our legs. We passed by Darren and Ann's compartment and saw him having an in-depth conversation with her. I pointed out to Etrician the three men I sensed earlier, but they had their blinds drawn and we could not see them.

'So how the hell do we go about this?' Hadriana enquired, with only an hour to go until we got to London. Time was pressing around us from all corners, and we were still no closer to coming up with a decent plan to save everyone from the three-hundred-ton train crashing.

The four of us sat down and put our thinking caps on. I saw a few ways of diverting the incident with Ann, but not the collision of the train. Moving the Jinn was next to impossible. Because he was commanded to guard the bomb, there was no way of moving him, unless one of the men had his lamp on him, but that was highly doubtful.

Slapping his hand down on the table making everyone jump Tyr smiled, 'I have it. We divide the train. Some stay with Ann. The others stay with the exploding part of the train and try to stop the bomb.'

'This isn't some cheesy 1930's black and white train robbery,' Hadriana exhaled heavily. 'I was thinking about using the emergency stop or get the conductor to stop the train, but then what? People in this period and in this country have never heard of bombs on a train. They wouldn't believe us, or they'd think it was a hoax.'

Rubbing my temple, I had to think about this and quickly. 'Right there are a few things we need to put into perspective and bear with me on this please,' I added as my thoughts were confusing even me. 'Firstly, track switchers, we need to know how many and where and what time they change. Tyr I need you to sort this one out for me if you don't mind?'

'Why?' he asked perplexed.

'In this period they only have one track line, not two. So I need you to buck up your powers, find out the track times from the conductor, then inform me afterwards so we can make a plan.'

'All right, but why would you need my powers?' he frowned, as he got up.

'I don't want to use the stardust. It's running out. If the train's breaks have been corroded and they won't stop, the train will speed up. I need you to be aware of the track changes and get in front of the train to change them.'

'And what are you three going to do?' he asked as he was about to leave the compartment.

'We're going to try and slow the train down. We need to stop it from getting to that tunnel.'

'WHAT!' Hadriana shouted, 'are you insane? Have you actually gone mad? I have no powers; I wouldn't even know where to start.'

Looking slyly at her, I smiled sweetly, 'No, you have no powers, but you can't die. So, you and Darren are going to be Ann's bodyguards.' Giving me a confused face, I elaborated. 'Think please, if they find out that we are involved, and we are trying to stop the train, they will have a Plan B and probably kill her in some other method. So you and Darren will be there to protect her.'

Giving me a sharp glare, she said, 'Darren is a human; if he gets shot he'll die.' Hadriana would, of course, point out the obviousness in a situation. 'It's fortunate for you and Etrician that the jinn is a myth. If used for wishes, they could do serious damage to anyone else.' A spark of knowledge flashed before me, and I felt so human and so slow that it took me this long to realise it. Initially, I had no idea how to make Darren and Hannah myths again. It was only when I was facing Morgana when she tried to use her magic on me, did I remember that myth magic doesn't work on legends. However, legend magic works on myths.

Raising my hands in front of me, I looked at them. I could make both Hannah and Darren myths again by using the aqua stone bracelets, which were magically created by the Ancients.

Etrician stood up. From the corner of my eye, I saw him stare at me. Slowly, my eyes lifted and met his; his eyes showed such deep concern for me. I didn't want to admit to everyone what had recently come to ahead. The Minister was right, after all, I was going to see his way and practically hand over Darren and Hannah on a silver platter, because I was the only one who could turn them back into myths.

'Thera…' he said softly, his voice almost pierced my heart.

My thoughts were becoming confused again. Would I have to turn him now or later? What difference would a few hours make to wait? 'Probably a lot,' I whispered to myself. 'It has to be done. I'll just have to command him until further notice.'

'What are you babbling on about?' Tyr asked, as he still waited by the doors.

Collecting my thoughts, I shook my head to rid my confusion. 'Straightforward is the way,' I said aloud. 'Tyr, go do your job, Hadriana come with me, Etrician… find a way to seal the doors of sound, it's going to hurt him, a lot.'

Heading out into the corridor, I looked back over my shoulder and glanced at the compartment, which housed the three evil men. Cursing the rules, I hated being unable to do anything. Now that humans surrounded us, the Ancients would get involved if we broke the golden rule and used magic in front of them. While Etrician and I would have to answer to our mothers, Tyr being the only myth was bound by law to obey the Ancients. As kind and helpful as Tyr was, he could potentially be the worst liability and put us all in danger.

In silence, we walked down the corridor and came to the compartment which Ann and Darren were in. Knocking gently on the door, I waited for it to open.

Ann Smith, a beautiful thirty-something-year-old, opened the door and smiled. 'Yes, can I help… you?' Her facial expression showed shock and confusion. 'Haven't I seen you somewhere before?'

'I need a word with my friend. Please,' I said, not answering her question.

Opening the door further, Darren came into view. Seeing us, he stood up, glowering. 'What is it?'

'I need a word with you. Hadriana,' I said to her.

She nodded and grabbed Darren and dragged him out, then threw him against the wooden panel behind.

'What are you doing to him?' Ann yelled, but Hadriana pushed her inside and closed the sliding doors quickly behind her.

'Thera, what the hell is going on?' Darren demanded. Glancing at his wrist, I grabbed it, pulling the sleeve down to see the bracelet and the semi-gleaming Aqua Stone set in the middle, feeling the power emit from it. I was about to touch the stone, but I stopped myself and shook my head. 'Why is Hadriana in there?'

Hearing a few compartment doors sliding open and seeing passengers peep out to see what all the commotion was about, I remained silent as I grabbed Darren and forced him to come with me. Trying to pull away from me, he was not strong enough to pull himself free from my vice-like grip. Abruptly stopping by our compartment, I knocked on the door. When I didn't hear anything from inside, I opened it slowly; gasping softly as there immediately behind the door was a thick wall of rock in front of me. The smell of fresh earth instantly sprang into my nose, and I smiled. Etrician smelled of the earth, the memories that came with its aroma lifted my spirits.

Placing my steady hand against the cold rock, closing my eyes, I whispered, 'Etrician.'

Feeling strange sensations coming from the rock, my eyes flicked open just in time to see a hand reach out through the stone. 'Holy shi-' Darren managed to say, just as I held onto Etrician's hand and he dragged me through the rock, with Darren tagging along behind for the ride.

Emerging from the other side, I gasped as I was thrown into an eerie green light. The whole compartment was encased with a thick rock. 'This is brilliant,' I said to Etrician, letting go of Darren.

'I can't breathe, there's no air in here,' he said, pushing against the stone.

'Well I'm going to fix that,' I told him, as Etrician was just visible under the small green fluorescent gems that sparkled in the ceiling of this mini-cave he created. Turning to Darren, I took a deep breath. 'I'm not giving you a choice in the matter Darren, it is going to hurt you, and for that I am sorry, but you will have to listen to me and obey me, again you have no choice in the matter.'

'What... what are you talking about?' he asked, looking a little frightened.

Grabbing his wrist with my left hand, I pulled it towards me; the bracelet gleamed from the eerie gems above. 'I'm going to turn you back into a full myth.' Stuttering from panic, Darren tried to pull away, but it was too late. With my other hand, I slapped it onto the bracelet, covering the Aqua Stone which immediately shone a brilliant blue light, and said the one simple word which would destroy Darren's humanity and turn him back into a creature of magic and allure. 'Release!'

Darren made a small involuntary gasp as he looked down as the Aqua Stone that had cracked under my command; viscous liquid that was the colour of the ocean streamed out and plunged deep into Darren's skin, piercing it as though soft paper. Darren yelled from shock. Stumbling back, he tried to stop the pure magic crawling up through his veins to the rest of his body. His eyes widened in terror, and that's when the pain began.

'Pin him down,' I yelled as Darren began to scream, his arms and legs flailing around, which would cause him more damage.

Etrician locked Darren's arms behind him while I grabbed onto his legs, which soon wouldn't be legs anymore.

As the minutes passed, agonisingly waiting for the magic to seep into every particle of Darren's body, he screamed out to make it stop but I couldn't and wouldn't stop it. We had come too far. 'My body feels like it's being stabbed by daggers,' he cried. 'Stop it now!'

Writhing but unable to throw us off as Etrician and I were too powerful for him, Darren's pain was so excruciating, he quickly passed out. Releasing his legs, I looked up to see his head lolling on his chest. Sighing with relief, I sat back. 'Put him on the floor,' I told Etrician.

Doing as I asked, he sat opposite me, ready to make a lunge for Darren if he was to act up again, which would be within the next five minutes or so.

'So tell me, you really did know all along how to do this?' He asked after Darren began to jerk his feet, instantly putting me on edge.

Glancing from Darren's feet to Etrician I shrugged. 'Only until I pieced it together, thanks to Hadriana. It's the Aqua Stone. It's legend magic, my mother created it. Besides my mother, I am a child of the ocean. I can unleash the magic within the stone for myself, but it never really occurred for me to try it on a human.'

'Part human,' Etrician corrected.

'Exactly. Darren's transformation only happened in water, but he was normal out of it. Unleashing the stone out of water well,' I glanced at him, 'this is the result. I need him immortal to protect Ann Smith.'

Etrician moved closer to me and took off Darren's shoes and socks; he would need them later. Sighing, he reached out for my hand. 'Thera, know this, I will always care for you, and I will do my best to keep you safe.'

I smiled and leant closer together, but something stopped me, 'But will you keep everyone else safe from me?'

The pained expression etched on his face again, and he lamented, pulling away from me. 'I… I cannot do that-'

'AHHH!' Darren had suddenly woken up. Within seconds, Etrician reached out and pinned him down, but his torso wasn't bothering me.

'Take his trousers off,' I yelled, as Darren's legs began to bulge, scales patterned his forearms and rippled down his body.

'What?' Darren and Etrician said together, as Darren tried so hard not to scream.

'If you don't take them off now they'll split, and I don't want you walking around with no trousers on, you'll get arrested!' I shouted at him. 'Take them off!'

Etrician moved me out of the way and managed to yank Darren's trousers off just before the slippery, long, brown tail bulged from his legs. Darren yelled out in such a screech it made my ears ring, his tail, forced me to move out of the way; the smell of salt quickly permeated the rock-room that Etrician had made.

'Damn mermen,' I panted, as the tail flopped up and down. Laying back on the ground, I took a deep breath, though became increasingly irritated as the flippers of Darren's tail kept hitting me in the face.

'Um Thera,' Etrician asked slowly, his voice sounding worried. 'Is he meant to do that?'

'Do what?' I frowned as I sat up. 'Oh, Atlas!' I yelped as Darren was scratching at his gills that had sprouted on his neck, he couldn't breathe air. 'Um,' thinking quickly, I looked at Etrician. 'Don't watch!'

'Huh?'

But before I could give him an answer, my hands clapped around Darren's gills and hefting his body, I kissed him on the lips, exhaling water into his mouth. In all fairness it was a pretty vile thing to do, as humans also think that exchanging bodily fluids is rather disgusting on some level; I too didn't particularly like it, but it was to save Darren from essentially asphyxiating.

Breathing in the oxygenated water, Darren's tail stopped flopping. After a few seconds, I stopped kissing him and quickly slapped my hand over his mouth. 'Right, you have enough water in your lungs to keep you happy for a moment or so.'

'Thera, how could you?' Etrician asked, looking hurt.

'Oh shut up,' I snipped, 'I told you not to watch.' I turned my attention back to Darren. 'Listen to me very carefully. I'm going to ask you some questions, and I need you to answer me, alright, don't speak just nod your head. I can't hear your thoughts because we're not underwater,' I added.

Darren nodded once.

'Good, now are you in pain?'

He shook his head.

Relief spread through me. 'Good, and do you feel like you are yourself again? Do you feel normal?'

He nodded.

'Good. Now, this is going to be the hard part, but I need you to listen to me. I hate doing this as… well… unless a myth is doing something wrong and need to be reprimanded, but I'm doing this for your own good. I am going to order you until I can pass over my power to Hannah when the time comes. But, in the meantime, you will listen to me and pay attention. Darren, you are going to transform into a human, while human you will obey me without complaint. Do as I say, now.'

Scowling at me in hatred, he suddenly cringed and arched his back in pain. Unable to yell out as I still had my hand clamped over his mouth, he made harsh yelps of pain deep within his throat. With his tail thrashing madly hitting Etrician and myself, I remained where I was. I couldn't let go.

The power of Darren's tail was immense. Almost cracking the walls of Etrician's rock-room, some illuminated gems from above loosened, falling to the floor like green rain.

Turning around to look at Darren's tail, it was slowly turning pink and dividing in two. Looking away, I stared down at Darren, looking for any signs of the transition on his neck. 'Etrician, tell me when he is human again so I can let the water out or else he'll drown.'

One of Darren's gills was visible on the left-hand side of his neck, and over a few seconds, it began to fade, though there was something in its place.

'Alright he's done,' Etrician said softly, as Darren's eyes grew wide in panic. Lifting my hands off, Darren spat out a large amount of water and coughed violently to get air back into his lungs.

Looking away as Darren got dressed; he laid back and tried to regulate his breathing. 'Kack on a stick,' he gasped, putting his hands over his head. 'Please don't do that again. That was awful and painful.'

'You won't have to go through that again.' I said and sat next to him. 'Welcome to the fold of mythology.'

'You mean that's it?' he asked, laughing softly. 'I'm a myth again? No more tattoo?'

Scoffing, I reached out and touched his neck. 'It's not a tattoo, but there is some sort of mark there.'

Sitting bolt up, Darren slapped a hand to his neck. 'I... I feel something, but I don't get it. If it's not a tattoo, then what is it?'

I shrugged. 'A mark of three lines that looks like gills. Normal mermen don't have that, but you aren't and never will be.'

Darren laughed lightly and shook his head. 'It's going to be strange being like this again.' Checking out his bracelet, he unclipped it and cast it to the floor. 'Don't need that anymore.'

Huffing, I leant over him like an ominous cloud. 'Right Darren, a few things you need to be aware of. Firstly is that you can't walk and I'm serious, you will have no balance as your brain, I suppose, has re-set itself.'

'What?' he barked, as he pushed himself up to a half-standing position then began to wobble. I gracefully jumped out of the way as he fell flat on his face with a mighty, 'oof,' escaping from his lips.

'I love saying I told you so... so I'll repeat it, I told you so,' I smiled wistfully at his failed attempt, wondering how he would cope with the new powers he would permanently have. 'Secondly,' I said, grabbing his attention, 'as I've told you before you have no sense of love, so-'

'Oh I'm sure that Ann or Saskia will-' but I quickly knelt down and pressed my hands on his mouth to quieten him.

'No, you are not listening; you have no sense of love. If you show any compassion towards Saskia, it will only be lust. It's not real love Darren.' I sighed sadly. 'You can't fall in love. In this state, you can barely feel infatuation. The only thing you need to remember is that caring for others, looking out for them is what's important. Promise me that you will not steal love from others. It will break the bonds that you have had from your human life, and you will forget your purpose. Promise me, Darren, that you won't succumb?'

He gave me a small smile. 'I will remember your words. And yes, I will promise not to hurt my friends.'

During the little chat that Darren and I had, Etrician had quickly destroyed the lumps of rock that formed around the room. In a cloud of dust he promptly opened the window.

Suddenly the door burst open, and Tyr's panicked stricken face instantly made me jump up to attention. 'What's wrong?' I asked.

Glancing around the room, his eyes glanced to Darren on the floor, but he didn't ask and to be perfectly honest, there was no need to at this moment in time. 'The track changes, there's one in about ten minutes. Well, it was ten minutes about five minutes ago!' he shouted glaring at me. 'I couldn't get in!'

'Etrician, go and check the Jinn, quickly!' In an explosion of dust, Etrician's body disappeared. It zoomed out the window, heading underneath the train.

'Whoa that was cool,' Darren laughed, still on the floor. 'I didn't know he could explode into dust.'

Ignoring him, I reached down and picked him up. 'Tyr, I need you to go and check on Hadriana and Ann. I'll be there shortly.' With a single nod, he left without another word. 'Alright you, one baby step at a time,' I told him.

'But I know how to walk,' Darren glared in frustration. 'It's one foot in front of the other but-'

Ensuring I had most of his weight, I helped him get some balance before we started to walk. 'Yes, exactly but. You can't comprehend how to do it anymore.' I held onto his shoulder and stopped him as he lifted his right foot and pitched forwards. 'Just find your balance first then we can worry about walking in a minute.'

The train then suddenly gave a great shudder, knocking both of us off our feet. People in the nearby compartments screamed and yelled in fright. In a heap on the floor, I looked up to the window, just in time to watch Etrician's dust cloud fly back inside. Forming instantly he said with shocked eyes, 'We're too late!'

'Atlas, damn it,' I cried, standing up. 'Get him off the floor and help move everyone to the back of the train.' Tripping over Darren's flailing legs, I made my way to the door and flung it open. 'We need to uncouple the engine from the carriages.' I ran down the corridor shouting, 'Everyone move to the back of the train!' People poked their heads out of their compartments in confusion and stared at me blankly. 'Get to the back of the train, do not ask, just do it!'

'I beg your pardon miss?' said one gentleman with a walrus-like moustache.

'Get to the back of the train! It's for your own safety, the train is going to crash. I need to uncouple the engine. Move it now!'

Seeing the look on my face, the man thankfully didn't question it, and sliding his door open fully, bellowed to the others in his compartment to get out.

With my heart beating like a hammer inside my chest, I yanked the door open of Ann's compartment. I saw the three of them staring in shock, unsure of what to do. 'Hadriana, take Ann and get to the back of the train. Tyr, to go the crossing ahead.'

'What is going on?' Ann asked as Hadriana grabbed her arm and yanked her out of her seat. 'I demand to know.'

Hadriana silently took Ann out and shepherded her down the end of the train, which was packed with people all yelling in fright. Everyone was now made aware that the train was going to crash.

Tyr and I took off towards the front of the train, still yelling at people to head down to the front when suddenly, I heard a loud crackle behind me. 'TYR, GET DOWN!' I shouted, flinging myself towards him, pushing him to the floor.

A bolt of electricity flew over our heads and hit a door's glass panel in front, shattering it to smithereens. A smoky wind suddenly picked up around screaming through the broken door ahead. Rolling over, I saw the men heading towards us; their hands sizzled from the magic they shot at us. Glancing past, Hadriana and Ann had somehow managed to sneak past them and joined Darren and Etrician.

'Get up,' I told Tyr, pushing him forwards.

'Where do I go?' he asked me, protecting his face from the wind.

'I don't BELIEVE this!' I shouted, annoyed by his unreliability. 'You're a God of wind, there's a wind blowing through this entire train, there are bad guys behind us! Bloody act like the God you are meant to be!'

Staring at me for a split second, realisation dawned on him and with a quick nod; he stood up and turning around, ran straight towards the broken window. Jumping into the air, he dived towards it and disappeared instantly, as though he became the colourless air around.

'Get up, you fool,' I told myself, 'they aren't going to wait until you get up again.' No sooner had I said that another bout of crackling electricity shot towards me, people screamed in utter terror as they were unsure of what they were seeing. 'The Ancients are going to get you, I swear to Atlas!' I shouted, scrambling up and heading for the door.

Yanking it open, I heard another crack and ducked to the metal part of the carriage on the right-hand side, just in time to see another bolt of blue light shoot through the blown window. Their aim was improving.

As the luscious green countryside of rolling hills changed into the pock-marked buildings of a new town we were approaching. Atlas knows where we were. I saw the coupling joints below me. There were four shock absorbers two on the end of each coupling joint, were hooks connected them with a large thick, rusty pin. Frowning at its simplicity, I reached down and pulled at the pin in the middle, but it wouldn't budge. 'Oh come on, I'm not that weak!' I chided myself.

Hearing movement behind me, I turned and grabbed onto a small ladder embedded into the side of the train and hoisted myself up. The billowing smoke blew into my face, making my eyes sting and water. Quickly bending down to shield myself, the winds screamed over the top of my head, making my hair whip around me. Searching to see if there was any way I could get to the second carriage and uncouple the joints there, I peered down and saw it was too far.

Cursing myself for my stupidity, I shuffled back along the carriage roof waiting. I knew that those men would appear at any moment; it was just a case of when.

Unexpectedly, I heard the sound of two zaps from underneath, but they didn't affect me. Confused, I didn't understand anything until I heard a roar of an angry man. Someone must have been shot.

Glimpsing the scenery, I noticed that the train was increasing in speed. It turned around a bend. Ahead I saw something that made my heart stop, the lever for the track changes. A frantic looking Tyr was beside them, not knowing which one to change.

I decided to make a break for it. Standing up, I shielded my eyes and taking a few unsteady steps back, took a running jump towards the coal carriage ahead. Smacking down hard onto the glassy black balls of solid fuel, I hurried to the side and peered over. Seeing a small ledge which was easily accessible to the very front of the train where the engineers. Carefully jumping over the edge of the sooty carriage I landed unsteadily.

More thick smoke puffed into my face, making it that much more challenging to see. Slipping a few times, I hurried as fast as I could, still trying to keep an eye on Tyr who was looming ever closer.

'Hey!' I shouted as loud as I could over the chugging engines below. 'Hey!'

As they were unable to hear me, I reached out, grabbed onto the inside of the engine room, and pulled myself towards it. My heart once again stopped at the sight I saw. The two engineers were sitting back to back on the floor bound and gagged. As soon as they saw me, their eyes stared in wonderment that someone had come to their rescue.

Jumping inside, I yanked the cloth from their mouths. 'The track changes, which direction should the train go?'

'Right,' they said together.

Turning, I stuck my head out of the window and waved, trying to get Tyr's attention, but he didn't see. 'Damn it,' I cursed, bringing my head back in. 'Have you got any water?'

'My canister,' one of the engineers said, nodding towards a small beat-up old canister of water on the floor beside his friend. 'You're not going to drink it are you?' he asked perplexed.

'No,' I frowned; shaking my head in case he didn't hear me.

'Well don't lose it, my wife got that for my birthday,' he complained.

Rolling my eyes, I unscrewed the top and went to lean out of the train. Up-tipping the canister, I immediately froze the water into a snowball and took careful aim at Tyr. 'Batter up,' I smiled, remembering the Base Ball games I saw Nathaniel and Henry watch in Bristol.

Throwing the snowball as hard as I could it zoomed through the air, magically manoeuvring it, it promptly smacked into the back of Tyr's head.

The train was approximately three hundred yards away from the change in the tracks. We had only seconds to spare. Jumping in fright from being hit, Tyr turned to see who had thrown it and caught sight of me, waving my arms, pointing to the right. Cottoning on, he threw the lever for the track to shift right, seconds before the train rolled on it.

'Come on!' I yelled, leaning out, I stuck my hand out for him to grab. Running for dear life, he quickly jumped. I pulled him upwards so fast he fell to the coal dust-covered floor and laughed.

I helped untie the men. 'Who did this to you?' I asked, unknotting their bonds.

'A little girl,' one of them told me with fear in his voice.

Whipping my head around to Tyr, we both looked at each other and said, 'Rhea.'

'What happened? Where did she go?' The men scrambled up and tried to take control of the speeding train, pulling levers, and twisting knobs and dials, but it did nothing to the train whatsoever.

'It's no good,' Tyr shouted over the engine as they fretfully pulled on the breaks, but nothing happened. 'The breaks have been damaged, there's no way to stop the train.'

'What?' the men yelled in panic.

'Calm yourselves,' I said in a firm tone. 'We need to unbuckle this part of the train with the carriages. They will eventually come to a stop, but we need to get you off this train, it will crash eventually.'

'How do you know all this?' one of the men said, his mouth agape in shock.

'It's inevitable,' I told him with a sad frown.

One of the men's eyes suddenly grew wide in shock as he looked past me. 'Get down he's going to shoot!' he shouted as he grabbed me and pulled me behind him.

Peeking around him, I saw everything in slow motion. The beefy hand of a man came around the corner, and from within his palm electricity crackled. He was aiming right at Tyr's chest.

CHAPTER TWENTY-SIX

ONE OF THE ENGINEERS SWIFTLY GRABBED ONTO TYR'S SHIRT AND PULLED him out of the way, seconds before the magic was fired.

Erupting in a bright blue flash of light, the electricity crackled and fizzed through the air. The energy zapped where Tyr had stood moments before, but instead squarely hit the human protecting Tyr.

Yelling, the weak human fell to the floor, smoke smouldering from his chest. Fortunately, for him, he would survive. As I looked up, I saw that the man had quickly left. Surely, he could have taken another shot. Unless he knew he had made a big mistake by attacking a human and had to flee?

Tyr got up and went to where the man had been seconds before. 'No, don't!' I shouted at him, in case he was still around. Not listening to me, Tyr stuck his head out of the window then jumped out.

'Is he crazy?' the other engineer asked as he had glanced to see if his friend was alright.

Ignoring Tyr for a second, I turned the human over and cringed. The smell of burnt clothing, smouldering flesh was enough to make anyone violently sick, but I had to keep my head together. Ripping my dress, I peeled back the burnt clothing of the man's overalls and pressed firmly down on the wound. 'This is no good,' I told the engineer who looked fretful. 'He needs to get to a hospital.'

'The breaks won't work,' he said, stating the obvious. 'Didn't you say it was going to crash?'

'Maybe it doesn't have to crash,' I said, thinking about what was happening. 'The entire train doesn't have to crash.'

'Well that's all well and good lass, but how do you stop a bleedin' train that's going fifty miles an hour with no breaks and eight carriages behind you making it that much more difficult to stop?'

'I'm going back to my original plan,' I told him. 'You take this here,' I ordered, showing him how to apply pressure. 'Keep it firmly on his chest, and when he gets to the hospital, tell them to apply maggots to his wounds.'

'Wait, what? Maggots?' he screeched in disgust. 'Who are you to say that? He's not dead!'

'No, but his flesh is. Maggots only eat dead flesh. They'll clean up his wound in no time, but promise me you will or else he will die from infection and you don't want to chance it, do you understand, it's important.'

He nodded solemnly then looked at his friend. 'Bert's only been on the train for a few weeks. Never imagined something like this though.'

'I'm sure, Mr...'

'Young, Bertram Young,' he nodded.

My stomach did a backflip, although the surname Young wasn't a rare name in Britain, it was just my luck that I could be standing next to Tara' great-great-grandfather. 'Oh for the love of Atlas,' I sighed. 'Right well I'm sure Mr Young will be right as rain in no time at all. But I'm serious about the maggots, it's been tried and tested.'

'Not in this country it hasn't!' he protested.

'Don't argue with me. I'm trying to save his life. Just do what I say, and he'll live.' Frowning at me with soot and sweat covered face, he nodded once. 'Good. Right now, I shall be back soon, I hope.'

'Where are you going? You're a lady! You can't go climbing out of windows and crawling over coal.'

'Ha,' I laughed. 'And who's going to stop me? You? Stay with him,' I said in a more serious tone. 'He needs you.'

Hitching up my ripped dress, I peered around the side of the train, although the coast was clear, there was no sign of Tyr either. Worried, I climbed out and placed my feet firmly onto the small ledge and had begun to make my way back towards the container of coal when there was a sudden loud BANG!

The jolt from the carriages had a ripple effect throughout the rest of the train. Shaking me from my grip my hand slipped off the side, and I fell. Scrabbling for purchase, my hands reached the ledge just below, though there wasn't much to hold onto. The wheels of the train chugged around rapidly and were very close to catching on my dress; just one corner and I would be trapped underneath. 'Why me?' I asked myself as I tried to think of a way to get up. 'Two options, one dropdown and wait to find the time to jump back on again or…'

'Thera, take hold of my hand!' Perplexed, I looked up to see Tyr on the roof of the train, his hand reaching down to me, but it wasn't long enough.

'Sure thing, I'll just extend my arm LIKE AN OCTOPUS!' I screeched at him.

Frowning, he carefully began to climb down, minding his footing as he did so. Still gripping onto the small ledge, Tyr grabbed me by the arm.

'Thank you,' I smiled, as he began to slide back towards the container full of coal. 'What was that bang?' I asked, jumping on top of the coal and sliding down the edge as the loose clumps were challenging to walk over.

'I don't know,' he said, turning back with a worried look. 'I tried to find the shooter, but he disappeared like he vanished into thin air.'

I breathed a sigh of relief. 'They've gone,' I told Tyr. 'That bang may be attributed to them, but we'll find out once we've sorted this train out.'

Jumping down onto the coupling joints behind the coal, I tapped Tyr on the shoulder before he went through the broken door. 'What's the plan?'

'Still the same one,' I pointed to the shock absorbers and the coupling joints. 'The pin has to be taken out, and the carriages unhooked from the engine. The heavier the train is, the more difficult it will be to slow down.'

He bent down to check them then testing the pin, it moved a little. 'I'm going to have to break it, but it would look suspicious. Perhaps Etrician might be able to pull it.'

'How long do we have until the next track change?'

'In about ten minutes,' looking at the bright orange sun that peeped over the horizon in the east signalling the dawn of what was turning out to be a horrifying morning, he shook his head, 'make that five. Because the breaks have gone, we're going faster.'

'How can we? The men aren't putting any coal to power the train.'

'It doesn't matter if the train is going down on a slight slant,' he said.

With the wind still whipping around my head, I tied my hair up into a knot, purely because I was getting annoyed with it and then peered around the broken door, seeing an empty corridor.

Stepping inside with Tyr close behind me, we quietly raced down the carpeted rocking passageway, checking every compartment to see if there was anyone inside. Passing three empty carriages, we came to the very last one and jumped in fright as I opened the door. Looking terrified, the people from the other carriages were all crammed in together like sardines. 'Etrician?' I called out, 'Hadriana? Darren?'

'HERE!' Hadriana cried as she jumped up and down amidst the large frightened group of people.

Pushing past everyone, she dragged Ann with her. 'Are you two all right?'

I nodded. Hadriana glanced at Ann, who appeared as though she was going to faint. 'Darren is sitting down squashed up in a compartment at the back. Etrician came back with Darren then followed the men.'

'They were following us,' Tyr informed her. 'One of them came after us as we neared the engine, but I haven't seen the other two.'

'They haven't come back here,' Hadriana frowned, 'but neither have I seen Etrician.'

Tyr and I exchanged looks. 'Neither have we.' I said instantly worrying. 'Tyr and I heard an explosion–'

'It was them leaving,' Hadriana explained as discreetly as she could, not wanting to confuse Ann more than she had already been today. 'I saw a blue light.'

'Damn, where is Etrician,' I sighed looking behind me, but I knew he wasn't there. I had a horrible feeling about this. 'Stay with the others, we need to separate the train,' I told Hadriana, nudging Tyr.

Turning around Tyr and I headed back through the empty carriages. Fear instantly prickled at my heart, and I began to panic. Etrician wouldn't just take off like that, and I'd know he'd fight to the teeth… so maybe that loud bang was him…?

Glass from the broken windowpane in the door crunched under our feet as we headed back out into the sooty air. Bending down we assessed the coupling joints, Tyr tried them again and moved the pin another inch. 'If Etrician isn't here, then there is only one explanation–'

'No,' I gasped, clutching my heart as I had thought of the possibility, but I didn't want to mention it. 'Please, don't say it… Just pull the pin out,' I told him, changing the subject quickly. 'I don't want anything to look suspicious. If the bolts are destroyed, and sabotage could arise in the newspapers, it would lead to questions, which no one would be able to answer, and it would change the timeline. But I've come to understand that the train cannot be allowed to crash.'

'Well, that's understandable, but if you want the pin to come out without it being damaged, then I do need help, it's a little meticulous.'

Helping him, I put my hand underneath the pin and hit it as hard as I could, jarring it; Tyr pulled as soon as it became loose and together, we managed to unclasp the interlocking catches. The shock absorbers slowly pulled away from each other as the engine continued to steam onwards, leaving the carriages to travel alone without power. Tyr and I became separated, each of us looking at one another expectantly; he was on the engine side, while I was on the carriage side.

'Stop the train, Tyr,' I called to him. 'By any means necessary, stop the train, do not let it crash!' The train began to speed ahead as the carriages, now that they had no driver, began to slow. 'It's important!'

Tyr slowly pulled away and rounded a corner, and he vanished, up ahead I saw a tunnel. The engine part had already raced on through.

The carriages with their heavy load of passengers situated at the back were as though an anchor, slowing down the unguided and unmanned cabooses. Darkness suddenly enclosed me as the carriages rolled on into the tunnel, the smell of the smoke from the train still lingered in the air, blowing through the first carriage as I headed back inside.

'Etrician,' I called out, 'please tell me you're here.' But there was no answer. Shaking my head in dismay, I dropped to the floor and cried. 'No, please don't,' I sobbed into my hands. 'Please don't... I can't do this without him, I can't lose someone else.'

'Thera,' came the sound of a familiar voice in the dark. Hearing the sound of heavy footfall, Hadriana rushed to my side, bending down she snatched my hands from my face to look at me in the dim pale light. 'What's wrong? Are you injured?'

'It's Etrician' I wailed. 'They've taken him. He's not on the train, he's gone, I know he has. They've taken him back to the present.'

Biting her bottom lip, Hadriana looked behind her. 'I can't leave merboy with Ann for too long. Thera, we need to stop the carriages. I know you've unhooked the front part of the train; I can already tell we're slowing down.'

I shook my head definitely. 'Not quick enough. There are a few more tunnels to get through. I'm not sure which one that the train crashes into. The train has to get out of the tunnel first. After that, we can go on ahead and get Tyr.'

'But what about Ann?' Hadriana asked frowning at me as though I forgot something important. 'Regardless whether we've stopped the train and saved it from crashing and everyone else on it, Ann still has to get down to

London for her sister. There's the bigger picture to think about too. No train means no visiting of family members and not being a midwife to the descendant of Hannah, who is still trying to exist back in our time.'

'I know, but I need to think, please shut up and let me think' I said fiercely. 'I can do this by myself. Darren is no help to me whatsoever even though he is a full myth, just let him protect Ann.'

'Idiot boy can barely walk,' she scoffed.

'Just go back to the others, and I'll sort the carriages out. Try and keep everyone calm-'

'Even though you're not?' Averting her gaze, I closed my eyes. Feeling a supportive hand on my shoulder, Hadriana said, 'we'll find him again. He hasn't been marked, so he is not needed for the Cabinet of Idols. If they've taken him, it's probably for a blackmailed swap, you for him.'

Wiping my tears, I took a shuddering breath. 'Too much to think about and too much to do.' Standing up, I brushed her hand from me and left without another word. I couldn't let Hadriana see me fall, not now when we were so close to finishing the race against time.

After half a minute or so as the carriages were still slowing down, they passed around a corner and bright sunlight flooded the exit of the tunnel. Sighing with relief at the prospect that we'd come to a slow stop and instantly planning a head on how to get Ann safely back to London, I saw something up front that made my heart stop. Tyr had managed to stop the train too early.

'Oh, Atlas no!' I cried.

Without a second thought, I leapt ahead of the carriages and placed my hands out by the shock absorbers, bracing for impact.

BANG! The carriages made instant contact, sending ripples of pain through my hands, arms and torso, up until the point they rattled my teeth. I heard more screaming at the end carriages, which came from another sudden jolt, but the force behind them was pushing me. I was unable to entirely stop them. I wasn't as powerful outside of water as I was in it.

'Thera!' came Hadriana's worried yell, as I saw her run along the corridor towards me.

'Stay... there,' I gasped, still trying to stop the carriages... it was working, but more slowly than I originally planned. Ignoring me, Hadriana brought out her bag of stardust.

'Let me help you stop the train.'

'NO!' I bellowed. 'You don't know… what it'll… do to me,' I strained with each word. 'I can do it… just give me a second.'

Digging my feet deeper into the stone-shavings, the wooden sheaves that were lined neatly in betwixt the metal tracks were being demolished one after another as they made contact with the back of my legs. I might not be that powerful as to stop tonnes of weight in mere seconds, but at least to a certain extent, I was indestructible. It made me wonder about that pin from earlier. Magic, it seems, was placed on it. They knew I wished to uncouple the train. They wanted to make it difficult for me.

Turning around briefly, I saw the engine looming ever closer. Tyr had just poked his head around the corner of the engine and was heading towards me looking panicked.

Hadriana crawled towards me on her belly, holding the little bag of stardust. 'No!' I strained again, putting as much power into my legs as I possibly could. 'Tyr!' I called.

'I wish your hands have power,' Hadriana said, taking a pinch of stardust and blowing it into my face. Feeling the dust land gently onto my skin, the power surged through my arms to my fingertips. Behind me I heard Tyr run, crunching along the gravel in quick long strides and skidding slightly. Abruptly a big gust of wind help to force the carriages back, but it carried the rest of the stardust onto the face of Ann who had decided to take it upon herself to find out what was going on with the train.

'NO!' I yelled. But it was too late. Ann sneezed and involuntarily shivered as the stardust was affecting her entire body. 'You idiot, Hadriana!' I bellowed, as the carriages had come to an abrupt halt with the extra power I had. 'You have done the most idiotic thing I could have ever thought imaginable.'

Pocketing the stardust, she gave me an annoyed look. 'Oh I'm so sorry,' she drawled sarcastically, 'and here I thought I was helping you out! You did want to avoid the crash at all costs, am I right?'

Throwing my hands out I said, 'You have given me more power, but do not forget I am still marked and will be under control by THEM! Did that not even occur to you? Also, the apathetic moron that you are, Ann got a dash of your dust.'

'Apathetic moron? How dare you?' she screeched.

'There's more daring words I can give you than that my girl!' I shouted.

'Enough you two!' Tyr bellowed between us. 'What's done is done, we can figure out a way on what to do later on. I've had a word with the engineers and told them about the broken brakes. If the train is repairable, we can let everyone be on their way. If it's not well then...'

'We're taking Ann directly to London,' I informed him. 'She's got to get to London.'

'Are you talking about me?' a soft voice spoke from behind us. Sighing I turned around to see Ann looking somewhat perplexed. 'Why do you want to take me to London so badly? What is so important?'

Hadriana and I exchanged a look of confusion, both of us unsure of what to tell her.

Thankfully, Tyr spoke up, 'We were aware that you were being followed and there was an attempt on your life... today as a matter in fact. We are here to ensure that you reach your destination, unharmed.'

Frowning, Ann turned around to search for something, or someone then looked back at us, tilting her head. 'Forgive me, but your friend Darren told me a different story. He said that you knew of who I was, and what I was doing and why I was travelling down to London. Regrettably, I had told him that I had suspicions I was being followed, but it was not confirmed.'

I sighed. 'Either way Miss Smith, you need to go to London. Tyr-' turning my back on Ann. 'Would you please see to the engineers?'

'Of course.'

As Tyr headed off, I got back onto the train and assessed the situation with Ann. I was unsure of what the stardust had done to her. The word power to a human could mean a great many things, superhuman strength, the ability to shoot energy from her hands, the capability to communicate telepathically, it was endless. And because Hadriana hadn't explicitly explained what type of power she was inadvertently giving to someone who was standing there gawping at us, I was worried.

'Do you feel, different?' I asked Ann, moving past her as I was going to see if Darren was all right.

A quizzical look appeared on her face, and she shook her head. 'I feel just the same as I had been not an hour ago. Why?'

Shaking my head, I looked at Hadriana. 'I'll be back in a minute.'

Ann reached out and grabbed hold of my wrist. 'Stop,' she yelled.

Somehow unbeknownst to me, my feet stopped. I struggled to move them but found I couldn't. Gasping in awe and panic, I turned my head to catch a glance at Ann. 'You can... order me.' Smiling at her, I laughed. 'You can order me!'

'What?' Gasping, she withdrew.

'Give me an order,' I asked her.

'I'm sorry I don't understand' she said.

Groaning I elaborated. 'You've told me to stop, and I have. Why did you want me to stop?'

'I would like to know what is going on,' she asked, her voice too polite to be commanding.

'Don't 'like' it, want it!' I told her. 'Put some force some passion behind it.'

Hadriana's mouth fell open in disbelief.

'Fine, tell me what you know about this train!' she commanded, but nothing happened.

'Thera, what are you-' Hadriana began, but I put my hand up to shush her, then I stared at them. Hadriana had inadvertently given power to my hands, and the dust must have fallen onto Ann's hands. Whatever she touched, she could command. 'Hold my hand, and then order me,' I told her slowly.

Ann looked inquisitive but did as I asked. Gripping my wrist, she ordered me to explain about the train. I felt relieved as the restrictions released. Still standing like a statue, I began to tell Ann about the train, and how we knew it was going to crash. I explained how we ended up in Scotland and knew she was going to London. All this time, Hadriana began to shout at me to shut me up.

After explaining everything to her, Ann seemed to relax, and so did the hold she had on me. Leaving her with Hadriana to process everything, I headed to the back of the train and found Darren cuddled up to two attractive young females. One was nibbling on his ear, giving him a delighted look. Upon seeing me, Darren frowned and retracted his hand from one of the ladies undergarments, who seemed to have a very flushed expression on her face.

'Out, now!' I shouted at him.

The girls blushed and giggled as Darren slunk out of the compartment, holding onto the sides for support, still wobbly on his legs. Clipping him around the head, I pushed him forwards.

'That was disgraceful!' I whispered harshly. 'You don't frisk anyone in this day and age like that, especially in public.'

'What?' he asked, sounding as though he hadn't done anything wrong. 'She only asked me to find her-'

'I don't want to know,' I shouted, grabbed his arm roughly and dragged him along. 'I cannot believe you,' I seethed, pushing through the people who were unable to find a seat. Now and again I got stopped by the passengers and had to tell them I'd be back to explain the situation, but one man got a little abrupt and stood in front of me.

'I demand to know what is going on at once madam!' he bellowed, spittle flying in my face. 'First, you call everyone's attention saying that everyone is to go to the back of the train as it's going to crash and now we've stopped. Clearly, we haven't crashed.'

Blowing out an exasperated lungful of air, I replied, 'No, I know. We managed to uncouple the train and stop the carriages. If the engineers can temporarily fix the problem, we can be on our way. The first carriage is inaccessible, but you can move to the next carriage if you are… cramped,' I smiled sweetly at him.

'And who gives you the authority to boss us around, Miss!' he said with contempt.

'I saved your lives.' I told him simply. 'If you think I have poor judgement well then I suggest you take it up with the train company. Come on Darren,' I said, tugging him along as he was ogling a lady with a large feather hat.

As we moved into the middle carriage, a few people followed and headed into their compartments, but none of them followed us as we moved into the last one at the front where Hadriana and Ann were now sat at the end of the train talking to Tyr.

'Ah yes you,' Ann called, swivelling around to look at me. 'Now that everything has been explained to me, I have some questions.'

'I'm sure you do, and I'm sure they can wait,' I told her, forcing Darren to sit on the floor behind me. 'Stay put and keep your hands to yourself!' I told him. 'Tyr what's the update?'

Frowning at what I said to Darren he looked from him to me, 'It's repairable up until Greenock. Everyone can get off and can wait for another train or find some other means to finish their journey.'

I agreed. 'We need to re-couple the train then.' Moving past Hadriana and Ann, who remained quiet during this time, I ignored their inquisitive looks. Jumping down next to Tyr, I thought of something and pointed at Darren. 'You,' I shouted, getting his attention. 'You do not touch, look or even talk to Ann, do I make myself clear?'

Hadriana raised her eyebrows and looked back at Darren who folded his arms and sulked, staring down at the floor. I turned around and followed Tyr to the rear of the train.

'What was that all about?' he asked me quietly as we were out of earshot.

I shook my head. 'Believe me, you don't want to know.'

With help from Tyr, together both of us managed to push the carriages towards the engine at the front. Before the carriages met the train, Tyr skittered round to the front to tell me when to slow down as the stardust Hadriana had given me had almost tripled my strength, leaving no room for Tyr to help me much.

Though I was thankful for the power, it was a significant burden to the world, and I cursed Hadriana for being so careless, even if it was done with good intentions.

'All right, Thera!' I heard Tyr shout from the front. Stopping, I moved around to the front, suddenly jumping a mile as one of the windows of the carriages slid down.

The pompous man from earlier stuck his head out and scowled at me. 'Who moved the train?'

Unable to answer him, I shrugged my shoulders. 'I'm not sure I um...' feeling a little hot under the collar so to speak, I pointed behind him, 'Oh my lord, what is that!'

Stupidly the man turned around, and I ran as fast as I could towards Tyr and the others who were helping to couple the carriages to the train.

'How is your friend?' I asked the engineer as he wiped his oily hands on a very oily cloth, which did nothing but smudge the oil further.

Giving me a concerned look he frowned, 'He's hanging in there miss. But I'm worried for him, I'm not sure he'll make Peterborough.'

'How far are we from it?' I asked feeling slightly worried that if this man had any connection to Tara, we were seriously messing with her timeline.

'A fair few hours I reckon, but he may not have that long, he's lost a lot of blood.'

I put a comforting hand on his shoulder, 'I'll take a look at him.'

Creeping to the front of the train where the poor human was in agony on the floor, I neared but then suddenly stopped as I heard something odd. Unknowing of the conversation that I was hearing, I began to translate the words from Latin.

'Why must I get into these situations? Filthy blighter firing electricity like that at me. As though he could make me a hollowed myth.'

With the mentioning of that word, my mouth fell open. Grabbing onto the side, I hoisted myself up, 'I know you're not human. Who are you?' I demanded in Latin, staring at the "human" who was sitting rather comfortably on the floor, scrubbing the front of his clothes, he clearly wasn't in any pain anymore.

'Are you a myth?' he asked in an abrupt almost icy manner, still speaking in Latin.

'No, I'm a legend,' I glared back.

His eyes showed surprise, but he didn't apologise for his tone of voice towards me. 'Hmph. I suppose you're going to reprimand me for getting shot, not that you really can reprimand me of course. Damn,' he sighed, 'now I have to move elsewhere.' Standing up, he pocketed the piece of my dress that was covered in drying blood.

'You've healed already,' staring at the pink part of his chest that previously was burnt. 'Well thank you for standing in the way, or else my myth friend would have been destroyed.'

'Destroyed?' he scoffed. 'Listen sweetheart that electricity wasn't anything like the Staff of Zeus alright?' That shocked me a little. He must have come back into the past from my time as well. The Staff of Zeus only came to earth just recently. 'Those people and that Jinn, they aren't from this time and come to think of it, neither are you.'

Feeling affronted, I stood up to my full height. 'That is none of your concern Bertram Young. You know of the myths, so I would like to know what you are doing here.'

'Ha,' he barked. 'Even if I told you, you wouldn't understand. You legends aren't meant to know, you have no business to know.'

He had the semblance of someone who was wise beyond years, yet apart from quick healing and the ability to travel through time, had no other power. The fact that he was speaking Latin too gave him away. I smiled. 'You are a Capturer, are you not?' If I was right, I really shouldn't be in his presence. 'Are you here in this time to stop and capture the Jinn?'

He raised one eyebrow, 'So you have heard of us? Oh well then, that changes a lot. Which legend are you?' He stared at me, shrewdly.

Smiling, I replied, 'Now you know I cannot tell you that. There are rules, and you should know how to play by them, time-travel and all that. But I'm curious why you're here?' I pressed.

He shrugged his shoulders. 'Probably the same reason why you're here. Time's been distorted, and the Ancients want to know why.' Snorting in disgust, he leant against the metal wall. 'I've been on stand-by for about sixty years. I only got given a chance to do their dirty work when my human cover, "died."'

'Let me guess, this all started in 1825,' I smiled.

A deep crease appeared on his brow, and he took a step towards me. 'What do you know?'

About to open my mouth to say something, I abruptly stopped. 'A favour for a favour?' I asked.

'Pah,' he scoffed. 'I don't do favours for legends.'

Turning on my heel, 'Fine, forget it then.' I was about to walk away when...

'Alright fine. What do you want?'

Facing him, I smiled sweetly. 'I want Renita saved from erasement. In my time, she's due to be erased from her mythological status, and I cannot allow that to happen. She is needed, she is wanted, and she cannot be thrown out of history.'

Looking up into the air to think, something clicked. 'Ah yes, I know the one you're referring to. Pygmalion's child, right? Yes, she is due to be erased in... Gawd blimey, you are from the future, aren't you, from 2011?'

I sighed, not responding. 'Do we have a deal? You save her and keep her from erasement, and I shall tell you what you need to know?' I stuck out my hand. 'When I make a deal I expect it to be kept or I shall be furious, and you don't want to make me angry, regardless whether I'm a legend or not.'

'Do I detect a slight hint of blackmail in your words?' he smirked, but nonetheless, he grabbed my hand and shook it. 'Deal. I'll save Renita from being erased, and you tell me about this time distortion.'

'A new Ancient, Drayman,' I began. 'Heard of him?' He nodded a dark expression on his face. 'He exists, and he's trying to gather legends into the Cabinet of Idols, myself included. There is nothing I can do. I've been marked by the Staff of Zeus that has fallen to earth. To cut a long story short,' I added as his face dropped in shock and I didn't want him to interrupt me, 'some humans have been given the ability to go back in time and disrupt the timeline of a girl called Hannah Smith who is needed for the future. She and another myth are to help claim back the Staff of Zeus.

There are certain points in time that we figured out that these humans will travel to, to disrupt the timeline. The dates are 1825, 1859, and 1882.'

Taking a deep breath, he glanced at me then folded his arms. 'Smith ey? Very common name. And those were the dates I was given to pay close attention to, though in 1825 everything went as planned and so did 1859. But this year... this year it was disrupted beyond repair. I had to get involved to see for myself what was going on, but never did I suspect this.'

'But you do realise you cannot change what is to come. It is now a burden you know of this knowledge.'

The Capturer laughed, 'Aye I know, lady. It's not really part of my job, sorting out the timeline but,' shrugging his shoulders he thumbed up towards the sky, 'they tell me what to do, and I do it.'

'So, you came from the future. Your human cover died? What does that mean?' I asked, but he shook his head.

'I can't tell you. It's not that I don't want to mind, but I'm bound by law to keep my trap shut. And it's got me into trouble from time to time, so I'm trying to be on my best behaviour.'

I sighed. 'Well as long as you're not going to find and destroy anyone then...' but something stopped me from continuing and giving him an odd look asked, 'your name, Bertram Young, is that some random name you've plucked from your head?'

'Why?' he asked, his eyes curious.

Shrugging I replied, 'Just someone I know of, who has the same surname...'

'Young isn't a rare surname,' he scoffed, almost sighing with relief.

'-...and who's a Siren.'

His eyes went wide, staring at me in shock. 'Oh, crap... Tara.'

I pointed a finger at him. 'No way! I knew it! Atlas on earth I knew it! That's just my luck I'd run into someone like you.'

'Someone like me? What's that supposed to mean?' he asked moodily.

'If I can figure out your secret, you're exempt from not telling me by law. So out with it.'

Giving up the pretence, he sighed. 'Tara was my daughter. But believe it or not, I'm just a normal human in this time, well,' he smiled glancing at his burnt clothes where he was shot with electricity to which a human would have probably keeled over and died after losing so much blood, 'near enough normal.'

'Tara and Nathaniel, they are your children. Although, didn't you say your human cover died? So, in actual fact, their father died. Yet, here you are, a Capturer. Please, explain.'

Disgruntled, he replied, 'For being a good boy for the Ancients for half a damn millennia,' he spat, 'I was allowed to remain on the non-magical plane as a human. I met Tara's mother, who was a Siren living as a human, we had the kids...' he stopped, a painful memory had resurfaced, and he shook his head. 'I was a crappy father, I admit it. We tried to protect them at every turn but Drayman, or Maynard, knew of us and knew of Gabby and what Tara was to become.' He shrugged, 'But my human body was killed. When I returned to the magical plane, I resumed my position as a Capturer and the Ancients gave me this task.'

'The new Ancient he's the eighteenth, do you know him. Do you know its Maynard?'

Avoiding my gaze, he nodded slowly. 'Oh, Yes. Before he was an Ancient I worked with him,' he practically growled in loathing. 'I hate that man with all my being!'

'I knew it!' I whooped again. 'Is Rhea causing all of this? I believe Maynard is stopping her screwing up his timeline. She's gaining some control back, isn't she?' He didn't need to tell me. From his hunched shoulders and still looking at the floor in concern, I had been right. 'Maynard is causing all this though,' I warned him. 'Don't let him open The Prison.' He frowned at me then, confused. 'That's his plan. He wants to-'

Someone coughed from behind, making both of us jump. Hadriana, Tyr and Ann were standing below. I faintly heard a small popping sound. Bertram Young had disappeared.

'Is everything all right?' Tyr asked me in Latin. Hadriana scowled at me then folded her arms impatiently.

'Hadriana, do you understand Latin?' I asked her, feigning a smile.

'Are you talking about me in a different language? That's really unfair, you know,' she said testily. 'I only know some, not all.'

'I guess not,' I continued in Latin. Looking at Tyr, I explained, 'I just met a Capturer, and no he wasn't after you,' adding quickly as he looked as though he was about to faint.

'Thank my father,' he replied, calming down from his shock. 'But why was he here and where is the other engineer?'

'He was the other engineer. He had to go; it would raise too many questions him suddenly healing. But he was here because of the Ancients.' I refrained from mentioning Maynard in front of Ann. I would tell the others when we were all together in the future. 'They told him to come here and sort out the distorted timeline. Of course, his usual day job would be to track down myths and erase them but, you're safe.' I smiled.

'Doing the Ancients dirty work, hmm.' Frowning in suspicion, Tyr sighed.

Sprinkling some of Hadriana's damned stardust over the other engineer, named Ernest, he promptly forgot about Mr Young. With the engine stoked, the coals shoved quickly into the furnace, the train slowly began to move in the right direction, carriages, and all.

Fields rolled past, craggy hills peeked out of the luscious landscape that was like natures fluffy green carpet, and forests blossomed around the edges of meadows that zipped by, dotted with little white wisps that resembled grazing sheep. The only thing that annoyed me was Hadriana complaining of feeling hungry.

I remained quiet most of the time. Standing beside Ernest, with Hadriana opposite me looking pensive about something as she gazed out of the window, I wanted to know what was on her mind, but I thought it rude to ask. Though she and I had known each other for a long time, this was a first that we'd spent so long together and I couldn't help but wonder if she was starting to regret it.

'Penny for your thoughts?' Hadriana asked me. I smiled softly; of course, she would be blunt enough to ask me what I was thinking. She was always so different from me.

Staring at Ernest, who was busying with the train, I thought it best to have a conversation with her in Old Norse. I didn't want him to know what I was talking about after all.

'About Darren and Hannah and the problems that they will face.'

'Ah. And the reason you are speaking in my language is that… you don't want him to overhear?'

I nodded. 'You were always so clever. Now that you have unintentionally given power to Ann which happens to be a power which I have been looking for to help me-'

'You want to use her,' she nodded at Ann, 'to banish you to the abyss? To stop you when your will is under control of Maynard?' she asked, folding her arms and looking at me slyly. 'She is in fact deceased in our present. How is that going to work?'

'I'll use your stardust and send me back here and ask her to do it.' Hadriana shook her head. 'I need someone to stop me. Etrician won't do it. He loves me too much to see me hurt. I just hope he's alright.'

'Hmm,' she glanced down and caressed Darren's bracelet. There was no power from it anymore, though I was curious as to why she wanted to keep it. 'I'm sure he is. He can't be killed, and he's not marked for the Cabinet, so they won't do anything to him.' She shrugged, not caring. 'But what was that other language you were speaking with Tyr? I have heard of it before, but it didn't register.' She wanted to change the topic as I gathered she found Etrician's disappearance tiresome.

'Latin,' I said in English as the Viking's had no equivalent to the word. 'I told Tyr that the other engineer wasn't human,' I continued in Old Norse. 'He's gone now, so just ignore it. It doesn't matter.'

Her right eyebrow rose. 'Uh, huh.'

Chugging along the tracks, houses soon came into view confirming that we were heading into the town of Peterborough. Blowing the whistle, the train roared loudly as it rolled into the station, Ernest quickly got out as soon as the train had stopped and ran to one of the offices on the far end of the platform.

Jumping out, Hadriana and I went to the broken carriage and found Tyr and Ann having an in-depth conversation while Darren was still sitting on the floor pouting like a spoilt told-off child. It made me smile.

'Right then,' I called, getting everyone's attention as I slapped my hands together. 'We have arrived at Peterborough station.' I looked directly at Ann. 'I suggest, since you know about us and our magic and we know about you and the O.M.C we're going to help each other out a bit, sounds fair?' I put it to her.

Pulling a face, she inclined her head for me to continue.

'We take you to London, free of charge, and you continue being your sister's midwife for her child. It's that simple. And if you don't do it, then we're going to come back and ensure you get it right.'

She raised her eye brow, placing her hands on her hips. 'Well since you have put it so forcefully, I guess I have no choice. Do I?'

'No, no, not really,' smiling at her.

'Very well,' she said.

Helping Darren on his still wobbly legs we walked past the grumpy passengers, I heard a conductor roar out that they had commissioned a train which would take everyone to London without any further delay. With a sigh of relief, our small group made it out of the station. And snuck behind a lane past a row of houses that faced the noisy station.

Blindfolding Ann and telling her to cover her ears for her own safety, Hadriana got out the stardust and sprinkling it around us, wished us to London's Paddington station.

Chapter Twenty-Seven

'Oy, watch out,' shouted a man as we accidentally transported right next to him. Hadriana shuffled Ann and quickly took the blindfolds off as Tyr helped Darren's wibbly-wobbly walking.

'Sorry,' I called, ushering everyone to the side of a busy platform where steam and smoke saturated the air. Squeaky carriages packed full of trunks and parcels rolled by, gentlemen and ladies with their children hurrying to catch their trains and ear-piercing whistles blowing around the country's busiest train station. 'Welcome to Paddington,' I sighed with relief as we were out of the way of people.

'People must have seen us,' Tyr mumbled looking around cautiously, trying to find someone who spotted us materialising from no-where.

'Nah,' I pooh-poohed him, 'it's way too busy for people to see us appear like that. Let's get out of here shall we?'

Moving along the edge of the extended platform, we took the main exit on the left, though it took a while as we bumped into trolleys and people along the way, always apologising. I found that saying "I'm sorry" was a constant thing in London, even during this period. Too many people in one area. Everyone's always in a rush, never one to stop and take a breather.

As we hurried out of the station, I looked back to do a quick headcount and stopped as I had counted five rather than six. My heart pained with guilt as I couldn't count Etrician. I felt utterly helpless, not being there for him. Those people would pay for what they did.

Gritting my teeth, I suppressed the lump in my throat. Even from just thinking about him for the briefest moment upset and frustrated me.

'So,' I said to Ann as we got out onto the street, which was a bit less encroaching as it was away from the station and fewer people to bump into. 'Where does your sister live?'

'Soho,' she said, pointing in the direction of East.

Hadriana raised her eyebrow at the mention of the place but didn't speak up.

'That's ages away,' Darren groaned. 'Let's get a carriage,' he suggested looking at Hadriana for financial support, but she shook her head.

'No, I'm all game for walking. Being stuck on a train that nearly crashed, I'm good with using my own two feet.'

'Well said,' Tyr piped up.

Rolling his eyes, Darren mumbled incoherently. Together we began to walk towards Soho, which, coincidently, was near the British Museum.

As we neared Edgware Road, Darren began to complain that his feet were hurting him. Though during the walk he had regained his balance and seemed more natural walking on his feet, however, he really didn't look like he wanted to walk anymore.

'This is just crazy,' he huffed, as we crossed the busy road of horse-drawn carriages. 'Why the Little Mermaid wanted to be human is just beyond me.'

'Ha, you're only saying that because you're not human anymore,' Hadriana laughed. 'You're experiencing the reverse effect. You want to have rubber flippers while she wanted feet.'

'Are you talking about Hans Christian Anderson's story?' I frowned, as I personally found the story annoying.

'Well, I meant the other version, but both are the same I guess,' Darren shrugged.

Tutting I shook my head, 'He was an idiot. Don't get me wrong his stories were very interesting, but the Little Mermaid story only began because he spoke to an unknown Water Nymph.'

'No way?' Darren gasped. 'Did he know who he was speaking with?'

'Nope, thank Atlas. If I knew who he'd spoken with, I would have to give her the lecture of the century. Stupid... idiotic... moronic... nymph...' I trailed off into one of my grumbling incoherent rants and suddenly realised that everyone was looking at me. Abruptly stopping, I shrugged. 'I never found out who did it.'

'So you're a Water Nymph?' Ann asked though I had already told her before. 'And how long can you live for?'

It wasn't a commanded question, but I thought it best I answer her with as much truth to it as I could.

'A very long time,' I smiled, as we passed onto Oxford Street, heading due East. 'Though please refrain from asking me questions. It's just a bit dangerous for you to know.'

'Yes, it is,' she said with a slightly worried look.

Addressing Hadriana in Old Norse, I asked, 'Is it possible to wish someone's memories away?' Tyr looked up at me, a surprised look on his face. 'Well?' I pressed her.

'Yes. You are thinking of changing her memories,' indicating Ann with the flick of her eyes.

'Hmm.'

Blowing out a breath of air, she shrugged. 'Well fine but you're going to have to be specific.'

'That's heavy-duty though,' Tyr frowned, not looking at me. 'You're messing with someone's life. Plus, what if the reason she joins that group, is because of her speaking with us?'

'Her life is already messed up,' I said. Ann frowned at us in confusion, having no idea about the argument we were getting ourselves into. 'Since we've come into the past, we've been shot at, chased,' I said beginning to count on what had happened, 'threatened, and almost pulverised in what could have been a very terrible train crash! Need I remind you that those things shouldn't have happened in the past. With that particular person I met on the train,' I added, not explaining to Hadriana about the Capturer, 'it just proves to me that the Ancients are aware that something has gone on. We can relieve their worries and our own if she forgets having any conversations with us. Along with Mr 'R', they need to create that little red book by themselves without our help. Tara was always talking about it. They had the impression that myths were once alive, but had died out. We need to keep that appearance.'

'Well that shut me up then,' he grumbled. 'Fine, I understand.'

'Can you three stop being so rude and speak in English?' Darren asked testily as he turned to look at us. 'You all sound German when you speak, I didn't catch one word of what you said and aren't I supposed to know all of earth's languages?'

'You weren't born a myth sweetie pie,' Hadriana smiled sweetly, grabbing his cheek and pinching it. 'So you'll never understand other languages.'

'Get off,' he shouted, slapping her hand away. 'What language was that? I want to know.'

'My native language,' she teased him.

'Oh forget it, damn Viking,' he murmured and stomped off ahead.

A few miles and an increasing amount of bickering later, coupled with tired, sore feet and hunger complaints from Hadriana and Ann, we finally made it to the junction at Tottenham Court Road.

I oversaw Ann as she was unsure where to go; left, presumably to where her sister was or right to the British Museum. It was signposted ahead and noticing this, she had an internal war with herself. I was suspicious about her intentions as soon as she mentioned her sister living in Soho, so close to the British Museum where the O.M.C. started. I was not that naive to believe it was such a coincidence.

'You have a choice,' I said to her softly, putting a comforting hand on her shoulder. 'But if you choose unwisely I cannot promise you a good future.'

'I thought she wanted to turn us in,' Hadriana said in her native tongue, 'you had the same suspicions then?' she asked me. I nodded once.

Ann shrugged my hand off her shoulders, spinning round to face me. 'I know you're talking about me. Though I do not know of what you are saying, I wish you would tell me outright on what you think of me.'

'You are an intelligent young woman,' Tyr said sadly, 'but you are human and are acting on the need to prove yourself right.'

Sighing heavily she stamped her foot like a child. 'I am right! You are real, you are here,' she gestured to Hadriana. 'The Fountain of Youth is real! People would kill for that.' When commanded to tell Ann what I knew, I had inadvertently explained the powers of Darren, Tyr and Hadriana. 'And you're The Tyr, the God of the Norse Mythology, alive and standing right in front of me. Do you know how lucky I am to be in your presence?' Tyr blushed and looked away from her; his shy side suddenly crept back. 'And you,' she pointed at me. 'A Water Nymph from Greek mythology.'

'Whoa there,' waving my arms to stop her. 'Don't you be classing me as a myth. I'm far from it.'

About to question me, Darren stepped up to her. 'What's your choice because we have other places to go to?'

Slightly relieved that Darren was picking up his slack and showing a little bit of responsibility, we waited for Ann's answer.

Staring at the ground in shame, she shook her head. 'I won't do it. I'll go to my sister's as was the original plan. I'm sorry.'

Taking a right towards Charing Cross Road, we followed Ann's directions to Greek Street, which I found highly amusing. Turning onto the road, Ann raced to an Edwardian style house at the end of a row of similar structured buildings, banging on the door numbered eighteen in brass numbers.

A few minutes later, a man opened the door. Frowning at first at the sight of Ann's face, he opened the door wide and flung his arms around her. Laughing he let go and kissed her on the cheek. 'I am glad you have made it. Please, do come in, she's been missing you so.'

Hesitant at first, Ann followed the man inside then upon entering the house, Hadriana brought out her small bag of stardust. About to throw it towards the house, I grabbed her hand and stopped her. 'Not just yet,' I told her. 'We will, but not just yet.'

Giving me a faint smile, she then sighed. 'So now that everything is settled and Hannah will most certainly be born, am I using the sand to take us back to the present? Mixed in with a little bit of stardust to take us back to my castle?'

'If you please,' I sighed. 'There are some things I have to attend to when I get back.'

'Etrician?' Tyr asked, placing a kind hand on my shoulder.

The lump in my throat instantly came back. 'I will deal with his disappearance, yes, but there is somewhere else we need to go.' A wave of panic rushed through me, and I almost felt as though I was drowning in fright. Shaking my hands, I inhaled deeply, trying to rid myself of this oppressive feeling.

'Where?' Darren asked as Hadriana prepared the spell to take us back.

Tyr and I made eye contact, and his brows knitted together. 'Greece, Darren. We're going to go to Greece and get this thing sorted out once and for all.'

With shocked eyes, he glanced at the others for sense. 'But we're not supposed to go there! It's dangerous, and now I'm a myth I'll be vulnerable, won't I?' pain was present in his voice. Like the others, he was now worried about his immortal life, but there was nothing I could do to ease it.

'I'm sorry, Darren. The staff is still in the hands of our enemy. We need to attempt to get it back.'

'Don't worry love,' Hadriana smiled at him, 'your mother will keep you safe,' she said, looking at me, and for once her words weren't patronising.

'She saved me a fair few times. Just because I'm immortal doesn't mean I don't feel pain you know.'

Tyr snorted and shook his head. 'Yes, the thing of it is Santorini asked us to protect Thera, not the other way around. Yet in some way, Thera has acted like a mother or a sister for all of us. But,' he turned and looked at me, 'we need to be helping you now.'

Reaching out, I grasped his hand and squeezed, mouthing a soft thank you.

Just as Hadriana was about to cast the spell to send us back, Ann poked her head out of the front door and stared at us. Hesitant about what she was seeing, she tilted her head. 'You're leaving now, aren't you?'

Leaving the circle that Hadriana had made, I walked up to the steps and held out my hand. 'It was nice meeting you, Ann Smith.'

Taking it, we shook hands. 'It was nice meeting you, but I fear you are about to ask me something.'

'You caught me,' I laughed lightly, but the severity of why I needed to talk to her pressed me urgently. 'I must ask you to do something for me, it's imperative.' A puzzled expression appeared on her face, but she didn't interrupt me. 'I need you to pass down a family motto if you will. I need you to say these words to your sister's child: "I command you to the Black Abyss where you shall remain until the time when I can summon you again." Can you remember that?'

Still, with a perplexed face, she nodded. 'I shall do. Though may I ask why?' She began but then shook her head, 'You know, I do not think I would like to know. I must leave it alone and stop asking questions. I will pass the words down as a family motto. You have opened my eyes to so much. I cannot thank you enough.'

'Ann!' called a lady from within.

'I'm coming. Listen,' she said, closing the door slightly, stepping towards me, 'I think I have figured it out that you are not from this time, though I don't want to know when there must be something I can help you with?'

Putting a delicate hand on her shoulder, I smiled. 'Keep to that motto and write in a little red book. You'll know what I mean soon enough.'

'Thera, we have to go now,' Hadriana called from below.

Leaning over the railings, I gave her a small wave. 'Well, goodbye, Ann Smith.'

'My name isn't Ann,' she shrugged. 'It's my nickname. My real name is Hannah. I'd thought I'd tell you something truthfully for once.'

'Well then Hannah Smith, I'll take my leave. And well wishes on your niece or nephew I'm sure you'll be a perfect midwife and aunt.' She smiled and nodded and headed back inside, closing the door gently, the lock clicking into place.

Sighing, I headed back down the stairs and joined the circle. 'Alright, Hadriana, make your wish and then send us back to the future.'

Hadriana brought out the stardust to erase Ann's memories that could jeopardise her future and blessed her family. Then with a dash of Father Time's Sand, she sprinkled it in the middle of our circle. After saying the date, the sand swirled around us once more; one after the other, we jumped back into our present.

As the sand settled, the dark dungeons of Hadriana's castle appeared before us. Without waiting, I bolted from the circle and headed down the passageway, my hair flying behind me. The two things I had to check, one was to see if Hannah was here and second, to see if Renita was still in everyone's memories.

Racing up the stairs, the new power surging through my legs, pushing me faster around the spiralling staircase, my feet clicking on the stone steps, echoing off the old cobweb laced walls.

Barging through the heavy old door that led back into the central part of the castle, I pelted down the large entrance hall and into the grand living room, forcing the door open with such power; it battered the wall, causing part of it to crumble.

'Hannah!' I gasped, staring at the shocked faces, making them jump.

'I'm here,' she waved, smiled at me from the settee by the roaring fire. Running to her, I enveloped her in my arms. 'I'm so glad,' I laughed, hugging her tightly, almost choking her. Letting her go, I smoothed her hair and smiled at her. 'Everything's alright? You're not fading anymore?'

'No,' she smiled.

Hearing thunderous footfalls behind me, the others had arrived.

'Hannah!' Darren laughed as he and Tyr raced over to her.

Moving out of the way, my eyes glanced around the room. Dagen looked positively bored, sitting on a chair by himself. Eleanor was with Jane, who for some reason, both seemed to be having a decent none argumentative chat. But where was... 'Renita,' I sighed in relief, seeing her curled up in a chair in the corner.

'She just fell asleep,' Jane told me as I walked over to her. 'Where's Etrician?'

'He got snatched by some of what we thought were the Minister's lackeys,' Tyr began and went to sit on the floor by Renita. 'Although now we're not sure that they are on his side in the first place. We think they were controlled by that other girl, Rhea,' Tyr explained. 'The Minister doesn't seem to be involved in messing up Hannah's timeline.'

While Hadriana slunk over to her sister, she grabbed a cigarette from Eleanor's pocket without asking and lit up. Jane moved away and went and sat by Darren and Hannah.

'What happened?' Eleanor asked her elder sister, no emotion in her voice. 'Sounds like it was thrilling,' she drawled.

'Shot, chased, threatened, nearly had a train crash... the usual,' Hadriana replied in the same voice, as though she was a completely different person around her sister, which I thought was a bit...odd. 'Etrician has been kidnapped by Rhea's little followers.'

Eleanor's eyes grew wide and stared accusingly at her sister. 'Rhea's followers? She doesn't have any.'

Replying, Hadriana just shrugged.

Something dark and sinister passed over Eleanor's eyes. Malice and a shady secret were hidden there, and though I did not know what she was keeping from her family, I knew it did not bode well.

'Are we going to find Etrician then?' Hannah asked the room, though looked at me for confirmation.

Eleanor's eyes swept to the floor, then balling her hands into fists, excused herself from the room. I watched Hadriana's gaze follow her sister then the door abruptly slammed shut.

Sighing heavily, I closed my eyes, trying to ignore another problem that we would face soon enough, Eleanor. 'Rhea sent some humans and a Jinn into the past.' I told them finally. Now was probably the best time to admit to Hadriana about the other engineer. 'Tara's father confirmed that.'

'Whoa, what?' Hannah and Darren asked. Hadriana's face screwed up and glared at me. 'He's dead!'

'The engineer,' I explained to Hadriana, 'Tara's father is a Capturer, he works for the Ancients and was sent in the past to sort out the disturbances that Rhea's lackeys were causing in the timeline. His human cover was being a husband and father to Tara, Nathaniel and Tara's mother. His cover died a few months back, but he is, in fact, an immortal.'

'Mind. Blown!' Hannah fell back against the cushions with her mouth open. 'I don't believe it. What else have I missed out on?'

'Tara's father, he wasn't after anyone, was he?' Renita had woken up and heard what we had been talking about. I smiled softly and shook my head.

'Oh,' Darren snapped his fingers and tapped Hannah on her leg. 'You were named after your great-great-great aunt,' Darren piped up. 'Her real name was Hannah. Her nickname was Ann!'

'Needless to say that the timeline has been restored,' I told everyone. 'The Ancients sent Mr Young into the past to discover why the timeline had been distorted. Now, the only thing is, does Maynard know about this? If this is Rhea's doing, she is pulling out the stops to ensure the obliteration of the T.A.T.'

Hannah's face contorted into utter bewilderment. 'But, isn't she being completely idiotic. It alters Maynard's timeline as well.'

Dagen, however, was the one who replied. 'Not necessarily. Remember Madagascar? There was a portal there. It may not be the only portal that's still open. Rhea knows that the T.A.T are the enemies. Get rid of the opposition and Maynard has got a chance for his plans to work without anyone poking their noses into his business.'

Darren groaned as something twigged. 'Oh, of course. Rhea must have gone through the transcripts at the hotel's library in London. Of course she would have known where to disrupt the timeline. Take out Ann Smith and you have no O.M.C or T.A.T.'

Hadriana let out a tired yawn then clapped her hands. 'Right kiddies, saddle up. We need to get to Greece. I want everyone gathered around and helping me out here. We don't know where in Greece we need to go and yes Dagen,' she said as he scowled at her, 'I am going, and you can't stop me.'

As everyone joined Hadriana by a table in the corner, I went straight to Renita and hugged her. Choking back the tears, I silently thanked Bertrum Young for keeping his end of the bargain.

'Hi,' she whispered. 'I'm glad you're back.'

I nodded. 'It's been an interesting journey,' I smiled. 'How have you been?'

'Tired,' she admitted, 'but before I fell asleep, my heart didn't hurt anymore. I'm feeling much better.'

I closed my eyes and smiling felt a single tear roll down my cheek. 'You, my dear, are going to live a very long and happy immortal life.'

With a slight frown on her face, she sat up and looked at me. 'I don't understand... how?'

'I made a deal with the Capturer, Tara's father. I'd give him information if he saved your existence and he upheld his part of the deal.' Grabbing her hands, I held them in mine and smiled at her. 'On the verge of leaving this world, I wanted to ensure that there was some good that I could do for you. I wanted so much to save you by keeping you from being taken away and erased from our memories.' Suddenly Renita burst into tears and fell into my arms, wrapping her own around my neck. 'Hey it's alright,' I chuckled softly as I rocked her gently.

'Renita are you all right?' Tyr asked from behind me.

'You don't have to tell anyone if you don't want to,' I whispered to her, as Tyr and Jane moved towards us. Stemming her tears, she withdrew from me and wiped her wet cheeks. Her black hair fell forwards covering her face. 'Come on, poppet,' rubbing her knees to cheer her up. I placed some hair behind her ears. 'You are going to be fine because we are all in this together. You're meant to be looking after me, you know?'

Laughing in a watery way, she nodded. Standing up, Jane and Tyr swooped in to see if she was alright. Offo and Eleanor came into the room seconds later and announced that there would be a light meal in the dining room.

'Thank Gods! I am starving,' Hadriana groaned.

'Ran out of food dear sister?' Eleanor drawled. 'One might have thought you'd spent our family's wealth on expensive hotels and inns? Or did our beloved Thera not allow it?'

Scowling at her, I ignored her comment and followed Dagen, Darren and Hannah out of the room.

'Darren, you're walking weird.' Hannah watched as he was losing his balance again. 'Are you feeling alright?'

'I'm fine, I just sort of forget how to walk properly.'

'Um, why?' She gasped. 'Holy kack, where is your bracelet?'

Hadriana shoved her long arm under Hannah's nose and showed her Dagen's broken bracelet. 'I've got it, merboy here, doesn't need it anymore, isn't that right, Thera?'

Cringing, I tapped them both on the shoulder and indicated to my left to a small cupboard by the grand staircase. Though Darren had no choice but to become a myth back in the past, I wanted to give Hannah the option of being one now or later. I knew that soon she would have to be one; it was just a matter of time.

'What is it?' Hannah asked. Darren remained quiet as I took a deep breath, trying to figure a way of how to explain it to her.

'I want to explain. I guess I've always known,' I began confusingly, 'though nothing really made sense until an incident on the train.'

'What train?'

Darren shook his head in hopelessness at my lousy attempt to explain to her what had happened. 'Look,' he began, 'Thera turned me back into a merman again. Well…' he said, gesturing to his legs sheepishly, 'she told me to become human while on land. Find it really odd though.'

'H-how?' Hannah lifted up her bracelet and held it out to me. 'Can you do it now?'

Darren grabbed her hand and forced it down. 'Hannah it hurts like hell,' he warned her. 'Like when it was back in Vietnam. It hurt like bloody hell. Only do it if you require the power. Because I'm a myth now I'm vulnerable to the staff, but you're not. Don't think you have to be a myth just because I am.'

Sadness passed over her eyes, and she hugged herself. 'I wish Nathaniel was here,' she whispered softly. 'He always knew what to say in difficult situations.'

'Yeah?' Darren growled, 'well he's not here, so you're gonna have to make these decisions by yourself. Don't go all lame on me because you have Nathaniel withdrawal.'

My hand flung to his mouth to shut him up as I heard the voices of Offo and Eleanor just outside. Peering around, I saw them amble to the dining room, though neither of them seemed as though they wanted to consider joining the others. Removing my hand from Darren, I placed a finger to my lips and pointed to them not twenty feet from us.

'They are aware of the situation,' Eleanor sputtered, almost frighteningly, as Offo closed the door to the dining room. 'We just need to keep them here as long as we can.' Pacing around, she was extremely agitated. But why, what had she done? And who was "they" that she was referring to?

'Excellent ma'am,' Offo bowed. 'And what of Mistress Thera?'

Snorting, she waved her hand. 'Never mind about her yet, its Hannah and Darren I'm worried about. She's already turned Darren. I could smell the stench of merman as soon as that boy entered the room. It won't be long until she turns Hannah too. Thera will bring them, there's no mistaking that, she's marked, end of. What about that idiotic Dinglewood, has he come back yet?' Eleanor began to pace and she went out of view.

Forcing myself not to gasp in shock, I inched closer, hoping not to miss a single word.

'No ma'am. He sent word that he has no news.'

There was a thump on the floor. I wondered if she's stomped her foot like a petulant child. 'Damn. Why isn't there anyone alive who can tell me about Thera's Amber Tree leaves? That stupid Hobgoblin doesn't know anything.'

'He knew about the pouch that you stole from Mistress Thera. Perhaps, if we ask her?'

Hannah's mouth fell open. 'Unbelievable,' she mouthed. Eleanor was a betrayer, not just to me but to her sister as well. Hannah and Darren stared at me, their faces mirroring mine. Complete and utter disbelief.

'No. She is not to know.' She groaned in frustration. 'Look, when Dinglewood gets back, tell him to take Hannah and Darren. He needs to watch them until Thera gets taken then we can start the ball rolling.'

'Very good ma'am,' Offo bowed, then quickly departed leaving Eleanor to pace a little more, until she messed her hair up a bit, then casually walked into the room as though nothing happened.

Waiting for a few moments, ensuring that Offo had gone away, the three of us crept out of the cupboard, stunned into silence. Closing it quickly, I made them follow me upstairs into the room where I was staying.

Upon closing the door, I expressed my concern. 'We need to get out of here now, get the others and go.'

'She has been acting weird ever since you left,' Hannah said, looking worried. 'Pacing, mumbling, walking out of the room, then coming back either looking concerned or happy. She's on the other side, isn't she?' Hannah spoke the words that I feared.

I had to think of an escape plan and fast. 'You two are the only ones who can get the Staff of Zeus which we believe is still in Greece. We'll get Jane to phade us there. Leave it to me to tell her the plan. We can't trust Eleanor or Offo.' Though what was annoying me was that Eleanor had my Amber Tree leaves but why? She wouldn't be unable to use them, only Santorini and I could. Going over to a chair where I flung the ripped clothes that Airmed gave me I routed through it and found nothing. The pouch had been taken.

It was apparent now what Eleanor was up to but even thinking about it was painful. Both she and Hadriana were like my own children in a way, I helped them through the transition into immortality, told them about a new hidden world. They called on both Santorini and me when they needed us for centuries. It was irksome. 'Damn Atlas I've been a fool,' I cursed, frustrated with myself.

Darren sighed, scratching his head. 'It's not your fault. But you're right, we need to get the others and get the hell out of here before Hannah and I get captured.'

Looking around for anything useful in the room, I saw a small dagger with a red and bronze hilt, with what looked like a bird's head at the end. Attached to the wall for decorating, I went over to it and smashed the plaque.

'What are you doing?' Hannah hissed, 'someone will hear that.'

Empowering it with magic, I nodded. 'Good, take it,' I said, thrusting it into her sweaty hands. 'You may need it for later. You need something to protect yourself with.' Seeing nothing else that would be useful, I motioned for them to follow me and together we hurried from the room, down the long carpeted hallway corridor towards the front doors. 'Get out of the castle,' I ordered them, 'I'll get the others, and we'll meet you by the lake.'

They nodded then both of them headed for the tall, heavy doors, running past the gleaming suits of armour, where soft lights flickered from torches on the walls. Turning right, I bolted to the dining room. Forcing the doors open with a bang, everyone immediately stopped and stared at me. Hadriana and Eleanor were sitting at the far end of the table, Eleanor's brows furrowed while Hadriana looked positively shocked.

All the plans I had been thinking of, went straight out of the window. 'We're leaving,' I said to the startled room. 'Now.'

Tyr and Dagen gave each other strange glances but began to rise out of their chairs, Jane and Renita looked between myself and Eleanor but remained still.

'I wouldn't advise you do that,' Eleanor said silkily, her eyes boring into mine.

'No? Well, I've just made that call. Jane, Renita, let's go.'

Eleanor suddenly stood up, scraping her chair, calling everyone's attention to her. 'You are not going, Thera. Everyone needs to stay here.'

'No, we don't, we're going,' I said forcefully.

Jane and Renita got up from their chairs and began to leave. Slapping a hand down on the table, making the cutlery clank, Eleanor gave a piercing shriek. 'You will not leave this castle!'

Turning to her as the boys hurried out first, followed quickly by the girls, I said, 'Eleanor, mark me. You will do well to remember your place within this world, child,' I spat. 'Do not incite my anger and stay with your sister.' Magically collecting water from three jugs from the table, I created a wall of ice behind me and left the room.

'OFFO!' Eleanor screamed. 'STOP THEM!'

As I hurried out of the castle with the others, the large doors ahead were open enough for all of us to get out. Icy cold blasts of snow forced its way inside the castle, snuffing out a few of the torches, throwing everyone into semi-darkness. I heard the wall of ice being hit heavily and then with one large bang, it came crashing to the floor.

Peering into the dark, I caught illuminated silhouettes of two people wrestling on the floor.

'Someone help, please! Offo, let go of me!' Jane whimpered, hearing her fists beat against the cloth on Offo's jacket.

'Eleanor, what have you done?' Hadriana shrieked from behind me.

'It's not your concern, sister,' she replied, enraged, hearing her run across the corridor her heels clicking quickly. I had to act fast. I wanted to avoid hurting her. Though she had done wrong, I still cared for the Von Reed family and Hadriana would never speak to me again if I hurt Eleanor.

Heading to Offo and Jane, who was still rolling on the floor, I ripped them apart; grabbing hold of Jane, I kicked Offo in the stomach, a pained grunt quickly followed. 'I'm sorry, Offo, but we can't stay here.' Together Jane and I raced towards the white light ahead. 'Go!' I shouted, making them bolt for the exit.

'Thera, don't you dare leave this castle!' Eleanor screeched behind me as I heard her follow me through the large doors and across the wooden bridge, where everyone stood huddled together, not moving as the troll had stopped them.

'Get out of the way,' I shouted to them, pulling back my fist. Scattering out of the way, I ran and jumped towards the troll, punching him straight in the face. With a loud painful roar, the troll flew back off his feet, hurtling through the air, crashing to the snow-covered ground meters away. 'GO!' I yelled again, leading the way back down the icy road.

'Thera no!' Eleanor screamed hoarsely. The snow fell quickly, coupled with howling winds that whipped our hair and stung at our eyes. 'Don't go-!' Eleanor called, but the winds stole her voice as we ran away from the castle.

The group headed down towards the large, foreboding lake, where ice had formed lightly across it. 'Hannah,' I called, running to catch up to her as she and Darren raced towards the water's edge. 'What are you-?'

'Change me now,' she urged, stopping meters from the lake. 'I can't do anything useful like this. I don't want to be a burden.'

'Are you sure? Once I do, I cannot undo it.' She nodded and reached out to me. Grabbing her wrist where the Aqua Stone bracelet still clattered against her bones, I yelled, 'Release!'

Hannah gasped and fell to the ground. I picked her up and saw the strange, vibrant blue liquid brake out of its stony prison and seep into her skin.

'NO!' Eleanor bellowed as she, Offo and Hadriana sped down the path, flying towards us. 'Don't go over the shrubs!'

I looked around for Jane, who stayed with Tyr, Renita and Dagen, all staring at us in horror. 'Jane, get the others and take them to Greece. We'll find a way to meet up with you.' Passing a load of odd shrubbery that made a strange border around the perimeter of the castle that was similar in appearance to those around Dian's home I said, 'You're going to Nisida Pachi.' Jane reached out and grabbed Renita, Tyr and Dagen, quickly forming a circle, and within moments a blinding flash of blue light erupted in front of me, and they vanished.

Heading to the lake, I began to feel very strange, as though my body was slowing down involuntarily. Hannah felt like a heavy burden as she squirmed with pain in my arms; reluctantly, I dropped her, mere inches from the lakeside.

'Thera?' Darren began. 'What's wrong?'

Feeling as though something was pressing down on me, I tripped up and fell, stumbling over my feet. 'Take her and go,' I said. Darren stared at Hannah, who was now writhing in agony. However, instead, he took hold of my hand and dragged me into the waters.

As my body lazily sunk into the depths, I tried to struggle against the strange feeling that wrapped around me, but to no avail. '*Got you.*' Someone whispered in my mind. Then, without warning, a shining white light illuminated around me, turning the water a garish green. Energy was instantly zapped from me and forced me to sink lower towards the lake bed. My entire being screamed out in pain that started from my back and rippled throughout the rest of my body; like blunted machete's piercing every inch of my skin, cutting into the muscle spreading corrosive acid through my veins.

Unable to move, something or someone was pulling me to the surface. Darren, in his merman form, swam to me, grabbing onto my hand and tried to stop me from rising out of the waters, his tail thrashing madly from the mini-whirlpool the light's energy was now emitting, but he wasn't strong enough.

Swimming with me, he yelled, '*What's going on?*' inside my head, but I could not respond, I wasn't allowed to respond. My body was no longer my own.

It was all over...No matter how much I tried, no matter how many people I had asked, how many ways I tried to escape what was coming for me: you really can't change your destiny.

Slowly my body lifted out of the murky waters that surrounded Castle Von Reed. My eyes, which still had some movement, swivelled in their sockets and locked onto Hannah. Hadriana and Eleanor crowded around her.

'It was Santorini,' Eleanor yelled as tears streaked down her face. 'He wanted me and a few others to help you... to keep Hannah and Darren safe. He didn't want me to tell you. It's all my fault.' She hugged a screaming Hannah who writhed around by the lakeside unable to stop the process of becoming a myth once more. I now understood the conversation she had had with Offo. Dinglewood must have been on her side from the very beginning. 'I'm so sorry.'

'*Thera!*' Darren called in my head. My heart wept from my stupidity of being too paranoid about even those who were closest to me. '*Thera, no, hold on!*' Darren yelled helplessly, but it was too late. Rising towards the ominous grey skies above, I was going to where the Fates had predicted. The Cabinet of Idols.

Hadriana, Eleanor, Darren and Hannah then vanished from my sight in a flash of blue light.

It was all over.

CHAPTER TWENTY-EIGHT

'WAKE UP, THERA,' A GIRL'S VOICE CALLED TO ME, SHE SOUNDED YOUNG like Jane, was it Jane? But no, it couldn't be. I told her to go to Greece, didn't I? 'Wake up now.' A sharp pain erupted on my back. My eyes forcefully flicked open, adjusting quickly to the brilliantly lit room with plain white walls, ceiling and matching chairs and a table in front of me. It looked like a clean room from a hospital, but it didn't smell like one, it smelt like lavender.

Looking down, I saw that I was standing up; my legs were locked together with golden shackles, and imprinted on them were old inscriptions of the Ancient's language. My arms were outstretched on either side of my body. My wrists too were shackled by golden printed cuffs, chained to the walls were a thick heavy metal pin embedded the chains into them. Testing them lightly, the chains barely moved. Applying more force, they wavered a little, but it would seem impossible to break them.

Frowning at the imprint on the cuffs, I made out, "Seal the power." Considering Hadriana beefed up my power, due to her sheer idiocy, I wasn't going anywhere.

Taking in more of my surroundings, I noticed that I was in a very tall, glass box, with a strange golden rod hanging directly above me. Immediately I tried to back away from it as it pointed down at me, but the shackles gave me no room to move. 'Damn, I think I'm…'

'Part of the magical exhibit of the Cabinet of Idols,' came the sweet voice again. 'Welcome.' Shuffling into view was a petit framed sun-kissed girl with, long brown hair that was plaited down her back. Her shiny hair enhanced a long silken sky-blue dress that reached the ground. Staring at me with dark blue eyes, she smiled widely at me. Instantly I knew who she was, but still, I was courteous towards the child.

'Hello, Rhea.'

A wide smile stretched on her face. 'Hello Thera, Daughter of the Ocean.' Sighing, she gazed avidly at me. 'You were by far, one of the hardest to capture, so feel honoured.'

'I'm not,' I replied icily.

The girl shrugged. 'Doesn't matter. You are now under our control, but I feel as if you knew that already. I also sense that you have gained power since the last time Garrick met you in Ireland. You can thank our informant,' her eyes went to her left and she smiled. 'Dian.'

'Dian?'

'Forgive me.' Came his feeble apology. 'I am so sorry, Thera.'

'Oh shut up, you insufferable idiot.' Rhea snapped.

It made sense now as to why we were found out in Ireland. Hadriana was right, it wasn't Dinglewood at all. Dian had been under Rhea's control when he got zapped by the staff. Though, I hid a smile. Hadriana's Witch Hazel obviously worked to conceal Dian's conversations at his home and Garrick's meeting with me at Hadriana's castle. At least Rhea didn't know about that.

'Did you know you used to be a Siren?' I asked, changing the topic.

Something passed in front of her, as though a fleeting memory of something she couldn't grasp, but recovering quickly, she shook her head. 'I used to be many things, but now I am here to extract the power from you so that when the entity is released, they can open The Gates.'

'Gates?' I thought it was a prison. Was there a difference?

Her eyes showed shrewdness. Taking a few steps towards the thin pane of glass that separated us, she tilted her head in wonder. 'I guess you never understood the purpose of the Cabinets. Though, I would have been surprised if you did. It's not common knowledge among myths or legends. It's Ancient's knowledge and being very close to them, I know more than most.'

Rhea sounded as though she was trying to get one up on me. Trying to sound more vital than she was. That just irked me. 'Don't you mean close to one Ancient?' her eyes narrowed. 'There is only Maynard, the eighteenth Ancient who will bring the downfall upon the earth. But surely you are aware of that?'

Eyebrows raised, she leaned on one leg. 'Of course.' But I could tell she was lying. 'When the entity is free they will unlock The Gate and its inhabitants will be set free. And humans will fall off the world and myths and legends will reign.'

Noting her "fall off the world" comment, I continued as though she hadn't uttered it.

'That's rather silly considering without humans there'd be no myths. The Ancient's created myths from humans, without them-'

'Yes I know,' she said venomously, suddenly angered. 'But there is a way to sustain ourselves from humans, to sever the ties, as it were. And it's all thanks to the centaurs,' she giggled, 'in more ways than one, we owe them our gratitude.'

Her simpering words infuriated me. 'You have destroyed dozens of herds with that monstrosity you hold in your hands,' I growled. 'Why are you thanking them?'

Rhea caressed the staff lovingly as though it was her favourite toy. 'I can't give away the surprise. I want to see the look on your face what you and the others,' she nodded around me, 'realise the truth of why you are all here together like caged rabid animals.' Her voice quickly became cold and spiteful. She was utterly full of hatred against us and I couldn't help but wonder if Maynard had planted these hateful emotions into her.

I wanted to know Rhea a little better, to understand her true motives and to see how much she remembered before she magically became a child, so I changed the topic. 'I hear you were saved from a fight with Tara, the black-winged Siren.'

Turning her back on me, she pulled at her flowing, cream dress and revealed part of her tanned back. Wisps of her mahogany hair clung to the stumps, but there was the evidence to suggest her wings had been ripped off. 'This is what happens when you piss off the other Ancients,' she spat furiously. 'Maynard saved me and gave me this,' she faced me and swung the staff around. 'There is nothing that Tara and her simpering friends can do now. We've won,' she grinned her dazzling white teeth. Staring at me for a little while longer, she sighed and turned away from me. 'There is just one more little job we need to do before we can begin. And I'm glad you will be able to do this,' she giggled.

Thoughts raced through me and I instantly remembered Santorini. He hadn't been captured, not yet. I barked out a laugh. Rhea's face whipped around to look at me. 'You'll never get my brother. He is safe and well and far away from your reach.'

Scoffing, she rolled her eyes. 'You think so little. For a legend, I expected better. Since you have gained that extra power there is no need for your brother, but there is need for him,' she said with an evil smile, looking away to something I couldn't see at the end of the room. Laughing airily, she gave me a smug smile then turned away from me. 'Maynard has the perfect plan set out for the world, and no one knows but me.'

Rhea glided away, her dress rippling behind. Walking off to the right, out of my peripheral vision, she began to mumble though I was unsure if she was talking to herself or others that I hazarded a guess was in the room with me.

Hearing a heavy door slam to my right, I waited patiently for extra sounds, the swish of a dress, the clicking of shoes against the pure white marble floor, but there was nothing. 'Is there anyone in here?' I asked the room. 'Hello?'

No-one replied. If there were others in the room, they remained quiet and rightly so. Talking amongst ourselves might prove hazardous if we let something slip that Rhea could use against us. 'Is there someone here? Just a simple yes would be beneficial to my sanity.' I called, straining my ears to hear something and then there was the slightest tinkle of chains. 'I heard your chains move.'

There was a groan beside me on the left. 'Yes I'm here, but I think you should shut up,' his voice sounded familiar...but I couldn't place the Russian accent. Russia was vast in size, and so were legends. It would be difficult to find out who it was.

'Hey don't talk to her like that,' someone on my right piped up, her voice was also familiar, but I had problems on her accent. Spanish in origin but it had a twist of Mexican and Incan? 'Don't you worry chica, we'll all get out of here.'

'Hardly,' someone's pessimistic very English voice sounded from the far right. Something twigged in my memory when I was in Avalon. Arthur was marked for the Cabinet also. I quickly assessed that he was speaking now. 'Though I don't know what the plans are, I doubt we'd be able to get out of here and stop whatever it is they're doing.'

'Arthur?' I asked, breaking the gabble.

Everyone abruptly stopped, holding their breath. 'Y-yes... Well, it's King Arthur actually, who are you?' came an uncertain reply.

Apart from Dian, I was relieved I'd found out at least one more legend that was trapped in this place... wherever we were. 'It's Thera, the Water Nymph.'

'Oh.'

Frowning at his lack of enthusiasm, I quipped, 'Well, don't jump for joy then.'

'Please address me as King Arthur. I do have a crown you know,' he said irritably.

'Uh-huh, well Avalon has turned to chaos since I was there last. Thanks to Morgana she's warped it into her own controlled world. I just don't understand why this is happening. We've got to put our heads together and do... something!'

'What on Atlas can a Vater Nymph do?' the Russian sniped at me. 'Throw vater at the leetle girl? Ha!' he barked. 'There is no one that can help us.'

'Vodyanoy!' I yelled, suddenly remembering the garish put-on accent. 'The Inca girl's right, you have no reason to speak to me like that!'

'Damn.' He sighed dramatically. 'Sorry, mistress but... vell I don't vant you talking to me,' he yipped annoyingly. 'You did not help me! No one did! There I vos sitting on my rock in the middle of my lake ven suddenly I felt something ripple the surface-'

'Oh, here we go again,' the Inca girl sighed.

'-then this bright beam shot down through the vater and snaked around and found me. It sucked me up,' making a sickening sucking sound which grew steadily louder there was then a sudden pop. 'I tried calling for your help, but you didn't reply and then, darkness. Then, I vake up to you lot shouting at leetle girl,' his voice monotone.

'I'm sorry I couldn't help you,' I said after a moment. 'I guess since I was taken and with Santorini, not here, any water-related myth and legend is fair game.'

He grumbled but didn't say anything, and I couldn't blame him. Because now I had been captured, everyone in my charge was in danger. I wondered if Jane and Dagen knew. Maybe they weren't aware yet? Thinking quickly, I had a plan. 'Hey, Rhea!' I called out, 'Rhea!'

'I say, what are you doing?'

'Chica don't be crazy, the girl has lost one too many bolas.'

'Hey, hey, hey, don't be calling leetle girl in here, she is in pissy mood right now. You'll make her extra mad!'

I heard the heavy doors swing open, footsteps coming towards me, everyone held their breaths again. 'You bellowed?' Rhea asked, looking stony. 'Come to barter for your-'

'I've had an epiphany,' I cut across her. 'The reason why I'm here is because of humans. After all, I wouldn't have been recently captured if it wasn't for those children from the T.A.T. I mean, you're right, we don't need humans. They pollute my rivers, dump toxic waste in my streams and spill oil into my oceans. At least some myths can do their job,' I shouted towards Vodyanoy. Pondering on my words, it looked like she was about to go, but I needed her to use me, to control me again. Rhea and Maynard thought they knew me; thought they knew the others, but they didn't. Hadriana, especially, was much more cunning. It was my one shot. 'Garrick said that I would see his way... but those were your words, weren't they? I've had enough of humans, use the staff on me, and you can use me to get Hannah and Darren. They are both "myths" now,' I air quoted, 'you need their power, and I'm willing to help you obtain it.'

The ball was in her court. Remaining quiet, I looked pitifully at the floor, waiting, hoping that she believed me. In truth, I had hated humans, but not all of them were bad. They were on the planet and myths needed them to continue existing.

After what felt like an age, I heard her sigh. 'Fine. You can help, after all, you can't escape, and what will happen to you will inevitably happen.' She smiled evilly. 'You Thera shall help us. We need you to go and find your friends and lead them here, and you'll do it without complaint!' Her brow furrowed. Darkness emitted from her eyes, it was quite scary to see an evil child who could look so sweet and innocent one minute and look like a demon incarnate the next.

Snapping her fingers, a bright red light flashed before me in its place was a large golden rod with Zeus' emblem at the top. Gleaming in its threatening way, I braced myself for the pain that was to come. Taking hold of it, Rhea caressed it gently then pointed it at me, 'Do my bidding!' The staff trembled in her grip then hearing the fizzing sound of electricity, a bright bolt shot point-blank towards me.

Pain shuddered through me like a million jagged pieces of glass, puncturing every inch of my body. Then it had gone.

Unsure of what my body was doing, I somehow managed to nod, though it was unwillingly. I once recalled Garrick mentioning that he knew of what he was doing when he was being controlled, but he could not stop it. Fearing the worst, I waited for the orders Rhea was about to issue.

Smiling evilly at me, she waved the staff. The thin screen of glass, as well as the chains all but vanished. A fresh, clean gust of air spread around me.

'Step out,' she ordered, my body willingly complied, but my mind screamed out 'No.' It was a very odd sensation, one which I didn't like. 'You will go to your friends, and you will bring them here to Pílios. You will not tell them anything about the Cabinet of Idols, you will lie that you were captured and you will force Hannah and Darren to come here. Do you understand?'

'Yes.' It was such a simple reply, but I wished beyond heaven and earth that there was a way for me to explain the truth to the others. My eyes were now Rhea's, my voice was now Rhea's. Anything that I was to say and see was because of her.

'Good, now go.' She pointed to her right, and my feet walked. I tried to glance to my right to see the others in their cells, but my head did not want to turn. Rhea had full control over me, and I couldn't do a thing to stop it.

My heels clicked across the pristine white marble floor, Rhea followed behind. Feeling the pressure of her will upon my own, it was maddening. Sighing, she went ahead of me and pushed the doors open.

'Thank you,' she made me say.

Passing the towering doors, there was a lengthy bright, blood-red arched corridor ahead, almost hurting my eyes. I sensed such a repulsive force of malevolence that pulsated from it. My instincts were to run the opposite direction, but Rhea's will forced me on. The pressure of this presence built up as I neared, though not too far ahead I saw an opening to the right and pleaded with my disconnected body to go that way—luckily for me, Rhea wanted to go in that very direction. My body felt lethargic as we neared the door. However, Rhea didn't experience what I felt and forced me to march on.

Another corridor; doors on either side were marked with Greek letters. Rhea stopped outside the third door on the right marked epsilon and made me open it. Refreshing cold air blasted into my face and splattered me with water. The source was a cascading waterfall which poured in from a hole in the ceiling of a very small, blue coloured room and fell through the floor where the bottom seemed endless.

'Bring the group here,' Rhea ordered. 'All of them.'

'Yes. I will.' My body suddenly lurched forward and made contact with the cold water, instantly revitalizing me, but it was short-lived as Rhea's hold on me was too strong to enjoy the water.

The naturalness of my powers took hold, and Rhea was able to guide me, to find who I was looking for. Using my abilities all too quickly, she found them. They were still at Hadriana's castle. This didn't bode well for the Von Reeds.

Phasing through the hundreds of miles of water, my body erupted out of the icy lake. Coldwater and shards of ice drenched Hadriana, Offo and Eleanor who were still outside of their castle. It made me wonder how long I was gone for. It felt hours.

Landing in a crouch on the bank of the lake, my body breathed in slowly. I stood up to face the others. 'Act naturally,' Rhea voiced in my head.

'Are you alright?' my lips moved, my eyes forcing me to look at the others who were shocked that I had come back. Darren was still in the water, his jaw opened in bewilderment as he leaned out of the water to talk to Hannah, who was rigid from disbelief.

'Thera?' Hadriana's question punctured the uneasy air that surrounded us, I was thankful that she suspected straight away.

My eyes shot to Eleanor, who frowned in confusion as she saw me. Rhea suddenly tried to access my memories, only seeing brief glimpses of what I had last said to the others. The words Greece flittered unwillingly into my mind, but the island I told the others to go to, cropped up. I felt Rhea smile from where she was in Pílios. She knew what she was going to make me say that would get everyone to the mountain of the Centaurs.

'The extra power,' I was forced to say, 'it's too strong for the staff. I managed to get away.'

'Extra power? What extra power?' Eleanor asked, turning to look threateningly at her sister.

Don't say it, I screamed out at the back of my mind where Rhea could not listen. Please don't say it.

Hadriana shrugged, 'A little mistake was made, and I gave her extra power. It's no big deal. It will wear off,' she said nonchalantly. Rhea didn't know Hadriana like I did. There were hundreds and thousands of memories of her. Rhea did not have time to filter through them all. This was the biggest flaw of Rhea's control over me. Underestimating my friends.

Hadriana had already cottoned on to me. She knew I was under Rhea's control, no matter the lies Rhea forced me to say.

'But how did you get back here?' Eleanor asked who wasn't as quick as her sister.

'I escaped. I found a door that had a waterfall that came from the ceiling and fell through the floor,' Rhea made me speak the truth. 'As strange as it sounds,' I was forced to smile. 'Then, as soon as I could, I found you.'

The plan was working, and Rhea had no clue of the mistakes she was making. Firstly, the argument that I had had with Eleanor and the accusations of her betraying us; the first thing I would have done was to apologise, regardless. Then, of course, I told the others to meet me on the island, I did not say that I would go back to the castle. Because of Rhea's obsessive tendencies to help Maynard, she was making mistakes that could be easily rectified if she had thought about them first. The big questions was how could I communicate to Hadriana?

'And you came back to see if we were all right?' Hadriana asked me coldly.

Rhea's annoyed thoughts passed through my head again. She was confused about why Hadriana would be acting like this towards me, but this was Hadriana all over. Forcing my memories open on Hadriana, Rhea made me reply. 'Not you, just Hannah and Darren.'

Smiling a little, Hadriana shrugged. 'Right so are we going to the others then? I don't fancy staying here, it's rather cold. Eleanor, are you coming with us?'

Frowning at me, Hadriana's impassive face obviously gave something away. 'Yes. Offo, you can stay here and wait for our guest. Tell them I won't be long.'

'Yes ma'am,' he bowed then walked off.

'Don't you think we need to take things with us?' Hannah asked, making her way towards us. I inwardly smiled. Her transformation to a real Water Nymph made her a mirror image of myself; sleek bodyline, with almost elfin-like ears, bright eyes and her hair fell in ringlets to her waist. My heart filled with pride as I saw her standing in the dusk's light that shone around us. A new Nymph had come into existence, a new daughter.

'Oh I think Hazel needs to come with us,' Hadriana said making a snap decision. 'I'll go and get her.'

Rhea checked through my memory and found that I didn't know a Hazel, so making me ask who Hazel was, Eleanor just shrugged in response. An oddity that Rhea didn't like.

'Was Rhea there?' Hannah asked me as she took hold of my hand. 'Is she still a child?'

'Yes,' I said sadly, Rhea half taking a backseat as I filled her in on the details of what was and wasn't mentioned. 'I asked her twice on whether she remembered who she was, but she didn't. I don't think she ever will.'

'Was Maynard there?' Darren called from behind, still in the water.

Turning around slowly, I shook my head. 'Not that I could see. But I didn't feel anything.' Rhea made me lie. 'Usually, I can sense an Ancient when they are about to appear or when they near me, but I didn't feel anything.'

'Do you think you should change Darren back into a human now?' Hannah asked me, smiling. 'He can't come on land looking like that.'

'Why don't you try it?' I asked, as Rhea wanted to test her powers, though she was unknowing of the plan I had in mind with Hannah at the end. Hopefully, if Ann's magic had been passed down, Hannah would be able to banish me.

'Let's get him some clothes first,' Eleanor said as she ran off towards the castle. 'Thera you stay with Darren and Hannah, I'll be right back.'

A few minutes later, as Hannah and Darren had a playful banter about never touching fish and chips again, Hadriana and Eleanor turned up. Reaching out, Rhea made me snatch the clothes from Hadriana's grip then throw them over to Darren. My eye caught sight of some holes in the ground, and I wondered where the Witch Hazel shrubs had gone to, but Rhea didn't notice them.

'Hannah, command him,' my voice sounded harsh and cold. Hadriana sighed behind me; Rhea turned me around to face her. 'What?' I demanded.

'She doesn't have to do it now,' Hadriana posed in her classical hands-on hip manner, 'you do it and hurry up about it, we need to get to the others,' she ordered.

'Darren, become a human,' Rhea made me say with a pathetic commanding voice. As Darren stared at me with a vacant expression, Rhea instantly got angry. 'NOW!' she made me roar.

Gasping in pain, Darren arched his back and slunk into the water. 'Crap, he'll drown,' Hannah yelped, as she dove in after him. Rhea found this all extraordinarily boring and made me sigh, folding my arms in impatience.

Breaking through the water, Darren gasped for breath as Hannah pushed his naked body onto the bank of the lake and magically siphoned the excess water off him as he got changed into dry clothes.

'Right, so let's get going,' I said impatiently, making my way towards Hadriana and Eleanor who like Rhea, found this annoying. However, there was a tiny glint in Hadriana's eye.

Nodding ahead, Hadriana said, 'We're heading back to the castle first. We need to get some weapons. Greece is dangerous. After you,' she said kindly.

Rhea made me nod and forced me to walk back to the castle where the troll was now standing guard by the bridge, holding a thick, wooden club. However, as I took two steps up the icy, slope, I slipped. In a flash of white, I felt something on the back of my head. It was as though I was doused with cold, oddly spicy water. Within a split second, I suddenly felt Rhea's hold slip from me, my body becoming my own. Gasping for breath, I pitched forward and placed my hands out to catch myself.

Eleanor and Hadriana rushed to my side, the look of pain on their faces. 'We know,' Hadriana said quickly. 'We know you are being controlled, we will follow you and do as she says.'

Euphoria gripped my heart, and I managed to genuinely smile. 'I'm sorry I doubted you,' I managed to say to Eleanor, as Rhea scrabbled to gain control of my body.

Smiling, she shook her head, 'I had to keep you in the dark. Santorini wanted me to. He's known for a long time about your future. He was told about what was going to happen to you when you visited the other plane in 1825. You can thank Urius, the Siren, for that.'

With everything making sense on how Santorini knew about the portal, on how to help me, sending four obscure myths to help, everything was in place for a reason. That was something I didn't doubt.

'What's your plan?' I asked the girls, but they refused to say.

'We'll just go along with her plan...' Hadriana said, but her voice was slipping from me as the pain of the mark on my back erupted again.

Before Rhea regained her control, I had to tell them what I knew. 'They want to open the Gates, not the prison. They want,' pain started in my temple, and I began to feel it fizzling down my spine. I had to hurry and tell them '-humans to fall off the earth,' I gritted my teeth from the agony of the evil magic as it coursed through me. My eyes locked with Hadriana. 'They don't need them anymore!'

Chapter Twenty-Nine

Though it had only been for less than a minute, Rhea was enraged about my body slipping from her grip. Though she had no idea about what happened, I hoped that the others would sort this out and cover their tracks. My eyes were closed, and I felt a metallic taste in my mouth. Aware and conscious, Rhea forced my eyes open and spat the taste out of my mouth. Blood dotted a thin covering of snow as the darkness began to descend upon the castle. Hadriana and Eleanor were by my side, concerned.

'Thera, are you alright?' Hadriana asked as she glanced at the blood beside me. 'That was the effect of the additional power I gave you, I'm sorry, I should have warned you.'

Rhea's placated mind understood what had happened gave her no cause to strike out or snap at Hadriana's idiocy. In fact, she found it quite interesting. 'No it's fine,' she made me say, as I stood gingerly. 'But we can't waste any more time. Forget your weapons. We don't need them. We have Darren and Hannah now.'

'I can phade us through the water,' Hannah piped up, smiling at us as she and Darren came over, both looked on edge as they saw me. I hoped that Hannah and Darren knew that I was not in control of myself.

Gathering in a group, Hannah commanded the lake to rise to her and circling as a maelstrom, moved us through the water to the tiny little island in the southern part of Greece.

In a big splash, we crashed onto the western waters of the island, Nisida Pachi. Swimming to the beach above was a dark, clear sky. Stars twinkled down so innocently, but it seemed that Rhea did not care to look at where we were, she was just happy that we were now closer to Pílios and that everyone agreed to go with her.

'Oh that's just perfect,' Dagen growled as we dragged ourselves out of the waters, sopping wet. The others, who were bowled over by a torrent of water when we arrived, sat up looking bemused. Pulling seaweed from her hair, Jane smiled as we waded through the waters, approaching the beach.

Renita laughed, waving at me. 'You're back!'

'Sorry that's my fault,' Hannah laughed, putting her hand up in apology. 'I guess I have forgotten how to use my powers.'

'Hey get back,' Tyr roared, placing his hands in front of Eleanor as she came up behind me. 'You leave them alone, betrayer!'

If I was in control of my own body, I would have given him a funny retort, but Rhea wasn't in the mood, in fact, she was curious. My head whipped around to face the youngest immortal. Rhea made me frown.

'Whoa calm it, it's alright, a misunderstanding,' Hadriana laughed forcefully, as she moved towards Tyr, blocking him from hurting her sister. 'It was a family argument, that's all.'

'A family argument?' Tyr asked as Rhea made me look at them, intently watching for anything suspicious.

'So the reason why I'm wet,' Dagen began pointing at Hannah, thankfully taking the conversation away from Eleanor and Tyr. I could always trust Dagen to warrant attention no matter what the situation. Glancing at me, he asked, 'So you did change her?'

'Yes, she did,' Hadriana cut across me. 'Not long after you left Hannah became a Water Nymph.'

'Oh good,' he nodded. 'I don't have to hate you anymore.' Rhea's personality came out and made me smile. She seemed to like Dagen, whereas the rest of us had significant problems with his attitude.

Hannah frowned and walked off in a huff.

Heading inland, I sat on a rock and watched the others having mini-conversations. Rhea was watching them closely, like an interested cat. Looking for weaknesses or signs in their personality she could exploit. Already taken a liking to Dagen, she watched him have a word with Darren who was hurriedly filling him in. As he finished, Dagen's eyes lifted into a surprised look but then sighed.

Eleanor, Tyr and Hadriana were having a conversation too, but theirs seemed to be a bit more relaxed, whereas Hannah, Jane and Renita looked extremely uncomfortable; having their backs to me as they talked. Rhea's sense of judgement was pathetic. She had no idea that they were talking about her controlling me. The naive child. Also, another thing that was a little off-putting, Rhea didn't mind being left out of the conversations. It was strange that she was content to not get involved and to sit on the sidelines and watch. Though Rhea was controlling me, she gave me some insight into her own personal life. She had been beaten down to a point where she didn't think herself necessary anymore and just left it to others. In a way, I could understand this as there had been times in my life where I was shunned for not knowing information. Rhea had been trampled and pushed to the side too often this was the norm for her. It was almost sad, and I would have felt sorry for her if she wasn't trying to do something awful that meant that humans would "fall off the earth", whatever that meant.

Clapping to get everyone's attention, Hadriana stood on top of a rock. 'Right, now that we have had time to talk about Hannah and Darren's new lives, we need to get moving.' Once again Hadriana managed to cover her tracks in case Rhea got suspicious. 'Thera, have you any idea where you were when you were taken.'

'What, Thera was taken?' Renita gasped, playing the part beautifully. 'What happened?'

'The staff was used on me, and I was taken to the top of what I think was a mountain in Greece,' Rhea made me say. 'I didn't find out much, but I do know that the extra bout of power I had was enough to escape the staff's clutches. Though no doubt that they will try and use the staff on me soon when I figure I am less powerful.'

Renita glanced at everyone for some form of confirmation, but they gave her none, so she just shrugged. 'If you say so,' she smiled. 'Well, there is a fair few mountains in Greece.'

'Well, we can be sure it's not Mount-bloody-Olympus,' Dagen interjected. 'It's probably going to be a bit obscure with a lot of protection.'

'Pílios!' Renita shouted, making everyone jump. 'It's the Mountain of the Centaurs, it's the perfect place! Centaurs have guarded the mountain for a very long time. Its full of secrets.'

Rhea was intrigued. 'What like?' She made me ask.

Renita grinned. 'There's a saying about the mountain that even humans don't know about, "Centaurs guard the world's treasure against mortal men, until the day the earth will unbalance again. Then when the earth is atop once more, can balance only then be restored." No one knows what it means, and it's funny, the centaurs don't even know either they just guard the mountain.'

'Who gave them that task to guard it?' Darren asked her.

Flicking her long black hair out of the way, she replied, 'Zeus.'

'That must be a pretty big deal to get Zeus involved,' Eleanor said. 'I've studied ancient mythology for hundreds of years. The reason why Classical Greek mythology is so widely known is that it's constantly talked about, ergo, Zeus is constantly powerful. To this day, he holds a lot of accountability towards the other mythologies. He is still one of the top dogs.'

'Hey, don't forget about Odin and Thor,' Tyr shouted at her.

'Or Osiris and Anubis,' Jane pointed out.

'Yes, yes whatever,' she snapped at them, instantly making them shut up. 'But whatever is on that mountain, we have to be prepared. So, how are we going to get there?'

Dagen raised his hand in the air and said with such a pretentious tone, that if I had control of my body, I would have hit him. 'Well, considering all of your powers combined are utterly useless, I can take us there.'

Looking offended, Jane scowled at him. 'Hey, I got us here in the first place. Don't you dare say my powers aren't as good as yours, you ungrateful snit!'

Rolling his eyes, he motioned for everyone to gather around. 'You don't have to hold hands,' he smiled in a smarmy way towards Jane, whose eyes could pierce like daggers. Standing between us, he placed his hands out beside him and took a deep breath. 'Pílios.' Unexpectedly a long circular crack formed around the group. Hadriana shot me a warning look, but Rhea didn't understand it. Was Hadriana going to bring out the Witch Hazel so soon? But I didn't have time to even think and nor did Rhea, as the earth became the sky and the sky became earth. Like a tilt table, we flipped up-side-down, ending in the earth. Everyone yelled in surprise at the abrupt motion as we began to move through the darkness. Dagen's magic was similar to phading but somewhat slower. However, within seconds of us moving, I felt a strange coldness creep down my back again and the same spicy smell of the Witch Hazel.

'You stupid cow,' I managed to gasp as Rhea's grip left me again. Grabbing onto Hadriana in the darkness, I pulled her towards me. 'Don't do this again, what do you want to tell me now?'

'Is she back?' Renita asked.

'Oh Thera, how could this happen?' Jane worried.

'The others are aware of the situation,' Hadriana replied.

'No, really! I hadn't bloody noticed the shifty eyes and quirky smiles. You idiot, girl!' I chided as I felt the pain beginning to emerge again. 'What else do you want to tell me?'

Hurriedly she said, 'The earth unbalancing, humans falling off the world, it all sounds so familiar. I think they are planning to unlock the Gates, the Gates of the Titans.' Trust Hadriana to know something that hardly anyone else did.

'Where are they?' I begged quickly, my back arched from the pain, almost like an electrifying spasm. 'I have seconds left, hurry!'

'The Gates. They were all locked up, can't you remember, you were there. You told me so yourself the day you made me an immortal!'

Gripping onto her arm to relieve some pain, I felt her wince under my strength. Then as the familiar sensation of being controlled again, I let Rhea take over my body and mind entirely and slipped into the memories of my past. Blissfully feeling and hearing nothing.

As a white haze vanished before me, I opened my eyes to a frescoed room. Pictures of hunts and gatherings, weddings and festivals decorated every inch of the walls in such vibrant colours they mesmerized me.

Lying down on a straw bed, I removed the scratchy sheets from me and stood up, revealing just a plain pale brown linen nightgown.

Looking to my left, a fluttering red cloth hung down over a doorway. Smiling as I smelt the waft of fresh bread, I moved towards it, pulling it back revealing a kitchen. A small table in front held two slices of bread and a jug of watered wine. Not hungry, I dashed out of the house and into the busy streets of the largest settlements on the island, Rayulos. Known far and wide for the largest festival of picking saffron, the markets were always bustling with traders from around the island and other countries too.

Excusing myself as I hurried past traders, merchants, sailors and priests who were on their way to a Bull Leaping event in the town centre, I met up with my best friend who was taking part in the village's main hunt. To become part of the village as a protector, you must hunt a deep-sea creature, but he told me that he didn't want to hunt any live animal and this posed a problem. If you were not a man, there was no need for you in the village.

I found him on the shell-strewn beach that hot, sunny morning, staring out at the ocean, his back hunched over, his head lowered.

Sitting beside him, I tried to calm him, but nothing seemed to work. Agitated at the prospect of the consequences of his upcoming failure, he picked up a shell and threw it in the ocean. And then something caught my eye. Two glowing blue stones had washed up on the shore. 'Keep this with you. Perhaps it will bring you luck.' I told him. I wished with my whole heart that he kept true to himself. He was more than my best friend. I loved him like a brother.

That evening, the hunt began, and a few hours later, when the sun dipped behind the angry mountain that pushed plumes of smoke into the air when the God and Goddess were offended, he returned empty-handed. As he said, he would fail, and failure meant death.

I was heartbroken, but I stood by him as no one else would.

He was sentenced to death as a sacrifice to the God and Goddess for appeasement the following afternoon. They pushed him with a spear up the angry mountain, and I followed, salty tears, slipping off my cheeks.

The Priests sang songs and said prayers and with his hands bound, they anointed him with oils and pushed him into the melted rock below. Grief-stricken at the thought that my life would have no meaning without him, I jumped after him, clutching onto that small little glowing blue stone I found the previous day.

As I fell to my death, I made a wish. That he and I would remain together forever. My wish came true.

The melted rock exploded outwards. Though we no longer had our bodies, our souls latched onto the glowing stones, and they were tossed into the sea. Soon, cold hands caressed us, and a soothing voice whispered, "I have got you, my children, my Water Nymphs."

The Ocean Herself gave us those stones, she had been watching us since we were children. We were pure, our essence good. "I had to destroy your island to bury deep the evils of this world and lock them away." She had told us, though we had no idea what evils she was talking about. However, The Ocean Herself tasked us then and there to look after the oceans, rivers and lakes. "It is to help other deities with their duties and to keep humans believing in magic. If there is no belief, the world will unbalance, and the humans will fall off the earth."

Those were the exact words I had uttered to Hadriana when I had made her immortal. She, Offo and her sister had just drunk from the Fountain of Youth, and they had only realised what they had done. 'You cannot tell anyone how you came by the fountain, nor can you tell them your true age for you cannot die in any way. An Ancient will be the only end of your existence.' Hadriana had taken it worse than the others and grabbed me by the collar of my dress, her knuckles white, her eyes wide in terror. 'How dare you do this to us?'

'I gave you a choice. You chose this path. Please keep the Golden Rule. Humans are to believe in magic. Never truly know it. If there is no belief, the world will unbalance, and the humans will fall off the earth.'

Hadriana, Offo and Eleanor would forever hate me for what I did to them. But thankfully they kept their word and had never broken the Golden Rule, not for anyone or anything.

'Thera, we're here,' Hadriana called into the darkness. Hearing Rhea's thoughts, she was now suspicious of Hadriana. Dagen turned the world right-side-up again, and everyone appeared slightly green. 'Damn, that really was the weirdest thing I have ever felt,' Hadriana moaned, standing up and helping her sister.

This time Rhea looked around to see if she was indeed on Pílios. Damp earth and luscious grass and colourfully closed sleepy, purple flowers formed around the group as they scrambled to stand. The sky was streaked with wisps of cloud, seeming eerie as it flowed slowly across the pale moon hanging overhead. In the distance, I could see the small lights of a town not too far ahead. Rhea made me frown as I stared at them, and I knew what she was thinking, "filthy humans."

Making me crane my neck, Rhea forced me to look up towards the top of the mountain, but this didn't help her. The peak was flat; dotted in trees. It was probably only useful for hikers and their footpaths which stemmed out in all directions; centaurs did their job a little too well.

'Now what?' Dagen asked, brushing his hands as though, mission accomplished.

'Your powers suck,' Darren laughed at him. 'That was crap. Was that the new way of phading?'

'At least I can,' he sniped back, folding his arms in defence. 'All you can do is blow bubbles out of your-'

'Enough!' Rhea made me say, which scarily sounded like me, I wondered where my own mind had gone to. 'Let's go take a look around, we may run into a centaur, and they could help us.'

'They won't do that,' Renita said defiantly, not moving as the others began to follow me up the hill. 'They have been entrusted with guarding its treasures that even they don't know about. They would never help us.'

Rhea was annoyed with Renita's testy jibe and continued onwards, ignoring her. I sat back and relaxed as Rhea's thoughts passed by quickly in a stream of processes. It seemed that Rhea knew about the centaurs and knew of what was in store for the others once they reached the mountain. Maynard wanted these new myths out of the way so he could get to

Hannah and Darren and use their powers. Mixed in with his other idols, they would open the Gates. She just needed the right power to do it...

Rhea's last thoughts confused me, but I would find out sooner or later. That was the damning thing. No matter who tried to stand in our way, no matter if Etrician came to the rescue, or if anyone had the time to banish me before it was too late, I did not see a plan forming in my mind...especially since it wasn't mine anymore.

Abandoned human houses and a logging company were situated on top of the mountain, and it made Rhea smile inside. She was on the right path, she just needed to position everyone, but she was aware she had to let go of me first to do it.

The others milled around, checking out the old rusty cranes and rotting old logs that were left when the humans vanished from the top, but Tyr had quickly cottoned on. 'Hey isn't this all centaur magic to make it look like there were humans here?'

'Yes you're right,' Eleanor said, smiling at him, but he wasn't having any of it. No matter what people had told him about Eleanor being the good guy, she still stabbed me in the back with a knife.

Tyr was loyal, and I liked him for that. Kind, sweet, slightly nervous and timid when I first met him, he really stood up to the line when he found out he was the only one who could stop Fenrir. Then afterwards, he found he could still be useful and was even happier still when he got his new hand. I also noticed the way he looked at Renita when we came back from the past. He couldn't wait to see her, and I knew he cared for her deeply.

Dagen walked around with a disgusted look on his face. 'Why do humans always destroy everything they touch?' he asked the group, immediately getting Rhea's attention. Dagen, on the other hand, had always been a problem. Sarcastic, bull-headed, egregious most of the time, Dagen had been there for us a few times and had even helped me on occasion. Though he acts tough for the girls, I have seen him upset when Tyr and Etrician have been talking and have left him out. Dagen lacks social skills, which makes him the person he is today, but I'm pretty sure he'll grow out of it once he had some humble pie.

Jane tutted and pointed away from him, 'have you seen the forest around here? They probably logged for a while then stopped and replanted what they took away from the earth. Don't be hard on humans Dagen or else you wouldn't be here.'

While Rhea used my face to scowl at her behind her back, I was imagining I was hugging Jane for her outstanding optimistic tendency to see the good in a lot of things. As blond as she was, Jane was remarkably intelligent on many things and others... not so much. Always afraid of her powers from day one, I tried to encourage Jane to use them as much as she could, and if it wasn't for her, none of us would be here today. She had saved us many times, for that, I am thankful. With each day, Jane had become more and more confident with her ability to phade, and I hoped that her father would be proud of her once she goes back home.

While everyone spaced out, Rhea quickly calculated their distance, and then her presence in my mind left me. Collapsing to the floor with a light thump, everyone raced to me, to see if I was alright.

Hadriana held me in her arms as she turned me over. Rhea was clever. She'd sapped me of my strength. I didn't even have the will to grab the others and flee. 'Thera?' she whispered as everyone crowded around me.

'Run.'

The ground began to tremble as though an earthquake. An old log cabin on the edge of the compound disintegrated within seconds as the crane and other vehicles that were left to rust jumped violently on their rubber tyres. Unable to hold me up any longer, I fell back down to the shaking ground and closed my eyes. It was all over.

BANG!

The entire surface of the earth vanished beneath me. Yelling in fright, we fell towards an unknowing future, but then after seconds of falling, our bodies stopped, magically suspended in mid-air.

'Well this is a dandy surprise,' came a Texan accent from the darkness around.

'Maynard,' Hannah and Darren gasped as they tried to get away, but whatever was holding us up wasn't letting us go. We were flies caught in a web.

'Well don't you two just look all fine and mythical, huh? Both finally turned, well congraaatulations!' he guffawed.

'You are crazy!' Darren bellowed. 'What the hell are you doing? Let us go you maniac!'

He tutted. 'Oh now, now Mr Hay I can't do that just yet, for ya see, I need this precious cute little Water Nymph to complete the set. Of course,' he sighed theatrically, 'I have the brother, he's a bit more powerful. But then again since Thera got zapped by the staff her powers have been waning all this time.'

My eyes flicked open, my heart pounded in my chest as I heard mention of him through the darkness around. 'Where is he?' I shouted as loud as I could. 'I want my brother back! Give me my brother!'

'Be patient little darlin' all good things comes to those who wait and I've gotta tell ya, I've been waitin' a looong time. Thousands of years to be exact,' he laughed. 'Now then, on to business. Rhea if you would be so kind?'

A great sudden shocked intake of breath was felt around the darkness as we looked in various directions to see what was going on. Then unexpectedly, a blinding light split through the darkness. Cold hands grabbed my arms and legs and dragged me back. 'No!' I shouted, trying to reach out to Eleanor and Hadriana as they saw me being taken away. 'Let go of me,' I cried, struggling with the little energy I had left in me. Having no idea who had hold of me, I thrashed about, but they were powerful.

A familiar corridor of red suddenly blasted my eyes as we entered, the strange gravity stopped, and I fell to the floor with a thud. Scrabbling up, I managed to kick at one of the people who had me. They fell to the floor with a recognizable "oof" I whipped my head round to see the one person I did not want to see here and under her control. 'Etrician.' My heart leapt into my throat as I sagged to the floor. My worst fear came true. 'No, no, not you, please no…'

Standing up and a little wobbly on his feet, his face was impassive as he reached for me again. The other man, as it turned out, was Garrick. Both of them looked like zombies, empty shells of their former selves. Reaching out to grab me, I withdrew my hand and slapped Etrician as hard as I could around the face. Dislocating his jaw, Etrician flew into the red-bricked wall beside me, cracking it in two.

'I'll do it to you too,' I warned Garrick as he advanced on me, the menacing Minister inching towards me this time, with caution. Standing up, I curled my hands into fists, waiting for him to strike. Like a cobra, he stepped forward to grab me, but I twisted away and kicked him in the stomach, sending him flying into the air. Having no time to look how high, I ran as fast as I could down the corridor, away from the horrid feeling that I briefly felt behind me.

Regaining control of my body and slowly recouping my powers felt alien to me. Checking to see everything was working, I pelted two fire blasts at the white doors ahead, which would lead me into the room of the Cabinet of Idols.

Bursting through the door, I checked the cabinets, one by one seeing for myself, who had been captured. Then, as I neared the end of the line, my heart stopped as I saw my brother chained in a cabinet, looking so tired and careworn. 'Santorini,' I gasped, pounding the glass trying to break it.

His head looked up, and he smiled sadly at me. 'I'm sorry I wasn't there for you.' A thick tear ran down his face. Despair took hold of me, and I sank to the floor.

'You were with me every single moment of every single day, but I missed you.'

'I missed you—THERA RUN!' he suddenly screamed, but it was too late. The sound of the electrifying fizz cut through the air and struck me on the back. Santorini's face showed such pain and anger at my own horrified face, he tried to lash out, but the chains were too strong for him.

Rhea's mind entered my own as the pain erupted all over my body. She was too gleeful at my being captured, too ecstatic. She knew that everything was going the way it should and that our little troop had lost.

CHAPTER THIRTY

MY EYES FLUTTERED OPEN TO THE FAMILIAR GROGGY SENSATION OF being struck by the staff. With my arms lifted, my body sagging and my legs unmoving, I found myself chained to the side of the walls in the cabinet. I sighed. After only moments of freedom that my body experienced, I was here once more.

'Santorini!' I called out as soon as my thoughts cleared. 'Can you hear me?'

'I'm here,' he replied, worry in his voice.

'Why are you here? You were meant to remain in the other plane, away from all of this. You must have known the consequences of coming here... so why did you?'

'Everything happens for a reason, and it has to happen in a certain way. There was no choice for me. Dinglewood contacted me. I knew you were already in danger, so I had to come. However, as soon as I got here, Etrician found me. It was all over. They brought me back here and told me to wait for you.'

'It's not his fault,' jumping quickly to defend Etrician. Santorini never really liked Etrician from the start as he was always too possessive over me and my wellbeing. 'He's being controlled.'

'I know, but it doesn't help that he punched me in the face!'

Even in these dark times, I still found a reason to smile, even if in a jocular manner.

'It is time now to break free from prison, ya?' Vodyanoy barked from beside me. 'Leetle girl is smart, no?

'Oh do shut up,' Arthur chipped. 'If I had a knife I'd cut your tongue out!'

'Oh, ho! Such big talk from vimpy leettle man with a magical sword that is not in his possession, huh? You can barely lift it.'

'I am a King, Sir! And don't you forget it!' he barked.

'ENOUGH!' Santorini and I shouted together. 'It's not helping anything,' I continued. 'Where is Rhea, what's going on?'

Just at that moment, I heard the heavy doors open with a loud bang as they bashed against the side of the walls. In long strides, a person entered the room, getting closer and closer and then peering round to look at me was the devil herself, Rhea. Staring at me with steel-like eyes, her arms folded. If looks could kill she began to pace. Threateningly patting the Staff of Zeus against her palm.

'Torturing you would only give me so much pleasure. But destroying you entirely, well, that's a different matter,' smiling evilly.

'You can't destroy legends,' Vodyanoy spat at her. 'We are here because of our creators... humans and myths. We will come back again.'

Throwing her head back, Rhea laughed maniacally, cackling like an evil witch. 'You idiot! All of you are complete morons. You have no idea of the power that Maynard, the eighteenth Ancient, has. And while you are all safely locked up, I'll tell you. Under this mountain, that is guarded by centaurs from mortal men, is the world's treasure.' Her eyes found me and flicked over to my right, where Santorini was. 'You see, it was Maynard's intention to use those pathetic members of the T.A.T., Hannah and Darren,' she shrugged, 'yet some little immortal gave Thera extra power and now Maynard has no use for them. But now there is enough magic from you guys,' she smiled, opening her arms wide, 'to release Calypso and for her to unleash the Primordial Gods on the world.' There was a collection of gasps from the other cabinets, some even cursed at her and pulled on their chains in anger. And you couldn't blame them.

Calypso was not as the mythology was told. Yes, she was beautiful and could turn any mortal men into animals, but it was Calypso who held the ability to unlock the Gates.

'No, you can't do that!' Santorini yelled at her. 'You'll destroy the world and tip the balance. It's monstrous.'

She laughed. 'Yes, it will be.' Raising the staff into the air, she shot a bolt of lightning. It struck a golden rod that was similar to the one that was dangling above my head. The rod fizzed and crackled from the power surge of the staff, and then quite suddenly, something came to life with a low thrum.

Hearing shouts and yells from outside in the blood-red corridor, I heard the door suddenly burst open. With hastened familiar feet, Renita suddenly came into view. 'Thera, I found you,' she smiled with joy. From behind, Rhea appeared and without a shadow of any hesitation, pointed the staff right at Renita.

'NO!' I screamed, unable to do anything as the electric bolt of light shot out of the end and hit Renita in the back, instantly disintegrating her into a cloud of ash. Her clothes fell into a singed heap on the floor.

'Whoops,' Rhea shrugged innocently.

I saw red. Pulling the chains with all of my power I managed to make them move, straining them from the magic that was keeping us locked in these cabinets, the thrum was gradually getting louder.

'YOU BITCH!' I heard Jane scream from down the corridor. Feet hammered the ground hard as they flew towards the cabinet-filled room.

Turning in defence, Rhea pointed the staff but then as I saw a glint of a blue flash of light on her face, it was clear that Jane phaded. Gripping the staff tightly, as it seemed to be her only weapon, Rhea spun around in a circle, trying to glance everywhere at once. Then out of nowhere, the blue flash of light happened right beside Rhea. Surprised, she hesitated for that split second too long, and Jane delivered a powerful uppercut under her jaw, then spinning on the spot, kicked her in the stomach. Dropping the staff, Rhea flew back and hit the wall with such force, it cracked on contact.

Jane turned and bawled her eyes out as she ran towards Renita's burnt clothes. 'No…please no,' she cried, picking them up and wailing into them.

'Jane, don't,' I soothed. My anger suddenly vanished and was replaced by indescribable sadness. 'We can't bring her back,' I told her, forcing the lump in my throat to cease from breaking the dam that I was keeping inside, willing it to not spill for a second.

Two sets of thunderous feet were soon heard approaching. Scared, Jane looked up to see who it was, but then doubled in more sobs as she picked up the clothes. Moments later, Tyr and Dagen came into view.

'She's gone,' Jane sobbed, passing the clothes to Tyr. 'Rhea… Rhea hit her with the staff at point-blank. I saw it as I came down the corridor.'

Tyr took the clothes from her and stared at them in muted pain. Carefully touching the cloth as though remembering she was still in them.

Dagen let out a painful gasp as he saw and looked away towards Rhea who was coming too. 'I'm going to curse you until your bloody children's, children's CHILDREN ARE DEAD AND GONE!' Pulling back his sleeves, he began to mutter.

'Hey kid don't, just leave it,' Santorini called after him. 'It's not worth it.'

Seeing a shadow form and grow below me, I glanced around and watched my body glow. Staring up, I cowered away from the metal rod that was now humming with a bright white light, I tried desperately to move from its direction, but I couldn't. 'Santorini, the rod above!' I called out.

'May Atlas help us,' I heard Vodyanoy sigh, already he had given up. Jane, Tyr and Dagen put their pain aside and came to the cabinet, all looking fearful.

'No, get back!' I ordered. 'Find Etrician and Garrick, they should be back to normal.' Trying to sink as far away from the rod as I could, the chains held me in place; cutting deep into my skin and drawing beads of blood that ran down my arm.

Jane banged on the glass to get my attention. 'We can't leave you!' She continued to beat a few more times but saw it was impossible. 'We all have to get out of here, we all have to be safe, that's all Renita ever wanted!'

'Please get back before it's too late!' Santorini shouted at them.

Tyr, still shocked into silence did as he was told. Dagen grabbed Jane around the shoulders and pulled her back quickly, just as the sound above was becoming almost deafening.

Everyone yelled out their cries of anguish and terror. There was no escaping it. Whatever this rod was going to do, was inevitable.

'I'm still with you, sister!' Santorini called. 'Forever and always!'

'I'm still with you brother. I love you through all of time.' Closing my eyes, I waited for it and yelled out an anguished screech. Within a split second the light grew so bright around me it almost penetrated my eyelids. Amidst the blindingly bright light, there was a large whoomph from overhead. Gritting my teeth, I felt it, whatever it was, covering my entire body and zapping the strength I had. Pulling on every atom, sucking out every magical aspect I carried. The pain was indescribable. Magically forcing power out of you is like taking out your cells with a white-hot needle that punctures every part of you.

Each legend screamed through the pain as their powers were being taken from them. Blood-curdling, agonising cries echoed in my head as I tried desperately to not let go of my sanity, to keep the pain locked up, I had to do it for my brother.

Then, without warning, the light stopped. A blissful numbness coursed through my body. Sagging as I was unable to support myself, I breathed deeply as though I had run a thousand miles.

'Thera are you alright?' Jane's shaken voice asked as the three of them reappeared by the cabinet. 'Oh Atlas, you don't look so good.'

'No, really!' Dagen snarled at her. 'Her powers just got sucked out of her, or weren't you looking?'

'Please, don't fight,' I gasped my voice barely audible. 'Go and... and get Hannah, she has to send us away, before it's too late.'

Jane and Tyr raced off while Dagen remained behind. 'I'm going to get you out,' he promised, gritting his teeth, placing his hands on the sheet of glass. 'BREAK!' he yelled. Though a ball of green light spurted from his hands and instantly made contact, the glass remained as it was. 'BREAK!' he shouted again.

'It's no use,' Santorini's almost strangled voice sounded beside my cabinet. 'It's Ancient's magic, no myth can break through it.'

Dagen frowned and rolled up his sleeves, 'Well if it doesn't like mythical magic, how about a good old fashioned punch!'

BANG! BANG!...BANG! BANG! With each blow, Dagen punched the glass with all his might, drawing blood from his knuckles. However, it refused to break under his strength. BANG! BANG!

'It's no use, boy,' Santorini told him again, some strength returning to him. 'Save your energy.'

After a few more failed attempts at pounding the cabinet, Dagen stopped, cupping his bleeding hands.

'I'm so sorry,' he said, looking at me in hopelessness. 'I'm so, so sorry.'

I smiled at him feebly, closing my heavy eyes.

'Thera,' Santorini asked, as Dagen went over to see if Rhea was about to wake up. 'Are you...' he laughed, 'I can feel your power still; you are alright?'

Scoffing I smiled. 'I'm alright, I'm just tired. I've never felt like this before... it's almost a human fatigue.'

'That's because it is,' groaned Rhea.

'Whoa!' Dagen yelped. I saw him just in time to kick the staff out of the way which lay mere feet from Rhea. Standing in front of it, he readied himself to attack, arms outstretched, waiting for her to do something, but instead she sat up against the broken wall and laughed softly.

Wiping blood from her forehead and wincing slightly from the pain, she stared up at the large rod in the ceiling and smiled. 'In about another minute.' The gentle thrum started again ever so quietly, and over a few seconds, it grew louder. 'Let's see who will become human and who will turn to stone,' she side glancing at the others who had become silent since they screamed in pain.

'St-stone?' gasped Santorini. 'How? We are immortal.'

'We didn't use to be,' I spoke quietly before Rhea answered him. 'You and I started out as humans. When we died the Ocean Herself brought us back to life and tasked us with helping her.' The light grew around us once more, and my stomach did an instant back-flip, waiting for the intensifying screaming pain that was to come any second.

'No, stop this,' Dagen yelled, as he threatened Rhea with magic, but she just shrugged.

Smirking she replied, 'Do it, hit me with your best spell, magician. It won't work. I'm immune to your powers.'

Baring his teeth like an angry cat he said, 'I don't believe that Tara's mother saved you, so you could do this!' he spat, 'to kill Renita and... and turn legends into humans. You'll upset the balance!' The light grew brighter and the thrum of noise became an ear-splitting blast.

Piercing through my every nerve and cell, I felt the power drain from me. Screaming out with the last breath I could feel in my lungs, a blissful almost comforting darkness soon loomed towards me. Straining so hard from the shackles, they cut deeper into my skin. Blood dribbled down my arms and fell to the floor making little scarlet pools.

'Your power is my power,' yelled Santorini. 'We are together, we are connected by magic. Stay with me, Thera!'

The pain was over in a second. My lungs shuddering for air I felt as weak as a day old kitten. 'Thera,' Dagen yelled, running to the glass pane and staring at me. 'Stay with us!'

'NO!' Rhea screamed as she dived for the staff as Dagen left it unguarded.

With a sudden flash of blue light that illuminated the room, Jane, Tyr, Hannah, Etrician and Darren appeared. Startling Rhea, she lost her balance and fell, her outstretched hands missing the staff by inches.

Hannah and Darren's faces were solely locked onto the staff. Both of them pelted towards it, just as Rhea reached for it. Piling on top of her, Rhea let out a muffled yelp. Pulling her hand back, Hannah cracked her hand against her back, making Rhea scream in pain. 'I never liked you, you lying little bitch!' Hannah seethed and punched her in the face. Rhea fell unconscious. 'Tara could fly better than you anyway.' Relinquishing the staff, Darren yanked it away from her grip and pointed it at the glass pane.

'Hold on, Thera,' Etrician begged, standing to the left of the cabinet, his face and arms had been cut mercilessly; he obviously took quite a beating.

Etrician glanced to the cabinets around me and looked worried, but I didn't understand.

Suddenly the thrum started up again, the rod in the ceiling of the cabinet began to glow.

'Get them out of there, it's going to take their lives; they are still powering it up!' Dagen screamed at Darren.

Darren was pointing the staff at the glass pane, but nothing happened. Looking at Hannah, he reached out for her hand, 'I can't do this without you.'

Clasping hands, the staff instantly shone a pale blue and shook in their grip. The tip gleamed brightly and sent a crackling bolt of electricity towards me, shattering the glass in seconds. The chains immediately snapped from the powerful magic of the staff and sent me flying towards the floor, but Etrician dived in and caught me.

In a split second, I heard another glass pane shatter and a light thump on the floor of the cabinet. 'Santorini,' I gasped, unable to even lift my head.

Cradling me, Etrician brought me out of the broken cabinet, brushing shards of glass from my hair, but I was still aware of the thrumming sound that continued to grow in volume. Darren and Dagen pulled Santorini out and laid him on the ground. He was white as a sheet which frightened me. Barely able to keep my eyes open, I forced them to see around me... for just one last time. The other cabinets where the legends were placed were devoid of life. The others had turned to stone. My heart was in my throat, but there was nothing I could do. I didn't know a way to turn legends back into their usual selves; it was all new to me.

'The light is still on,' Jane said in a panicked voice.

'It will continue to...' I wheezed, my hand fell limply to the floor, inches from Santorini's as his half-closed eyes found my own. 'Hannah, send us to the Black Abyss please...'

Etrician hugged me tighter to him, my head lolled, unsupported. 'No,' he cried, tears streaked down his face.

'You have to,' I whispered. 'Calypso cannot… have the power to open the Gates. If she does…the Primordial Gods… will break free and humans will fall off the earth.' I took a shuddering breath, my lungs felt unable to hold much air in them. 'Do it now and get out.'

'I love you,' Etrician whispered into my ear, gently kissing me on the cheek. 'I will come for you; I won't let you leave me like this.' Two fat tears fell onto my cheek, and I smiled.

Trying to move my body to see Hannah, I looked up at her sad face. 'Hannah, I give you what little power I have for you to control Darren Hay,' saying loudly and clearly. Reaching out for her, she bent down and grasped my hand, a faint yellow spark flashed between us. 'You will have the power to command him, to turn him back into a merman and to stop him from stealing the hearts of your friends.'

Hannah wiped her own tears from her face and knelt down beside Santorini, and I. Etrician moved out of the way, glass cracking underneath him, unable to look at me anymore he turned away, stifling a sob.

'Please, banish us,' I begged.

Hannah carefully placed my hand in Santorini's, he gripped it as best he could but was unable to hold onto me for more than a second. Like me, he had, but an ounce of power left and nodded, smiling at me. 'Thera, Santorini, children of the Ocean Herself, I banish you to the Black Abyss where you shall remain, until the time comes, I can summon you again.'

Feeling my body relax that my wish was granted, I was removed from the pain and anguish of losing my powers and swept into the void of darkness in the Black Abyss. Holding onto Santorini as I once had when we left our human lives for the new magical ones we were now unable to live.

CHAPTER THIRTY-ONE

Hannah

THEIR BODIES VANISHED IN AN EERIE SWIRLING BLACK MIST. WHY THERA had asked me to do this made no sense, but she obviously had a good reason. Controlling my breathing from fear of bursting into tears, I stood up and glanced at the other legends. All of them were hanging in their chains, all of them stone. Then an almighty BOOM sounded underneath, and the room began to shake.

'The building is collapsing,' I heard a scream from down the crimson corridor. Whipping my head around, I saw Hadriana and her sister, Eleanor, run towards us, carrying a lifeless Garrick in their arms.

A strange shudder that felt like it came from beneath us cracked the glass panes of the other cabinets, making it easier to get the statues out.

Standing up, I turned to Jane. 'You need to get these legends out of here; maybe we can find a way to restore them.'

'Where to?' she asked fretfully, her eyes glancing from each of the unbroken cabinets behind me.

'The island that Thera asked you to meet her on, hide them there.'

'Dagen help me with them, I can't move them all,' she asked.

'I'll help too,' Etrician said, scrunching up his face and taking a deep breath.

The loud noise from the strange rod which was embedded into the ceiling above us grew louder, but it began to flicker. There were no legends left in the cabinets for it to work. Appearing from the corner of the room, a large crack zigzagged to the centre of the ceiling.

Hadriana huffed, 'We need to do something with Rhea. We can't leave her here.' She stared around the room. 'Where's Thera and Santorini?'

'Thera told me to banish them to the Black Abyss,' I told her. Anguish flickered across her eyes, and she quickly shook it away. 'We need to get out of here,' I pressed as I saw more cracks around the walls, revealing strange dark shadows in between.

'We'll meet you on the island," Jane shouted as she Etrician and Dagen, holding a legend each, phaded from the room.

'There are just two more legends from here,' I said, spinning around to see them at the very end. 'Darren and I can take them; Thera mentioned a waterfall or something. I think she was telling the truth even if it was Rhea controlling her, I can sense it.'

Hadriana nodded and holding her hand out, uttered a small spell, and the Staff of Zeus flew into her hand. Uttering another spell, she, Eleanor and Garrick vanished in bright blue light.

'Damn, not light are they?' Huffing Darren grabbing hold of a nearby statue. 'Hey, what about Bitch-face?' he nodded at Rhea.

Hadriana suddenly popped back into view. 'I'm taking her,' Hadriana said darkly and striding across the room, reached down for her.

'Where?' I asked dumbfounded. 'I know exactly where I can put her until she grows up.'

'No!' A booming voice sounded behind us. Hadriana's eyes widened in horror and muttering her spell vanished once again. Darren and I turned to see Maynard, standing on the opposite side of the room, a livid expression on his face, making his face turn red.

'RUN!'

Darren and I hefted the statues and hurried as quickly as we could into the red corridor, where I felt a strange evil presence that lurked nearby.

'I can sense the water,' Darren said through gritted teeth as he hefted up the statue to an odd standing position and went to a door marked epsilon in Greek. Putting his hand on it, he nodded. 'It's behind this-' but he couldn't finish his sentence. There was suddenly a deep rumble from beneath us, making the floor violently shake, throwing us off balance and hurtling to the floor. The statue's too rolled onto their sides, but thankfully remained undamaged.

'Oh no,' I gasped, seeing the white room behind me continue to flicker with light as the gold rod was wobbling in the ceiling like a loose tooth.

The ground, mirroring the ceiling, cracked open like an egg, as a massive earthquake juddered underfoot. 'Quick go!' I shouted at Darren.

'Running back to Tara, are you?' Maynard drawled behind us. I turned to see him hovering just above the ground, moving slowly towards us. As bits of the ceiling rained down on him, it was repelled by a protective shield. 'Problem is I can't have you running back to her with everything you know.' He came upon us too quickly. Darren pushed by and together we made it to the room where a large waterfall cascaded from the ceiling and poured into the floor.

'Just kill us then!' Darren snarled. 'You have the power to do it.'

His smile slipped a little, and he squinted as though he was thinking about it. 'Can't say that it hasn't crossed my mind, but annoyingly as you two are now myths, I can't kill you without collaboration with the others,' he said darkly. 'I may be powerful, but dang it, I have my limits. Not that you'll remember.'

Reaching out to us, there was another large bang beneath; rattling the entire room which splitting the walls into several parts. Maynard hesitated. Coming to my senses, I lurched forward and pushed Darren headfirst into the strange waterfall. He instantly turned into a merman, and the statue slipped from his grip and fell through the floor. 'Hannah, come on!'

Maynard placed his hand on my shoulder. You can't outrun an Ancient, I thought, defeated. 'You both will forget what you know!' Purple streaks of light shot out of his finger and hit Darren and me squarely in the chest, pushing me and the last statue into the waterfall.

Taking hold of Darren, I willed him to stay human as we twisted in the refreshing water. Darren then started yelling, but I didn't understand why. Memories began to become foggy, and I felt myself forgetting the simplest of things, but one thing stuck in my mind. I wanted us to be taken back to the little island where we would meet everyone else, whoever everyone else was.

Seagulls cried overhead as I lay on the wet beach of wherever I was. Coughing, I spat out the grit and saltwater and stared at the imprint my body made on the soggy sand. Feeling the waves still wash over my feet I sighed and tried to remember how I got here but nothing came to mind. Sand dunes that were speckled in tufts of grass, swayed in a gentle wind in front of me. Dawn was slowly creeping over the horizon behind. Though it didn't tell me where I was, and I still didn't understand how I got here.

Rolling over, my wet clothes sticking to me, I jumped in fright as I saw an oddly shaped wet statue to my right. Staring at it for a few more seconds and seeing the look of pure agony on its chiselled face, I backed away. 'Weird.'

'Hey…' a voice on the wind reached my ears from behind me. Turning, the silhouette of a familiar-looking boy stood on top of the dunes, the light shone over him, looking like something from a cheesy movie. 'Hannah, is that you?'

Squinting, the boy skidded down the dune and came to a stop near me. 'Darren?' I asked as I stood up to greet him. 'What on Atlas are you doing here? Actually, where is here?'

Darren shrugged. 'Oh, look you have a statue too.' Moving past me, we carefully walked to the statue and looked at its face. 'That's odd. Your statue looks similar to mine.'

'Do you think we were shipwrecked or something?' I asked, looking around for any signs of life and not seeing a thing.

'Um… not sure,' he scratched his head. 'I don't remember being on a boat, but then again, I don't remember much, do you? Hey, your ears look weird?'

About to query him, I heard a happy shout from our left. Making both of us jump, a lean russet-haired girl with short-cropped hair and a taller girl with ringlets down to her waist, came towards us. Moving towards Darren, I hid behind him, putting him in front of me.

'Oh cheers,' he spat, trying to move out of my way.

'Are you two alright?' the lady with long ringlets asked. She had a cut on her cheek, but I didn't ask how she got it.

'Look Had's, they didn't break,' the younger-looking lady pointed to the statues beside us. 'I'll get Etrician and ask him to move them with the others.' Without another word, she left and headed back down the beach wherein the distance, I saw a small group of people that I hadn't noticed before.

'We need to get back to the castle and prepare. That bang that felt like an earthquake, well that was Calypso being released. Etrician saw it happen,' she sighed heavily. 'I can't believe it's come to this.'

Frowning at her strange words, I made an 'Oh' with my mouth but kept quiet. Confused, Darren and I watched her as she put her hands on her hips bizarrely looking at us.

'Are you two, alright? You're acting as though you haven't got a clue what I'm on about.'

'Um yea... we kinda don't,' Darren managed to say. 'I don't think we've met before,' he said, offering his hand, 'I'm Darren Hay, and this is Hannah Smith.'

The lady's jaw opened, and she took a step back. 'What the-. What are you playing a? This really isn't funny.'

'Where are we?' I asked, ignoring her question. 'I want to go home now... or well back to Bristol I suppose. It's warm here, so I take it we're not in England.'

'Don't you...' she inched towards us, 'don't you remember who you are?' she asked, worried.

Unsure of how to respond, I whispered to Darren. 'Do you think she knows about the T.A.T.? Because if not, we'd only upset her or freak her out and the world isn't ready for that yet. Besides, I don't think Tara would like it.'

'Agreed,' he whispered back.

'Hannah, Darren... you're myths now, don't you remember?' Not responding to her question, she pried further. 'What was the last thing you remember?'

Closing my eyes, I said, 'Just a letter that came to Bristol through our letterbox, but who it was from, I can't recall.'

'Me neither,' Darren confirmed.

The lady looked perplexed at what Darren and I were saying. Moments later, the lady with short hair returned with a tall, muscular African man, who was extremely cute.

'Don't talk to them,' the lady said as the man was about to open his mouth to speak. 'I think Maynard has done something to them. I saw him before I took her away. They can't remember anything since Thera contacted them. Must be at least three weeks, nearly a month of their lives.'

'A month?' we asked, practically shouting. 'No wait,' my heart began to hammer in my chest, my palms sweating. 'Y-you know Maynard? Where is he? What happened to him?'

'Didn't he die?' Darren asked. 'Amjee never found his body.'

The lady sighed despairingly. 'Etrician, take them back to Bristol. They are no good to us while they have no idea of what has happened to them. I'll ask Dinglewood to keep an eye on them. He's proved quite useful since I gave him extra power all those years ago before he got lost in Avalon. If it wasn't for me, he wouldn't have got Santorini.'

'Who is now banished to the Black Abyss with Thera,' the man growled.

She looked sad and wanted to get off the topic. 'We'll be here when you get back.'

I picked up on her words, such as "power" and "Avalon" but I couldn't trust her. She didn't introduce herself to us, which I thought was very fishy indeed, but there was a more pressing matter to deal with. 'Whoa wait a minute!' I called, as the women were about to walk off. 'Are you saying that Darren and I have lost our memories? We've, in actual fact, lost an entire month's worth of memories?'

Both of them nodded.

'Well, how the hell do we get our memories back?' Darren demanded.

The women looked at each other and shrugged. 'If and when we find out something, we'll contact you.'

'So, you're the good guys?' I asked, as they turned and slunk off, both wiggling their arses the same way.

Stopping they turned around and smiled. 'If you think we are, then we are.'

The very sexy looking man called Etrician grabbed our hands immediately after that and without warning, we plunged into the earth. The smell of dirt went right up my nose, making me want to sneeze, but having no sense of direction, no point of origin and no real understanding of what was happening to us, I decided my sneeze would wait.

Fresh air suddenly flooded my senses, and I took a deep breath of the familiar smell of a cold winter's night in Bristol. 'We're home!' I laughed as I ran to the front door. 'Hey, how did you know where we lived?' I asked the man as he followed us, but stopped just outside of the gate.

'It's my job to know where the survival of the world lives,' he smiled. 'I pray you get your memories back soon. Keep safe.'

Suddenly sinking into the earth, the man disappeared.

'Bugger I'm wet and cold,' Darren shivered as he ran up the steps to me as I banged on the door. 'It's been snowing, look,' he pointed to the windowsill of the living room which had a soft coating of snow. 'I can't wait to have a hot bath.'

A light came on in the entranceway, and the golden metal flap of the letterbox opened. 'Who is it?'

'It's us,' I laughed, peering through the opening to see Tara's eyes stare back at me. 'Let us in please, it's freezing, and we're wet!'

'Oh my God!' she yelled. Hearing the key getting thrust into the lock, it clicked open. Yanking on the door, Tara flung herself onto us. 'We've missed you guys so much! It's been ages! Where the hell have you been?'

'That's a good point,' I smiled as she let go and stared at us. 'We've lost our memories.'

Her eyebrow raised in surprise. 'Well, that's not helpful to us now, is it?'

'Why?' Darren asked as he moved her out of the way, fed-up of standing outside in the cold. Heading inside, I closed the door behind me with a slight bang.

'Well, you are meant to be explaining these,' she said, gesturing us into the kitchen. Turning the light off in the entranceway, Tara carefully opened the squeaky kitchen door and flicked on a small light. 'These look.' Picking up a box that was marked to everyone, minus Darren and myself, Tara opened the lid. Inside were little boxes, each with someone's name on it. 'It's jewellery,' she whispered, picking up the box that had her name on it. Opening it up, she revealed a ring with a white stone set in the middle. 'Saskia has one too. A letter came with it saying that you'd explain what they were. You two got bracelets didn't you?'

Darren and I held our wrists out. Darren had lost his, but for some unknown reason, the stone that were set in the middle of mine had broken. 'Ah, well I can't explain that,' I said sadly. 'It's best that you don't put the jewellery on. Not just yet. Wait until Darren, and I get our memories back, whenever that is. We don't know what they'll do.'

Frowning at the little ring, Tara nodded and put it back with the others. Sighing, she yawned and glanced at the kitchen clock by the cooker. 'You guys look tired. I think we need to go to bed. You can freak everyone out in the morning when they find you're here,' she smiled. 'I'm glad to have you back, though.' She paused and turned to Darren. 'It was quieter since you left.'

'Get stuffed,' he quipped but gave her a smile.

Giggling, she bid us goodnight and headed back to bed.

Sighing, Darren put the kettle on and together we sat at the kitchen table. 'Why does it feel that we were in a battle but escaped and now... ironically we've forgotten everything?' I asked.

'Sod's law,' Darren shrugged, getting two cups. 'But I do have a feeling this isn't over, Hannah. Something's coming, we knew this already before we left, we knew it wasn't over, and I think even though we did whatever we did in that month, I think... I think it made it worse.'

I nodded in agreement. 'I guess we'll just have to see.'

With half a smile, Darren faced me, leaning back on the cooker, a cup of tea in his hand. 'Yes, we'll just have to wait and see.'

The end...
For now...

ABOUT THE AUTHOR

A E Kirk is a writer of sorts. Mostly she writes fantasy or science-fiction for young adults as well as horror. After travelling most of Asia in 2012, Abi now lives in Devon, UK and is constantly inspired by the views of the sloping idyllic landscapes around her.

Printed in Poland
by Amazon Fulfillment
Poland Sp. z o.o., Wrocław

60133665R00222